PRAISE FOR RAC

"Rachel Grant's smart, edgy, high-energy romantic thrillers deliver a real rush. The suspense is intense and so is the romance. Fascinating heroines, cool heroes, and intelligent plots. Grant sets a new gold standard for romantic suspense."

—*New York Times* bestselling author Jayne Ann Krentz

PRAISE FOR *TINDERBOX*

Named to *Kirkus Reviews*' Best Books of 2017

"Unexpected and intense from the get-go. With irresistible characters, a rare setting, and an inventive, high-powered plot, it's a smartly crafted gem of a story."

—*USA Today*

"This first novel in Grant's Flashpoint series offers a multilayered, suspenseful plot that's strengthened by its appealing characters, strong attention to detail, and a healthy dose of romance . . . An exciting tale that offers an entertaining mix of action and romance."

—*Kirkus Reviews* (starred review)

PRAISE FOR *CATALYST*

Named to *Kirkus Reviews*' Best Books of 2018

"The second novel in Grant's Flashpoint series offers intelligent romantic suspense that moves with the urgency of a thriller."

—*Kirkus Reviews* (starred review)

"From ravaged South Sudan to opulent Morocco, Rachel Grant's *Catalyst* reveals both a sophisticated thriller and a sizzling romance."
—*New York Times* bestselling author Toni Anderson

PRAISE FOR *FIRESTORM*

Named to *Kirkus Reviews'* Best Books of 2018

"Grant expertly braids together action and romance in a propulsive, page-turning suspense thriller."
—*Kirkus Reviews* (starred review)

"Romantic suspense done right and to the max. Don't miss it."
—All About Romance

"An enthralling, heart-pounding masterpiece!"
—*New York Times* bestselling author Annika Martin

DANGEROUS
GROUND

DISCOVER OTHER TITLES BY RACHEL GRANT

FLASHPOINT SERIES

Tinderbox
Catalyst
Firestorm
Inferno

EVIDENCE SERIES

Concrete Evidence
Body of Evidence
Withholding Evidence
Night Owl
Incriminating Evidence
Covert Evidence
Cold Evidence
Poison Evidence
Silent Evidence
Winter Hawk
Tainted Evidence
Broken Falcon

ROMANTIC MYSTERY

Grave Danger

PARANORMAL ROMANCE

Midnight Sun

DANGEROUS
GROUND

RACHEL GRANT

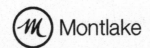

Published by Montlake, Seattle

www.apub.com

Amazon, the Amazon logo, and Montlake are trademarks of Amazon.com, Inc., or its affiliates.

ISBN-13: 9781542029285
ISBN-10: 1542029287

Cover design by Caroline Teagle Johnson

Printed in the United States of America

This one is for Elizabeth Winick Rubinstein.
It was a longer journey than either of us expected,
but you never gave up. Thank you for always pushing
my work to the next level and for believing in me.

A NOTE TO THE READER

Chiksook Island and all the cultural, historical, and geological features described in this book are fictional; however, the setting is based on several real Aleutian Islands that have ruins and debris left behind by US and Japanese soldiers after World War II in addition to extant prehistoric sites and modern villages occupied by the Unangax̂ people.

ONE

Whidbey Island, Washington
September

Dean had done some risky and dangerous things in his ten years as a wildlife photographer, but nothing that could send him to federal prison. But then, this wasn't an assignment from *National Geographic*. He wasn't going to remote, frigid Alaska to photograph polar bears under the aurora borealis. And while he would certainly be expected to take photos of birds, his role on this expedition wasn't that of a photographer at all.

He wasn't even going as himself.

He'd cleared the first major hurdle and now approached the group of scientists and engineers on the tarmac waiting to board the plane. He was just minutes from takeoff, which was the point of no return.

Federal prison might await him at the end of this flight or expedition, but he'd worry about that after he found his brother.

Two women and three men stood in a cluster, watching uniformed marines load supplies into the back of the cargo plane. Dean joined the group and was about to introduce himself when the engines of a small fighter jet on the runway fired up.

He ripped open the pack of disposable earplugs he'd been handed before being permitted onto the restricted tarmac and quickly inserted them. Everyone waiting for the flight watched the fighter jet prepare to take off, so Dean used the opportunity to check out the five people also heading to Chiksook Island.

It was easy to guess which of the two women was the archaeologist. Dylan had said she was tall and beautiful. Both women were attractive, but the one with lighter-brown hair had a good six inches on the other.

Until yesterday, when Pollux Engineering had given him the list of scientists and engineers slated for this trip, he'd known only her first name, making reaching out to her impossible. Now, standing just feet from her at long last, he couldn't tell her his real name if he wanted to avoid prison. Avoiding prison might not be his *top* priority, but it was high on the list.

Fiona Carver's shoulder-length honey-brown hair had gold and red highlights that he could believe were natural. While human subjects were not his specialty, he'd donated his skills over the years to photograph models and actresses on location with various animals to raise money for habitat preservation and protection. He'd since become friends with many in the film and fashion industries, and he knew enough about both to recognize that Fiona had either been blessed by the hair gods or she had a really excellent stylist.

There wasn't a speck of makeup on her lightly freckled, pale-cream skin, but then this military flight to a remote island in the Aleutian chain for government-contracted fieldwork wasn't a makeup-wearing sort of trip for most people.

The fighter jet hurtled down the runway just as the military ground crew signaled for Dean and the other civilians to board the waiting aircraft.

This was it. Stepping onto the plane meant no turning back. If he was caught, he could kiss his perfect life and career goodbye.

So be it. He'd risk anything for his brother. Dylan would do nothing less for him.

Finding Dylan was Dean's number one priority.

He followed the archaeologist up the ramp of the small turboprop transport. She settled into a seat in the middle of the inward-facing row that lined the port side. Dean passed her, going deeper into the jet, closer to the cockpit, and took a seat, leaving one spot open between them. There were a dozen seats total—six on each side of the fuselage—for just six passengers. Only a total dick would choose the empty seat between them.

Thankfully, no one on this team proved to be a dick. All six passengers spaced themselves on both sides, with open seats between one another.

In the center of the compartment, field equipment and supplies were strapped down. There was a month's worth of food and gear for the fourteen-day expedition to Chiksook Island—more than enough in case a storm caused delays for their return flight.

The no-frills seating inside a plane heavy with supplies wasn't much different from some of the flights he'd taken on assignment for *National Geographic* or *Smithsonian*, except this wasn't an expedition to stalk and photograph big cats or the elusive pangolin.

He wasn't even sure *how* he was going to search for Dylan. If he was safe and sound in the field camp or in the tiny Aleut—or as the locals preferred to be called in their own language, Unangax̂—village, he'd have emailed Dean and postponed the LA visit instead of being a no-show.

The last correspondence Dean had received that was unequivocally from Dylan had been sent from Chiksook Island nearly six weeks ago. The email had come from Dylan's personal email account and described the project and Fiona, in addition to listing restaurants he looked forward to frequenting during his upcoming trip to LA. Remote fieldwork always made Dylan long for fine cuisine.

A few days later, Dean received another email, supposedly from Dylan but which could have been sent by anyone with access to his work email account.

When Dean was unable to get in touch with Dylan, he'd wasted no time in contacting Pollux Engineering for an explanation of that last email, which stated that Dylan was going off the grid for a few months. Pollux informed Dean that his brother had flown home to Seattle and promptly taken a leave of absence, and they had no information on how to reach him.

The military wouldn't provide Dean with a manifest of the flight—which had been a transport like this one—because it violated operational security. He'd had to rely on Pollux Engineering's account.

Had Fiona Carver been on the boat that evacuated Chiksook and the transport flight that followed? Could she confirm Dylan had flown home?

The only way to get to Chiksook Island and its heavily restricted US Navy property was to be a member of the Aleutian Pribilof Islands Association, which was the federally recognized tribal organization of the Unangas, or to be hired as a contractor working on the Environmental Impact Statement for the proposed submarine base project.

Given that Dean couldn't claim Unangax̂ affiliation, he'd instead "borrowed" the name of an ornithologist he'd worked with years ago and applied for Pollux Engineering's last-minute call for an ornithologist. A mated pair of rare birds might be nesting on Chiksook, and Dean had no qualms about taking advantage of that situation. He had a wildlife biology degree and knew enough about birds to bluff his way through. But given his fake identity, he couldn't reveal his real reason for being here to the others on the team. Not without risking federal prison.

He pulled out the disposable earplugs and tucked them in his pocket. As he settled in, he studied the other passengers. He would question each in turn, but his first order of business was to question the woman his brother had been dating in the months prior to his disappearance.

He reached out a hand to her and flashed a smile that never failed to please. "Bill Lowell, ornithologist."

She shook his hand, her smile polite. "Fiona Carver, archaeologist. Pollux Engineering hired you to find the gray buntings?"

He nodded. "I take it you don't work for Pollux?"

She shook her head. "Civilian navy employee, not a contractor."

He glanced toward the open end of the aircraft and the tarmac of Naval Air Station Whidbey Island. "Is this your base?"

"No. I'm on the Kitsap Peninsula. Near the shipyard."

That checked out. Dylan had said she lived a ferry ride away from Seattle. But Dean had discovered Washington had a lot of ferry runs, several of which terminated in the Seattle area, so instead of narrowing Dean's search for Dylan's girlfriend, that piece of info only made it broader.

"Is this your first time going to Chiksook?" he asked.

"No. Fourth trip in six months. Between the historic World War II site and prehistoric sites all over the island, I've been busy."

He grinned. "Excellent. You can show me the ropes, then."

Her pale-green eyes narrowed ever so slightly. "I'm sure I'll be too busy with my fieldwork."

"I can start my search for the gray bunting anywhere." He shrugged. "Might as well start wherever you're working. It gets lonely in the field."

She kept her expression mild, even though he was being pushy and presumptuous. Her eyes gave her away, however, sparking with a not entirely unpleasant heat. He guessed his persistence both irritated and amused her.

This didn't exactly endear. Dylan had been missing for weeks, and his girlfriend had yet to show any sign of caring.

Had she already moved on?

Faint freckles dotted her nose and cheeks, and his eyes were drawn to a darker freckle just to the right of center on her full, pink bottom lip. His camera would love that freckle, and he itched to pull it out and

5

start taking photos with her backlit by the open ramp. What else would his camera reveal?

"Are you afraid of bears or something, Mr. Lowell? Hoping I'll protect you from the dangerous beasts?"

He laughed at that. "Bill, please. And no, I'm not afraid of bears." That was true. He'd spent enough time photographing them to have the utmost respect for their power and beauty, and he knew how to stay out of their way. "Especially given that there aren't any bears on Chiksook or any of the Aleutians west of Unimak Island. In fact, on Chiksook, foxes and caribou were introduced in the fifties for hunting excursions, but otherwise, the only fauna you'll find are rodents and birds."

She smiled and tilted her head in acknowledgment. "Then why are you so eager to join me in the field?"

He shrugged. "I'm just a fan of the buddy system when it comes to fieldwork."

"For your bird search, you'll have to stick to the roads to cover the most ground, so you'll be fine alone. While the environment is rough, it's easy to get a bearing even without a compass. It's all green tundra and grasses. Trees can't survive due to the low temperatures. Easy to find your way around when it's not foggy, and utterly beautiful with or without rain, snow, and fog.

"I'm afraid accompanying me in the field would hinder your search. I'll be working in one place for days at a time, and you'll need to keep moving if you're going to search the entire island."

She'd been deliberately patronizing with the bear comment, but he had it coming, given how pushy he was being. He respected that. Plus, he felt his first rush of actual like for Dylan's new girlfriend as she described a place that was also known for being one of the foggiest, rainiest, windiest, and basically most miserable places in the United States. She didn't speak of the negatives as others might. She liked Chiksook Island. It showed in her sharp green eyes.

"Anyone could twist an ankle at any time," he said with a wink.

She rolled her eyes even as she gave him a genuine smile, and his gaze fixed on the lip freckle. It was a perfect focal point for the composition of her features, which, as Dylan had described when he'd first told Dean about Fiona on the phone two months ago, were stunning not for their perfection but for the lack of it. Her eyes were a bit wide, her chin a bit sharp. Together, they were a thing of beauty.

"Tell you what—you can radio me if you trip and bust your ankle."

"Deal," he said, transfixed by that perfect stray freckle. Her mouth was another bit of charming imperfection, with the bottom lip fuller than the top. He'd photographed—and, truth be told, slept with—models who'd paid good money to have their lips puffed to perfection, and this wasn't it. But on Fiona, it was deeply alluring.

Which was the kind of thought he absolutely shouldn't be having about his brother's girlfriend.

Her eyes narrowed at his unwavering stare, and she pulled her lip between her teeth, hiding the spot . . . and telling him she was aware of the power of the freckle.

She turned and faced forward, toward the scientists on the other side of the fuselage, ending their conversation.

He had to find a way to pull her back in. He needed information, and she might be the only one who could provide it. "Sorry. It's just . . . I dabble in photography, and the way you're backlit with the tail open right now, you'd make a stunning subject."

She gave him a side-eye, letting him know he'd just made things worse. She was a scientist heading to the field, and he'd reduced her to a pretty face.

So different from the models he'd dated, whose livelihoods depended on them being seen as nothing *but* a pretty face. In that world, if he wanted to get a woman's attention, all he had to do was pull out his camera and use a little flattery to coax her into letting him take her picture.

In those situations, he could always tell if he was going to get laid simply by looking at the photos he'd snapped on the camera's digital screen. If he photographed Fiona Carver now, the image would reveal a decided *no*. Which, he reminded himself, was a good thing.

She's Dylan's girl.

Had Dylan told Fiona about him? Probably not. And if he did, he probably wouldn't have mentioned exactly *who* Dean was.

Months ago, Dylan had admitted that when he started dating again, he'd learned the hard way that he couldn't tell his dates his brother was Dean Slater, the wildlife photographer known for his photos of animals in their natural habitats on all seven—yes, *seven*—continents. According to Dylan, a lowly volcanologist couldn't compete. His dates were more interested in hearing about the brother who was off exploring the world, not the scientist who studied it.

After that, Dean had been determined to fix Dylan up with a model he knew. She was perfect for his brother and eager to meet him. But once the LA visit was on the calendar and plane tickets were purchased, Dylan had refused the blind date on the grounds that he had a girlfriend. He went on to tell Dean all about the brainy and beautiful archaeologist he'd met while working on Chiksook Island in the spring.

Dean had been happy his brother had met someone, even as he feared Dylan was getting too serious, too fast. Dylan was still raw from his divorce. The guy needed to learn how to casually date. Sex didn't have to mean commitment.

But then Dylan vanished, and Dean didn't hear so much as a peep from his brother's new chick. The one he was wild about and who was wild about him.

Had they broken up? Did she know no one had heard from Dylan in weeks, with the exception of one abrupt email that claimed he was going off the grid?

If, for some unfathomable reason, the email was real and Dylan actually had gone off to find himself, did she know where he was? And even more important, was beautiful and brainy Fiona Carver the cause?

———

The new ornithologist was hot, but he had an air of full-of-himself that billowed out in waves, like too much aftershave. He was too smooth, and Fiona wasn't a fan of the *I want to photograph you* pickup line. She'd heard that one before, also from a scientist hoping for a field fling.

The usual ratio of men to women on the Chiksook expeditions was four to one, with the majority of both genders being heterosexual. Given the ratio, guys looking to hook up didn't waste time before making the first move, but this had to be a record. The ramp at the back of the plane hadn't even closed yet.

She glanced at his hand. No ring and no cheater band. At least there was that. A fisheries guy on the last trip had been married and thought that was a selling point. He'd gone so far as to pitch, *"What happens on Chiksook stays on Chiksook."*

She told him she preferred to post everything on Facebook and would be happy to tag the guy's wife. And then she showed him his wife's page and threatened to send a friend request.

She loved fieldwork, but sometimes people could make the whole experience miserable.

She rolled her shoulders, eager for the jet to take off. The noise of the flight made conversation difficult, and she had a book to read. Plus, she was impatient to get back to the island. They'd been called out of the field abruptly last time, thanks to a problem with the generators. She hadn't been able to collect the samples she needed for testing and analysis. The quick evacuation had also meant she'd left the prehistoric village site exposed to the elements, and the elements that battered Chiksook were not to be underestimated.

She didn't think she'd gotten a full night's sleep in the last month as she agonized over the state of the site. It was possible she'd made a significant find that could alter theories on trade routes during the Iron Age, or she'd found artifacts made with meteoric iron. But it was all speculation without the actual tools and rocks. The site had been buried for over a millennium until she'd uncovered it, and it was now exposed in one of the harshest environments in the United States.

A storm could have compromised the structure. The artifacts could have been washed away, the dwelling flooded.

She frowned at the open cargo-bay door, wondering what the delay was. They needed to get this party started before she completely lost her mind.

She startled when a guy in uniform with a military police armband came running up the ramp. Irrationally, she feared he was there for her. She wouldn't go to Chiksook today. Wouldn't return to the site. She'd failed at her one job.

She exhaled to dispel the ridiculous fear, then glanced around the jet interior, catching the look of alarm on the new ornithologist's face before he managed to hide it.

What is he *afraid of?*

"Which one of you is Trevor Watson?" the MP asked.

The geologist seated across from her raised his hand. "Me."

"I need you to come with me, sir."

"I can't. We're about to take off. My job is mission critical."

"Yes, sir. Orders from the base commander, sir. You must come with me."

Trevor frowned and unbuckled his straps, then stood. They all knew you didn't argue with MPs.

"Grab your bag, sir," the MP said.

Trevor unclipped his duffel bag from the rack above him, then scanned the faces of everyone inside the plane. Fiona held his gaze and shrugged. She was the only navy employee on this flight. Everyone else worked for Pollux Engineering. If this was some kind of internal company issue, she knew nothing about it.

The moment Trevor was off the plane, the ramp began to rise. Several people let out pent-up breaths, including the bird guy.

"That was weird," Cara said. "Anyone know what that was about?"

"No clue," Fiona answered. The engines flared to life, making further conversation difficult, and she settled back in her seat. She'd text her boss for an explanation when they landed on Adak. She'd hoped to consult with the geologist about the site stratigraphy.

Her gaze returned to the bird guy, and she found he was studying her with an intense look; then he gave her a confident—maybe even smug—smile.

She shook her head. There was something charming about him. She even almost found the smugness appealing, and that made no sense whatsoever. Ornithologists weren't usually the big egos in camp. It was the geologists and volcanologists you had to watch out for. Except for that one—Dylan Slater. He'd been kind and smart and a professional to his core.

She glanced around the group again, but she knew what she'd find. Dylan wasn't here. He wouldn't be back, which made her belly twist.

There wasn't a volcanologist on this expedition at all, but maybe one was being flown in with the team from Anchorage. In two days, Fiona's field assistant would be catching a flight from Elmendorf Air Force Base just outside Anchorage, along with other scientists, but until then, Fiona would be the only archaeologist in the field.

With her on this flight were Roy and John, both engineers of one type or another—she always forgot the exact specialties—and Cara, a marine biologist. Fiona had worked with everyone here except the bird guy with Paul Newman–blue eyes.

Like Newman, Bill's hair was blond, but his was a bit darker with sun streaks, which made sense if he spent a lot of his time in the field chasing birds. He had lines on his face that gave him a weathered look. Rugged and appealing. Comfortable and confident.

That had to be where the egotistical vibe came from. He knew exactly how good-looking he was. She'd bet his cheesy lines and brooding stare worked like magic to make women's panties disappear.

They all donned headsets to hear the pilots' instructions as the plane rolled toward the runway. There would be no flight attendant or refreshments on this flight, except for what Fiona had brought with her. Still, she preferred this to commercial flights any day. Plenty of legroom for her longer-than-average legs and no unexpected overnight layovers in Chicago or Denver. Layovers on Adak—where this flight terminated— happened occasionally, but it wasn't the same as being stuck in a hotel in the Midwest or Rockies. It was an island that was beautiful and brutal and utterly exhilarating.

She leaned against the headrest and closed her eyes, feeling the rumble of the plane's engine at her back. Between the noise of takeoff and her closed eyes, Hot Bird Man wouldn't be able to get her attention, and she would enjoy a moment of peace knowing she was finally on her way back to Chiksook.

Did he really expect her to help him settle in on the island, like she was some sort of concierge and not a fellow scientist with a job to do?

She wished she'd sat next to Cara. She hadn't seen her since she'd left the last expedition early and wanted to hear all about the woman's misadventures in the intervening weeks. They'd have plenty of evening hours over the next fourteen days to catch up, so she hadn't been concerned with seating on the flight. A mistake, apparently.

The jet aligned with the runway. The engines revved, the plane vibrating beneath and behind her. Fiona opened her eyes a tiny bit and looked askance at Hot Bird Man.

He looked tense. Fear of flying, maybe?

They raced down the runway, and the nose of the turboprop lifted. His shoulders seemed to relax, and he appeared to settle back in his seat as they rose into the air, yet he was strapped in like the rest of them, so the difference was subtle.

Maybe he didn't suffer fear of flying so much as fear of takeoff?

She opened her eyes all the way and unabashedly studied his profile. While his eyes and hair reminded her of Paul Newman, that's where the resemblance ended. His nose was broader and his brows were thicker. A trim beard framed his lips and covered his chin and cheeks, and she wondered how those bristles would feel against her skin.

She jolted at the unwelcome thought, and the motion drew his attention. His gaze turned to her, and his intense blue eyes lit with an amused heat. As if he knew exactly what she'd been thinking.

The guy was full of himself.

Except she *had* been thinking inappropriate thoughts that involved his mouth.

She glanced across the aircraft to where Cara sat. The woman's gaze bounced from Fiona to Hot Bird Man and back, and she flashed Fiona a speculative and knowing grin.

Fiona rolled her eyes. She didn't do field flings, and Cara knew it. She had a list of reasons why it was a bad idea, starting with personal experience, but there was also the issue of her professional reputation being jeopardized in a way that male scientists rarely had to fear for doing the same deed.

Cara just grinned. She didn't share Fiona's concerns and had in fact hooked up with one of the engineers in May. She'd claimed it was worth it because the nights were darn cold. Fiona had to admit, she had a point there.

Again, her gaze strayed to Hot Bird Man.

No. No way. Nothing good ever came from field flings, even when the guy was a hot birder with Newman eyes.

What happened to Dylan Slater was proof enough of that.

TWO

Dean didn't think his heart settled to an even beat until they'd reached cruising altitude. The MP's sudden appearance inside the jet had probably taken five years off his life. But they were in the air now. His fake ID had worked, and they were on their way to the Aleutians and Dylan's last-known location.

The woman across the fuselage from Fiona's seat unbuckled her straps and crossed the space, dropping herself into the empty seat between Fiona and himself. She strapped in, then offered her hand to Dean. "Cara Santiago. Marine biologist. You must be the new bird guy."

The engine noise meant having to pitch their voices a bit higher to be heard, but conversation wasn't impossible. He smiled and shook her hand. "That's me. Bill Lowell." He'd practiced saying the name over and over the last few days so it would sound natural.

"Have you ever worked in the Aleutians before, Bill?"

He'd done several photo shoots on the islands, including the birds of Attu, the bears of Unimak, and the fauna of a few other islands. Five years ago, on one such expedition, he'd been asked to photograph a Unangax̂ elder, one of the two dozen survivors who'd returned to the Aleutians after being taken to Japan to serve as laborers during the war.

The resulting image had run on the cover of *National Geographic* and had become an iconic image of both the Unangas and their struggles during and after World War II, and the article that accompanied it chronicled their ongoing fight to preserve their culture and language.

Bill's experience, however, was likely to be far different, so he simply said, "I've been to Attu, of course, but haven't done fieldwork elsewhere on the islands."

She smiled. "Well, you're in for a treat, then."

The diminutive woman was quite pretty, with glossy brown hair, deep-brown eyes, and dark skin that all signified her Hispanic heritage. Dylan had probably mentioned her on one of their many phone calls, but Dean didn't remember details.

His brother much preferred phone calls to emails, which had proved frustrating when Dean tried to gather all the information he could on the Chiksook project. Emails provided departure and return dates but little in the way of details, such as who had been on each expedition. Fiona's was the only name Dean could remember, and even then, he'd had only the first name to go on, plus the fact that she was an archaeologist. He hadn't even known her employer.

The Register of Professional Archaeologists hadn't listed a single Fiona in Washington State. But then, now he knew she wasn't a contractor, she was a federal employee, so listing herself there wouldn't be necessary.

But just because he couldn't remember if Dylan had ever mentioned Cara didn't mean they hadn't been friends. Everyone—with the exception of Dylan's ex-wife—liked him.

Dean gave Cara his most charming smile. "True, if you like brutal winds, freak storms, bad or nonexistent roads, limited water, and rubberized frame tents for shelter."

She laughed. "Who doesn't?"

"Were you on Chiksook when the main generator blew out last month?" he asked.

She shook her head. "No. I left the expedition after a week because I had the data I needed for that round." She nodded to Fiona on her other side. "Fiona was there at the end, though."

And there was the piece of information he'd been hoping for. Fiona had been on the island at the end of the last expedition.

"Tell us what happened, Fi," Cara said.

She grimaced. "I don't really know. I was on my way to the village site with Christina that morning when we got a call on the radio saying a storm was coming and the generator blew out, and we were to evacuate immediately to beat the storm. We made it back to camp in time to catch the last of two boats."

He was desperate to know if Dylan had been on that boat. Once he was safely settled on the island and certain he wouldn't be ejected or arrested, he could risk asking. "That must've been scary," he said.

She shrugged. "We've had to evacuate quickly before. The frustrating part was not being able to return within a few days. I waited on Adak for nearly five days for the generator to be repaired, but one thing after another delayed it, and I had no choice but to fly home. I can't believe it took over a month to fix it." She sighed. "But here we are. Sometimes I think this project has been cursed."

"How so?" Dean asked.

"One contract tangle after another. Equipment malfunctions. The contractor in charge of delivering fuel to the island had a fire onboard the barge that could have been catastrophic. Thankfully, no one was hurt, and the barge made it back safely—but that particular shipment was never delivered, which meant we had to cut short the June expedition. Now it's September, and I'm supposed to be done with fieldwork and writing my report, but instead I'm heading back to finish recording the village site and finally document the World War II base. I'll be lucky if we can wrap this up in two weeks."

"You left out the part about the volcanologist," Cara said. "I've been dying to hear what really happened."

Dean relied on all his deeply trained patience—a necessity when waiting for the perfect shot—and kept his face blank, the same stillness he employed in the wild.

Fiona's brow furrowed, and she gave a quick shake of her head. "I don't have any firsthand information, and I refuse to smear anyone based on rumor alone."

What the hell does that mean?

"C'mon, Fi. You must know something. Weren't you two tight?"

"Tight" was one way of putting it. Perhaps the relationship was supposed to be a secret? Were there no-fraternization rules between navy employees and contractors?

"Cara, you know what happens when people repeat rumors. I'm uncomfortable with the whole thing. You want gossip, ask Trevor for the details."

Cara let out a bitter laugh. "Convenient. And why in the world was he pulled from the jet?"

"No clue." Fiona frowned. "I wanted him to look at some rocks and artifacts from the village site, since Dylan won't be able to finish the analysis. Dylan said the metal could be from a meteorite, which would be a pretty big deal. Now we're going to the field with no geologist and no volcanologist. Have I mentioned this project is cursed?"

"Hopefully Trevor will be able to get another flight. I'm sure Sylvia is losing it at Pollux right now."

Cara referred to Sylvia Jessup, a midlevel engineer at Pollux Engineering who was Dylan's boss. Well, and now Dean's—or rather, Bill's—and probably Cara's too.

"I'm going to head back to my seat and catch up on my reading." She nodded toward Dean. "But I wanted to welcome you to the project and Pollux. Sylvia asked me to look out for you." She turned to Fiona. "And I wanted to ask if you want to bunk together. Unless I get a better offer."

With Cara sitting between them, he barely caught Fiona's smile and the amusement in her eyes as she shook her head, clearly having a good idea of what Cara meant by *"better offer."* "Christina arrives the day after tomorrow, so she'll bunk with me. Maybe if there aren't any other women on this expedition, you'll get lucky and get your own tent."

"Well, that would make it easier if a better offer comes along." She gave Dean a sideways glance, and he got her message loud and clear.

If this were a photography assignment, he'd eagerly take her up on the offer. He was a fan of short, proximity-driven flings that could go nowhere. But he wasn't here on a freelance assignment, and getting laid ranked dead last on his list of priorities.

Cara might be able to give him information on Pollux and Dylan's role in the company, but she hadn't been here when the project had ended abruptly five weeks ago, so it wouldn't be worth cozying up to her to find out what she knew.

No. He had to focus all his energy and attention on Fiona Carver. Even if it meant hitting on his brother's girlfriend.

———

The landing on Adak was bumpy as usual, and Fiona found herself gripping the straps that pinned her to the seat as she prayed this wouldn't be the time the pilot missed the runway. She let out a sigh of relief after the wheels touched down and the jet finally came to a screeching halt. Still, she sat there with her hands clenched tightly on the straps and breathed deeply.

She should be used to the hard landings by now, but each time, she felt the terror anew. She was fine with flying in general; it was the unpredictable weather in the Aleutians that terrified her. At least the next leg would be a helicopter, which generally meant an easier landing.

After taking one last deep breath, she unbuckled her harness and stood and stretched. Her gaze met Hot Bird Man's, and he gave her a sympathetic smile. Clearly, she hadn't hidden her fear as much as she'd hoped.

She hated showing weakness, especially to the male scientists on these expeditions. Two decades into the third millennium, and many of her male colleagues still looked for ways to minimize or belittle the contributions of women in the field. Bill Lowell's smile was friendly, though, so maybe he wasn't one of those.

She'd find out soon enough. One thing about working on Chiksook—you got to know everyone on the team well. Camp was a series of rubberized tents—two researchers per tent, gender-matched. They would all dine in the same cook tent and share the laundry/shower tent. Her off-hours would be spent in the cook tent playing cards and sharing stories or alone in her solitary cot, passed out from exhaustion.

Weather days happened often. When it was impossible to work, they spent their time in the cook tent socializing or in the office tent working on their reports, or helping others with their analyses if there was nothing that could be done on their own portion of the Environmental Impact Statement.

Even though some were contractors and some were government employees like her, they were a team in the true sense of the word, because if one part of the project got behind, they'd all lose. This EIS needed to be finished so they could all move on to the playoff round—remediation.

For that reason, Fiona would be on the lookout for the gray buntings as she recorded the prehistoric site, and she expected Bill to be on the lookout for World War II debris hidden in the six-foot-tall grasses.

She grabbed her backpack, which contained her most urgent supplies—laptop, change of clothes, Rite in the Rain notebooks, waterproof camera, sleeping bag—and followed the others down the open ramp at the rear of the jet. The rest of her gear would be unloaded with the field supplies and sent via barge to Chiksook. Weight restrictions on the helicopter made prioritizing supplies necessary.

"What happens next?" Bill asked as he descended the ramp beside her.

"If the copter is ready and the weather clear, we'll hop right to Chiksook," she said.

An hour later, they were still in the tiny airport terminal. There'd been a mix-up with the helicopter charter, and it wasn't due back to Adak for another hour.

Fiona rubbed her temples. Nothing was going right. To make matters more difficult, they couldn't charter a boat because it was too late in the day to set out to sea.

"You okay?" Bill asked.

She let out a heavy sigh. "Not really." She closed her eyes and, for the ten thousandth time, pictured the housepit she'd been excavating five weeks ago. Untouched. Dug into the earth.

For the first time in her career, she figured she'd experienced the same awe and excitement the archaeologists who'd excavated Ozette in Washington State or Pompeii in Italy must have when they'd realized what they'd discovered.

Ozette had been capped by a mudslide, Pompeii by a volcanic eruption. Both had happened in an instant, capturing a moment in time. Dylan Slater had visited the site with her that last week they'd been in the field together, and he'd surmised that the mudslide that had engulfed the village had been a lahar flow triggered by a volcanic eruption that had occurred fifteen hundred years before.

What she'd uncovered of the housepit was so utterly pristine, she wouldn't be surprised if a half-cooked salmon dinner remained in the hearth. Except she hadn't been able to properly protect the site, and it had been exposed for five agonizing weeks.

She huffed out a breath and answered Bill's question. "I was yanked out of the field unexpectedly—I mean, even more unexpectedly than usual for the Aleutians—and I was in the middle of recording the most amazing find. I'm worried about what the intervening weeks have done to the site and am pretty much desperate to get back."

She didn't think she'd ever said those words out loud before. She didn't want to believe she was superstitious, but part of her worried verbalizing her fears would make the damage real.

There was something in Bill's eyes that echoed her desperation. Like he had the same frustration at the delay, but considering he was new to the project, she couldn't imagine why that would be, except for a general irritation at the *hurry up and wait* aspect of fieldwork.

"How about you? What does this delay mean for your work?"

He shrugged. "Don't really know yet. I guess I'm still hoping we'll be able to get to the island today."

No sooner were the words out of his mouth, though, than the charter company manager stepped out of his office. "Sorry, folks. A medical emergency means the helo is now on the way to Dutch Harbor. It'll be back in the morning to take you to Chiksook."

She told herself to be glad the helicopter was where it needed to be, providing aid in a crisis, and pulled out her phone to call the Aleut Corporation. The five of them needed lodging for the night. In minutes, the task was done. "I got us both sides of a duplex," she said to the group. She led the team of five out of the terminal.

It was a cool evening—in the midfifties—and the sun looked like it would set in another two hours or so. The wind whipped up, blowing her hair around her face. She'd forgotten to braid it earlier and would regret that lapse when it came to combing the tangles out of the curls. She glanced at her watch. "The diner closes in an hour. If we want to eat out, we should head there now."

John shook his head. "I'm going to grab something from the store and go straight to the rental. I've got work to catch up on."

"Me too," Roy said.

Cara glanced from Fiona to Bill and then at Roy and John. "I think I'll head to the duplex too. I'm beat, and I packed sandwiches just in case we got stuck here."

Fiona met Bill's gaze. Did she want to have dinner alone with Hot Bird Man?

He smiled. He really had a stunning smile, but she suspected he knew it. "Guess it's just you and me, then."

Part of her wanted to retreat, to say she'd changed her mind and would grab dinner from the store with the others. But that was ridiculous. They were colleagues who would be sharing meals and company for the next two weeks on Chiksook.

She smiled back and said, "I guess so."

Cara and the others set off for the rental office to get the keys, while Fiona led Bill the short distance to a small café. They settled into a table situated on the side of the living room that had been converted to a restaurant dining room.

"Tell me about your project," Bill said after they'd placed their orders.

"I found a housepit that was covered in a mudslide—likely triggered by volcanic activity, according to a volcanologist."

"The guy Cara mentioned on the flight? What was she talking about, anyway?"

"Yes, that volcanologist. She was asking why he was sent home the day before we were evacuated."

"Sent home? He didn't evacuate with the rest of you? Why?"

She frowned. Saying he was sent home early was one thing—everyone who worked on the project knew that much—but she really didn't want to spread rumors when a man's professional reputation could be on the line, and as a federal employee who played a role in the contractor selection process, she didn't want to say anything that might show bias against Pollux, given that they were unlikely to be hired again after their handling of the Chiksook EIS. Some things that happened in the field would always be beyond anyone's control, but then there was negligent management, and she couldn't help but believe Pollux had suffered from more of the latter than the former.

Bill worked for Pollux, so her lips were sealed.

"I'm sorry, but as I said to Cara, it's not something I'm willing to discuss. So, back to my site. Assuming you don't know Aleutian prehistory, the housepit site is a pretty amazing find. Given that there aren't any trees in the Aleutians, the Unangas, which, I should probably mention, is the preferred name for Indigenous Aleutians in the western dialect spoken on Chiksook. Unangas is plural and Unangax̂—with a circumflex over an *x* on the end—is singular. Anyway, the Unangas dug their homes into the earth. They were semi-subterranean pits sometimes lined with rocks for the walls, and driftwood or whale bones were used for roof beams. Over the beams would be layers of more wood and bone, grass—whatever was available—but it all would be capped with a layer of living sod. Basically, imagine a hobbit house but with the opening at the top, with ladders to descend. From the outside, it would just look like a small hill.

"I found what I believe is a village, but so far I've only uncovered one intact house and one collapsed one. The roof openings had been covered by a lahar mudslide, and it appears the interiors are pristine. Like Ozette or Pompeii. I was in the process of recording both houses when we were pulled from the field. I found some interesting artifacts—your standard stone tools but also a few nontoggling harpoon heads with bilateral barbs. Harpoons are usually made out of bone, but the barbs in this instance were hammered metal. Possibly iron. If it's iron, it changes everything we know about trade routes from the Iron Age, but it's also possible they were utilizing meteoric iron, which has been documented in a few prehistoric sites."

She held back from mentioning that Dylan had one of the metallic rocks and a harpoon with him when he'd left the island, and she was in the middle of a battle with Pollux to get both artifacts back. She'd given them to him to see if he could identify the metal, but the next day he'd been sent home without warning.

Pollux claimed Dylan had likely left the harpoon head on Chiksook—but there was no way to find out until she got to the island. Between that and the tools left in the field—the site had been covered with tarps that were meant to only protect it overnight, not for five weeks—she was something of a wreck with worry.

She was supposed to be on the island already, searching Dylan's tent.

Fifteen more hours. She could wait. It wasn't like she had a choice.

"Sounds like an interesting find," Bill said, and his tone was genuine.

"It's the kind of site that people go into academic archaeology for but rarely find."

"But you aren't an academic," he said, his blue eyes probing.

Goodness, those eyes. It wasn't just that he was handsome, it was the focus and attention in his gaze. It wasn't hunger she saw there, but it might be on the same continuum. All she knew was, she liked being on the receiving end, which in itself didn't sit well with her. He wasn't her type, so what was the appeal? But still, his stare triggered the same kind of fluttery feel that came with attraction that flowed both ways. A pleasant feeling she hadn't felt in far too long.

And that was a problem. She did not want to be attracted to Bill Lowell. She didn't want to be attracted to anyone she met in the field. Never again.

She felt the jab in her heart that always accompanied such thoughts. Regan had loved the field fling, but her sister had been a free spirit in a way that Fiona would never be.

"Fiona?" Bill said softly, and she realized she'd been sucked into dark memories once again.

She shook them off and put on a bright—but fake—smile. "No. I don't have any interest in academia. The last thing in the world I want is to spend ten years excavating the same damn site and then twenty years writing it up. I don't want tenure. I don't want to teach.

But hopefully some lucky grad student who *does* want those things will have the chance to excavate the site in cooperation with the Aleut Corporation. It's outside the APE for the proposed base, so with the proper permits and consultation with the Unangas, it could add a great deal to what we know of Aleutian prehistory."

"A-P-E?" he asked.

She shook her head. "Sorry. I used the NHPA term—*area of potential effect*. You'd be more familiar with the NEPA term, which is *study area*."

"Ah," he said, but he still sounded confused. "And what is NHPA?"

She frowned. She wouldn't expect an ornithologist to know all the regs behind her part of the EIS under the National Environmental Policy Act, any more than she knew the finer nuances of the Endangered Species Act or the Migratory Bird Treaty Act, which were the drivers for his work. But she'd worked on enough multidisciplinary NEPA projects to at least know the acronyms for the laws that governed each segment of the NEPA document. This all was NEPA 101 for Dummies.

"NHPA is the National Historic Preservation Act of 1966."

"Oh. Yeah. Right. Sorry. I was just confused because if it's outside the APE, why were you digging there in the first place?"

She supposed that answer made sense. Sort of. "The Office of History and Archaeology and the island's Unangax̂ residents insisted on a full historic and prehistoric inventory—even if only to define areas where navy personnel are not allowed to go. Christina—my assistant, who actually knows tons more about Aleutian archaeology than I do but who doesn't have a master's degree so she can't be the principal investigator—and I were recording the site as a Traditional Cultural Property—TCP—and did some shovel test pits to determine if there were physical remains as well when we found the housepits."

"Christina is one of the people who will arrive the day after tomorrow with the Anchorage contingent?"

She nodded.

Their server returned with their waters, which Fiona gratefully took, being dehydrated from the flight. She hadn't wanted to tempt fate by drinking in the airport terminal before an hour-long helicopter ride. The last thing she needed was a full bladder on a bumpy flight.

She drank half her water before setting the glass down and giving Bill her own measuring stare. "So how long have you been doing this kind of consulting work?"

"Eight years . . ." He scrunched one side of his face, like he was calculating something, then added, "Yeah, eight. I'm a recent transplant to the Pacific Northwest, though. A job with a wildlife refuge fell through. Was lucky to get this contract. Moving is expensive."

"How did that happen? I mean, I thought the bird box was the first one checked from the NEPA list, but then at the last minute, I hear there was a gray bunting sighting?"

"Not a sighting. A call. I guess one of the maintenance crew who was sent in to repair the generator was something of a birder. He reported hearing the calls of a mated pair of gray buntings on one of his outings. Once it was officially reported, it became a problem."

"I'm guessing he won't be hired back." Reporting the birdcall had cost the navy thousands of dollars, and if Bill found the pair was still around, the cost could go into the hundreds of thousands.

"You don't approve?" he asked, tension in his tone.

She shook her head. "I didn't say that. I'm a firm believer that an EIS should be done right. The whole point is to determine the harm a project such as this will cause and mitigate the effects as much as possible. If a mated pair of rare birds would be harmed, we need to know about it, just like we need to know the locations of all cultural materials so if the base is expanded beyond the original plans, engineers will know which areas to avoid."

He nodded as if satisfied with her answer. She'd bet whoever hired him at Pollux only gave lip service to the mission of environmental science and remediation, or minimization of effects on cultural and natural resources.

Pollux was all about the engineering end of things and would skip the entire environmental process if they could—which was the attitude of a few people in the navy as well. The engineering firm hired good people, but management was very much of the mind that pleasing the client—in this instance, the US Navy—by sidestepping environmental law to save money and time was the goal.

Fiona worked for the navy, but her job was to ensure navy projects didn't harm cultural and historic resources, or, if they did, to mitigate or offset those harmful effects as much as possible.

That meant her military bosses, including the admiral who commanded the base, weren't always happy with her. The times they *were* happy came about when her work led to smoother relations with local tribes who had to be consulted on a government-to-government level in compliance with treaties, or when archaeological research and findings generated good publicity for the navy in the Pacific Northwest.

"What do you think of Sylvia Jessup?" she asked, referring to the Pollux engineer who was Bill's boss.

"Oh, no. You won't tell me about the volcanologist, I'm not going to talk to you about my boss—who I've never met in person, by the way. Technically, I'm a contractor, not an employee of Pollux, but still."

She grinned. "Fair enough."

Their dinner arrived, and they settled into eating. Their conversation took on a lighter tone as Bill talked about his work on Attu Island several years ago. He was charming and funny, sharing stories that were self-deprecating and yet still demonstrated his expertise.

She'd always had a thing for men who were super competent but could still laugh at themselves, and Hot Bird Man with Newman eyes fit the bill.

Fiona was picking at the remaining food on her plate when Cara appeared.

"Changed your mind?" Fiona asked.

Cara shook her head even as she pulled out a chair and sat down. "I already ate. I tried to call you, but cell service is intermittent right now. It could have waited, but I figured I could use the walk." She grabbed a fry from Fiona's plate and popped it in her mouth. She chewed and groaned. "I forgot how good the fries are here."

Fiona laughed, glad that whatever brought Cara here wasn't urgent, or she wouldn't be stealing fries. Plus, she didn't mind the interruption. Dining alone with Bill had begun to feel a bit too intimate. Frankly, she'd been enjoying the time with him too much.

The waitress came to their table, and Cara ordered a Coke. When she left, Fiona said, "So what's going on?"

"We have another crew member."

"What? How is that possible?"

"He arrived late this afternoon, before we even got here. I think. It's a little confusing. Here's the weird thing: he's a geologist. Trevor's replacement."

"What? And he was already here?" Fiona sat back in her seat, even as Bill leaned forward.

"How on earth did they get that arranged so fast?" he asked.

Cara shrugged. "I'm just as baffled. All I can think is that's why Trevor was pulled from the flight? Maybe they already had this guy en route? But I can't for the life of me figure out why. Could this have anything to do with Dylan Slater?"

Fiona furrowed her brow. "I don't see how. I mean, Dylan was sent home because—" She cut herself off even as both Bill and Cara gazed at her sharply.

She'd consulted with her boss at the navy, Graham Sherwood, about Sylvia Jessup. Graham had directed her to talk to navy attorneys about how to best enter what she'd witnessed between Sylvia and Dylan into the record, and they'd specifically warned her not to speak of it with anyone from Pollux.

28

One slip could give Pollux grounds to sue if they weren't selected for the next open-ended, on-call contract. Given that the EIS was worth several million to Pollux, they would seize on anything they could to keep the navy as a client. Much as Fiona liked Cara, and now maybe even Bill, she didn't want Pollux involved with the next phase.

She was quite done with Sylvia Jessup.

She shook her head as if to brush away her near-slip. "What did Sylvia say?"

"I only managed to speak with her for about thirty seconds before we got cut off, but she said Victor Neff is to be made welcome on the team, and he's a vital addition to ensure we get the EIS done on time."

Cara snatched another fry from Fiona's plate. Before taking a bite, she said, "Anyway, Victor took the third room in the guys' side of the duplex, so, Bill, you're bunking with us in our extra bedroom."

He nodded. "I promise I'll behave."

Cara laughed. "Where's the fun in that? This is the last time we'll have access to alcohol for two weeks. We should pretend we're back in college and play drinking games until three in the morning."

Fiona groaned. "No way. I am not playing Never Have I Ever with any of you." The last time she'd played that game, it had been around the campfire at field school when she was twenty-one, with her baby sister, Regan, by her side. She'd learned a lot about her sister that night and had made the mistake of vowing to be more adventuresome moving forward.

She took a long look at Hot Bird Man and wondered what a game like Never Have I Ever would reveal . . . and got strangely flushed just thinking about it.

Nope. No way. No field flings. She'd learned that much from Regan and her own mistakes.

THREE

Dean didn't want to like Fiona Carver. Well, he wanted to *like* her, because he wanted Dylan to have found someone worth caring about, but he didn't want to be attracted to her. Didn't want to notice how her eyes crinkled when she smiled, or how damn smart she was, or the way she paused before she said anything about Pollux Engineering, demonstrating a thoughtfulness in her speech that he found rare in field expeditions. In his experience, once you got people away from the office, they loosened up and said things they'd never reveal otherwise. But not Fiona. If anything, she was more mindful, given her role as sole federal employee on this expedition.

He found her decisive, take-charge ways appealing. She'd secured lodging for the lot of them before anyone else had thought to grab their phones.

She also knew something about Dylan, but she wasn't talking—and he was more desperate than ever to know why. But he didn't think playing drinking games would do the trick, mostly because he was certain she'd never agree to play.

He placed his pack in the closet of his bedroom in the small former military base housing unit that was now owned by the Aleut Corporation. It was nearing ten, and the sun had set. He was tired but also wired after a long, stressful day of flying on a military jet under a false identity in an attempt to find the only person in the world who mattered.

He plucked one of his cameras from the pack. He'd brought four cameras with him on this trip, and this one was his favorite. The moon would be rising soon. He could get pictures of the twilit night and more of the ruined buildings and stark landscape after the moon rose. He grabbed a coat, hat, and fingerless gloves—the temperature had dropped rapidly once the sun went down, and the wind would probably be high—then stepped into the living room.

Fiona and Cara sat on the couch, sharing an open bottle of wine. The glass in front of the empty plush chair reminded him he'd planned to join them.

Fiona's wool-sock-covered feet were up on the couch, with her arms wrapped around her knees. Her curly hair was loose and touched her shoulders, and there was something achingly beautiful about the relaxed, casual pose. The professional was off for the night.

He should stay. Maybe she'd open up in this setting. But he had his coat on and the camera in his hands. He couldn't pull back. "Sorry. I was thinking this would be a good time to go for a walk. See if I can get some photos of nocturnal birds on the hunt."

"Seriously?" Cara asked. "You're going to have two weeks of that starting tomorrow."

He shrugged. "What can I say? I like birds."

Fiona let out a soft laugh, then cocked her head. "You up for company?"

He shrugged, determined to keep his responses casual, when her request was better than he could've hoped for. "Sure."

She looked to Cara in question, but the shorter woman shook her head. "No way. I'm going to enjoy real walls and plumbing and being out of the wind while I can. Have fun, though."

"I'll grab my gear," Fiona said and ran into her bedroom. She returned a minute later with a polyfill jacket, rain shell, fleece cap, and wool mittens. She grabbed her boots and sat on the couch to don them, then pulled on the other layers that would protect her from the wind.

They set out, the wind greeting them at the front door, but it wasn't as sharp or bitter as they were likely to face in the coming days. "I was thinking of heading to the ruins," he said. "There are probably nests in the debris."

"Sounds good."

They walked along the main road that paralleled the shoreline in silence. A strong gust swept at them from behind, and Fiona shivered as she crammed her hands into her coat pockets.

"I'm surprised you wanted to join me," he said. "You could be in a warm house having wine with Cara."

"There will be plenty of time to hang out with Cara on Chiksook, and I'm a big fan of night walks. I live in a small town on the Kitsap Peninsula where I can walk by myself at night, and it's one of my favorite ways to lose my stress so I can sleep. I was planning to go out later by myself, but it's nice to have company too."

Seeing an opening to get her talking, he asked, "Is your life on the Kitsap Peninsula stressful?"

"Work is. Always. But that's true for everyone, isn't it?"

Damn. Nothing about her personal life. "I suppose. I'm curious, though: Why is being an archaeologist for the navy stressful?"

She gave him a sideways look, and he figured he'd made another mistake, like not knowing what NHPA stood for. If he'd done this kind of contract work before, he'd know all about what archaeologists for the navy did. He cursed Dylan for not sharing more about the other disciplines he worked with in the field, but Dean probably had only himself to blame. He hadn't paid close attention to the stories Dylan had shared.

"There are individuals in the navy who'd like to believe the military is exempt from having to follow environmental and historic preservation and protection laws. Take this project, for example. Navy brass wants this submarine base so badly, they initially tried to bypass the EIS process. As if the need for military might trumps the need for clean air or water."

"But it's not that simple."

"It's never that simple. As you know from dealing with loss of bird habitat. The ripple effect can be devastating, but we can have the base *and* protect endangered species. *And* honor agreements with Alaska Natives."

"And yet, the entire reason the navy wants to build this base is because of the melting ice caps," Dean added. He'd done his research on the rationale behind the project; he knew exactly what the navy planned.

"Yeah. Global warming is opening up a new Northwest Passage. One that will be in Russia's and China's control if we don't establish a stronger presence here." She kicked at a rock as they walked. "I want the navy to have their sub base, but I'm not going to roll over and rubber-stamp their plans without doing a thorough evaluation of the effects for the Environmental Impact Statement they're paying me to do. I won't compromise my professional reputation by signing off on an inaccurate or half-assed EIS. But sometimes the pressure from the top is strong for me to do just that." She shrugged. "So it's stressful."

"But not stressful enough to make you rethink your decision to stay out of academia."

She laughed. "Yeah, no. Different kind of stress. And, stressful as it is, I also love my job. I mean, look at what I get to do. I'm on Adak Island in the Aleutians, and I'm going to spend the next two weeks on Chiksook on the government's dime. I'm going to record one of the most amazing sites I'll ever be blessed to find, and I'll also record a World War II site. I love travel and learning, and I'm going to learn new things and even possibly expand the knowledge base of prehistoric Unangax̂ dwellings, and even what it was like to be here during World War II. No two days will be the same on this expedition. It will be cold and miserable and exhilarating and wild."

Dean was one of the lucky few whose job was his passion—and he was paid damn well to do it. He'd reached a level in wildlife photography most only dreamed about, and the words he used to describe his job were so very similar to what Fiona had just said, a passion for travel and learning. A similar need to understand the environment and the past to understand why wildlife behaved the way they did today, and the knowledge that his photos would educate and expand knowledge of the species he captured in a moment in time.

Sometimes a photo was just a photo. And sometimes it was a lesson in animal behavior. He'd bet sometimes a site was just a site for Fiona, but then there was Chiksook.

Her words triggered a rush of pleasure, but given who she was, the feeling was unsettling. And yet not unsettling enough.

They reached the point where the road skirted the end of the runway, and he paused, first looking down the long, paved expanse, then turning to face Kuluk Bay. Clouds were spotty, allowing stars to peek through, the water dark gray in the speckled light.

He turned again, this time looking down the shoreline, and lifted his camera to snap pictures of the rocks in the bay, the coastal road, and the housing development they'd just walked through.

It wasn't a particularly pretty image—the light was all wrong—but it felt good to have his camera in his hands, adjusting the settings to get the best possible shot even in poor conditions. This he knew how to do. He was an expert in this one area, and it was good to remember that, given how off-kilter he was by having to pretend to be someone else.

By having to pretend that he didn't know Fiona Carver had been sleeping with his brother, but she didn't seem to give a damn about the fact that he was missing.

The camera in his hands gave him confidence. Reminded him of who he was. He'd made it this far. Tomorrow they'd arrive on Chiksook.

I'm coming, Dylan.

Fiona had wandered toward the water as he snapped away. Now his lens found her. Her silhouette was striking against the dark sea beyond the bay.

He adjusted the settings to make the most of the light and shadow. "Mind if I take your picture?" He had to shout to be heard over the wind and splash of the waves.

Through the viewfinder, he could see her wry smile, probably because he'd reminded her of his comment on the jet earlier. "Go for it. But no posting it online and identifying me. I don't do social media, and I don't like having my picture posted."

That explained why he'd been unable to find her online from the scant information Dylan had given him. But also, she had nothing to fear from him on this point. As a photographer, he didn't post any images online that he wasn't prepared to lose control over. Pinterest and other social media sites were a nightmare for protecting photographers' copyrights. "No problem."

He snapped away, appreciating that she didn't try to pose for him or hold still. She just continued what she'd been doing before, walking slowly along the shore, occasionally scooping up rocks, studying them, then tossing them in the water.

After spending the evening with her, he could see how she was just Dylan's type. Which of course meant she wasn't Dean's type at all, even if he found her attractive. Even if they shared a similar passion for their work.

He and Dylan might be fraternal twins, but they couldn't be more opposite when it came to relationships and their taste in women. Dean highly doubted Dylan had ever gone on a date that hadn't turned into a serious relationship, whereas Dean had only had one serious relationship, and it would remain that way.

Dylan's multiple breakups over the years only firmed Dean's resolve. The divorce was simply the latest and worst. Dylan had left Southern California and moved to Seattle to start over.

When Dean reached out to Elise to ask if she'd heard from Dylan, she'd made it clear she didn't care that he was missing, and he couldn't understand how someone could promise to love and cherish till death,

Rachel Grant

then three years later not even be able to muster concern for his disappearance.

Yet, a year after an ugly divorce, Dylan had been back in the dating game and waxing poetic about his new girlfriend on the phone.

As Dean snapped more pictures of beautiful Fiona in the darkening twilight, he couldn't help but wonder how serious the relationship had been for her. All he could think from her reactions to the few mentions of Dylan's name was, *not very.*

The last thing Dylan needed was another woman to crush his heart.

Dean lowered his camera. "Ready to keep walking?" The words came out terse, and he hoped she'd assume it was because he yelled to be heard over the wind.

She fell in by his side without a word as he continued down the road to the ruins of the old military base.

"Does Chiksook look like this?" he asked as they approached the crumbling buildings.

"Parts of it, but Adak has more housing and structures that were built after the war. Chiksook was still in use as a radio tower and staging point, but not nearly so extensively, so most of the ruins date to the war, not after."

"What kind of ruins are there? The battles happened on Attu and Kiska." He'd seen the ruins on Attu and visited the memorials when he was there to photograph birds a few years ago.

"The requisite Quonset huts, Pacific huts, pillboxes, elephant magazines—"

"Elephant magazines?" the wildlife photographer in him couldn't help but ask.

"They're munition storage made with 'elephant steel.' It's a turf-covered bunker meant to be nearly invisible from the air, so if a Japanese plane flew over, it would just look like another bump on the mountain."

"Sort of like the prehistoric homes you were talking about at dinner."

"Kind of, except the magazine has a circular opening in the hillside, not the top, but a similar built-into-the-earth design. There are also remains of things like generator buildings and other concrete structures, as well as collapsed wooden buildings. A gun emplacement. All the things you'd expect to find on any coastal base from that era. Plus, there's all sorts of debris that litters the island. It's surprising how well things can hide in the tall grasses. I've found more than one object by tripping over it."

He smiled. "Sounds painful."

She nodded. "It is. It really is."

"So maybe the buddy system is a good idea after all."

"Yes. For me—I'll be traipsing across marshy ground and tall grasses with Christina. You'll be in a vehicle most of the time so you can cover the most ground. None of us can spare the time to accompany you. I'm surprised Pollux didn't hire a team to find the gray buntings."

"I was all they could scrape up at the last minute." *Thank goodness.* He doubted his knowledge would hold up with a real ornithologist to question him in the field.

He paused on their stroll to take a picture of one of the dilapidated structures. The gray sky was getting interesting as they left behind the few lights of the small town.

He scanned the night sky for birds. Even though Adak was known for an abundance of bald eagles, they were unlikely to be out at this time of night. His best bet would be to spot an owl hunting, but that would be pure luck, given that he hadn't questioned locals on nesting locations.

"Doesn't look good for a bird sighting this time of night," Fiona said, clearly reading his reason for scanning the buildings and sky.

"I knew it was a long shot. Frankly, I just needed some fresh air."

"Me too. But I'm curious why *you're* anxious?"

He studied her face, so utterly tempted to tell her so he could get some straight answers, but he'd gotten this far. He wouldn't blow it now. "No particular reason. Just new employer concerns."

"Are you hoping the contract will turn into something more permanent?"

"Yeah. Benefits would be nice."

"At least it gives you a chance to test the water with Pollux."

"What do you think of the company?"

"Oh, no. No way. As a federal employee, my lips are sealed."

There was a light in her eyes that surprised him. She'd warmed up to him over dinner.

He raised his camera and snapped a photo of her without looking through the viewfinder. "What, are you afraid I'm recording this or something?"

She laughed. "I knew you were Sylvia's spy from the moment you stepped on the plane."

"She'd have to pay me more if she wanted a mole. I'm not getting nearly enough for this job."

She crossed her arms and gave him a stern look. "Not my fault. We go with government rates for all professionals."

This time he couldn't resist and raised the viewfinder to his eye. He took a step back and adjusted the focus. She was beautiful in the starlight, all deep blues and grays with a gray sea behind her. Her freckle was lost in the darkness, but tomorrow he'd remedy that and photograph her in daylight with green hills. If he could get her to lose the cap for a few photos, he'd be able to capture her perfect golden-brown hair. In the sun, the reddish hues would glow.

Once again, she didn't pose for his camera. Instead, she shook her head. "So that line on the plane . . . it wasn't really a line? You're a photographer?"

"I dabble in photography, yes. I've even won a few awards." That was true.

"For photographing birds?"

"And other wildlife." Best to stick close to the truth.

"I'll have to look you up. Do you have a website?"

Thankfully, Bill Lowell's website didn't include his own headshot, and he hadn't updated it in three years. Even more important, internet service on Adak was spotty, but even better, on Chiksook there would be enough coverage only for sending and receiving emails. "Feel free to google me."

"Maybe I will."

Her smile kicked his heart rate up a notch. It was natural and . . . flirty. He knew that look. He'd seen it dozens of times through the camera lens, watched it come to life when he developed film in the darkroom.

For this trip, he'd brought only digital cameras, but suddenly he wished he had his favorite film camera. He wanted the surprise of watching one of her many expressions come to life in the darkroom, a mystery revealed.

There was something about Fiona. She had this calm about her, even though he knew she was anxious about the archaeological site. It was like she had an unshakable center, and it was so appealing.

He could understand Dylan's attraction, even felt a tug of it himself, and that never happened with the women Dylan dated. Not even in high school, when they were the Slater twins, athletic and academic rulers of the school. Dylan had dominated on the football field and track, while Dean had been king of the baseball diamond and swimming pool.

Dylan had been named homecoming king, and Dean had nabbed the prom crown, but it had never been a competition between brothers. Their classmates had simply taken turns in the voting, giving the honors to the sport of the season. And true to form, Dylan had dated one girl his entire senior year, while Dean had enjoyed the freedom of being both popular and single.

It wasn't until Dean's junior year in college that he'd finally had a real relationship that lasted. And Violet was nothing like any of the women Dylan fell for with frightening regularity. But then, there was and would never be anyone like Violet.

A hand strayed to his chest and rubbed the violet tattoo, as he always did when she came to mind. Violet had given him so much, including the career he had now. A career he loved almost as much as he'd loved her.

But there was much to love about his line of work. The hunt. The agonizing patience. He even loved the misery of a 110-degree desert heat while waiting for the perfect shot as much as he loved twenty-below in an Alaskan wasteland while waiting for a polar bear and her cubs to make an appearance.

He loved windy nights on remote Aleutian Islands, strolling in the dark with a beautiful woman while waiting for a bird to make an appearance. He loved taking beautiful women to bed after the exhilaration of an intense shoot.

In the distance, he heard the soft *what . . . what . . . what* call of a short-eared owl, and he smiled. He really was living his best life.

He lowered the camera and searched with unenhanced vision, spotting a small shape on the roof of one of the dilapidated structures as the moon rose behind it. He raised the viewfinder to his eye and zoomed in. Sure enough, it was a short-eared owl.

They weren't common for this island, but not unheard of either. He snapped several pictures. These would be keepers, as the moonrise and the crumbling structure combined with the owl's fixed, knowing gaze gave the image an eerie feel. He could sell these shots. A good price could pay his bail if he ended up getting arrested.

"What is it?" Fiona asked.

"Short-eared owl. Third building over. On the roofline." She didn't have binoculars, so he offered her his camera. "Want to see?"

"Yes, please."

She stepped beside him, and he draped the sturdy strap of his camera around her neck—no one was allowed to touch this baby without wearing the strap—then pointed the lens toward the round-headed raptor.

She let out a soft gasp. "Oh! He's beautiful. I mean, if it's a he."

"It's hard to tell with short-eared owls. The females are slightly larger than the males and maybe darker. But that's difficult to gauge in this light and without both present."

"Well, it's beautiful, whatever it is."

He looked down at the woman holding his favorite camera, as she gazed with rapture at the tiny bird thirty meters away. The rising moon gave her skin an ethereal glow.

When was the last time he'd shared this kind of moment with another person? Again, Violet came to mind, and he brushed that thought away. No. He'd never feel that way again. This didn't compare.

Usually, in moments like this, he was the one holding the camera. Or the moment of discovery was planned, expected even, as part of the expedition. Tonight was random; that's why it felt . . . special.

"Take a few pictures if you want," he said. "I've got more than enough memory cards for the next two weeks." He bought them in bulk, like they were Costco bags of Halloween candy.

"I don't know where to begin. I've never used anything more complex than a point-and-shoot."

"I've already set the shutter speed and adjusted the light meter for these conditions and that depth of field. You're good to go." He moved her finger to the shutter release button. "Fire away."

She did, and after she took a few, she lowered the camera to look at the screen, which showed the last image taken. "I took *that*?"

He smiled at her obvious joy. "You did."

"Well, I kind of cheated, but still, it might be the prettiest photo I've ever taken."

"I'll email it to you."

"I'll have it mounted and framed and tell everyone who will listen that I was the photographer. I think we need to name him. The owl, I mean."

His grin deepened. He liked this side of her. "And what would you name him—or *her*?"

"Well, the way the moon is just peeking above the ruins . . . Luna?"

"We'll just have to consider Luna as gender neutral."

"We should probably give him a Unangax̂ name. Next chance I get, I'll find out the Unangam Tunuu word for *moon*. Until then, his name is Luna."

"I like it," he said. And he did, no pretense. He stood way too close to her but had no desire to retreat. "If you want, I can give you photography lessons when we're on Chiksook."

"Really?" Her face lit with excitement. "That would be amazing. Learning how to use a real camera is one of those things I've always wanted to do but have never had time for."

"First weather day, you'll get a lesson." And he'd enjoy every moment like this one. Standing close. Teaching her . . .

She chuckled. "Don't think that means you'll get out of it. Weather days happen way too often out here."

The light in her eyes combined with the soft ripple of her laugh was downright enchanting in the moonlight. "I'm counting on it." On instinct, he dipped his head down, making a move without thought. This was as natural as breathing, as ingrained as scratching an itch.

Fiona leaned in, lips ever so slightly parted, but then she dropped back. "Bill, don't. Don't ruin this. I don't do field flings. Ever."

All at once, he was zapped back into the moment. His name was Bill. She was Fiona. His brother's girlfriend.

And he'd almost kissed her.

Even worse, she hadn't said a word about Dylan as her excuse for refusing his advance. She didn't do field flings. So what did that mean when it came to Dylan? How serious had she been about him?

42

FOUR

He'd been so damn close to kissing her, and she'd almost let him. She didn't even know how she'd had the brainpower to back away; the pull had been that strong. She'd been a rocket defying gravity. Or at least, that was what she told herself, but deep down she knew it wasn't gravity-defying strength that had granted her the ability to resist. It had been fear.

She didn't know Bill Lowell. He could be a liar. Married. A predator. Or even all three. She didn't take chances like that. Not anymore. Let Cara take the risks. Fiona didn't need to live on that edge.

But still, even though she'd managed to put a stop to Bill's kiss, that didn't mean she hadn't spent the rest of the night imagining his mouth on hers.

She'd managed to sleep, but only fitfully, as she alternated between dreams of Bill Lowell in the moonlight and the weird questions around Dylan Slater's abrupt departure.

But why should one man make her think of the other? Did the attempted kiss make her think of Sylvia Jessup and the advances she'd made toward Dylan?

At last it was dawn, and she had an excuse to get out of bed. She'd go for a run. It would get her adrenaline pumping and clear her head. She quickly pulled on waterproof running pants and a rain shell over the thermal underwear she'd slept in, donned her running shoes, and then was out the door.

It was cloudy, and she guessed rain would begin to fall shortly, but it didn't look like it would be a nasty storm. She forced herself to stretch, even though she wanted to set out before the rain started.

As she warmed up, the door to the duplex next door opened, and a man stepped out. He must be Victor, the new geologist. And her heart sank as she realized he was dressed for a morning run too.

She'd really wanted a quiet solo run, but it would be rude to take off when she hadn't met him yet. It was never a good idea to start on the wrong footing with a guy you were going to be stranded with on a remote island for two weeks.

"Hey there. You must be Victor the geologist," she said, without interrupting her stretching.

"And you must be Fiona the archaeologist." He began his own stretching routine.

"How did Pollux get you here so fast?"

"I'm from the Anchorage office."

It was odd that he'd arrived yesterday, instead of taking the military flight from Anchorage tomorrow, but as long as Pollux stayed within their budget, their travel decisions were none of her business.

"You must be new, then." Pollux Engineering's Anchorage office wasn't large, and she'd worked with everyone there at one point or another since this project began.

He nodded. "Just hired this week."

"So what happened with Trevor? Why was he yanked from the flight?"

He shrugged and continued stretching. "Don't know, and Pollux isn't talking."

Not surprising but still strange. Trevor had been the one to tell Fiona about Sylvia's allegations against Dylan. Did his being plucked from the jet have something to do with that?

She'd finished stretching but had paused to talk. Now, before she could set out, Victor asked, "Mind if I join you?"

44

There was really no way to say no and not look like a jerk. Nights in the cook tent could get awkward, and that was the last thing she needed after a long day of fieldwork.

"No problem. But fair warning—I'm slow. Running isn't really my thing. I only do it when there aren't any other exercise options."

He smiled, and she noticed Victor was handsome in an unconventional way. His features were uneven, and he had acne scars that, like Edward James Olmos, only added to his appeal.

Thoughts of the actor made her think of binge-watching *Battlestar Galactica* with her siblings during the good times, and her heart squeezed. Her brother and sister were both lost to her, but in different ways. The grief was similar, though.

She needed to learn how to hold on to the good memories of her brother, without feeling the stab of pain. Much as she could think of her mother and feel the loss of the woman she'd been while knowing it was not yet time to grieve.

She shoved the thoughts aside. She was in an incredible place that few got to visit, and she needed to focus on the moment. "Ready?" she asked Victor.

He nodded, and they set out, following the same route she and Bill had walked the night before, running along the road that paralleled the beach. They passed the end of the quiet runway and continued on, jogging in front of the military housing ruins where she'd photographed the owl.

Again, that almost-kiss flashed through her mind. She'd wanted it, which wasn't like her. What was it about Bill Lowell that made her forget all her rules? She didn't even know the guy, yet she felt twittery just being around him.

And she *never* felt twittery. Not even with any of the three men she'd had long-term relationships with. But Bill wasn't anything like the men she'd dated and thought she might someday love, so what was his allure?

Aside from the fact that he was hot, that is. She wasn't usually swayed by pretty faces. In fact, she generally preferred men like Victor, whose imperfect faces held their own beauty. Given her own less-than-perfect features, she always appreciated less obvious beauty.

Bill Lowell's beauty was more than obvious. It was in-your-face perfection, with those Newman-blue eyes and rugged lines.

Victor kept pace beside her, and he didn't even do that thing where he tried to subtly increase her pace by slowly picking up speed. "How long have you been working for the navy?" he asked, his voice not even winded.

"Eight years," she said, showing no such ease with the workout. "Got the job when I was fresh out of grad school." She would have let the conversation end there—talking and running wasn't her thing at all—but it was rude to not show interest in return. "How long have you been doing NEPA work?"

NEPA—the National Environmental Policy Act—was the primary driver for his work on this project, but most geologists she knew worked for the United States Geological Survey. It was always interesting to meet a geologist in the private sector doing environmental work.

"Five years," he said. "Like you, I started working right after grad school."

He looked to be a few years older than her thirty-five years, which meant he'd gone to grad school later.

"Have you done a lot of work in Alaska?"

"No. Mostly down in California. Studying tsunami activity for USGS."

"Oh. You must know my friend Dr. Michal Addison, then." Addison was one of the world's foremost experts on tsunamis and was a fixture in the Bay Area, giving Chicken Little–type lectures on the end of the world, which predicted that the Big One wouldn't be devastating for its shake; the real problem would be the tsunami that followed.

"Oh yeah. Michal. Great guy."

Fiona stumbled. Michal Addison was a woman.

Should she correct Victor? That would be embarrassing. But then, how could he not know? Michal Addison was legendary for her work studying tsunamis. Clearly, Victor wasn't as experienced in his field as he'd claimed.

How well did Pollux vet their hires? Bill didn't know the basic list of laws that fell under the NEPA umbrella, and Victor didn't know Michal Addison's gender.

She supposed it was possible Victor had only read Addison's reports. If he'd never gone to one of her many talks, he might not know.

But then, why pretend he knew Addison by calling her *"great"*?

Geology was like archaeology—everyone knew everyone, either in person or by reputation. There was no way a man who'd worked in California as a geologist wouldn't know Michal Addison was a woman.

"Yes," she said, keeping her eyes on the rocky ground. "Great guy."

When he didn't say anything in response, she knew she hadn't imagined his error. He didn't know Michal.

Unease filtered through her. Before she left for Chiksook this morning, she would reach out to her boss and ask about Pollux's vetting process. Not knowing NHPA was one thing, but not knowing one of the foremost experts in your field? That made no sense.

————

The boat pitched to starboard as it went over the top of the wave and dipped into the trough. Dean gripped the handrail mounted to the cabin exterior as water sloshed over the high gunwale and splashed his face and raincoat. It was time to head inside the cabin, as the sea had taken a dramatic, rough turn on their two-hour crossing from Adak to Chiksook.

In the distance, the southeastern edge of Chiksook was taking shape as a dark spot visible through the light fog. He snapped a photo with a small but high-quality waterproof camera. It didn't feel right to be out here without a camera in his hand, but he wouldn't risk his favorite one in this rough water.

The morning had been nothing but frustration, as there was no helicopter available to fly them to the island. But finally, in the early afternoon, Fiona had managed to arrange a charter boat for them, and now the island was in sight at last.

Irrationally, he didn't want to go inside, as if that would somehow delay their arrival or make the island less real. He zoomed in with the camera and could make out details of the shoreline, so he snapped photos, forever capturing the island on disk to assuage his superstitious thoughts.

He'd set foot on Chiksook within the hour; then his search for Dylan could finally begin.

The boat dropped into another trough, and he got a face full of water as a wave splashed over the rail. Icy water soaked his collar, but he was too relieved to finally be here to care.

He pulled open the heavy door to the passenger cabin where the rest of the team rode in dry, warm comfort and slipped inside before the boat took on another wave. Fiona glanced up, her eyes skimming his dripping hair and wet raincoat. She smirked. "Told you so," she said in a singsong voice.

He let out a bark of laughter. She had, indeed, warned him they'd hit choppy seas as they neared the island. But he'd wanted the cold, fresh wind on his skin, to see the island with naked eyes. When he and Dylan were boys, they'd had a bit of the spooky-woo connection that some twins shared, and he'd wondered if he'd feel it again upon seeing Chiksook.

But he'd gotten nothing—no twin vibe, no sense Dylan was near. He didn't want the void of feeling to worry him. After all, the connection had faded in adulthood. But still, he'd hoped.

He unzipped his coat and hung it to drip on the rack next to the door. He needed to be Bill the ornithologist and tease Fiona right back. "Nice to know you're the kind of person who doesn't hesitate to say *I told you so*."

Cara laughed. "Get used to it. Fiona is always right."

Fiona flashed a smug smile. "It's a gift."

The new geologist, Victor Neff, stared at Dean with an intense focus he found worrisome. Was it possible Victor and the real Bill had crossed paths at some point?

And how the hell had Pollux gotten the guy to Adak so fast, two days in advance of the rest of the Anchorage contingent? Why not wait and have him fly in with the others?

Victor's gaze turned to Fiona as she told Cara a story about learning scuba in the cold Pacific Northwest. As she spoke, Victor's hard stare gave Dean pause.

There was anger in his eyes. Hostility.

Dean had seen Fiona and Victor go running this morning, had even felt a small jolt of irrational jealousy—or maybe it was concern for Dylan that had tugged at him. He wondered if Victor had also made a pass at Fiona and was now angry she'd turned him down.

She *had* turned him down, right?

Damn. He had far too many conflicting emotions when it came to beautiful Fiona Carver. He really shouldn't have tried to kiss her last night, and yet, he had to admit it had been the perfect act to maintain his cover. Bill Lowell didn't have an agenda beyond finding a mated pair of gray buntings. It was natural for him to flirt and make a move, as long as he didn't cross a line that made the situation uncomfortable.

Thankfully, there had been no discomfort with Fiona today. If anything, she'd been more relaxed, given that they'd gotten the awkward moment out of the way. He had a feeling she was used to being hit on in the field, and it probably wasn't always as mutual as last night's almost-kiss was. Because one thing he was certain of—Fiona had leaned in. She'd wanted his kiss even as she'd been sensible and put on the brakes.

Dean settled in a seat separate from the others for the rest of the journey. He examined his notes on gray bunting nesting habits. He'd read everything dozens of times and had listened to their calls until they were so familiar, the birds filled his dreams. He'd studied up on other birds he was likely to find on Chiksook, but last night he'd realized he should have spent more time reading NEPA documents to familiarize himself with the EIS process.

Knowing the names of other regs like NHPA was as basic as it got, and he'd failed.

He couldn't focus, though, as the boat neared the island. He tucked his papers away and watched as they entered the bay. A long dock extended from the shore, beckoning them.

After weeks of trying to figure out how he could get to Chiksook, he was finally here. He took a deep breath, willing his eyes not to tear.

The answers to what had happened to the only person in the world who mattered to him, the brother he'd shared a womb with, the baby he'd communicated with before either of them could form words, were on this island. They had to be. The truth waited for him.

And deep down he knew, if Dylan wasn't here, he had nothing left to hope for.

FIVE

Fiona shook hands with the cook and two maintenance workers. All three men had been on the island for several days to oversee the setup of camp. The new generator was up and running, and the laundry and shower tent had been moved closer to the kitchen tent so they could share water, but otherwise the camp was much as they'd left it five weeks ago.

As a group, they crossed the camp to the team barracks. Fiona paused in the aisle between the two rows of pale-gray rubberized tents and faced the five researchers. She'd become the de facto leader of the group when she arranged for housing last night and then for the boat today. "Since the rest of the team won't be arriving for another day, we each get our own tent for the night. Pick a tent and make yourself comfortable." She looked to the cook, a beefy man with deep lines on his face and a bulbous nose. "How long do we have until dinner?"

"Dinner is in the oven and will be ready in an hour."

She nodded, feeling a tinge of disappointment. If they had a later dinner, she might have had time to drive to the site. After dinner, it would definitely be too late to set out.

At least she could search for the artifact and stone in Dylan Slater's tent. She studied the two rows of facing tents and made a beeline for his, which had been the last one on the right.

Unfortunately, Victor was ahead of her and aiming right for it.

"Victor," she called out, "if you don't mind, I'd like to claim that tent."

He paused midstride, his spine stiff. He hesitated for a moment but then nodded and turned to claim the one directly across from it. He faced her, his expression . . . carefully blank. She suspected he'd been irked by her request. "What's so special about that tent?" he asked.

"A volcanologist who is no longer on the team might have left geological samples from the archaeological site inside. Easier to claim the tent for my own than to ask if I can search yours."

"Fair enough," Victor said, and stepped up on the wooden pallet that acted as a porch for the tent he'd claimed.

The gray tents were slightly rounded on the upper corners but had a center ridgeline that gave them a soft point. The design was all about minimizing wind resistance, but it always reminded Fiona of a dollop of whipped cream.

While the walls were rubberized, the tents had hard doors that latched and locked, and Fiona was always glad she didn't have to spend extra time in the wind unzipping the door. She entered the tent she'd called dibs on, noting that Bill took the one beside hers, and Cara grabbed the one across from Bill, next to Victor. John and Roy took the ones on the ends of both sides. The cook, boat captain, and the helicopter pilot—who would arrive tomorrow with the rest of the team—each had their own tent, and the maintenance guys shared a fourth tent, but those were on the other side of their little village, by the office, laundry/shower, and cook tents. Two latrines were set up side by side and slightly offset from camp. No one wanted the latrines too close to camp, even though the greater distance meant a longer walk in the cold wind and rain.

Inside, her tent was just like all the others—two cots, two sturdy footlocker-type trunks for gear, two plastic folding tables that were serviceable desks, and two folding chairs. Under the tables were plastic storage bins for other supplies and odds and ends.

Fiona dumped her carry-on bag on top of the footlocker next to the cot that would be her bed for the next two weeks. The rest of the gear was being off-loaded from the boat by the crew, and in a few minutes, she'd head down and grab a dolly to haul the heavier gear to the tent. For now, she had a change of clothes, her computer, and her sleeping bag. The bare necessities.

She flopped on the cot and stretched out. Exhaustion overwhelmed her, which was ridiculous because she hadn't *done* anything today except take a long boat ride. But travel stress was always exhausting, and she needed to cut herself some slack.

Discomfort stirred in her belly. She'd called her boss this morning and expressed concerns about both Victor's and Bill's qualifications. She felt somehow disloyal for making the call. Both men had been nice. For all she knew, they could be supremely competent. But if they were going to run into trouble getting the EIS completed and signed, her boss needed to know the potential pitfalls now, while there was still something that could be done about it.

She didn't owe Bill or Victor her loyalty. She didn't even owe Pollux loyalty. She'd been hired by the navy and had taken an oath to uphold the Constitution when she started the job. That was where her loyalty lay—to her country and the laws that governed her work. Period.

She closed her eyes. She was so damn tired. The moment her brain relaxed, though, images of Bill Lowell's face as he'd leaned down to kiss her filled her mind. She'd had that fluttery prekiss feeling in her belly and had leaned in slightly, ready to receive.

It had to be his eyes. She'd always been a sucker for blue eyes.

She shook away the image just as there was a knock on her door. "Fiona? It's Bill."

Speak of the devil.

She sat up and took a deep breath, preparing to face him. It wasn't good that she was attracted to him. She'd told him her no-field-fling rule, and he seemed the type to respect it, but what if she threw caution to the wind and made a pass at him?

She was more than aware her resolve could weaken. It had been a long time since her last relationship, and as Cara would point out, nights were cold here.

"Come in," she said, loud enough to be heard over the wind that buffeted the tent. That was a reason to forgo being on the end. The middle tents had a layer of protection.

Bill stepped into the room, his gaze scanning the small space before landing on her. "Hey, sorry to bother you, but I found this bag in my tent. It's women's clothing, and knowing you were here during the last expedition, I thought maybe it could be yours?"

She shook her head. "No. At least it shouldn't be. The tent you chose wasn't mine, but I suppose things could've been moved around." She tried to remember whose tent it was. Maybe Cara's? Or had she been on the other end? The projects blurred together sometimes. She only remembered which tent had been Dylan's because she'd been eager to search it for the last five weeks.

The bag was a large Pollux Engineering canvas tote, which were ubiquitous in camp, and she'd used them herself many times, but she never took the bags home with her, because if she did, it could be considered accepting a gift from a contractor. While the value of the item was below the prohibited threshold, it was still a bad idea, and she believed in playing it safe in all things.

She rose from the cot and glanced into the bag in his hands. A pair of high-quality long underwear covered the items beneath. She moved the wool underwear aside—thinking if no one claimed them, she'd be happy to add them to her wardrobe—and revealed several sheer, colorful undergarments. She pulled out a lacy bra that was designed for sex appeal and not for support, dangling it in the air.

No woman in her right mind would wear anything this uncomfortable while hiking across the marshy ground. Women here invested in high-quality sports bras for the field. A good bra was vital because sometimes the team traveled to and from project locations via boat, and the waves were not kind to a busty woman.

She gave Bill a skeptical look. "Really, you thought this was mine?"

His piercing blue eyes lit with a tiny bit of humor and a lot of heat. "I wouldn't know what you wear, but the long underwear looked to be the right size."

Considering her long underwear was under several layers of bulky clothing, she was impressed he could guess her size, but then she remembered they'd shared breakfast in the duplex together after her jog, and they'd both been stripped down to their base layers. So not surprising he might be able to guess her size, just as she hadn't been able to help noticing his thermal shirt had hugged his torso in a way that let her know he led a very athletic lifestyle.

His build was as impressive as Dylan Slater's had been. And Dylan was a broad-shouldered former athlete. He'd played football in high school and college.

She'd liked Dylan enough that if he'd ever shown interest in her, she would have said no to the field fling but might have accepted a date when they were back in Seattle.

She did not believe the rumor. If anything, he was the victim.

She dropped the sexy bra into the bag and gave Hot Bird Man a look. "This definitely isn't mine."

"Bummer," he said softly.

She flushed with heat that wasn't entirely unwelcome, even though it should have been.

He stepped back and looked down at his feet. "Sorry. I shouldn't have said that. It was inappropriate and wrong."

It would be *so* fun to flirt with him. But he was right. She, after all, was the one who'd set the boundaries. "It's okay. But yeah, probably not a good idea moving forward." She took the bag from his hands and said, "This could belong to Cara or Sylvia, I suppose. Pretty sure it's not Christina's, who is too sensible to bring something so ridiculous to Chiksook."

Bill scanned the tent that would be her home for the next two weeks. "Did you find the geologic samples you were looking for?"

"I haven't even checked yet. I was so exhausted, I decided to lay down for a bit before starting my search."

"I'm sorry I interrupted you."

She shrugged. "It's fine. I shouldn't be so tired."

"The logistics of this trip would tire anyone, and you handled the bulk of it for all of us."

She smiled. "That's why I get paid the big bucks."

"You're a government employee; I highly doubt you're getting big bucks."

"Medium bucks, then."

"Want help searching?"

She hesitated. She didn't know Bill, and the lockers could contain someone's personal belongings. But then, it wasn't her stuff either. And both men who'd last shared this tent had worked for Pollux Engineering—Bill's current employer. Even if he was a contractor, he technically probably had more right to look through the items than she did. "Sure."

She went to the locker at the foot of her bed and removed her bag from the top. She flicked the dual latches and lifted the lid. Basic supplies—emergency blankets, flare gun and flares, dehydrated food packs, matches and flints, windup flashlights, windup radios, rope, and paracord. The whole standard kit filled an old navy surplus backpack. There were more bags just like it in the supplies shipped in advance of their arrival, and they were each given a new pack at the start of the project that also had a fully charged field radio. They were expected to carry these supplies every time they hiked away from their vehicle, in addition to their field gear packs.

Still, she emptied the bag and checked all the pockets, in case a stray artifact had been tucked away and forgotten. The only other item in the footlocker was a quality three-season sleeping bag. "Damn, I'd hate to leave a bag like this behind," she said. One thing the navy didn't provide was sleeping bags. She always brought her own and had invested in a good polyfill one because, in this climate, down would kill you fast if it got wet. She met Bill's gaze. "Does Pollux provide your sleeping bags?"

"No."

"Then this was left behind by Dylan or Trevor."

"The guy who was booted from our flight was in this tent too?"

"Yes. It's possible Trevor left this here knowing he was returning. One less thing to haul back and forth."

She dropped the bag into the footlocker and latched it closed. From there, they inspected the storage boxes under each table and found a pair of worn hiking boots.

"It's pretty common to bring more than one pair on these trips, so you can switch out if one pair gets soaked. Those could have been missed in the pack-up because it was done in a hurry. Same with the sleeping bag—although it's odd that the bag was in the footlocker and not on top of the cot."

Bill picked up the boots and inspected them from toe to heel, as if they might hold secrets to the universe. "These belonged to the volcanologist."

"What makes you think that?"

He showed her the boot treads. "These soles have walked on a lot of 'A'ā," he said, using the Hawaiian word for lava flows that had a jagged surface.

"Forget birds. You should be an investigator."

He smiled. "I've spent a lot of time on the Big Island. I know what 'A'ā does to boots."

She took the boots and placed them in the other locker, next to the sleeping bag. "I'll send an email to Pollux about the boots and bag."

She turned to the footlocker at the end of what would be Christina's bed when she arrived tomorrow. "Please let the artifact be there. I really don't want to get into a bigger fight with Pollux about Dylan."

She knelt before the box and flipped the double latches, took a deep breath that included a hope and a prayer, and lifted the lid.

She startled a bit at seeing the metal clipboard with an inch-thick compartment for storing notebooks, pens, and other supplies.

"That belongs to Dylan Slater," she said, feeling a little breathless.

She remembered how he'd wrapped both the stone and the tool in Bubble Wrap. The tool made sense, but the rock might have come from a meteor and was more metal than stone. It was more likely to damage the clipboard box than to be damaged by it. She'd said as much, and he'd winked at her and said, *"Bubble Wrap works both ways. It'll protect the clipboard my brother gave me when I got my PhD."*

She'd laughed and made a joke about the inexpensive gift for such a momentous occasion, and he'd explained that it also came with the camera that was his most prized possession. After he placed the stone and the tool inside the compartment, he'd flipped the aluminum clipboard over and showed her the engraving on the back.

Now she held the clipboard in her hands—the place where she'd last seen the artifacts—but before opening it, she turned it over to read the inscription again.

Now it's your turn. Conquer the world, and don't forget to take pictures. —Dean

Bill stood so close, his scent enveloped her as his fingers traced the inscription, almost as if the words meant something to him. "Dean?" he asked, his voice a bit hoarse. Probably because she'd turned the heat up to high when she'd first entered the tent, and it was getting a bit warm.

"His brother. Some sort of photographer, I think. Fashion, maybe? At least, Dylan mentioned a lot of models and his brother being something of a womanizer. But he gave Dylan a camera and taught him photography. Dylan took photos of my site when I asked him to come out and take a look at the artifacts, and his photos were so much better than the average site shots. One of the reasons I'm interested in taking you up on your photography lessons."

Bill had a strange, almost shuttered look as he nodded to the clipboard. "Open it."

She did, and her heart fell when the only items inside were a stack of field notes, some hand-drawn maps, and three yellow Rite in the Rain field notebooks.

"Dammit."

"Why haven't you asked Dylan where the artifacts are?"

She frowned. Did he really think she hadn't already thought of that? "I tried. But Pollux wouldn't give me his number, and I haven't been able to find him."

"You don't have his number?"

She met his gaze and frowned. Why would she have Dylan's number? Or maybe the question was, why would Bill think she had the man's number? "No. I never thought to ask for it."

He gave a sharp nod of acknowledgment. His intensity about this didn't add up. Maybe he had heard the rumors about Sylvia and Dylan after all?

She cleared her throat. "I should have gotten his number when I gave him the artifacts, but I had no way of knowing he would leave Chiksook without warning."

A new suspicion bloomed. Was it possible Bill had been sent by Pollux to investigate? Could he really be Sylvia's spy, as he'd joked last night?

She locked her jaw closed. She wouldn't get into this with Bill. His loyalty had to be to the company that employed him.

She unhooked the metal flap that held down the papers and notebooks and pulled them out to flip through, but she was distracted instead by what removing the papers had revealed.

A spiderweb of broken glass marred the face of a smartphone.

SIX

Dylan's boots. Dylan's clipboard. And now, Dean held Dylan's smart-phone in his hand.

"I don't understand why Dylan would have left this behind," Fiona said. "I gathered the clipboard had sentimental value, if nothing else."

The clipboard *was* sentimental. There was no way his brother would have left it behind. And he couldn't imagine Dylan abandoning his field notes any more than he'd take an artifact for analysis and not return it. "None of this makes sense to me either," Dean said, keeping his words neutral, given that he wasn't supposed to know Dylan. "Just because the screen is cracked doesn't mean the phone won't work. I have the correct charger; we can power it up."

"It's probably locked."

That wouldn't be a problem. Dylan always used the same passcode, their birth month and day. "Still worth a shot."

She took the phone back. "I have a charger too. I'll charge it and see if I can verify it belongs to Dylan Slater. My boss will likely need to go through channels to return it to Pollux." She nodded to the clipboard and field notes. "Given that he also left behind data collected for a government contract, we need to do this by the book."

While her words were probably correct, he had a feeling she didn't trust him. He'd probably made her uneasy with his interest in Dylan's stuff. He'd overplayed his hand, which meant he had no choice but to comply. His best hope was sneaking into her tent when she was in the field and unlocking the phone.

What would he find stored there? Why had Dylan left it behind?

With nothing left to search, Dean had no more reason to continue questioning her. He left her tent and returned to his own. It had been a stroke of luck to find the clothing left behind—giving him the perfect excuse to knock on her door after she'd announced to them all which tent had belonged to Dylan. But why the thermal underwear and lingerie had been left behind was another mystery, albeit a less worrisome one.

He flopped down on the cot and looked up at the ceiling of the pale-gray walled tent. He was here, at last, and the items found in Dylan's—now Fiona's—tent told him he'd been right to risk federal prison in coming here. Dylan never would have left the clipboard behind, and it made no sense that he hadn't taken his cell phone, unless the cracked screen was only the beginning of the damage. He wished Fiona had plugged it in right then and there, so he could have seen if it worked.

Patience.

He now needed all the skills he'd honed when stalking wildlife. When he was on assignment, he could spend days waiting for the right shot. He needed to think of this in the same way.

Except . . . it was hard to imagine a scenario in which Dylan's disappearance wasn't urgent. Five weeks was a long time, and here in the Aleutians, even a single day of bad weather could be deadly. Five weeks? It would be damn near impossible to survive that long without aid of some kind.

There was a Unangax̂ village several miles west of here. Dean would go there tomorrow—using the search for the gray buntings as his excuse—and see if they knew anything. He might even be able to tell them who he really was. He had connections among the Unangas, and he wouldn't be shy about using them.

Before dinner, Fiona went to the office tent—where they had a modem that offered limited connectivity—and emailed her boss from her laptop.

Graham,

Following up after our phone call this morning.
Finally arrived on Chiksook about an hour ago.
Any word on Lowell's or Neff's background and experience?

She felt a trickle of unease at writing the sentence, but the question had to be asked. If neither man was qualified to do the work, the EIS could be invalidated, which would mean their work would have to be repeated, adding months, if not another year, to the EIS process.

She took a deep breath and continued typing.

Also, there were a few items left behind in my tent. I think they belong to the volcanologist who was fired, Dylan Slater, but don't understand why he would leave the items behind—his cell phone, hiking boots, and clipboard field desk with notes. Unfortunately, the artifact and stone sample are still missing. None of the items left in the tent, with the exception of field notes, appears to belong to Pollux, and the clipboard was a personally engraved gift from his brother, not something he would aban-don. Have you had any luck in tracking him down through Pollux? I don't want to turn the items over to the Pollux employees here because I'm certain they would just give them to Sylvia Jessup and . . . you know my reservations there.

Please put more pressure on Pollux to provide Dylan's contact information so I can reach out about the artifact.

Thanks,
Fiona

Pollux had said Dylan had decided to use his accrued leave time to go off the grid for a few weeks as the investigation into his conduct played out. She didn't doubt Dylan needed a break after Sylvia's allegations, but she would also expect that he would stick around and defend himself.

It was all just so weird, and she was more than a little uncomfortable doubting the allegations of a well-respected woman engineer, but what she'd witnessed didn't jibe with Sylvia's account. In fact, she'd seen the exact opposite.

But she also didn't want to be the kind of person who automatically discounted the word of a woman, just because she both didn't like the woman in question and was friends with the man.

The door behind her opened, and she quickly hit "Send" without reading through the email. She didn't want anyone here to know she was asking questions about Bill and Victor.

She turned to see Victor Neff.

"Good. Looks like the internet is working?" he said.

It took a moment, but finally her computer played the whoosh sound of a sent email. Even an email that short with no attachments took more than a few seconds to send from this remote place. Of course, once the sub base was built, this whole island would be a hub of connectivity.

"Yep. Working," she said.

"Excellent. I need to email my wife."

She hadn't realized he was married, but they hadn't talked about their personal lives during their jog this morning. "I'm sure she'll be happy to know you arrived safely."

"Any luck finding what you were looking for in the tent?"

His gaze held an intensity that was similar to Bill's. What was up with these two men and their interest in her missing artifacts? "Sadly, no."

"Bummer. I can check and see if they went to the Anchorage office, if that helps."

She'd already made inquiries there, and it had been a dead end. No one at Pollux wanted to talk about Dylan, and they'd formed a united front. Victor was new, so maybe he *could* help, but they'd probably give him the runaround too. Plus, there was the fact that he might not be the qualified geologist he presented himself as.

Nope, best to leave it for Graham to follow up. As a supervisory-level federal employee and the civilian in charge of the EIS—he answered only to the admiral and other officials who would sign the final document—he had the clout to get the information needed.

"It's fine. I'm sure they will turn up."

She closed the lid on her laptop and slid it into her field bag. "See you in the cook tent. Dinner should be ready soon."

He dropped into a chair and was setting up his computer as she left the tent. She decided to swing by her tent to stow her computer bag before heading to dinner. Since her tent was on the end, she opted to walk around the back way, then stepped into the aisle between tents.

She stopped short at seeing Bill on the pallet that served as a front stoop for her tent.

He was facing away—as if he'd just stepped out of her tent.

Had he entered her tent while she was emailing her boss?

But she hadn't seen him push the door closed, so she couldn't be sure. "Hey," she said, her tone not exactly friendly.

64

He spun around as if startled. "There you are. I was just knocking to see if you were ready for dinner." He smiled, giving her the full power of his megawatt looks, with that trim beard that would probably look deliciously scruffy in a few days' time.

She had zero belief the man was unaware of the power of his smile combined with his intensely gorgeous eyes. Was he hoping to distract her after she'd caught him exiting her tent?

But had she? Or had he just been there, knocking, as he'd claimed?

After all, why would he go in her tent when it would be so easy to get caught? She had to be imagining things.

"The buddy system doesn't extend into camp. I'm perfectly capable of walking all the way to the cook tent by myself."

He held up his hands. "Sorry. Didn't mean to offend. Just being neighborly."

She closed her eyes and tried to figure out if she was being a bitch or not. Did she have reason to be suspicious of him? Last night she'd wanted to let him kiss her.

Something about Bill Lowell threw her off. He didn't add up. She rubbed her temples. "Sorry. I think I'm cranky from travel and hunger. Let me drop off my laptop, and then I'll give you a tour of the cook tent and, if the food isn't ready, the rest of camp."

His smile returned, and she felt that damn flutter again. "I'd like that."

———

That had been damn close. He really had knocked on her door to see if she wanted to go to dinner, but when she didn't answer, he figured she was already in the cook tent and saw an opportunity to see if she'd plugged in Dylan's phone.

He'd been in her tent only long enough to spot the phone on the table. Plugged in. He touched the button, and the screen lit. It was working. He'd typed Dylan's PIN, and it unlocked.

His whole body had flooded with adrenaline in that moment, but he couldn't risk checking the contents now. Tomorrow, when she—and everyone else—was in the field, he'd be able to swipe the fully charged phone and comb through it. He'd hit the button to lock it again and quickly stepped out of her tent, thankful that no one was around.

He'd just stepped off the pallet step when she spoke. Damn muskeg ground cover made for silent footsteps around here.

She was suspicious. He knew it, so he dialed up his smile and took the offensive, calling out her manners. Her reaction told him she hadn't seen him actually leaving her tent. She had doubts.

He needed to play up the attraction angle—as if that was the reason he'd been on her step—while still not coming across as an ass who refused to respect her boundaries. He needed to get her to flirt with him. Let her think she was the one who was pulling him in like a magnet, no matter how much he tried to resist.

He needed to coax her like he would any woman in front of his camera when he was bent on seduction. He knew how to get women to flirt, vamp, and make the first move.

Could he do that with Fiona without a camera between them?

Dylan's life might depend on it, so he had no other choice.

SEVEN

Fiona never slept well at the start of a field project, and the first night on Chiksook was no exception. Between the wind buffeting the tent, her odd suspicions of the two new team members, and the fact that at first light she'd head to the archaeological site at last, her sleep was fitful until the last hour before dawn, when she finally sank into deep REM sleep.

She woke with a jolt upon hearing a knock on her door, followed by a male voice. "Fiona? Are you still here? Everyone is heading out, and you weren't at breakfast."

Shock filtered through her as she sat bolt upright and checked her phone for the time. But her phone was dead. Which was why she hadn't heard the alarm.

A female voice—Cara's—added, "She must've set out early, before any of us were up."

"Shit," she muttered, then projected her voice to the door. "I'm here."

"You are?" Cara shouted. "Can we come in?"

She was still in her mummy bag as she rubbed her face and tried to get her bearings. "Yes. Sure. Crap." She hit the button for the bedside LED lamp, and nothing happened. The tent was warm, but the heaters ran on gas, not electricity.

The door opened to reveal Cara and Bill, both dressed in the layers that would see them through a day of fieldwork with shifting weather conditions.

She held up her dead phone in one hand and pointed to the dark lamp with the other. "Power is out. Something must've happened to the line to my tent." She flopped back on the bed, groaning. This was not how she wanted to start her fieldwork.

On the bright side, now that she was wide-awake thanks to a big hit of panic, she realized she felt well rested. Even sleep saturated, in spite of several hours of fitful sleep.

"It's not the end of the world," Cara said. "The cook set aside a breakfast for you, and Bill packed your lunch so the cook could clean up."

She smiled at Bill, who'd held up an insulated bag on cue. "Bless you," she said, meaning it. The man was her new best friend for making sure she didn't start off on the wrong footing with the cook by messing with the cooking and cleaning schedule.

She rose from her cot and dropped the thick mummy bag that had kept her toasty warm in spite of the cold, windy night. She wore the same thermal underwear for pajamas that Bill had already seen her in yesterday morning, when they'd had breakfast together after her run with Victor, so there was no reason to be shy when she needed to get moving.

"I've got to run," Cara said. "I'm sharing a vehicle with Roy, and he's anxious to head out. Victor and John left before the rest of us were up, apparently, and they took two vehicles—we weren't sure if you were with one of them, but the cook said he hadn't seen you this morning, and he was up at five."

She did the math on the vehicles. "So if John and Victor each took a vehicle, and you're riding with Roy, that leaves only one left."

"Looks like we're working together after all," Bill said with an amused smile.

One of the reasons she'd planned to get up early was to claim a solo vehicle, since the archaeological site was on the other side of the island from where the others would be working today. She closed her eyes, regretting very much the times she'd scoffed at the idea of working with Bill. "Please tell me you think your mated pair of gray buntings are on the west end of the island, because that's where I absolutely must go today."

Cara flashed Fiona a bright smile. "I'll let you two work that out. I'm off. There's a radio for you in the office tent, along with an emergency kit."

She slipped out the door and closed it behind her, leaving Fiona alone with the man she'd be working with for the next eight to fourteen hours, depending on the weather.

Bill cleared his throat. "I suppose I can start in the west. But it'll cost you."

His deep voice had a slightly teasing tone that sent an anticipatory shiver down her spine. How did he *do* that?

"What's the price?" Damn, did her voice sound . . . *breathless*? She hoped it came across as sleep-fogged.

"This afternoon we head to Mount Katin for the bird hunt."

"That's fair. But why near the volcano?"

"Just a hunch," he said with a shrug.

"There are several scatters of World War II debris on the slopes of Mount Katin that I need to record. I can get started on that while you look for buntings."

"*Gray* buntings. For this project, not all buntings are equal."

She chuckled. "My bad." She nodded toward the door. "I'll meet you in the office tent in ten minutes, and we can set out."

"You don't want to eat first?"

"If you drive the first shift, I can eat on the road. It takes at least an hour to get to the site."

"All right, then." He set the food pack on her footlocker and left her alone to get dressed.

As promised, ten minutes later, she was dressed and ready. Thankfully, she'd prepped her field gear last night, so it was only a matter of throwing food in the bag, getting dressed, and visiting the latrine.

She then remembered she'd need the car charger for her phone and returned to her tent to grab it. Her gaze landed on the cracked cell phone she'd started to charge last night but then unplugged in favor of charging her own. She touched the wake button. It had a 20 percent charge.

She considered bringing it with her to charge on the drive, but there was no point, considering she didn't know Dylan's PIN. She powered it off. Usually, she trusted everyone in camp—they had locks on their doors, but nobody used them. But she felt a little off with her questions about Victor and Bill, so she returned the phone to the storage compartment inside Dylan's clipboard, behind the papers exactly how she'd found it, and returned it to the sturdy metal footlocker. Best to keep it out of sight for now.

From there, she went to the cook tent to thank the cook for making sure she had food and to ask the maintenance team if they could check the power line to her tent, then filled her stainless-steel insulated mug with a hefty amount of coffee. Even though she had managed to sleep in the end, she had a feeling she was going to need the caffeine jolt to get through the long day.

Given the variable weather, everyone worked as long as possible on good weather days. Fourteen hours in the field wasn't unheard of, but there was a storm forecast for later today, so this was more likely to be eight to ten, maximum. She hoped Bill would be content to spend much of that at the site before moving to the volcano. Sleeping in and missing her shot at her own vehicle today had cost her. But then, she probably shouldn't go to such a remote part of the island by herself, and Christina wouldn't arrive until sometime after noon today.

As she made her way to the office tent, she looked up at the sky. The Anchorage contingent should get here ahead of the storm, which wouldn't hit until late afternoon or evening. And hopefully the barge with more supplies—including enough fuel and vehicles to support a twelve-person field crew with varying project areas—would also reach Chiksook ahead of the storm. The barge was supposed to have arrived days ago, before any of the researchers were here, but like everything else, there'd been problems and delays.

She stepped inside the office tent, and her gaze met Bill's entrancing blue eyes. If she'd gotten up early, she would have checked her email before setting out, but there was no time now. She'd just have to hope her boss said Bill Lowell was the world's best ornithologist and she was worrying for nothing . . . because like it or not, he was her partner in the field today.

———

Dean had hoped to get a crack at Dylan's phone today, but he'd take this as the second-best scenario. Alone with Fiona for the entire day would give him plenty of opportunity to get a fix on what she knew.

It still nagged at him that she'd given no indication of how well she really knew Dylan. She claimed she didn't even have his phone number? That made no sense. What had happened between them at the end? Did she dump his brother? Did she break his heart?

Dean had a hard time imagining Dylan breaking up with *her*. She was too perfect for him, and he wasn't one to give up on relationships easily. If he'd had his way, he'd still be married to his cold ex-wife.

The fully enclosed side-by-side UTV bounced over the rough old road, making it difficult for Fiona to eat her breakfast burrito and drink her coffee, but she didn't complain. She was too darn grateful to "Bill" for making sure she had food for the day and still getting a relatively early start.

He couldn't have planned that piece of luck any better.

"So, how old is this archaeological site we're going to?" he asked.

"We don't have carbon dates or soil analysis—I hadn't collected samples yet when we were yanked from the field—but when Dylan examined the site, he said the volcanic eruption that triggered the mudslide occurred about fifteen hundred years ago."

Dean kept his focus on the road and grip tight on the steering wheel to keep from giving away any emotion. "When did the volcanologist have a chance to visit the site?"

They hit a deep, muddy stretch, and his solid grip kept them from sliding off or getting stuck, as he kept them moving through the thick, slick mess that could barely be called a road.

When they reached slightly more solid ground, Fiona's breath whooshed out very audibly—he didn't take his gaze from the muddy track to look—and she said, "I'm glad you're driving. I hate this part. Christina usually drives."

"See now, I knew we'd make a good field team."

She let out a soft laugh. "You're good at this."

"Lots of practice, plus I enjoy it."

"Oh. So you're reckless and like taking risks."

"Absolutely. C'mon, didn't you get a little rush back there? Wondering if we'd make it?"

"Ahh. And an adrenaline junkie."

He unequivocally was an adrenaline junkie, and his addiction had served him well—he had no problem taking risks to get the perfect shot. He'd have loved the thrill of sneaking onto this project, if he wasn't so worried about Dylan.

"Yep," he said. "Unashamed and unabashed adrenaline seeker."

"Like I said, reckless. Have you ever jumped out of a perfectly good airplane for no reason?"

"I *love* skydiving."

"Climbed sheer faces of rock?"

"Half Dome is next on my bucket list."

"Free solo?"

He shook his head. "Oh, hell no. No adrenaline is that good. I always use ropes."

"Okay, we can be friends, then."

He laughed. "Whew. Do you climb? If you do, and we can be friends, maybe we could go sometime."

"No. My climbing days are over."

She didn't offer a reason, which made him wonder if she'd had a bad experience. "Well, maybe we can hike together sometime."

"I believe we will today, in fact, when we climb Mount Katin."

"I meant for *fun*."

"Let's get through this field project before we start planning hiking dates. I mean, we might hate each other before the end of the first week."

She had a point. When she found out who he really was, she might be a tad angry. And then there was the fact that she'd probably dumped his brother. His loyalty would always belong to the brother who was his only remaining family and who'd been his best friend since they'd shared a womb.

EIGHT

The road ended abruptly at a cut bank too steep to drive down to cross the shallow stream, requiring them to park and hike the last mile to the site. Fiona studied the terrain as they trudged the final mile of the journey she'd been obsessing over for the last five weeks and three days.

In rocky areas where the vegetation was light, things looked much as she remembered, telling her that maybe, just maybe, the site would be okay. Except this was treeless, wet tundra that *always* looked the same.

But then the spongy, wet muskeg—Alaska's version of a bog—gave way to tall grasses, where a person could almost get lost. Even she, at five nine without shoes, found it hard to see more than a few feet in front of her as the sedge grasses neared six feet. Bill was a large man—at least five inches taller than she was—and his head just peeked above the ground cover.

They cut a trail through the grasses, following her compass bearing, and the grasses popped back up behind them, hiding their path.

Five weeks ago, this hike had been much the same, and the beating of her heart intensified as she hoped that was another indication of how the site had fared. If the storm that roared through the day after their departure hadn't been strong enough to alter the landscape, maybe the tarps had held up.

"Careful," she said. "There's some WWII debris hidden in the grass up ahead. Rusted-out vehicle parts."

"How did they get a vehicle on this side of the stream?"

"There used to be a bridge. It collapsed and rotted decades ago."

A few minutes later, they came upon the debris, and despite the warning she'd given, *she* was the one to trip over a jagged piece of metal hidden in the grass. She stumbled but managed to stay on her feet, then said, "Found it," with a grumbling laugh.

"You weren't seriously going to come out here by yourself today, were you?" Bill asked.

She gave him a chagrined smile. "I suppose that would have been unwise."

"Uh-huh. Between the potential for getting the vehicle stuck in the mud and the hazards hidden in the grass, there's a lot that could go wrong, and it would be dangerous if you were alone. Frankly, I'm curious as to why John and Victor set out alone."

"They're probably going to the APE—or rather, study area—which doesn't have these high grasses or much in the way of World War II hazards. The land for the proposed base is much more level and sits on a sheltered bay. It's more seismically stable because the volcano is generally only active on the south flank. Mount Katin is lopsided, like Saint Helens after 1980. The eruption that covered my archaeological site fifteen hundred years ago took out the south face of Mount Katin, and the active fumaroles are mostly found on the southwest flank."

"So you're saying that if the volcano should decide to erupt today, we're in the primary blast zone?"

She chuckled at his dry tone. "Technically, yes, but there was also a lahar flow on the north side forty-five years ago that swamped part of the World War II base—which is why the base and radio tower were abandoned and that cove was deemed not ideal for the new submarine base. The proposed base is on the easternmost edge of the island—as far as one can get from the volcano on Chiksook." She smiled. "If it makes you feel better, Dylan assured me Mount Katin is pretty quiet these days. Not nearly as active as some of the other Aleutian volcanoes. He set up all sorts of sensor thingies to let us know if she starts to rumble."

Bill chuckled. "Sensor thingies?"

"I believe that is the technical term, yes."

"You've gotta stop using such big words. I'll never keep up."

She laughed, then skirted around more rusted-out vehicle parts hiding in the grass. "I'll do my best to stay away from SAT words."

They climbed a slope, leaving the wide valley of tall grasses behind. The village site was on the top of this hill.

Almost there.

The ground was slippery, forcing her to grab hold of the low ground cover and scramble up the wet, mossy slope. It wasn't the most graceful maneuver to navigate a slick forty-five-degree hillside, but it got the job done.

They reached the top, Bill having made the climb without being reduced to all fours. She rose to her feet and brushed off her muddy hands, then pulled her fingerless wool gloves back on. A quick glance showed the slope of the land and the grasses still hid the housepits from view.

She could barely breathe as she led Bill across the uneven ground and over a low rise. At the apex of the mound—which could well be another housepit buried by the mudslide—she could finally see the patch of earth she and Christina had dug into six weeks ago.

They'd removed the vegetation, exposing soft, wet soil beneath. The layer below that was where it got interesting. Mud and ash had capped the housepit. There'd been a partial collapse fifteen hundred years ago, and the rocks that lined the walls and the whalebone that provided structure to the roof had been the first things she'd identified. But then they'd found a chimney or entrance hole that had been covered and sealed by the slide, without filling the structure beneath. They'd removed the cap and had even been able to partially enter the pristine home. She'd collected the harpoon head and a metallic stone for Dylan to analyze, and she'd photographed what she could.

The last time she'd been here, she'd covered the opening with a tarp and weighed it down with rocks to protect the site for one to two nights—weather days were always possible, so she'd known it could be more than twenty-four hours before she returned. She'd never dreamed it would be five weeks and three days, during which the temporary tarp would be battered by wind and rain.

Her heart sank as she took in the condition of the site now. The blue tarp was gone.

She held her breath and moved closer to get a better look at the exposed opening. It might be okay. Once upon a time, the house had been built to withstand the weather.

But when she got close enough to see the hole, it wasn't okay. It was nowhere close to okay.

The opening was much bigger now than it had been five weeks and three days ago. The earth had given way to the elements. The roof had collapsed—and so had the rounded wall.

The pristine housepit—a find that could rival Pompeii or Ozette for offering a snapshot back in time—was destroyed.

She stared at the ruins in shock and horror. Her stomach churned, and she thought she might retch. This was the worst-possible scenario.

She'd left the housepit vulnerable. It was all her fault.

A single word escaped her lips. *"No."* It was a cry and a plea and all she could manage to choke out as emotion swamped her.

Every sleepless night, every minute of anxiety she'd lived with the last five weeks, had come to fruition. This was her worst nightmare in Technicolor. She couldn't stop a sob from escaping her throat.

Never in her life had she shed a tear at work. But then, she'd never been responsible for the destruction of a site that could easily be designated a National Historic Landmark.

The Unangas had trusted her to record their Traditional Cultural Property, and she'd *destroyed* it.

She held her gloved hands to her mouth and tried to hold back both a wail and tears. She was a professional. She didn't cry. Not in front of coworkers.

Bill moved to stand close beside her. "You okay?"

All she could do was shake her head, her gaze fixed on the jumble of rocks that had been perfectly lined up to form a semi-subterranean wall. A wall that had survived for more than fifteen hundred years, until she'd exposed it and left it vulnerable.

"What's wrong?" He waved an arm toward the rocks. "Is that bad?"

His question was reasonable. Archaeological sites often looked like nothing more than a jumble of rocks. A layperson—or anyone who hadn't seen the site five weeks and three days ago—wouldn't recognize the difference.

All she could do was nod. She managed to push air through, just enough to say, "Very bad." Then her throat seized again. She really was going to puke.

He raised an arm and hesitated, but then he placed it around her waist, under her pack, and pulled her against his side, offering comfort.

She was so shattered that she allowed it—even appreciated it—and turned to lean into him.

The ground beneath their feet gave way.

———

Dean pulled Fiona tight against him as they dropped at least six feet into the earth that had opened up beneath them. It must've been their combined weight when he pulled her close that triggered the collapse. He hadn't realized they were standing on part of the site.

Another room in the house? If so, it was much bigger than he'd expected.

He landed on his back, rocks gouging his hips and ass, while others tumbled from the walls and pelted his sides and head.

78

He would be bruised, but not broken. A good thing, because a broken leg out here would require a helicopter rescue, and they'd learned during their time on Adak how difficult it was to get a copter in the air in any kind of hurry.

Fiona had been reckless to even consider coming out here alone, no matter how desperate she was to get to the site.

Thanks to his hold on her waist, they'd landed face-to-face, chest to chest, him beneath her, his back slightly bowed by his pack, cushioning him from the rocky ground.

Fiona's eyes were wide—her devastating grief of a moment ago lost with the shock of the fall. When she realized she lay upon him, she started to push off his chest to stand, but he tightened his arms around her, holding her down.

"Wait. We need to make sure the ground is stable before we move." He brushed a few wisps of hair that had escaped her braid to the side so he could examine her face. Didn't look like she'd been pelted in the head with anything, so that was good news. "You hurt?"

She shook her head. "I—I don't think so?" She shifted, her hip coming into unpleasant contact with one of his favorite body parts.

He grimaced and tightened his grip on her again, preventing her from doing more damage.

Her eyes widened. "Sorry! Are you . . . okay?"

"Been better, to be honest." His voice came out higher than he'd like, and he couldn't help the small laugh that erupted at the ridiculousness of the moment.

She surprised him by letting out her own startled laugh. The way her body vibrated against his had the opposite effect of her hip jab a moment before.

He'd been pummeled by dreams of holding Fiona in a similar fashion the last two nights and had woken up to guilt at lusting after Dylan's girl. Now he had her in his arms and was far too consumed with wanting to cheer her up after her obvious desolation at the collapse of the site.

He released her and said, "I think the rocks have settled. Before you move, you need to look up and see what we're dealing with."

They were down inside the housepit, and there was a slight overhang where the roof hadn't collapsed yet. They didn't need more soil, rocks, and debris to collapse on top of them. It was going to be hard enough to scramble out without risking more destruction. Every move Fiona made would have to be careful to keep from undermining the structure further.

She planted her hands on either side of his head, raised up, and stretched her neck to see the precarious overhang.

She wore layers of clothing, yet he had a flash of what it would be like to have her on top of him like this in bed, her chest thrust outward above his face. It almost felt like a premonition.

This will *happen between us, beautiful.*

No. Not the time, and definitely not the woman.

"Oh, hell," she muttered softly.

Yes, hell indeed.

She slowly rose, moving gingerly—no longer a threat to the family jewels or the structural integrity of a fifteen-hundred-year-old house made of rocks without mortar and covered in sod.

Pebbles made a dash for the low point in the loose soil, which lacked the moisture content of the top layers that had been exposed to the elements. It wasn't dry by any means, but it also wasn't permafrost.

And beyond the collapsed area where they had fallen, he could see more rooms in the semi-subterranean house. There were more chambers. Intact.

He wished he had Dylan's expertise right now. He'd know how stable the layer of ash was that capped the site. Could he crawl into the other chambers and photograph them?

Once Fiona's body was extracted from his, he very slowly, very carefully removed his pack and pulled out his best camera. He was thankful it had been protected by both case and pack during the fall, but now he needed it in his hands.

He focused on the dark chambers beyond their bubble of destruction and snapped photos, using the zoom lens to gaze upon rooms not seen by human eyes for fifteen hundred years.

"Can you see anything?" Fiona asked, her voice breathless.

"Yes, wonderful things."

NINE

Fiona let out a soft, exhilarated laugh at their replay of Howard Carter and Lord Carnarvon's exchange at Tut's tomb nearly a hundred years ago. She hadn't intended it, but subconsciously, the words had slipped out, and Bill, bless him, knew the next line.

"Are you teasing me, or is there more?" she asked, because she couldn't blame him if he'd fudged to complete the script.

"There's more. A lot more."

She couldn't suppress the soft keening sound she made any more than she'd been able to suppress the sob earlier.

Part of the site had collapsed, but there was more. A lot more.

Except now, another portion had collapsed, and that jeopardized the remainder.

She pulled out her phone—which she'd charged on the drive—to take her own photos, but it wouldn't boot up. *What the hell?* This was a new phone.

Had there been a power surge in the line to her tent that fried her phone? Perhaps the generator problems hadn't all been fixed, and her tent, being first in the row, had taken the brunt.

She pulled out her work camera, the one she'd had to sign six forms and put up her kidney as collateral to check out from the power-hungry supply misers on base, and discovered the fancy rechargeable battery was also dead.

"I will name my firstborn after you if you get photos of everything. This might be our only chance to document this."

"On it." The camera's shutter sounded repeatedly.

"Right now, you're my favorite person in the world."

He laughed. "Glad to be of service. I hope you believe in the buddy system now."

She was thoroughly chagrined for how she'd treated him in the first minutes of their meeting. Standing behind him, she leaned her forehead on his shoulder and admitted, "You win that round retroactively."

"Ah, Fiona, I expected a longer battle."

There was something about the way he said her name. It was a caress. Like he'd said it before. Like he *knew* her. And that was the strangest thought to cross her mind in this situation.

She took a deep breath and focused on the small opening that appeared to be an adjacent room. The housepit was a web of different chambers. She'd known some of these dwellings were built like this but hadn't dared to hope to find more than the single room.

"How big is this place?" Bill asked.

"I have no idea. It would be great to use ground-penetrating radar to get a feel for the extent of the site or lidar to map the interior. Hell, even a magnetometer would be a miracle out here. Most of these kinds of houses are just a single oval room. But archaeologists have recorded collapsed ones that had a central hub with several branching chambers. This must be one of those."

He looked at the screen on his camera. "I'm getting a shine on the rocks in some of these pictures. Might be more of what you found before. More pieces of meteorite."

It was only a narrow opening to the next chamber, and Fiona didn't dare move closer to see inside, given how unstable the walls and ceiling were. "Please tell me that's a good camera for low light and hidden chambers."

"It's the best money can buy, and I know how to use it."

"Not all heroes wear capes. Some carry cameras."

"Want to record a video? Get a three-sixty view of the pit?"

"Yes, please."

"Okay. I'll start recording; you narrate as I turn."

She did, giving the date, time, weather conditions, and everything else she could think of to describe and document the find.

She didn't have a large-enough tarp to cover this new opening, and there was no way to protect it from the elements. This would be the most intact this portion of the site would ever be.

Excavation was, by its very nature, a destructive process. Every dig she'd ever been on destroyed the thing they were studying, but this was different, and this site, with its perfect preservation, would have been treated differently, perhaps not been excavated at all in favor of remote sensing with lidar, GPR, and magnetometers, all of which could map the site without destroying it.

And maybe that would still happen, but this part, without a doubt, would not survive the coming weeks or months. It had now collapsed twice after the first portion had been exposed. She would call higher-ups in the navy and ask for resources to protect the site, but it was probably too late to save it.

Rocks high in the wall to her right shifted and threatened to fall.

"We need to get out of here," Bill said.

She studied the opening and loose earth where they'd fallen. A few large rocks remained. Enough to give her footholds. She tested the lowest ones with her not-insignificant weight. Halfway up the slumped wall, she'd run out of rocks.

"I'll give you a boost if you need it."

"But how will you get out?" she asked.

"We'll deal with that after we get you out."

There wasn't really much choice.

She gingerly started to climb, trying to prevent the wall from collapsing further or, worse, bringing down the rest of the ceiling. Halfway up the six-foot slumping wall, she started to slide down again.

Bill planted his hands on the place where her thighs met her butt and pushed, giving her the leverage she needed to clamber up and over.

They'd now lain chest to chest and he'd had his hands on her ass. This was *not* a normal day at the office.

She scrambled up and out, then scooted back as if the ground were a thin skin of ice formed on a winter lake. She turned and faced the opening, lying flat on her belly, still thinking of it as fragile lake ice, and said, "Hand me the packs."

He did, and she crawled backward with both bags, moving them away from the gap in the ground. When she started to crawl forward again to offer Bill a hand, he said, "Nah. I got it. Move out of the way."

She moved to the side, then all at once Bill backed up, then bolted forward, vaulting up the six-foot wall like some sort of wildly talented summer Olympian. He moved so fast, the earth didn't have time to collapse beneath him.

Once he'd cleared the lip, he crawled away from the ledge like she had. She retreated with him, moving back until she was certain they were on solid ground. But what did she know? She'd thought they'd been standing on solid ground before.

They were both breathing heavily as they lay in the sloppy, wet moss. She rolled over to look up at the gray sky above and took a deep breath.

"So what does this mean for the site?" he asked.

"I honestly have no idea. The collapse isn't good, but there's so much more here that could still be intact. I feel awful about the damage, but maybe . . . maybe data can be salvaged after all? Maybe parts can be preserved. I was just thinking it would be great to get lidar out here to map it. But the navy will never pay for that. I need to visit the village here on the island and talk to the Unangas, tell them what we found and what happened to it. They were the ones who asked me to record this as a Traditional Cultural Property."

"You want to go there today?"

She sighed. "No. I need to contact my boss first, tell him what happened. Legal might need to get involved. Technically, it's not my fault—it's not like I had any other choice—but really, it's totally my fault, and legal is going to want to approve the language that explains the situation."

"It's not your fault at all. You didn't know it would take this long to get back to the field."

"I shouldn't have exposed so much and removed the cap on the hole. When I realized it was likely an intact house, I should have stopped and left it closed. So it *is* my fault."

"But isn't . . . your whole purpose to dig in sites like this?"

"My purpose is to *find* them. Digging is destructive. I should have stopped the moment I realized what I'd found."

"But how could you do that? You had to expose it to know what it was."

"Yes and no." She considered that day she and Christina had found the site. It had happened three days before Dylan was booted from the team and four before they all were yanked from the field. At what point was she certain she'd found an intact Unangax̂ house?

"We scraped off the moss and humus layers, followed by the tuff and ash from more recent volcanic eruptions. Below that was a layer of lahar—the volcanic mudflow that capped the site." She remembered the thrill of it, knowing it could have covered something important. "The Unangas told us there was a village in this area. Their oral tradition tells of the time the volcano was active and they'd abandoned the island for safer ground, only to return and find their village gone. So when we found the lahar—a thick layer from a big eruption—Christina and I were excited. We were certain we'd find cultural layers beneath, not sterile soils followed by basalt that predated human occupation of the Aleutians."

In short, they *knew*. They'd exposed the site to confirm it.

"But the lahar could cover a massive expanse. It probably does. You didn't know the village would be here."

"No. It was an educated guess based on oral tradition and the land-form. Access to fresh water. Proximity to fish and other resources."

"You're determined to blame yourself for doing your job."

Was she? Or was she just being honest? Maybe it was a bit of both. They could have left the house sealed when they'd found what was, for all intents and purposes, the door.

But even more than opening the door, they'd cleared a large expanse of moss, tuff, ash, going all the way down to the lahar—including the portion that had collapsed today. They would have covered the exposed areas with the layers they'd carefully removed had they known they were about to be evacuated. Being exposed for over five weeks must have weakened the roof.

"We uncovered a lot of the site down to the lahar. That's what we were standing on when it collapsed."

It really is my fault.

"Are you going to get in trouble?"

"I'm sure headquarters will have some choice words for me, but no, not in the sense that I was negligent. We had no idea we'd be leaving so soon, let alone that we'd be gone this long."

Bill went silent, and she figured he'd accepted there was no point in trying to talk her out of feeling guilty. Did that ever work with anyone? Guilt wasn't easily logicked away.

"What do we do now?"

"I need to record the damage as best I can. If you could take more pictures, I'd really appreciate it. I don't know what the deal is with my phone. All I can think is there was a power surge to my tent last night. I swear this project is cursed."

They spent the next hour documenting the damage. He took at least forty kabillion photos, and she followed along, creating a photo log that described the visible damage. More of the shiny rocks were spotted in the collapsed room. Were the rocks really debris from a large meteorite?

Trevor had tagged along with Dylan the day he'd visited the site, and the geologist and volcanologist discussed the possibility that a large meteorite might have struck Mount Katin several thousand years ago—after the volcano formed but before the most recent cone-building events—because Dylan had seen superheated quartz-icicle-like things that were often found near impact craters. He speculated the crater might be underwater, but the debris field extended to land.

Trevor had concurred with his findings and said he'd take core samples to look for associated tsunami soils that would indicate a meteorite had struck the area.

Neither Dylan nor Trevor was on Chiksook now, though, to tell her the results of their study. She'd been so busy with her other projects once she'd returned to the Kitsap Peninsula, she'd managed only to shoot off an email to Pollux asking for Trevor's findings on tsunami soils, and hadn't followed up when she didn't receive a reply.

Were the metallic stones part of a many-millennia-old meteorite strike? Prehistorically, had the Unangas found chunks of meteorite and incorporated the pieces into their homes and tool kits? Or did the metal simply indicate a more extensive trade system than had been previously theorized based on the existing archaeological record?

The prehistoric village site raised so many questions and was without a doubt eligible for listing in the National Register of Historic Places under Criterion D: the site was likely to yield information important to prehistory, plus the site had the required integrity.

Well, it had integrity before she'd kicked the domino that caused everything to tumble down, that is. But still, enough remained for inclusion in the National Register.

An hour later, they sat down on the edge of the site to enjoy a midmorning snack of hard-boiled eggs, cheese, and salami. The amount of hiking required, long days, and unforgiving wind required protein-heavy snacks and meals.

Fiona sipped her water and chewed on a pepperoni stick as she looked out over the site. Without thinking, she leaned her head on Bill's shoulder.

The moment her temple touched the shell of his raincoat, she realized the inappropriateness of the action and even had to wonder why it had felt natural in the first place.

He stiffened. She could feel the tension in his body even through the slight contact that included at least three layers of clothing separating her temple from his skin. She wanted to jerk her head up, but that would only draw attention to the awkwardness of the moment.

She decided to play it casual. No big deal. She let out an audible sigh and said, "It's been quite a day, and it's only eleven a.m."

His shoulder relaxed, and the awkward moment passed. Or maybe she thought it did simply because she wanted it to be gone. Whatever it was didn't matter, because he was playing along. "Is your work always this exciting?"

She snorted and lifted her head, still sitting close but no longer leaning on him. "Hardly."

"What are your days usually like?"

"Usually I'm in a cubicle on the Bangor sub base, managing contracts, working on reports, following up with tribes or the State Historic Preservation Office, trying to guide projects through the compliance process."

"A lot of bureaucratic hoops in addition to the technical work? That must get old."

"It does. But then there are projects like this, where I get to go to restricted islands and find wonderful things. Well done with the King Tut reference, by the way."

89

"Thank you. I'm a Tut fanboy, to be honest. I've even been to the museum in Cairo."

"Now I'm jealous. I've never been to Egypt. Never been to Africa at all."

"I did a sh—evaluation there. Even got a VIP tour of the pyramids."

"Seriously? They don't have their own bird experts?"

"I'm sure they do, but I know the right people."

"Damn. I need to get to know your people." She chuckled. "I have several friends who are actual Egyptologists and they've done zilch for me."

"Yesterday, on the boat, you were telling Cara about an underwater dig you worked on in the Caribbean. That had to be cool."

"It was. I have been lucky. I'm not an underwater archaeologist—I mean, I don't have a degree in nautical archaeology or anything—but I know scuba and did a field school in Jamaica, which was basically a summer in paradise going scuba diving twice a day, then drinking rum and dancing to reggae music all night."

She closed her eyes, remembering that carefree summer. Regan had been a senior in college and doing her own field school, but Aidan had been able to take a week vacation and visited her. That had been during the good times, when she and her big brother had been allies.

She missed that brother. She grieved his loss, even though Aidan was still very much alive.

"You're describing a different woman from the one I'm working with today."

"We can't always be carefree and young."

"Amen to that."

His words made her wonder what had been the event that pushed him into responsible adulthood.

"Do you still dive?" he asked.

"When I can. I sometimes wish I'd pursued nautical archaeology."

"I love diving. Photographing marine wildlife is one of my favorite hobbies. After we go hiking, we can go scuba diving together. It's even more important to have a dive buddy than it is to have a fieldwork buddy."

That made her smile, and she pushed away sadness over her brother and questions about Bill's dark past, whatever it might be. "I thought we were going to hold off on making plans until after we know each other better. Besides, that summer in Jamaica kind of ruined diving in cold Puget Sound for me."

"Hey, earlier you said I was your favorite person in the world. I'm striking while the iron is hot. You'll have to deal with the cold water, though, because I think it's too soon to start planning a tropical vacation together."

She laughed. "But think of the hikes we could do in Hawaii!"

He grinned, his blue eyes narrowing in a sexy way. "Okay then, putting tropical vacation back on the table."

She'd bet he looked amazing in a wet suit. Or better yet, no suit at all . . .

She shook her head. This was not the time or place. She had a job to do. She finished her snack and rose to her feet, dusting herself off. "I'm going to do a pedestrian survey of the area, make sure we didn't miss anything. When I'm done, we can head to the volcano."

"Can I help?"

"No. I really need to walk it myself. You might not recognize something as cultural."

She set off, doing five-meter transects up and down the landform. She dropped blue pin flags in a few places where she found pieces of metal—a reminder that the US military had been all over this island during World War II—and red flags in a few places that she thought might be other semi-subterranean houses. If there were more intact houses, she might be able to forgive herself for the destruction.

Right now, the guilt of it weighed on her.

91

What would have happened if she'd missed the boat that day? There had probably been enough supplies to last a few days. They would have come back for her after the storm passed. She could have ensured the site was completely closed and protected.

She should have taken that risk, but it hadn't even crossed her mind at the time.

Bill also walked the area as she conducted her transects, but his path didn't intersect with hers, and she appreciated that he gave her room to work as he photographed the area.

There was something about his body language when he had the camera in his hands. She'd noticed it that first night on Adak. Something had shifted from the moment he'd started taking pictures.

Lots of birders were excellent photographers, so that was no surprise. What caught her attention was that without the camera, he seemed almost . . . anxious. Worried. But when the camera came out, he was like a cigarette smoker finally getting a nicotine fix. It calmed him in some way.

She didn't know anything about cameras but guessed the one he was using had cost a lot. It wasn't the kind of camera one usually brought to Chiksook. The EIS didn't require *National Geographic*–worthy images. Point-and-shoot was all they needed.

That he was willing to bring expensive equipment—and at this point, she'd seen him use no less than three different cameras—not just to Chiksook but also out to the field made her wonder at his finances. A guy who was desperate for a last-minute contract after a job fell through wouldn't necessarily be loaded.

Why risk his good cameras? Pollux Engineering was supposed to provide him with a camera for this job, so even if he didn't have a less-expensive one to bring to the field, he could have gotten one at no charge.

It was another little piece that nagged at her. He wasn't familiar with the NEPA process. He'd been far too interested in Dylan Slater's forgotten gear. He'd brought not just one, but at least *three* expensive cameras into the field. His charm and looks weren't enough to stop the camel's back from starting to bow.

She reached the end of her transect and found a rock to sit on to jot down some notes. Several birds took to the sky when she sat, and she realized they'd been hidden in the low vegetation.

Bill had his back to her and didn't turn when the birds called out to each other.

"I don't suppose any of those are the birds you're looking for?" she asked when he failed to notice the activity.

He turned, looking almost startled to discover a dozen birds flying overhead. What had he been so focused on that stopped a birder from noticing birds?

She wanted to blow this off; after all, she'd be offended if he tried to tell her how to do her job, so she shouldn't tell him how to do his. But she couldn't let it go.

He aimed his camera at the birds and, she presumed, snapped away. He was too far for her to hear the snick of the shutter.

He lowered the camera, letting it hang from the strap as he approached her. "No. Not gray buntings, but they'll go in my inventory. Thanks for the heads-up."

"How are you going to calculate the potential number of takes an operational sub base might trigger?" She kept her voice neutral. Casual question. *Not suspicious of you at all.*

He paused, looking at his camera screen, and she had the distinct feeling he was trying to figure out how to answer her. Finally he said, "I won't be calculating potential takes on this trip."

She gave a stiff smile, trying to keep her response friendly sounding, because his answer was . . . odd. "Yeah. Well, that would be impossible given that they haven't given us the engineering plans yet."

There were a lot of factors in determining takes under the Endangered Species Act or the Migratory Bird Treaty Act. She'd heard complaints from other ornithologists that the two acts even had different definitions of the term *take*, and sometimes they had to write one section for ESA and another for MBTA, if the study area was home to both endangered and migratory birds.

"Yeah, that would help for sure."

"Plus, for your take calculation, you'll need to look at the electric facility and power lines. I mean, that alone would require an APP."

She specifically didn't say "Avian Protection Plan" instead of APP, because she wanted to know if he was familiar with the acronym at all.

"Yeah. All of that. It's a lot to factor in with endangered birds to consider."

Unease slid through her. The gray bunting was a migratory bird, not an endangered species. ESA didn't apply here. And he, the ornithologist hired to find a very special migratory bird, should know the difference far better than an archaeologist who knew squat about birds.

Her suspicion was only heightened by his continuously vague answers, but she didn't know enough about ESA to really grill him.

Except . . . every archaeologist working in Cultural Resources Management knew that Section 106 of the National Historic Preservation Act was the primary driver of their work. Similarly, every wildlife biologist working under NEPA could cite Section 7 of the Endangered Species Act for the exact same reason.

"At least consultation as outlined in Section 27 of the ESA has teeth to make sure all forms of 'takes' are taken into account under NEPA." The statement was a word salad with extra croutons. If he was the ornithologist he claimed to be, he'd correct the section number or ask what the hell she meant. She had no idea how many sections there were in the ESA, but she doubted there were more than twenty.

Bill shifted to scan the horizon. He didn't want to meet her gaze. "Yeah. I'll make sure all potential takes are counted."

Fiona studied his back, trying to even out her breathing so he couldn't hear the sudden panic his words just triggered.

There was no way in hell Bill Lowell was the ornithologist with NEPA experience he claimed to be.

TEN

He blew it. He hadn't had enough time to study for this role. He'd looked at the regs but clearly hadn't memorized them, didn't know the lingo.

And Fiona had noticed.

Dammit, he *knew* gray buntings were migratory, but he got tangled in the regs, and he'd just made it worse from there. He'd probably made multiple mistakes but had no clue what they were.

Less than two weeks ago, he'd seen Pollux Engineering's call for an ornithologist. The preliminary fieldwork for endangered species had been done months ago, and no endangered birds were known to nest on Chiksook. The report of the gray bunting call had triggered a new study with the focus on migratory birds, and the original ornithologist was no longer available.

Dean saw an opportunity and had wasted no time calling in favors. He had an investigative reporter friend who wrote exposés on endangered-species trafficking. She cultivated sources on the shady side and was able to help him. A few phone calls and $1,000 later, he had a fake ID in the name of Bill Lowell that would pass close examination.

He'd scoured Bill's website for background information and combed through the regs for NEPA work. He'd read the bird section of a few EISs he'd found online. But clearly, ten days of cramming government regs wasn't enough to pass the social conversation test. A true expert on the Endangered Species Act or the Migratory Bird Treaty Act would use words like *take* with ease.

They'd have worked on enough EIS documents to recognize the difference between NRHP and NHPA—the National Register of Historic Places versus the National Historic Preservation Act. It was his confusion over NHPA that had tripped him up the first night. And now he'd somehow screwed up the regs he, as an ornithologist, should know backward and forward.

They hiked back to the side-by-side in silence, Dean well aware that anything he said to correct his mistakes would only make it worse, as he couldn't be certain what his errors were beyond confusing endangered with migratory. And an attempt to correct that one would only highlight his confusion over the very law that was his reason for being here.

Was she afraid of him now?

He considered coming clean, but given that she'd lied about her relationship with Dylan, never mentioning that they'd been involved, that could be a bad idea. He needed to keep his focus and not forget that he should be suspicious of *her*.

Until she admitted there was more to her relationship with Dylan than the working one she'd described, he didn't have a lot of faith that what she'd said so far was true.

It was entirely possible she had something to do with Dylan's disappearance. That could be the reason she was so closemouthed about his exit.

The thought had been in the back of his mind from the start, but as he got to know her, he'd brushed aside the concerns. Because he liked her. He didn't want her to have betrayed his brother.

It was time to drop the wishful thinking and start probing her for information.

Now they would head to the volcano. It was a pathetic starting point, but it was all he had. He would revisit the sensors Dylan had placed and monitored. He'd spent his days out here studying Mount Katin. Maybe he'd find some clue to what had happened there.

It was almost a shame he had Fiona with him now, as she'd expect him to do ornithological things. He'd go through the motions and take photos and hope his cover would last a few more days.

They reached the side-by-side. As Dean reached for the keys, Fiona said, "I'm driving."

"I thought you didn't like driving out here?"

"Now that I've seen the condition of the roads, I'm okay with it."

She was lying, which was a bad sign. She *was* scared of him. And now she had a need to be in control of their vehicle.

He had no choice but to give her the keys. It was a small gesture, but it might go a long way toward regaining her trust.

———

The main study area where the other scientists and engineers would be was on the far side of the island. Between Fiona and the group of people she knew and trusted was one rather large volcano.

Bill wanted to do his bird hunt around the volcano, so she took the road that skirted the lower slopes and headed to the far side of the mountain. Once she rounded the southern slope, her field radio should be able to connect with Cara, Roy, or John.

She'd feel better once she wasn't isolated with Bill.

She really wanted to go back to camp and check her email, see if her boss had information on Pollux's vetting process, but that wasn't possible. She kept coming back to the question: Why would anyone fake being an ornithologist?

A paid vacation on Chiksook Island this was *not*.

The sky filled with low, gray clouds. The predicted storm looked like it might arrive earlier than expected. Wind buffeted the vehicle, making her glad they'd finished recording the damage to the site and were in the enclosed side-by-side. She just hoped the rain held off until they were back at camp, because the roads could get swampy.

As anxious as she was about the storm and her suspicions, she went through the motions of aiding his survey and pulled over whenever there was a new bird sighting. He would take pictures and write down the time, date, and location while she checked her phone—still not taking a charge, making her more certain the battery had been fried—and pretended everything was just fine.

After more than an hour of driving and stopping, they were finally in radio range of the study area. Fiona used the excuse of more birds to pull over again.

"I've already got pictures of song sparrows. They're super common here."

"Oh. Sorry. I couldn't tell what they were. While we're stopped, I want to radio the others and check in."

She reached for her pack, pulled out the radio she'd picked up from the office tent this morning, and turned it on.

Nothing happened. The red LED power light didn't glow. There was no static. It was dead.

She'd left it off this morning to save the battery while they were out of range anyway. It should be charged and ready to go. Like her phone.

She'd been afraid before, but now . . . she couldn't breathe.

Last night, she'd seen Bill on the front step of her tent. Had he been inside? Had he messed with her phone? Was that why her alarm failed? Was that why the phone wouldn't take a charge now?

This morning, she'd entered the office tent to pick up her radio and Bill was already there, waiting. Alone. Had he sabotaged her radio?

"Give me your radio." Her voice was low and deep, a result of the difficulty she was having drawing in air.

"Why? What's wrong?"

"Give me your radio!"

Bill frowned at her sharp tone, then shrugged. "Sure." He reached for his pack in the back seat and plucked out his two-way radio. "Have at it."

She yanked it from his hand and turned the knob.

Nothing happened. No light. No static.

Nothing.

Her gaze swung up to meet Bill's no-longer-attractive blue eyes. "Did you do something to the radios? To my phone?"

He reared back. "Uh, no. Why would you even think that?"

A storm gathered and would be rolling in soon. They were alone on a remote road on a remote island. There were about two dozen Unangas living in a village on the southwest coast, four Pollux employees in the study area on the east end of the island, and a boat captain, cook, and two maintenance men at the camp in the southeast. And she couldn't reach a single one via phone or radio.

They didn't bother with satellite phones out here, because cloud cover made them unreliable, but right now she wished she had one anyway on the off chance today would be the day it would work even with the ominous, dark clouds overhead.

She couldn't name her suspicions while she was alone with him, not while she was trapped without a radio, phone, or anyone who even knew exactly where they were.

She was certain at this point he wasn't an ornithologist. But what was he?

Who was he?

"Is your phone working?"

"I assume. I haven't looked at it since last night."

He pulled out his phone and handed it to her.

Her heart sank as she hit the wake button. It was dead.

She covered her mouth with her hand. Her whole body shook.

"It was working fine when I plugged it in to charge last night. I swear."

"How did you wake up this morning without your phone?"

He held up his wrist, which sported a sturdy field watch. "Wristwatch. I don't like relying on phones and things with such short battery life." He looked at his dead phone. "Maybe this is all just . . . I don't know. A bizarre coincidence?"

"Right. Every piece of electronics but your camera and this vehicle is dead." Dread shot through her, and she checked the dash, feeling faint relief at seeing the gas gauge showing three-quarters of a tank.

"I don't know why our phones and the radios are dead."

"Was the power working in your tent this morning?"

"I don't know. I have a battery-powered lamp I brought with me. This morning I grabbed the phone from the charger and shoved it in my pack without checking it. You think there was a power surge that took out both our tents and blew our plugged-in phones?"

"Maybe." His not knowing if the power had tripped in his tent too could be a convenient excuse. But it also could be the truth.

But then, he'd lied about being an ornithologist, so why should she believe him in this?

She put the side-by-side in gear. "We're heading to the study area. We need to check in with the others."

She mentally dared him to challenge her decision, but he simply said, "I think that's a good idea."

ELEVEN

Fiona was freaked out, and Dean didn't blame her. What the hell was going on?

Had a power surge taken out his phone? It was possible his and Fiona's tents shared a line, given they were next to each other, but were they the only ones affected?

And what was the deal with their radios? The emergency field kits were assembled and maintained by the maintenance team. Was it a coincidence that the two bad radios went to the same two people whose phones had been fried?

Was it possible someone had figured out who he was and why he was here?

Was someone trying to stop him from finding Dylan?

There was a part of Dean that was aware Dylan might be dead, but he refused to entertain that scenario. He would operate on the belief that Dylan was alive until he was faced with irrefutable proof otherwise.

This wasn't some bullshit thought experiment with a cat in a box.

Dylan was alive. Dean would find him.

The messed-up electronics supported that belief. Because why would anyone mess around with their phones and radios unless they had something to hide?

Dean chose to believe the thing they were hiding was his brother.

I'm here, man. If ever there was a time for some Wonder Twin power, it's now.

He closed his eyes and pictured his brother the last time he saw him. Several months ago. Dean had flown north to Seattle to see Dylan in his new, post-divorce life. They'd done the whole Seattle circuit. During the day, they'd visited the troll under the bridge and Gas Works Park, followed by a ferry ride across the Sound in the late afternoon. To their great luck and astonishment, a pod of whales had crossed the ferry's path—several passengers who were regular commuters said it was only the first or second time they'd seen whales from the ferry—and Dean had taken several magnificent photos he'd subsequently sold with limited licensing to the Washington State Department of Transportation's ferry division and the Seattle Metropolitan Chamber of Commerce.

After the ferry ride, they'd watched a Mariners game in a Pioneer Square bar—it was an away game, or they'd have gotten tickets—and then they'd enjoyed live music in a blues bar.

It had been the first time Dean had seen Dylan happy in so long, he hadn't even commented on the fact that Dylan still wore his wedding ring. He got it. Dylan wasn't ready to date, and the ring was a big deterrent.

At least four women had approached them in the bar, and once eyes fell on the ring, they skedaddled. Some stuck around to flirt with Dean, but he was there for his brother and not a hookup, so he'd politely declined. That night in Pioneer Square, he hadn't looked twice at any of the women who'd approached them, and neither had Dylan.

So when Dylan had gushed about Fiona on the phone a few months ago, Dean had been elated his twin was dating again, even if he worried Dylan had gotten too serious, too soon—again.

He told himself he'd always worry about Dylan, that it was in their DNA. But now, as he bounced across the marshy tundra with Dylan's latest love at the wheel, and she'd given no indication she cared about him one way or the other, plus their radios and phones had been nuked, he decided his worry over Dylan's infatuation with Fiona Carver was more than warranted.

The shit of it was, there was no one for him to turn to. He was on his own and had been from the start. For the last ten years, Dylan had been the only person Dean could truly trust.

He preferred it that way. The fewer people in your inner circle, the less you had to lose. He had sex when he wanted it and lots of friends among the beautiful and talented in the LA area. He was invited to all the A-list parties. He knew his assets: he was good-looking and had an awe-inspiring career. He was at the top of his game, and his work was in demand by all the major wildlife organizations. Movers and shakers in Hollywood wanted to associate with him, and it was fun because he didn't *need* anything from the same celebrities who were so eager to court him as a friend.

If someone turned out to be a dick, he simply deleted them from his contacts list and moved on, which was a luxury few who moved in the same circles could afford.

Dean had a good life and was happy. He had his camera, his career—which included travel to all seven continents—sex without messy emotions or heartbreak, and his brother.

But then Dylan disappeared . . . and nothing mattered anymore. He'd lost the most important piece of the equation that gave his life balance.

He kept his focus on the road ahead as Fiona navigated the rough, muddy track better than he would have expected. She might not like driving on these roads, but she was good at it, even when she was in a hurry—which she was now.

She didn't trust him. Before this day—probably this afternoon—was over, he'd have to tell her everything and hope she'd keep his secret. Maybe even help him. She had Dylan's phone, after all. And his field notes.

But he couldn't tell her yet. Not when she was terrified of him. And not when he wasn't sure if he could trust her.

"We're almost to the study area. It's large, though, given that it would have all the infrastructure required for the proposed base. I'm not sure where we'll find everyone."

"How much of the area is accessible by vehicle?"

"Not a lot, but we'll see parked vehicles if they're far from the road."

It took a full twenty minutes to drive across the study area, searching for parked side-by-sides to indicate where the others were working.

"Maybe they went back to camp?"

"I can't imagine why they'd cut out early when the rain hasn't started yet. The rule is to work when you can, and right now, we can."

"Head to camp. If they're there, we can ask them why they quit early." Much as he'd wanted to go to the volcano today, that wasn't happening. The suggestion to go to camp might earn him some trust points, and he needed all he could get right now.

She did a big, sweeping U-turn and headed in the direction of camp. They'd done quite a circuit today, crossing the entire island to get from the archaeological site to the study area while skirting around a volcano.

"How far to camp from here?" Dean asked.

"Twenty minutes or so, if we don't get stuck in the mud."

"Not to be superstitious or anything, but I think you need to knock on wood now. Given how this day has gone."

She glanced around the interior, then lifted her hand from the steering wheel and knocked on her head. "That'll have to do."

The road was slippery, and her focus remained on the road as they drove in tense silence for at least ten minutes. The vehicle rounded a curve and the view of the water and gray sky opened up. She squinted into the distance. "It looks like the helicopter is coming in. The rest of the crew is arriving." There was relief in her voice.

Dean shifted forward, looked in the direction she indicated, and saw the bird, but . . .

It was rising. And getting smaller.

"Um . . . it looks like it's leaving, not arriving." He glanced to the side to see her reaction.

She pursed her lips, and her brow furrowed as she focused on the small retreating dot in the sky. "That doesn't make sense."

With her focus on the sky, she didn't see the pothole until the side-by-side lurched and her chin hit the steering wheel.

She cursed and shifted back in her seat, returning her focus to the road. "We've booked the helicopter for the duration of the project. It stays here so we can evacuate if needed. Same as the boat. There's no reason for it to be taking off so soon after delivering the rest of the crew."

He cleared his throat. "Well, not unless they're evacuating."

"But . . . why would they evacuate?"

Dean figured they were still ten minutes from camp, but they were on a slope, up above the sea-level camp, and the rain clouds remained just high enough that when the four-by-four rounded a bend, the view below opened up. Even at this distance, he could see choppy water. In the foreground, he could just make out a dark-gray cloud in the general vicinity of where the camp should be.

Fat raindrops landed on the windshield as he stared at the cloud and tried to make sense of it.

"That cloud doesn't look . . . normal," Fiona said.

There were lots of dark clouds thanks to the threatening storm, but they were much higher in the sky. He frowned and lifted his camera to his eye so he could zoom in. "It's smoke, not a cloud."

"Smoke?" Fiona's voice took on a new level of alarm. "What . . . how?"

"It would explain the helicopter leaving." Through the lens, he scanned the pier and then the water. In the far distance, he just caught sight of the boat. He snapped a photo, or Fiona might not believe him as he said, "The boat's gone too."

"What? The boat *and* the helicopter? We've been abandoned here?"

He turned the camera to the rows of gray tents as smoke billowed from the center of camp.

"It looks like it," he said, his voice dry as he gave her the worst of the news. "One of the tents is on fire."

He hit the record button to capture video. Through the lens, he watched the dark cloud shift and shimmy—then a massive orange plume lit the sky, billowing outward as a thunderous noise split the air.

TWELVE

Fiona slammed on the brakes. This . . . wasn't possible. She hadn't just seen their camp get incinerated in a massive blast.

Had they guessed the blast was coming, and that's why they'd evacuated? Had the electrical problems somehow ignited the gas lines? The massive fireball had looked like it encompassed all the tents.

Every single tent had been heated with gas. Something must've gone catastrophically wrong. And yet, it was hard to believe anything that catastrophic could be . . . an *accident*.

Her hands shook as she hit the gas on the side-by-side. Surely the boat or helicopter would come back to get them, now that the explosion was past.

The rain picked up, the patter of heavy drops on the hood gaining tempo. The rain would douse the fire, thank goodness.

It took more than ten minutes for her to descend the slippery slope near the camp. By the time they were in range to truly see the damage, fog had rolled in.

Bill continued using his camera as a telescope. "The boat is gone."

"Maybe you just can't see it in the fog. Surely they'll come back for us."

"I don't think so. Not with the storm coming in. They got out just in time. It's probably why they left when they did. Before we were back."

"So they were all called in because of the fire and told to evacuate. But because our phones and radios didn't work, we're stranded."

She could hardly wrap her brain around it. Was it all some horrific accident, or was it deliberate?

The timing with the storm was convenient but also made the deliberateness of it all improbable. The storm was predicted but was supposed to hit later in the day.

The vehicle headlights cut a small swath through the fog as they rolled closer to the smoldering gray mess that had been their camp less than fifteen minutes ago.

The tents were gone. All of them. Completely destroyed.

She stopped a fair distance from the wreckage. No telling if there was another fuel tank ready to blow.

"They must've called for an evacuation after the first tent caught fire," she said. Her voice had a dull sound to it—disbelief, probably, or maybe it was the roaring in her ears that could only be shock or alarm.

"And with the storm coming in, neither helicopter nor boat could wait, especially when they had no idea when we'd return." Bill's voice was equally flat.

In that moment, the steady rain turned into a downpour, proving the captain and pilot had made the right call. If anything, it was possible they'd waited too long, given choppy sea and air between Chiksook and safety.

"The helicopter can't come back for us in this."

"No. Not today."

They were stranded and didn't have a phone or radio. The office tent was destroyed, so no Wi-Fi either.

No shelter. No food.

She glanced up at the sky. Water wouldn't be a problem, but heat would.

Without shelter, with this storm, they could die out here. It wouldn't even take long.

At least the rain was putting out the cinders that continued burning after the explosion. She looked to the man on her right. She didn't trust him. And now she was stranded with him.

They had to work together if they were going to survive the next twenty-four hours until rescue could arrive in helicopter form.

"We need to see if there's anything we can salvage," she said, her brain clicking into survival mode. "We need food. Shelter. Fuel. And a damn working phone."

"We can go to the Unangax̂ village. Don't they have phones?"

She nodded. "I was thinking that too. But we might not be able to get there in this storm. There are a few sections of road heading that way that are particularly bad."

"Every side-by-side is supposed to be equipped with emergency shelter and other basics," Bill said. "Let's see what we've got."

She reached in the back and grabbed her heavy-duty raincoat, the one she avoided wearing at all costs because it was stiff and didn't breathe. But this storm required it. If they'd had working radios, they'd have known the storm prediction had changed for the worse and would have headed back to camp sooner.

Today was one disaster after another, but this one . . . this was unfathomable.

She pulled on the heavy raincoat before opening the side-by-side door in the two-handed grip that quickly became second nature here, as the wind was known to rip doors from their hinges if one wasn't careful. Before stepping out into this kind of storm, she'd usually pull on her rain pants, which were thick, yellow rubber overalls, but it would be impossible to perform that maneuver in the tight cab, and she'd be soaked before she got them on if she paused to don them in the wind and rain. She'd just have to dry off her pants tonight in a cramped two-person tent.

Things were about to get cozy between her and Bill.

He'd donned a similar raincoat, and they met at the back of the side-by-side. A full fuel can was strapped to the back, thank goodness. They had plenty of gas to get to the village.

Bill opened the rear storage compartment, and they both leaned in, taking shelter from the pummeling rain, and rummaged in the supplies. Flare gun and flares. Waterproof matches and a butane lighter. Rope and paracord. Windup flashlights. Several packets of modern meals ready to eat—MREs—along with protein bars and powdered milk and powdered electrolyte replacement. Basics that would see them through a day or two.

She had more protein bars in her pack, and Bill probably did too.

She frowned at what *wasn't* there. "There should be sleeping bags and a tent. These vehicles are supposed to be stocked with emergency supplies in case we're stranded overnight or in a big storm during the day."

"I have a feeling that the missing tent and sleeping bags are no accident."

Her belly churned. His words matched her own suspicions. It was all just way too convenient. "The broken radios and phones weren't an accident either." And the same two people were in charge of all these things: the maintenance men. She didn't even remember either of their names, but they'd been on the island for days, installing the new generator and prepping camp for the team's arrival.

But then, the generator replacement must have been a different team. The one guy had reported the gray bunting call at least three weeks ago.

She'd been worried about Pollux's vetting of their geologists and ornithologists, but now she had to wonder how well the navy had vetted the maintenance crew. Or were they hired by Pollux too? She didn't even know.

Bill met her gaze. "Everything that's happened was deliberate."

She could barely form the single-word response. "Yes." She took a shallow breath and managed, "We're stranded without supplies. On purpose."

———

Dean made a beeline for Fiona's tent. He didn't give a damn about his own belongings, but her tent had held Dylan's clipboard and his phone. If anything survived this mess, please let it be those items.

The pouring rain had doused the fire, and less than thirty minutes after the blast, the only sign of the fires were small plumes of smoke that dotted the ruins of camp.

There was something to be said for having very little wood as a structural element. The pallets that had served as front stoops for each tent would've incinerated, but everything else appeared to have melted, and the icy rain had halted the damage before it became a gooey, charred mess.

The rubberized sheet that had covered the structure was a blackened blob, but—again thanks to the rain—it was cool to the touch, and Dean peeled it away to get to the items buried beneath.

He located the footlocker first and flipped the latches.

"That's not the one with the sleeping bag," Fiona said. "It's in the other footlocker."

He shrugged, relief too great at seeing the clipboard had survived the blast. He tucked it into the bag they'd grabbed to carry any supplies they could salvage. "Could come in handy," he said, knowing it was a weak excuse at best. "Let's grab the bag from your bed and the one in the footlocker."

She ripped at the rubberized sheet that covered her cot and cursed. "My bag is destroyed." He stepped beside her to see the charred and melted sheet adhered to the shell of her sleeping bag. When she'd pulled at the sheet, the shell of the bag had ripped open. Now rain poured down on the exposed polypropylene filling.

He said a silent prayer that the second footlocker had survived as well as the first. The latches had melted, and the metal box was dented, but it was still sealed. He kicked at the latches, and they snapped. He opened the box and gave thanks for the sight of the orange stuff sack packed tight with the quality bag. He quickly crammed it into their sack. While he was at it, he grabbed the backpack with the extra survival gear and slung it over his shoulder.

"Good idea," Fiona said.

"Let's see if we can find that other phone. Maybe it will work?"

"It's locked."

"Maybe we can find a way around that." He'd tell her the truth later. After they had supplies and this place was far behind them. He couldn't freak her out now. He turned for the collapsed table and began digging around in the melted plastic.

"Why are you looking there?" she asked.

All at once, he realized his mistake. "I saw it on the table this morning."

Had it been there? It had been dark in her tent with just a gray light penetrating the walls.

She said nothing, just turned to search for her laptop, which she found, but it was smashed beyond repair. She grabbed a few items of clothing—fleece and wool that would keep her warm—but left the rest of her belongings behind.

"Food is more important," she said impatiently as he continued to search for Dylan's phone. "We need to see what we can salvage from the cook tent. We can call from the village."

He tightened his jaw. It was too much of a jumble for a complete search, and he couldn't afford to freak her out more than she already was before they were safe for the night.

113

They moved on to Dean's tent from there, where he salvaged a few items of clothing and grabbed his waterproof camera and all the batteries and spare storage disks. If the solar charger worked—and they got some sun—he could charge the batteries and stay in business, documenting whatever the hell was happening on Chiksook Island.

They did a spot-check of the other tents, but it was clear that everyone else had managed to gather their belongings before the blast. Their cursory search didn't turn up any personal items.

From there, they went to the cook tent to see what could be salvaged. They found a box of ramen noodle packets that had been inside a sturdy storage box that survived.

"This is gonna be just like college. Ramen and electrolyte drinks."

Fiona gave his joke a weak smile.

On impulse, he pulled her to him and wrapped her in his arms. "Hey. We're going to get through this. We've got a sleeping bag and a vehicle with gas, plus ramen. A helicopter will come for us tomorrow. We'll be fine."

She hesitated, then leaned her head against him. For one brief moment, he felt her whole body relax into his, a surrender. A need for comfort so deep, she set aside her distrust.

It had been ten years since he'd held anyone with this kind of intimacy. Sure, he'd had sex, but never intimacy. Never this emotional exchange that could be felt through layers of rain gear, fleece, and wool.

He'd been buck-ass naked and inside women and hadn't felt this kind of emotional exchange.

Not since Violet.

But then, after Violet, he'd never allowed anyone past the walls he'd built around his heart. Only Dylan had keys to that fortress.

And this was Dylan's girl.

He released her and remembered his role. They had to get out of here. He had a bad feeling they *weren't* alone, and every second they delayed was a risk.

She found a dozen protein bars and added them to their bag of goodies. "Dibs on the chocolate peppermint LUNA one."

"No way. Everyone knows peppermint is the best. You want the best one, you've got to earn it."

"Aww, can't I interest you in a peanut butter fudge LUNA? We've got at least five of those."

His heart squeezed. That was Dylan's favorite. He managed to maintain his teasing smile. "We can arm wrestle for the peppermint one."

She pursed her lips and squeezed his biceps. "I have a feeling you have a distinct advantage there."

He gave a shallow grin and resumed searching by peeling sheets of burned plastic from the collapsed shelves. "It's a risk you'll just have to take."

They found jars of instant coffee in addition to regular ground beans but opted for instant so they wouldn't need to track down filters or a press. He grabbed a small pot for boiling water for coffee and ramen, along with bowls and utensils. Their travel mugs were already in the side-by-side from this morning.

At the other side of the pantry area, Fiona shoved aside a folding table and revealed a small, ancient freezer built like a tank. "Oh yes," she said, reverence in her voice.

Dean knelt next to her, offering up his own hopeful affirmation. He wrenched it open, and his eyes feasted on the contents. Beef, chicken, and fish, frozen in solid bricks and sealed in airtight plastic. Frozen as they were, they would be easy to pack and would keep for a few days. "Hallelujah," he said softly.

"Oh, thank goodness," Fiona said. "This is better than peppermint LUNA."

While she shoved the bricks of frozen meat into a canvas Pollux Engineering bag they'd found in the debris, he continued searching and found an old ammo box filled with small cans of Sterno cooking fuel.

"Sweet. We can cook the meat and boil water with these if we can't build a fire." He grabbed the ammo box by the handle. No point in leaving any fuel behind, and the metal box could come in handy too.

Their bags—and arms—were overloaded. Between meats and other items, they'd managed a decent haul of food. From there, they moved on to the office tent.

But the office tent was no more. Had this been where the initial fire had started or the epicenter of the blast? The theme from *Gilligan's Island* ran through his head, the line where it listed the luxuries they lacked, starting with "no phone."

Thankfully, they had a motorcar. And it was time to get in it and get the hell out of there.

———

They piled their haul into the back of the side-by-side. The overflow went in the back seat. If nothing else, Fiona figured the frozen meats could be given to the Unangas as a thank-you for their assistance.

She kept telling herself they would be fine once they got to the village. There would be an easy explanation. It was all one horrible accident. A nightmare, sure, but not deliberate.

But deep down, she didn't believe it. Not when Bill had lied about his expertise. Not when all communication was cut off right when she needed it most.

The rain had seriously pummeled the road. It was questionable as to whether they'd make it to the village, and they still didn't have a tent. They'd checked the other side-by-sides that were parked by the pier, and none had a tent or sleeping bags. And their spare gas cans were gone.

But the most disturbing fact was . . . Fiona thought one side-by-side was missing.

But she could be wrong. It was possible the cook and maintenance team didn't have a dedicated vehicle. But if they did, there should be five vehicles in camp, not the four that were accounted for.

The keys to all the remaining vehicles were nowhere to be found, so they would continue on with the side-by-side they'd been using all day. They had one full gas can, but that was it. With all their driving today, they'd used half the tank. They'd have to be judicious in deciding where to drive. Right now, the Unangax̂ village was their best bet. But if they couldn't make it that far, where would they sleep?

They could probably find shelter in a rock overhang or the World War II ruins, but the World War II base was on the north shore, to the east of the volcano, easily a two-hour drive, given that the road there was worse than all the others. It used to be accessible via road, but between the lahar flow and several collapsed bridges, the main road could no longer claim the lofty title.

No, their best bet was to go straight to the village.

"Do you want me to drive?" Bill asked.

She didn't, not really. She wanted to be in control. But she wasn't good at navigating the sloppy, muddy ditches that threatened to snag a vehicle at any time. She sighed and handed him the keys. "It's probably for the best."

He surprised her by wrapping an arm around her waist and pulling her to him again. His lips brushed her forehead. "I'm not a threat to you, I promise."

She wanted to sink into him like she had as they stood amid the ruins of the cook tent, but she wouldn't let herself. Something had happened between them in the kitchen. And it was unsettling, even though she didn't know why. And now here he was, his words practically an admission she had reason to fear him by acknowledging her unspoken suspicions. Nothing made sense. Not his reassuring words or her desire to escape into the comfort he offered.

She shifted her body, and he dropped his arms. Freed, she circled the vehicle to climb into the passenger seat. One thing was certain, as soon as they were settled into someplace safe and dry tonight, they were going to talk.

———

The road was worse than he'd imagined. For starters, it was a road—perhaps the only one on the whole damn island—that they hadn't driven today, so it was completely unfamiliar. It was also straight-up terrible, a series of pits filled with water with the occasional boulder thrown in.

And then there was the fog. A thick fog reduced visibility to ten feet, then five, so he couldn't see the pits and boulders until he was aiming for them. The side-by-side was more maneuverable than the *Titanic*, but not when there was only five feet of warning that the road was going to disappear up ahead.

If he went too slow, he risked getting mired in the muddy track. Too fast, and he'd play chicken with a boulder. Boulders always won.

Eventually, though, it was a water-filled mud pit that got the checkered flag. They'd only made it a third of the distance to the Unangax̂ village when he got stuck in a deep pit.

He rested his head against the steering wheel as he braced himself to step out into the fog. If Fiona drove and he pushed, maybe they could escape the mud.

But where would they go? There was no way they were going to make it to the village tonight. Not in this fog and rain and mess of a road.

"You drive. I'll push."

She met his gaze, and he saw the fear in her eyes. She hadn't been comforted by his promise earlier that he wasn't a threat to her. If anything, it seemed to make her concerns worse. He'd pointed out the elephant in the room before they'd had a chance to talk about it.

Once they had shelter, he'd tell her everything.

And she'd damn well tell him everything she knew.

Problem was, without a miracle, their only shelter might be this tiny side-by-side, and if that was the case, they needed to get it someplace sheltered and out of sight for the night. He still had the distinct feeling they weren't alone out here.

He climbed from the vehicle. He had to fight the wind to close the door as she climbed across the console into the driver's seat. "Punch it," he said when she was settled.

The rear driver's-side tire spun and spun, getting zero traction.

"Stop. Let me see if I can get some rocks in place. Give it something to grip."

He trudged through the mud along the side of the road and looked for football-size cobbles. He found a few smaller rocks and tucked them into the muck in front of the rear tire. He hadn't bothered with gloves because he wanted to be able to position the stones just right, and his fingers ached with the cold of the clinging mud.

He needed at least two more cobbles before they should make an attempt. If there weren't enough, the ones he had found would just disappear into the mud, wasted effort. He returned to the side of the road and continued searching. He'd ask Fiona to help, but one of them should stay warm and dry, and she knew this island better than he did. She'd know where to find shelter. He needed her if they were going to survive, and that meant keeping her warm and functioning.

They'd been left behind on purpose. Did whoever blew up the camp know he was Dylan's brother? Or had they just guessed he wasn't who he'd presented himself to be?

Had Fiona guessed even before today? Had she told someone her concerns?

The radio and phone sabotage raised a helluva lot of questions.

Hell, could he even trust her? Maybe it was her job to make sure he missed the boat.

These concerns ran through his mind as he found and placed more cobbles in front of the rear tire.

There were enough now to give it a try. He positioned himself at the rear and to the side, so if the vehicle were to rock backward, he wouldn't get caught and run over.

"Punch it," he shouted again.

She did, and he pushed on the corner, giving the vehicle an extra nudge. The tires spun, then gripped, and it bounced out of the hole. She kept going, moving steadily to keep from getting stuck again, and he jogged after her, ready to jump in when they got past the low spot in the road that had collected so much rainwater. She neared the top of the hill, the vehicle slipped a bit, but she pumped the gas, and it made it up.

She might not like driving these muddy roads, but she was good at it.

The vehicle crested the rise and made it to the hilltop. He jogged after and reached the top—just in time to see the side-by-side disappear into the fog and rain.

THIRTEEN

She hadn't planned on abandoning him; she'd merely seized the moment and kept going. But she hadn't gone more than a hundred yards when guilt weighed on her. Leaving him out here with nothing was leaving him out here to die.

She couldn't do that.

But she couldn't stay with him either. Not when he could be the biggest threat of all.

If she could get to the village tonight, she'd send someone back for him, but there was no way she'd get to the village without his help. They would get stuck again, and getting out was a two-person job.

It was time for a new plan. She would take the supplies she needed and leave him the vehicle. He was, without a doubt, following on foot. He'd find the vehicle. He'd have shelter and food. She'd be gone with half their food and the sleeping bag. It was only fair she take the bag, since she was leaving him the shelter of the vehicle.

She even knew where she'd go. Not far from here, there was a Japanese airplane wreck she'd recorded during an earlier survey. It was tucked up against a rock face and covered in tall grasses and shrubs. The plane was big enough for her to take shelter in. She might even be able to build a fire and dry out her clothes. Smoke wouldn't be seen in this rain and fog, and besides, she doubted Bill would pursue her once she realized he had the vehicle.

She just needed to get enough distance between them so she'd have time to grab what she needed from the back before setting out, but she couldn't go too far or she was likely to get stuck again.

She found the perfect place to pull over and tucked the side-by-side behind a rocky protrusion covered in thick shrubs.

She reached into the back and grabbed a bag of food, swapping out bricks of meat for ramen and protein bars and making sure she had packs of powdered milk, powdered protein, and powdered electrolytes. She shoved what she could into her field pack, which she would strap to the larger emergency pack that held a first aid kit, among other basic necessities. There were mylar emergency blankets, flares, waterproof matches, a lighter, and flashlights as well. She would need all of that and more now.

Her gaze landed on the thick yellow bib rain pants in the back seat. The field pants she wore now were water resistant, but the resistance wouldn't hold up for long in this weather. The yellow Helly Hansens would do a much better job, but they took too long to put on, and Bill would catch up to her soon.

She grabbed the pants, then dropped them back on the seat. No time. She'd just have to get wet and dry out in the plane.

She shut off the engine but left the keys in place and circled to the back of the side-by-side, buffeted by wind with every step. She grabbed the emergency frame backpack and dropped the food items that hadn't fit in her smaller pack inside. She opened the ammo box and transferred several cans of Sterno into the frame pack, then stuffed the sleeping bag inside. She was about to cinch it closed when she spotted Dylan's clipboard peeking out of one of the canvas Pollux bags.

Why had Bill been so eager to find the clipboard? It was the first thing he'd gone for.

And he'd been desperate to find Dylan's phone. But at least that one made sense, as it might have been a working way to call for help, if they could unlock it.

She grabbed the clipboard and crammed it down the back of the already stuffed backpack. It was bulging, but the flap and straps would prevent anything from falling out, and the sleeping bag would remain nice and dry inside.

She quickly clipped her field pack to the frame of the larger pack, then hoisted the entire thing onto her back. Holy hell, it had to weigh at least forty pounds. But she'd deal. She had to. The plane was less than a mile from here. She could make it.

She closed the back of the vehicle and set out, taking a path that would leave the fewest footprints but knowing it was futile in the mud.

Hopefully, he'd be so grateful to have the vehicle, he'd decide not to pursue her. After all, she'd left him food.

The first part of the hike was the hardest—a steep, muddy hillside with a forty-pound pack in pouring rain. Her feet slipped and her muscles strained and she found it hard to get enough oxygen.

Maybe that was panic?

She couldn't be sure; she just knew it sucked as she grabbed shrubs to keep her from sliding down and losing the ground she'd gained.

As she'd known would happen, her pants quickly soaked through, the icy water penetrating all the way down to her thermal underwear. At least her torso remained warm and dry.

She made it to the top and dropped to her knees to catch her breath, the heavy pack weighing on her, threatening to press her into the soft, muddy earth.

She'd been overly optimistic about her physical condition and ability to handle the heavy pack. But she'd made it. She had to give herself credit for that. She'd get to the plane and settle in. Dry out. Wait for the storm to pass. She had enough food to last a few days. Surely a helicopter search party would show up once the storm abated. She had a flare gun. She'd be found.

She pushed to her feet and forced herself to keep walking.

She followed the easiest path for the first fifty yards or so, then pulled out her compass to get a bearing. It would be easy to get lost out here, given the limited site distance, but she was fairly certain the Japanese plane was to the northeast of her position. If her phone worked, she could look up her field notes and get the exact UTMs. She also had paper maps and could plot her course if she could see enough features to triangulate. But right now it was more important to get distance from the side-by-side. She'd worry about finding the plane once she was certain Bill wasn't following her.

———

Relief swamped him when he found the side-by-side with the keys inside. Okay, so she wasn't trying to kill him.

She had, in fact, left behind enough food to see him through a few days and his own field and emergency backpacks.

What did this mean? Should he push forward to the village or go after her?

She had the sleeping bag. He could only presume she had a plan for shelter, given that she'd left him with the vehicle.

What was her goal here? To lose him because she was in on it with whoever had blown up the camp? Or was she simply acting out of fear?

He'd just about decided to try to make it to the village and sleep in the vehicle, if necessary, when he noticed one more thing missing from the side-by-side: Dylan's clipboard.

Why would she take that? It was of no use to her . . . unless she was part of whatever was going on and knew the notes were valuable.

He looked to the steep hillside she'd parked next to and could just make out the path she must've followed up the hill. It couldn't have been easy for her—her boots weren't built for climbing slippery hillsides, as he'd seen this morning on the way to the site, and her pack must be damn heavy.

Now he wondered if leaving the vehicle behind was a red herring. Hell, for all he knew, the Unangax̂ village was a red herring. Maybe it wasn't occupied year-round. Maybe they'd been evacuated too.

She could be sending him off while she met with her conspirators. Maybe she'd lead him to Dylan.

Hope flickered in his chest.

He cursed the fact that he hadn't been able to pack a gun for this trip, but he'd been well aware that while his bags wouldn't be scanned by an X-ray machine for the military flight, they were subject to inspection, and it was a risk he wouldn't dare take. But if he had, he'd have a weapon now—more than the knife that was clipped to his hip and was considered reasonable for this kind of field project.

He quickly set to work, filling his own packs with everything he'd need. She'd left him more than half their supplies, including the small pot and dishes, probably because she couldn't fit more into her bags. But he wasn't burdened with the sleeping bag, so he managed to cram the remainder into both packs and used the clips that attached the packs together. He grabbed the keys from the ignition and secured them in a zippered pocket. If he couldn't find her, he'd have to come back here to weather out the storm, and he wasn't about to take chances the vehicle would be gone.

One thing being a photographer had taught him was tracking. He was no Navy SEAL or Army Ranger, but he knew how to follow a nearly invisible trail, and he knew how to do it in good weather and bad. He doubted she'd do much, if anything, to cover her tracks. Like a lioness on the savannah, she'd be more concerned with finding her prey—or in this case, shelter—to waste time attempting to erase her trail in the pouring rain.

He set out, following her path up the hill, noting the places where plants were torn out at the roots—places she'd grabbed to halt a fall.

She'd mentioned a fear of rock climbing, and he wondered if she'd suffered panic at losing ground on the steep hillside.

Not his problem. Right now, Fiona Carver was the enemy.

———

It had been at least an hour since she'd left the side-by-side, and it was time to pull out her map and get a real bearing. The airplane was near. She was sure of it. She could just make out the low slopes beneath the cliff where the plane had crashed over seventy-five years ago.

Her shoulders ached from the heavy pack, her hands were frozen from the chilly rain, and her feet had blistered in her boots from the hike that was more strenuous than she'd expected to do today.

She dropped the pack to the ground and rolled her shoulders. She'd pause just for a minute and enjoy the relief of not carrying forty extra pounds. She crammed her hands up the opposite sleeves of her coat so her cold fingers could find warmth on the skin of her arms. She wore wool gloves, but they were the fingerless kind, so the tips were cold and uncovered. She should have switched out for mittens after she'd climbed the steep hill, but she'd been too anxious to make progress to stop and change.

She'd do it after she studied the map. But first, she would drink water and get warm. She wanted to sit but was afraid if she did that, she wouldn't have the strength to stand again.

She was nearing her limits and was aware fear had reduced her capacity today. She could usually handle more strenuous hikes than this, even in the rain.

As an archaeologist in the Pacific Northwest, she didn't have the luxury of working in only good weather.

The rain had lightened considerably since she'd set out. It was still cold and miserable, but sight distance had increased, and it was back to being a steady rain and not a deluge. It was light enough, in fact, that now that she'd stopped walking, she could make out noises that weren't weather-related.

Like the snap of a shrub underfoot.

Fear shot through her as the noise registered. No fox or other critter to be found on this island would be out in this.

Slowly, so as not to make her own noise, she turned.

Something slammed into her, and she fell, dropping to her back on the ground as Bill Lowell pinned her down and stretched over her, bringing them eye to eye and chest to chest. She sank into the spongy muskeg as the full weight of his body pressed her into the slippery, muddy moss.

His voice was low and dangerous as he spoke with his face just an inch from hers, his blue eyes no longer bright but a stormy gray to match the dark sky. "Why did you take Dylan's clipboard, Fiona?"

His weight on her made it impossible to breathe or speak. She pushed at his chest, suffocating. Panicked.

She was going to die here, but not from exposure. He was going to smother her.

He shifted his weight, and she took in a deep breath, but she was still pinned. Trapped, and she might be hyperventilating. It was hard to know in the moment.

"Do you know where he is?" Bill asked, his voice louder now but no less menacing.

"I—I—wh-what?" The stuttered words were all she could manage as she tried to get air.

He'd shifted again, and now rain hit her face directly, and she couldn't turn or dodge it. This must be what water torture felt like, trying to breathe but unable to get air without taking in liquid.

She wriggled beneath him. Unable to raise her hands, she tried to use her hips and knees. But the soft ground swallowed her, and she sank farther down, reminding her of childhood stories of the dangers of quicksand.

No. The real dangers in this world were mud and rain and lying hot bird men.

"Where is Dylan?"

"Can't . . . breathe." She gasped between the feeble words.

At last he moved, perhaps realizing she couldn't answer if she died of asphyxiation. He rolled to the side but kept a leg and arm flung over her, holding her down. "Where is Dylan?" he demanded again.

"Why would I know where Dylan is? And . . . what does it matter to you? Who *are* you?"

"Because last I heard, you're his girlfriend. Nice to finally meet you. I'm his brother. Dean."

FOURTEEN

Dean watched her face as his words settled in. Confusion. Surprise. Anger. In that order.

She scratched at the arm that pinned her, catching his bare wrist between glove and coat, but his skin was numb from cold, and he felt only the faintest trace of her touch. She could be opening a vein and he wouldn't notice.

They were finally at the crux of the situation.

"Where is Dylan?" he asked again.

She shook her head. "I don't know!"

His hand was so close to her neck, which was exposed at the front, as rain dropped down on her face and filled the yellow hood of her raincoat. It had to be sliding down her back, chilling her to the core.

He itched to place his hand on her exposed skin; his cold fingers would let her know he was in control here, and she would answer him.

He'd never before threatened or harmed another human being—at least, not outside of a sport where it was part of the game—but he'd reached a new level of desperation. A new low in his evolution from man to monster.

He'd lost Violet. No matter how hard he worked, how hard he fought for her, he'd lost her. But that had been a losing battle to begin with.

He wouldn't lose Dylan. Couldn't. He'd do absolutely anything to find his brother. He'd risk federal prison by impersonating an ornithologist. He'd tackle a beautiful woman and watch her rain gear slowly fill with icy water that would kill her in a matter of hours if she didn't get warm.

But he wouldn't put his hand on her throat.

Violet would be appalled.

He released her and scooted back, the voice of his dead wife shaming him. It had been years since Violet had spoken to him like that, even in his mind.

Fiona curled up and rolled to her side, putting her back to him. He could tell from the shudder of her body that the water that had been trapped in her hood had filtered down and soaked her side.

She wore wool and fleece, which remained warm even when wet, unlike cotton, which would mean death out here. Her body might even heat the water, like a wet suit, but still, they needed shelter and a fire ASAP or hypothermia could—*would*—set in. If he took her back to the side-by-side and they turned it on for the heater, she'd get warm, but they'd quickly run out of fuel.

She must've had a plan, a destination in mind.

"We need shelter," he said. "Where were you headed?"

She pulled her knees up to her chest and said nothing.

Shit. He'd fucked up. Big-time. She was now more afraid of him than of dying from exposure.

"We need to talk, Fiona, and we can't linger out here. Someone might be following us, and you're soaked. Please. Let's work together and find shelter. Make a fire. And then you can tell me why you and Dylan broke up or where he is. Whatever. I won't hurt you. I just need to know the truth. I just need to find my brother."

Slowly, she rolled over. It was like each shift of position pained her, but then, her whole body could be seizing with fear, cold, or aches he had yet to learn about. She'd hiked uphill in the pouring rain with a heavy pack. She could be flat-out done for the day.

If that were the case, he'd have to carry her and both their packs to safety. She was tall and strong. She had to be 150 pounds, minimum. Probably more. The packs would be another sixty to seventy pounds.

He worked out regularly to remain fit for the job, and his work often involved extreme conditions, heavy packs, and remote locations, but this . . . this was too much. No way in hell could he do it, not all at once. And not uphill in the rain.

She met his gaze. "I don't know why you seem to think Dylan and I were dating. We were colleagues, nothing more. I liked him, but there wasn't any attraction beyond respect and friendship. And I have no idea where he is now. All I know is he was fired. Rumor has it, he sexually assaulted his boss, Sylvia Jessup."

Fiona watched Bill's—or rather, Dean's—face carefully for his reaction. At the same time, she took in the subtle resemblance. They had a similar height and build, and she realized she'd mentally compared them more than once based on that. But their facial features were different enough that the resemblance wasn't obvious, so she didn't need to kick herself for not connecting all the dots. It was there in the blond hair and probably the jawline, but Dean sported a beard while Dylan had always remained clean-shaven throughout the expedition.

It had to be the eyes that had thrown her off. She'd been so focused on Hot Bird Man's Newman eyes, she'd failed to see the resemblance to the hazel-eyed volcanologist who'd left the last field expedition in disgrace.

It all came back to her now, the night in the office tent when Dylan showed her the inscription on the clipboard. He'd mentioned his brother the photographer—his twin—and for some reason, she had it in her head they were identical. Dylan was supremely good-looking, and she'd mentally imagined what it must be like to be presented with two of them. Beautiful bookends to make an awkward girl tongue-tied.

She remembered now that Dean wasn't a fashion photographer. He photographed wildlife, and Dylan had said he was quite successful.

One twin was a volcanologist and the other traveled the world taking pictures of animals in their natural habitats. It was hard to imagine two more appealing careers. To her mind, anyway.

Now she looked into Dylan's brother's eyes, and the man was an entirely different kind of handsome from Dylan. Two flavors of perfection.

She should have caught on when she'd noticed the expensive cameras and ease behind the lens, but she'd been too wrapped up in those blue, blue eyes and the gentle—but enticing—flirtation when he had those fancy cameras in his hands.

What had been the point of that flirtation? It didn't make sense, given that he'd had it in his head that she'd dated his brother. It couldn't be a competition thing between twins, because he clearly cared about Dylan or he wouldn't be here under a false name.

The shock of it all almost made her forget the cold that was slowly sapping her energy.

She'd been just as shocked when Dylan had been sent home abruptly. The volcanologist had been nothing but kind to her, and she'd found Sylvia's behavior toward Dylan problematic. What she'd seen with her own eyes was enough to make her doubt the allegation. But Fiona hadn't been there when it happened. All she could do was fail to support Sylvia's account by not repeating it when people asked. And she sure as hell wouldn't testify on the woman's behalf, not when the interactions Fiona had witnessed were the opposite of what the woman claimed.

If Dylan had asked for a statement on Sylvia's conduct, Fiona would have agreed to provide it. But he'd never reached out, even though they all knew Fiona had witnessed a few choice encounters between boss and subordinate.

Now she was face-to-face with Dylan's handsome, angry brother, and the guy wanted to know why Fiona had lied about her relationship with Dylan? *What relationship?*

Every muscle in her body ached with cold and other pains too numerous to mention, but she forced herself to roll to her feet and stand. She was as wobbly as a newborn colt and in a whole lot of pain, but lying in the icy muck would kill her. They needed to get to shelter. She needed fire and food before her body seized.

"In my pack, you'll find a field map in a plastic case. There's a Japanese plane wreck marked on it. That's where I was headed. It's big enough for shelter. We can probably build a fire inside." She reached for the bag she'd dropped moments before she'd been flattened to the ground, but before she could wrap her fingers around the strap, her knees buckled.

He swooped forward and caught her before she landed in the mud. Her cheek pressed to his chest, and she closed her eyes against tears. She felt no comfort in his arms. He might have saved her from hitting the ground this time, but he'd also put her there.

She pushed against his chest to regain her footing. She couldn't rely on him. Couldn't trust him, any more than he seemed to trust her.

"I'm fine," she lied.

"No. You're not."

"I will be. Once we get to the plane. We'll build a fire. Eat."

"And talk."

"Yes. And talk." She reached for the pack again, but her fingers were too numb to lift it.

Dean swore and grabbed it. "Where is the map?"

She thumped on an outside zipper pocket with her club of a hand, then tucked both hands under her coat and all the other layers so her fingers met the warm skin of her torso. It was a little scary that her belly felt the cold but her fingers hardly registered the heat of her own skin. Like waking up in the middle of the night with a dead arm, but she was wide-awake.

Dean pulled out the map, and she used her club hand to signal where the airplane was and where she thought they were, then tucked it back under her layers, against her skin. Feeling was returning, and her fingers ached with renewed life.

This was next-level pins-and-needles pain.

He pulled out his own compass and took a bearing. The fog had lifted enough for a few more landforms to be visible in the distance, and she was impressed that he knew how to triangulate their location. But then, he'd probably been on many shoots where GPS wasn't available and he had to use old-fashioned maps and rulers to find his way.

Somehow, that made her trust him more. He wasn't so different from Dylan after all. She'd always been impressed with Dylan's competence in the field. He'd been one of the people she'd most looked forward to catching up with on these projects, a person she'd enjoyed as a friend, as Cara was a friend.

But she'd never felt a *burning attraction that went both ways* sort of vibe. They were colleagues who enjoyed hanging out in the cook or office tent at the end of the day.

"I—I liked Dylan," she said. "But that was all. And I'm pretty sure it was the same for him."

"He told me otherwise," Dean said. His voice wasn't angry, but she didn't know what it was. This conversation would be easier once they were safe inside the World War II wreck and had food. A stiff drink would, frankly, be welcome at this point, but that wasn't among the emergency supplies, unfortunately.

If she survived this, she was going to get good and drunk off her favorite rum, and she wouldn't even feel guilty about it.

Her breath hitched as her brain repeated the *"if"* in that thought.

"It looks like the plane is a quarter of a mile from here. I'll take the packs and find it, drop them off, then come back for you."

Her brain rebelled at the idea of being left behind without supplies. "No. I can walk. I can carry my pack."

He gave her a look that said he highly doubted that. He slipped his pack from his back and unclipped his day pack from the frame. "Mine is a little bit lighter. You carry it. I'll carry yours plus my day pack."

She was giving up the sleeping bag, but either way, she had to trust him. They wouldn't survive the night without each other, so she gave a sharp nod. She slipped the pack onto her back and cinched the shoulder straps while he buckled the waist strap and the chest support. She felt like a toddler but was still glad he took the initiative.

Her body was shutting down.

He cinched his day pack to the frame pack that already had her pack attached, then hoisted it onto his back. She guessed he was carrying fifty to sixty pounds, and her load was down to about twenty-five.

He led the way across the muskeg. She nearly lost it when they had to traverse a loose talus slope, but she kept her feet until almost the end, when a rock rolled beneath her and she went down hard, her knee jamming on the cold stone. She wasn't sure if her ankle twisted or her knee was more than bruised; all she knew was her entire leg hurt, and she didn't want to put weight on it right then.

She would, though. She had to, no matter how painful. She could maybe do it without the pack. "I think the plane is just over the next hill, tucked against the cliff face," she said between gasps of pain. "Take my pack. Find it. I'll follow in a bit."

He held her gaze, his eyes showing concern. All signs of anger were gone from his face and body language. After a long moment, he gave a sharp nod. "I'll come back for you."

"No need. I can do it." Even if she had to crawl. She'd get there.

He took the packs and disappeared over the rise. She watched him go and took several deep breaths to prepare herself for what she had to do. Food and shelter awaited her. Dean Slater was the mechanical bunny at a dog track. She would chase after him and win this round. She had to if she wanted to survive the night.

FIFTEEN

The Japanese wreck was as described, tucked up against a cliff face. It was covered in vines and grasses, nearly hidden by the vegetation, as it had burrowed into the dirt when it crashed seventy-five years or so ago. To Dean, it looked like an American Douglas DC-3, but it was Japanese, so it must be a licensed version of the aircraft, sold to Japan before the war.

It was ironic that the old wreck of a plane could look like salvation, but that was exactly what it was. It would give them shelter, and, if they were very lucky, they'd find a way to have a sustained fire for heat.

He entered through the crack in the tail and crawled through the narrow opening, noticing that a whole lot of rodents and other critters had taken refuge here in the last seven and a half decades. The interior smelled of rotted animal carcasses and droppings, but it was blessedly dry and large enough for them to camp inside. He set the packs down in the center of the fuselage and scanned the interior. He'd clear a spot for a fire, but he needed to get Fiona. Housekeeping could wait. She couldn't.

He crawled through the opening again and set out, his focus narrowed on one purpose: get Fiona warm and see to her leg. If she'd busted an ankle, they were doomed. This was the kind of terrain where a broken leg meant death. He never should have let her walk across that talus slope in her condition.

He was half the distance to the place where he'd left her when he came across her body, collapsed in the muskeg.

His heart seized as he took in her motionless form, facedown in mud. Had she collapsed while crawling and drowned in the mud?

He dropped to his knees and yanked her over.

Her body was lifeless, her face coated in wet brown soil.

NO. No. No. No. no. *no.*

Images of Violet's last moments came to mind. It had been the most devastating hour of his life, but at least with Violet, they'd been prepared. They'd both known it was coming. They'd said what they'd needed to say.

He swiped the mud from Fiona's face, then checked her pulse. Slow but steady.

"Breathe, Fi."

He wiped the mud from her nose, then tilted her head back to open her airway and pressed his mouth to hers, creating a seal with his lips. He pinched her nose closed and breathed out, sending air into her. Her chest rose, showing her airway wasn't clogged. He raised his head, and her breath expelled, chest lowering. He breathed into her mouth again, watching her chest rise and hoping to hell he wasn't too late. He'd breathe for her as long as she needed, but he damn well hoped her body would take over fast so he could get her inside the shelter.

They were so close.

All at once, she gasped and coughed, and he felt as if his heart might explode at seeing life infuse her body. He'd faced a lot of scary moments, but nothing compared to this.

Even with Violet, they'd *known* what she faced. They'd had a plan.

But this . . . everything was unknown. Everything was terrifying.

Once he was certain she was breathing on her own, he scooped her into his arms and made the trek to the crashed airplane. Fiona hadn't told him if the Japanese pilot and crew had died in the crash. The plane was intact enough that they might have survived. But it didn't matter. The wreckage that might have killed during the war would now be life and refuge to Fiona and him.

He pulled her through the narrow opening and lay her down on the floor in the center of the fuselage. Once she was protected from the wind and rain, he had a choice to make. He decided that stripping her of her wet clothes and stuffing her in the sleeping bag was the best place to start. They needed to get her core temperature up first and foremost. Then he could build a fire and check on her leg. They had emergency cold packs to ice the knee or ankle, if either one was more than bruised.

She muttered as he began to unsnap her thick yellow raincoat. "Dean, why did you think Dylan and I were dating?"

Her eyes remained closed, and it was clear she was only half-conscious. Her body was shutting down to deal with hypothermia. Otherwise he'd have taken the time to answer her question with care. Instead, he just said, "Shhh. I'll explain later. You're hypothermic. I'm going to undress you. I promise, I'm not taking advantage. I'm trying to help you get warm."

"You don't want to undress me?" Her voice carried a small pout, which made him smile.

Oh, Fiona, you have no idea. But you're not mine and never can be.

It crossed his mind that she was out of it enough that her words about Dylan could only be true. They hadn't been involved.

But that didn't make sense. Why would Dylan lie?

He'd assumed from the start that Fiona was the liar, because Dylan never, ever lied.

But Dean was peeling the clothing from the semiconscious body of a beautiful woman who wasn't, and had never been, Dylan's girlfriend. And he wouldn't have considered it in a sexual way, except she'd asked that pouty question.

Fiona was attracted to him, as he was to her.

He shook his head. He needed to focus on what was important. "Tell me if any part of you is injured badly enough for me to look at."

She ran her hand from chest to thighs. "I might hurt here."

139

She'd clearly lost her mind in the cold. "You don't do field flings, Fiona. Ever."

She let out a soft laugh. "I know. But also, we might die tonight."

"You will *not* die tonight. I won't let you."

She reached up and stroked his cheek, her fingers brushing among the short whiskers of his beard. "Thank you." She shook her head lightly and sat up. "I can undress. I think. If you hand me the sleeping bag?"

Relief filtered through him. She wasn't delirious, and she wasn't half-dead. She'd just needed several minutes to get her faculties together. Once again, he was reminded he *liked* this woman.

He pulled out the sleeping bag and turned his back. "I'll clear a spot to build a fire. We can use one of the busted windows as a chimney."

"I'm supposed to complain that this is an historic site, but I think I don't care at this point."

"Sweetheart, if we were taking shelter in one of those intact houses in the village site, I'd still be making a fire."

"Yeah. No. I don't think I could ever do that."

"Good thing we're not there, then."

"You don't know what those houses *mean*, though."

"I do, actually. And I honor the history and culture they represent. I would do everything I could to protect the house, but I'd still make use of the hearth. If it was the only shelter available, we'd have to use it to survive."

He remembered Violet's last days and the things he would have sacrificed if it would have given her more time. He'd have given his own life for hers, but brain cancer didn't allow for those kinds of deals.

Burning pieces of a World War II wreck didn't even trigger a blip on his guilt barometer. He hadn't caused this situation, but he'd damn well make sure both he and Fiona survived it.

"I can't . . . I can't get this zipper. My fingers aren't cooperating. Can you help?"

He turned to see she was still clothed but struggling with the zipper of the sleeping bag. Of course she needed the bag ready before she stripped. He took it from her and quickly threaded the two opposing zipper pulls, then seated the pin in the slot to close one side of the bag. It was a wide base-camp-style bag, not the narrow mummy-style preferred by backpackers. Not only was it a deluxe, extra-wide bag, it also had zippers on both sides that opened from both ends and a separate zipper to attach the foot box. According to the tag, it was rated for three and a half seasons, which meant it could be used in temperatures as low as ten degrees Fahrenheit.

With careful zipper management, they might both be able to fit in the bag and still trap enough heat to make it work. It would be a damn cozy sleeping arrangement, but it would keep them alive, which was all that mattered.

While he zipped the sides and attached the foot box, she peeled off her layers of wet clothes, finally reaching the base layer of wool. It was his fault even her undergarments were wet. He'd let her lay there in the pouring rain as the water filled her hood.

The mud on her face was beginning to dry, flaking off her skin and showering the floor of the fuselage. "Was I . . . facedown in the mud?" she asked, staring at the dirt that had rained on the floor.

He cleared his throat. "Yeah. You were unconscious and not breathing when I found you." Everything that had happened to her was his fault. He shouldn't have let water fill her hood. Shouldn't have pinned her to the ground as he had.

"Thank you for saving me."

"I shouldn't have left you alone. It's my fault."

She shook her head. "No. I'm the one who left the side-by-side. I shouldn't have run."

"Why did you?"

She tried to work the buttons on her wool long underwear. "I'd keep this on, because it's still warm, but it's so damp, it'll get the sleeping bag wet."

"I've got a T-shirt you can wear." It was cotton, but at least she had something dry to wear in the bag as she warmed up.

He undid the buttons at her throat, opening the neck wider to make it easier to pull over her head; then he turned his back, giving her a semblance of privacy while she finished stripping and pulled on the dry long-sleeve T-shirt he'd plucked from his bag.

With his back to her, he repeated his question. "Why did you run? And why did you take Dylan's clipboard?"

He heard rustling as she slipped into the bag he'd prepared. She let out a soft purr of relief as she settled into the warmth. Finally, she said, "Because I was afraid of you. I had no clue who you were. All I knew was there was no way in hell you were an ornithologist with any kind of ESA Section 7 experience."

"Section 7? That's what I screwed up?"

"Among other things, yeah. It's pretty basic lingo."

"And Dylan's clipboard?"

"I wondered why it was so important to you that it was what you looked for first in my tent. It didn't make sense."

"I was past pretense at that point. Too desperate to collect everything we could to try to find him."

"Find him. You think he's . . . *here?*"

Dean turned around and faced her. She was tucked deep in the bag, lying on the floor of an old, rotting Japanese airplane. Dried dirt flecked her face, her perfectly highlighted hair was in a tangle around her head, and her eyes were wide with curiosity.

She looked vulnerable, with her beautiful face framed by the hood of the puffy bag. Color was returning to her cheeks as she settled into the warmth.

"He has to be here. If he's not here, then . . ." His voice trailed off. He couldn't put the alternative into words. He cleared his throat. "I came here to find him. It's why I lied to get hired by Pollux. It was the only way to get to the island." He'd tried to bribe his way here, but that had failed. Chiksook was remote and restricted for reasons both cultural and military. The two combined were a nearly impenetrable barrier, no matter how much money he threw at the problem.

One thing he had in abundance was money. Little did it help him here.

Fiona cleared her throat. "And why . . . why do you think Dylan and I were involved?"

"Let me get the fire going. Get us some food. Then we'll talk."

She nodded. "Do you mind if I just lie here?"

He couldn't help but laugh as he shook his head. "Uh, we'd have words if you *didn't* just lie there. Do you realize you weren't *breathing* twenty minutes ago? Get warm and keep breathing. That's your only job."

"For once, that's a job I can do."

He took that to mean she was still beating herself up about the archaeological site. After everything that had happened today, Fiona Carver still harbored guilt over the damage to the site.

He rummaged through the plane, looking for something, anything, burnable. He had small emergency fire-starter bricks, and they had those cans of Sterno, but it wasn't enough for the kind of heat they needed, plus they should save the Sterno for cooking.

Twigs and vines had grown into the cracks of the plane over the years. He gathered the dry, dead branches into a pile, along with rodent bones and the skeletons of a few larger mammals that had died inside the plane over the decades.

The plane had been used for cargo, and he salvaged a metal container to use as their fire pit, and beneath it found a wooden pallet that would probably provide a half hour's worth of fuel. It was a start, but not nearly enough.

He shoved aside a sheet of rotted canvas that covered a metal shelf bolted to the side of the plane—and wanted to sink to his knees and offer a prayer of thanks. The canvas had hidden wooden boxes. A quick count indicated there were two dozen, each one more than two feet long and about fourteen inches deep and wide, with thick wood handles on the sides.

He pulled one box from the shelf—it was heavy, at least fifty pounds. That meant the wood shell had to be sturdy. And thick.

He set the box on the floor; it hit with a loud thunk, but the aged, dry wood held together. He unhooked the metal latches. Inside were large rounds. Antiaircraft ammunition? Not that it mattered; big bullets didn't interest him. He was far more excited by the thickness of the wood.

That's what she said.

He snickered at the internal joke. Too bad it wouldn't be half as funny if he said it out loud.

He focused on the wonderfully thick wooden sides of the box. If he slowly fed a small fire, this box would last at least two hours. Probably longer. And they had two dozen to burn.

Slow-burning thick wood was the best wood.

He shook his head even as he let out a soft laugh.

"What's so funny?"

He cleared his throat. "Nothing. Just being juvenile in my head. I found some boxes we can burn. We have enough wood to dry your clothes and cook dinner."

And once her core temperature was up and long underwear dry, he could join her in the sleeping bag, and they could rest for the night, letting the fire die to conserve the precious wood.

They could stay here for days. All they needed was water, which was raining down on them in waves. He could fill one of her silicone collapsible field buckets from a stream he'd spotted pouring down a groove in the rock face behind the plane.

They would survive the night and several more to follow.

He dug around in the plane looking for tools and found a crowbar. He emptied the ammunition onto another shelf and then used the crowbar to pry apart the wood, repeating the process with a second box and making a small mound of firewood to get them started.

He pulled the metal box close to where she lay in the center of the widest part of the fuselage. He then cleared a spot beneath a broken window with vines growing through it and proceeded to set up a fire, starting with the wax-infused fire-starter brick, a few crumpled pieces of precious paper—blank—from Dylan's clipboard, followed by a bird's nest of dried twigs and vines combined with other debris he'd gathered from the plane. Last, he arranged the kindling in a circle, forming a tent over the other items with long sticks from the ammo box.

With one match, he set off the paper and fire brick. He leaned down and blew on the flame and brick, and in moments the bird's nest caught, glowing red with each long puff of air sent to the heart of the flame, much as he'd breathed life into Fiona earlier and watched her chest rise.

Smoke filled the plane, and he used the crowbar to widen the hole in the window to increase airflow. Soon the smoke was being sucked outside and warmth began to radiate from the metal sides of the makeshift fireplace.

Once the fire could survive on its own without suffocating them, he used paracord from the emergency kit to make a clothesline that extended from one side of the fuselage to the other, then draped Fiona's clothes over the cord.

"You're good at this," Fiona said, her voice a bit drowsy but otherwise strong.

"This isn't my first Aleutian storm."

"You weren't lying about having been here."

"No. I had an assignment a few years ago to photograph birds. I do have a wildlife biology degree. I might not know the Endangered Species Act chapter and verse, but I know enough about birds and wildlife in general to get by."

"Do you specialize? In wildlife, I mean."

"Not really. I've been lucky." He closed his eyes and gave a small thank-you to Violet for the financial support she'd provided that had given him his start. "I had a financier who funded my early expeditions, which meant I could spend months abroad in different environments. On land. Underwater. Jungle, desert. You name it. I was able to spend far more time on expeditions than the National Geographic Society or other wildlife organizations could fund, and it gave me the opportunity to gain a diverse portfolio and develop connections that opened more doors. I get to pick and choose my jobs now, and if I don't get the shot I want in the allotted time frame . . . I can linger, because I'm not relying on grants. Get the perfect shot. Patience is key in my business. I can afford to be very, very patient."

It was a luxury to extend expeditions at will, but then, he didn't need the photos to pay the bills. For the most part, he lived within his photography income, but if he failed, he had reserves. Vast reserves.

His gaze lingered on the beautiful woman in the puffy bag. *Patience.*

The word slipped through his mind, but it had no place here. No place with her. She might not be Dylan's girl, but his twin had, in essence, called dibs. And Dean would never, ever violate the rules they'd established as teens.

Dylan wanted her. He'd made that clear with his claim they were involved. No matter how attractive Dean found her, he could not, and would not, have Fiona Carver. Patience be damned.

She sat up. With the puffy hood tied around her face, the sleeping bag stayed with her, an orange lion's mane. "How did you get on the team? Is Bill Lowell a real person?"

146

"He is. I worked with him about five years ago in Costa Rica. He's the real deal. Wouldn't screw up Section 7."

"Well, he might. ESA is a US law. If he worked internationally, he wasn't working on Environmental Impact Statements."

"True, but Costa Rica was his vacation. He lives in Florida and does most of his fieldwork there, which meant it was safe for me to borrow his name and credentials. Pollux was in too much of a hurry to do more than a phone interview. Bill was hired on the spot by the head of the EIS project."

"Sylvia didn't hire you?"

"No. I gathered after the fact that she had someone else in mind, but it was too late. Her boss picked Bill. Er, me."

"That's quite a risk. If you'd been caught, you'd have been arrested and charged with a federal offense."

"No one really had reason to suspect, though, did they? I mean, why would anyone fake something like that? It was a risk, sure, but it didn't feel like one until I was on Whidbey Island, ready to board the plane." His gaze scanned the interior of their aircraft refuge. "And frankly, this part is feeling like the bigger risk now."

She let out a harsh laugh. "Fair point."

He reached for her bag and pulled out the collapsible bucket. "I'm going to get us some water. Keep an eye on the fire."

She nodded, and he crawled through the tail opening. The rain had slowed, but the stream flowed with vigor. While the water filled the bucket, he studied the plane. It was covered with vines and dirt, a natural camouflage. He never would have seen it if she hadn't handed him that map. It was the perfect hiding place. Even the smoke from the fire was lost in the fog.

They would be safe for the night.

He let out a thankful sigh and grabbed the bucket. Minutes later, he was back inside and pouring water into the metal pot they'd grabbed from the cook tent and setting it by the fire to boil. He then stripped off all his outer layers down to his long underwear and hung them on the line. The interior of the plane had warmed to the point that he wasn't miserably cold in his thick undergarments, but he wasn't exactly warm either. If his sweater and pants weren't damp, he'd keep them on.

He turned his focus to cooking dinner. He'd originally planned on ramen noodles and protein bars, but they had meat and a fire and would be better off saving the portable food for when their options were limited. Plus, he was hungry.

He placed two vacuum-sealed bags of chicken in a bowl of cold water to thaw, then set about searching for a pan or fork to use as a spit for cooking. He hadn't thought to grab a separate frying pan, and they needed boiled water.

"Can I help?" Fiona asked.

He shook his head. "You know your job."

"Breathe and get warm. I know. But I'm feeling better."

"I don't think you want to be crawling around the plane in nothing but a flimsy T-shirt. It's damn cold. Plus, it's getting dark, and we need to conserve flashlight batteries." They had a crank flashlight, but he'd save that for later. He'd turn the crank to charge it after they ate.

"I suppose. But it feels weird just lying here while you do all the work."

"Tell me what you know about this plane, then, while I search."

"The allied code name for this kind of plane was 'Tabby.' I think it crashed in 1944, after the Battle of Attu. There were no remains inside when I recorded it, which makes me think that at least some of the crew walked away and carried anyone who was dead or injured with them. The Tabby is really just a Douglas DC-3."

He smiled, pleased with himself that he'd guessed correctly. When he was a kid, he'd been obsessed with planes and had dreams of being a pilot. He'd never quite outgrown the obsession, even though he'd traded in the pilot dreams for photography before he'd graduated high school.

He fed a few of the larger sticks into the fire, then resumed searching the nooks and crannies of the plane for supplies, finding a few tools that might come in handy and lots of dead rodents, which, he very much hoped, would not.

He returned to the shelves with the ammo boxes and pulled down another one. He emptied it like he had the others and set it aside for dismantling later. He did the same with two more boxes, then reached for a fourth. One more and he'd go back to searching.

He opened it . . . and couldn't hold back a grin. He let out a low whistle. "Well, one of our Japanese soldiers was doing a little smuggling."

"What did you find?"

"Alcohol stash." He pulled out a blue-green bottle and held it up to the firelight. The distinctive color said it all. He'd seen piles of these when he photographed animals in the South Pacific, near other World War II battle sites.

"Sake," Fiona said.

"Yep." He was more pleased with the other bottles in the box, which he held up for Fiona to see. "And whiskey. Several bottles."

"You know, I don't even like whiskey, but right now it sounds like heaven."

He set it aside. "We'll have a splash after dinner. Don't want to risk drinking on an empty stomach after the day we've had."

"That's reasonable."

A few minutes later, he finished searching the plane and had a tin plate that would work as a frying pan for the meat. He sliced the slightly thawed chicken into thin strips for cooking over the fire. He would round out the meal with boiled ramen noodles in chicken broth. It wouldn't be gourmet by any means, but he was so hungry, he didn't care about the lack of cooking oil or seasonings.

Fiona sat with the bag around her but open, revealing the T-shirt. Her cheeks were red, and with her hair coming loose from her braid, she looked tousled. Like they'd just enjoyed a good, rousing fuck and then she'd pulled on his shirt.

His gaze fixed on that freckle on her bottom lip. The firelight made him itch to take out his camera. The photo would be gritty and sexy, with the traces of dirt on her face in the dim but warm light and rotting wreckage that surrounded her. The sleeping bag manufacturer would make a fortune if this were an ad.

But this photo would be just for him. A beautiful woman bent on survival. There was nothing sexual about her pose, but damn, he felt the pull of desire for the strength she exhibited. The line of her neck as she tilted her head and stared into the flames. The firelight reflected in her eyes.

He'd photographed actual supermodels, but none of them had ever been more alluring than Fiona Carver right this moment.

A sizzle and a pop sounded before he felt the sting of burning fat on his skin. He glanced down to stir the searing chicken and brushed his hand on his thigh to dispel the burn. He probably should be focusing on the task at hand and not the woman who might hold the answers to his brother's whereabouts. After they ate, they would talk.

He served up dinner in the bowls he'd salvaged from camp, the chicken strips mixed with the noodles and broth. She cupped the bowl with both hands and let out a soft moan as she held it up to her nose. It was a low, sexy sound that triggered yet another reaction.

He needed to ignore both the sound and his instinctive response. She might not have been Dylan's girlfriend, but his brother must've wanted her. Was it simple infatuation, or had he been in love with her, as he'd hinted on the phone?

Dean shook his head against the thought and took a bite of his meal, letting out his own moan of pleasure. There was nothing like an improvised meal at the end of an intense day in the field, and today . . . well, it ranked on an entirely different scale of intense.

He forced himself to eat slowly and noted she did the same. They were rationing, just in case, and the meal wasn't large. They had to be careful, and eating slowly would let their bodies know they were getting the protein and carbs they needed, and the hunger would dim, at least, before the bowl was empty.

She finished and set the bowl aside. "Thank you. That was one of the best meals I've ever had."

He didn't doubt it, and it wasn't because his cooking was stellar. "You're welcome. Will you tell me about Dylan now?"

She nodded. "I think I could use a cold pack on my knee, though."

He cursed. He'd forgotten about her injury. "Sorry, I meant to get you that as soon as your core temperature was stable." He reached for the bag with the first aid kit. "How is your leg?"

"It's going to be fine. Just sore." She unzipped the foot box on the bag and showed him her bare foot and ankle. "Ankle isn't even swollen. It was just a twist that hurt in the moment. My knee"—she unzipped the bag from the bottom to expose her calf and knee—"is more bruised than anything. Ice will help with the swelling, but I should be able to walk on it tomorrow."

The wind whipped at the side of the plane, and the sound of rain tapping on the metal hull intensified. "I'm not sure we'll be going anywhere tomorrow."

"We need to call my office. Let them know where we are."

"Absolutely. But you aren't up for hiking to the village, and the road is a mess. We'll reevaluate the situation in the morning." He snapped the first aid cold pack to activate it, and the bag turned cool under his fingers. A shame to be wasting the pack when it was likely to drop to below freezing tonight, but the nearest snow was on the upper slopes of the volcano, a few miles away. He grabbed a bandanna to protect her skin and knelt in front of her, examining her knee before placing the wrapped pack on the lateral side just below her kneecap.

The skin was red and the swelling minor, but still, he had the urge to press his lips to the injury. But then, he wanted to run his lips all up and down her legs.

Her throaty words from earlier came back to him. *"We might die tonight."*

She'd been joking, hadn't she?

After all, she didn't do field flings.

Dylan wants her. She's off-limits.

Fingers touched his hair, and he realized he'd been kneeling by her leg for too long. He lifted his gaze to meet hers, and he saw a heady mix of heat and desire that he was pretty sure matched what his own eyes were saying.

He cleared his throat and scooted back. "I think it's whiskey time."

She let out a pent-up breath. "Thank goodness."

He rose and grabbed the bottle he'd set aside just for this moment and threw another wood scrap on the fire, before settling by her side to watch the flames. He broke the seal on the bottle and offered it to her; she took a swig, then handed it back.

He studied the label. It was an American distillery, making him wonder where the Japanese soldier who'd smuggled it onto the cargo plane had gotten it. His mouth twisted in a bittersweet smile. "This is Dylan's favorite brand." He took a long, slow drink, then set the bottle between them, appreciating the burn as the amber liquid went down.

After a long silence, she lifted the bottle and took a second pull, then lowered it and said, "You need to know, Dylan was my friend, but we were never involved."

"Is," Dean corrected. "Is your friend." He refused to speak of his brother in past tense.

"Is," she repeated. "Why did you think we were involved?"

"He told me you were dating the last time we talked on the phone."

"When was that?"

"Eight weeks ago. Before your last trip to Chiksook."

"I have no idea why he would have said that. I never spoke with him at all between trips to Chiksook. As I said before, I didn't even have his number."

"Which explains why I found no correspondence between you when I finally got my hands on his computer."

"Then why did you believe it?"

"Two reasons: one, Dylan never lies, and two . . . it was his desktop computer, not his phone. He doesn't text on his desktop. And the only emails I could find there were work-related. He must have his laptop with him. We found his phone last night." He paused. "For what it's worth, he said the relationship was serious."

"What was the context? Why did it come up?"

"We were planning his trip to LA. He hadn't been down to visit since he moved north. I had invitations to a couple of events, including a launch party for an ad campaign featuring a model I know. I wanted Dylan to meet her. He was so crushed after the divorce, he needed to start going out again."

"So you were trying to convince him to spend his vacation, in which he was supposed to hang out with you, with some model he'd never met . . . and suddenly he tells you he's madly in love with me?"

Put that way, it did make a bit more sense. But still, he wasn't ready to believe it. "You're forgetting the part about how Dylan doesn't lie."

She scooped up the bottle again and handed it to him. "Sorry to say, your brother wasn't perfect. He lied."

"Isn't. He isn't perfect."

"Isn't," she repeated.

He took a swig and handed the bottle to her, and she took her own drink. After a long pause, she said, "I think Dylan was being sexually harassed by Sylvia. Or at least, there was something odd going on between them. I had the sense he didn't like working for Pollux at all, but he liked this project and wasn't ready to walk away from it."

"His ex-wife worked with him at the US Geological Survey. She dumped him for another coworker eighteen months ago. He couldn't stay in California after that and didn't want to work for the USGS anymore. The job with Pollux was a chance to do the work he loved but for a different agency. I don't see him getting involved with a coworker after that experience."

"But you thought he'd get involved with me?"

"You don't work for Pollux."

She nodded. "Okay, but none of that explains why you think he's still on Chiksook Island. He left the day before the rest of us did."

"Did he? Did you see him get on a helicopter or a boat?"

She frowned, her gaze fixed on the fire. "No," she said after a long pause. "I was in the field with Christina all day. Dylan was supposed to come out to the site after he did some work checking sensors in the volcano."

"*In* the volcano?"

"There are lava tubes and caves that are accessible from the north shore. After I showed him the metallic rock, he said something about maybe seeing something like it in one of the tubes or caves near one of his sensors. He was going to check it out, then return to the site after we'd exposed more of the lahar. It's why we opened up more than we should have, why the site was so vulnerable."

"But Dylan never showed up at the site that day."

"He didn't. When I got back to camp that night, I went looking for him, but Trevor said he was gone. Sent home earlier in the day. Sylvia was gone too, and Trevor said she claimed Dylan had assaulted her. It was all so abrupt and bizarre. There were no witnesses. It was all he said/she said, and frankly, it was always Sylvia who was inappropriate with Dylan, to the degree he was uncomfortable and hinted as much."

"I will never believe Dylan would make a pass at—let alone assault—his boss."

"For what it's worth—and from what I saw—I agree. But anyway, according to Trevor, Dylan had been flown home and put on unpaid leave while Pollux investigated. Dylan and Sylvia left on the helicopter. Together. But that seemed weird too. I mean, if someone had assaulted me, I wouldn't be eager to spend time on a helicopter with them. I was told Sylvia caught a military flight back to Whidbey, while Dylan flew home commercial."

Dean startled at that. "I was told Dylan was on a military flight—and the navy refused to give me the flight manifest, which is one of the reasons I believed Dylan never left Chiksook. There is no record of him leaving, as far as I can tell."

Fiona's brow furrowed. "The helicopter charter would have records of how many were flown to Adak, even if they didn't provide names."

"They refused to answer either way. Military contract, operational security. They gave me the full runaround."

"So no one has seen Dylan in five weeks?"

"No one. You would be one of the last people to see him, if you saw him that morning."

"I did. We had breakfast together and made plans to meet up."

"Was Trevor there?"

She frowned but finally said, "No. I don't think so. Christina wasn't there either. She tended to sleep in and eat on the drive." She gave a wry smile. "Gracious, was it just this morning that I did the exact same thing?"

Dean nodded, feeling the same way. This morning felt like a month ago. A glance at his watch said it had only been eleven hours. Eleven hours and a site collapse, a camp explosion, one near-drowning, and a hypothermic reheat in a Japanese World War II airplane, and now he was stranded on an Aleutian island with a beautiful woman and not a single step closer to finding his missing twin.

Or was he?

This all had to be related to Dylan's disappearance. Something was going *on* here. Nothing that happened today had been an accident.

"How did you find out Dylan was—supposedly—sent home?" she asked.

"After I received an email from Dylan's work email address—anyone at Pollux could have sent it—saying he was taking a leave of absence and going off the grid for three months, I tried to reach him. When I couldn't get a hold of him, I contacted Pollux, and they made it sound like Dylan had been evacuated with the team."

"That was definitely a lie."

"And I had no way of knowing that, because no one would talk to me." Dean took another swig of whiskey, then breathed deep as it burned. "I knew from the moment I received the bogus email that something was off. Dylan would never take off like that without talking to me first. We're close. Always have been. Best friends since the womb. He might run off for a few months—I'm not saying *that* part isn't like him; he did as much when he found out his wife was leaving him—but he would absolutely contact me, just like he did then. Which means he never left Chiksook." He glanced toward the broken window where the smoke escaped into the night. "He's out there somewhere. And I need to find him."

SIXTEEN

Fiona's heart broke a bit at the pain in Dean's voice. She could relate to his pain and his fear on a deep level, one he absolutely didn't want to know about. Not now. Not while he was so adamant he could find his brother.

She knew from experience, sometimes the finding was more painful than one could even fathom.

But at least now she understood him. Even more than he realized. But also, his suspicions were explained. The hostility he'd shown when he knocked her down on the hillside.

She knew the pain of a lost sibling. And Dean and Dylan were twins, a dynamic she couldn't relate to. With Regan, she knew only the older sister role. The responsible one. With Aidan, she was the middle sibling. The one who would never be good enough. And then, in her teens, he'd stepped into their father's role after the accident.

Aidan would always view her more as a dependent than an equal, not much different from how he treated their mom. But the difference was Mom couldn't make her own decisions anymore, while Fiona was just fine without Aidan in control.

"Who is older?" she asked Dean.

He tilted his head. "It doesn't matter. We're twins. The same age. Technically, no one is older."

"I know. Just curious."

"Truth is, we don't know who's older. My dad's best friend was a twin, and when Dad found out he was going to have twin boys, he asked for advice. The one thing Uncle Leroy said was to never, ever tell us who's older, or it will start to *matter*. So my dad made sure when we were born, both birth certificates recorded the same time of birth. We know one of us was born ten minutes after the other, but no one—with the possible exception of my dad, who took it to the grave—knows who came first."

"I'm so sorry your dad is gone, but also, that's really sweet."

He smiled, and his eyes held warmth that made her heart do a little flutter. He picked up the bottle and stared at it, then said, "Our dad was a great man." He glanced up and added, "To you, Pop," then took another drink.

She took the bottle from him and said, "To your pop." She silently added her sister and father to the toast, took a long, slow sip, then offered him the bottle again.

"That's it for me. Not a good idea to get wasted right now, much as I want to."

She set down the bottle between them. As tempting as it was to escape into the happy haze of alcohol, it was also dangerous. "Agreed."

He moved the bottle to the side and scooted closer to her, now that the whiskey wasn't in the way. "We need a plan."

She nodded again. She'd been thinking the same thing. She leaned her temple on his shoulder, feeling drowsy now that she had an almost full belly and was warm again. The fire lit their haven with a cheerful orange glow. Her eyes fixated on the flames as a warm buzz infused her. Just a few sips of whiskey and she could feel her senses dulling. Good thing she'd stopped there. It wouldn't take much to get her drunk right now, and she needed to keep her wits.

"I'm sorry you're in danger because of me." His fingers drummed the floor between them, and she had a feeling he was fighting the urge to take her hand in his, to give and take comfort.

Sparks popped and danced in the small metal bin that served as their hearth. "We don't know that I'm in danger because of you. This might have happened—probably would have—even if you'd never stepped on that plane." She closed her eyes and thought about last night in the office tent, when she'd emailed her boss. "I told my boss I was concerned you and Victor aren't qualified. Maybe someone in camp was intercepting emails."

"Victor? He's on my short list, but why do *you* suspect him?"

She explained his mistake with Michal's gender.

"Damn, that's probably even worse than messing up Section 7."

"It's certainly close, especially for a USGS geologist who's supposedly from California. Why do *you* suspect Victor?"

"Trevor was pulled off the flight at the last minute and suddenly this geologist shows up like a miracle? It's a little hard to swallow."

"But is Trevor involved too?"

She felt Dean's shrug as she leaned against him. "No clue," he said. He wrapped an arm around her shoulders—even better than holding hands, really—and it felt so natural. "Right now, my biggest concern is that we're not alone on this island. I don't think we're the only ones who missed the boat. If it weren't for the wicked rain, I'd be concerned we can be tracked here from the side-by-side, but I watched our trail wash away behind us. We're safe as long as Victor—if it's Victor who set up the explosion—doesn't know about this plane. Does Pollux have your field maps?"

She shook her head. "Nope, we're doing the archaeological survey with navy employees only. No need for Pollux to have historic and cultural resource maps or location information. It's a separate section of the EIS, and the actual site data aren't subject to FOIA. Sites are protected."

He let out a deep breath and said, "Thank goodness. We can sleep at the same time tonight, then, instead of taking shifts. We're both going to need all our energy tomorrow if we leave this shelter."

Something stirred low in her belly at the knowledge they'd be sharing the sleeping bag. There wasn't any other option that didn't include one of them freezing to death.

"You still want to go to the village tomorrow?"

He nodded. "Maybe you can check your email, see if your boss replied. Find out if there's a plan to rescue us."

She yawned. "It's worth a shot." She rose and shed the sleeping bag. "I'm going to step outside and take care of business, then brush my teeth."

"There's a spot under the broken wing that offers a little shelter from the rain."

She nodded. "That was my plan." She cleared her throat. "We're supposed to pack out *all* waste, but given that this plane itself is garbage that's been rotting here for over seventy-five years, I'm going to ignore the regs for the duration of our time here. We've got enough crap to worry about without worrying about actual . . . *waste*. Just make sure anything we leave behind is biodegradable and buried."

"Deal."

She pulled on her thick yellow raincoat but didn't bother with anything else. It would just be in the way, and she didn't plan to be outside long.

All she could think as she took care of business in the shelter of the broken wing was how glad she was that her period wasn't due for three weeks. It was always a hassle to have a period during a field project, but in this situation, it would be extra irritating.

She was shivering by the time she was back inside. The temperature had dropped by at least ten degrees after the sun went down. The rain was now mixed with flecks of snow. There was a chance they'd wake up to a blanket of white tomorrow.

Back inside, she used water Dean had boiled to wash her face and hands; then she brushed her teeth while Dean slipped outside to take his turn in their makeshift latrine. While he was gone, she inflated their one small sleeping pad that had been in the back of the side-by-side with the emergency supplies. At least their sleeping bag had bands to attach to the pad. They wouldn't slide off it and would each get a small amount of thermal padding.

After their bed was set up, she paced the cold plane, bracing herself for the coming night.

He crawled into the plane through the back, then stood and faced her. "We should conserve wood and let the fire die."

She nodded. They would probably be too hot in the bag with their combined body heat. It would be a waste of good wood.

That's what she said.

She mentally groaned at her own internal joke. How would Dean react if he knew where her mind was going right before they had to share a sleeping bag?

He nodded to the bed she'd set up. "You climb in first. I'll slide in beside you."

She did as he suggested and watched as he peeled off his long underwear, stripping down to boxer briefs. She was caught off guard by his sculpted chest. She'd known he was strong but hadn't expected this . . . utter perfection.

But then, he must spend more months of the year in jungles, deserts, and on tundra than in the city, and a man had to be fit for that kind of lifestyle. Clearly, he worked out to maintain the shape he was in.

Her gaze landed on a tattoo just left of center on his chest. Purple flowers. Violets?

Before she could get a good look, he pulled a shirt out of his bag, covering up both the tattoo and his perfect, sculpted chest and shoulders. Then he donned a pair of sweatpants, covering his muscled thighs as well.

She stifled her sigh. It was better this way, since they were going to be sleeping wrapped like the stuffing in a burrito, but still. She might not have *minded* having his bare skin against her.

He caught her gaze and gave her a smug smile, reminding her of the first moments they'd met. The man wasn't short on ego, but then, with a body and face like his—and a skill with the camera to match—he had plenty of reason to be smug. And Dylan had said his brother was something of a playboy. The women he dated tended to come from the glitterati of LA.

Given his profession, he wasn't a man who could make or break any woman's career. All he could do for them was give them pleasure.

That women flocked to him said something about his talents in other areas. Maybe she should reconsider her no-field-flings rule. Find out if he delivered on his smug promises.

"You know, *I* turned my back when *you* were undressing."

She chuckled. "Yeah, but I stripped naked. You had boxers on. Also, you could have said something sooner. I'd have given you privacy."

"And deny you the pleasure of ogling me? I would *never*."

Now her chuckle turned to a belly laugh. His abundant ego worked for her. There was a refreshing lack of pretense. "I'm glad you get me. Your body is impressive."

"Thank you. I work hard enough on it; it's nice to get some appreciation."

If she had a pillow, she'd throw it at him. Instead she said, "Stop bragging and come to bed. I'm tired."

"You just can't wait to touch this."

Now she snorted. But dammit, there was a little bit of truth there.

I mean, if I have to be pressed up against some stranger all night long . . . might as well be a slice of perfection.

He spread out the wood in the fire pit so the fire would die but maybe preserve some charcoal for tomorrow morning. The light dimmed as the flames divided among the pieces of wood and shrank. "Scoot over. I'm going to need some room."

Yes. Yes. You will. Your shoulders will take up so much real estate, they should have their own zip code.

She pressed her body to the right zipper to give him as much space as possible, and a moment later, his hard, sculpted body was sliding next to hers inside the bag.

It was a *tight* squeeze. So tight, her arms were trapped. She tugged down the zipper at her shoulder. Cold air would lick her skin, but with the hard body at her back, she'd be warm enough. And she'd be able to move her arms.

He settled in, tucking his knees behind hers and wrapping his arms around her so she spooned against him. "Sorry. This is the only way we'll both fit."

"I know. It's fine."

And it was. Not because he had a nice body but because it really was their only option.

His face was in her hair, and her ass was pressed to his crotch. If she were shorter, he could breathe in this position. Sometimes she felt guilty over being tall, which was ridiculous given that it wasn't exactly a personal choice.

"Sorry you can't breathe."

"I'm fine."

They lay there in silence for several minutes, both their bodies tense. This was going to take a little getting used to.

The firelight slowly dimmed, and the interior of the plane grew darker and darker. Her body relaxed by slow degrees. Rain pattered on the roof, and she wondered if it was more snow than rain, hence the quieting of the storm.

He cleared his throat and said, "I feel I should warn you—and apologize in advance—there's a ninety percent chance I'm going to get an erection at some point tonight. It's . . . kind of unavoidable, given your ass is . . . snug against me. But I'm going to try not to, and I just want to say, I wouldn't . . . do anything. It's just biology and physiology. Hard to ignore when there's a beautiful woman in my arms."

"Well, that last line goes a long way toward earning my forgiveness. In advance."

"It wasn't a line. It's obvious why Dylan is attracted to you. You're the full package. Beauty, brains, skilled. Professional."

The compliments were nice, but he was wrong, which kind of undermined the good parts. "Dylan wasn't—*isn't*—attracted to me."

"He is. He described you to a T, and the first thing he said was you're beautiful and brilliant."

"I'm neither of those things. I mean, I do okay, but I'm hardly special in looks or smarts."

"I think you're wrong there. And so did Dylan."

"I promise you, Dean, Dylan *wasn't* attracted to me. Not in any real way. There was no . . . *zing*."

Not like I feel with you.

She jolted at that. This was not the time to explore that thought train.

"I don't believe it. Not after the way he talked about you."

"When we first met, we did the usual checking-each-other-out thing. Both single and of similar age and all that, but by day four or five, we'd settled into an easy friendship. I liked him, even appreciated his looks—but it wasn't anything more than enjoying working with a good-looking, kind, smart man who wasn't a dick on the job. Those can be rare in the field. Especially the engineers. No social skills and with an inflated sense of their importance."

She rolled over, which wasn't easy in the tight bag, but she wanted to see his eyes so he'd *get* it. It took a ridiculous effort—like making a sixty-point turn to get a car out of a tight space—but eventually she was looking at his eyes in the dim light. "You don't have to compliment me to get me to help you find Dylan. I'm on board. I'll do what I can. I'll take you to the volcano where he was working. But don't try to make our friendship into something it wasn't."

His eyes showed confusion, which wasn't at all what she'd expected. Finally, he said, "I can't help but think there was more on Dylan's side, given what he said. You just didn't notice."

It made no sense, the way he clung to this belief. But it was probably hard to accept his brother had lied. Because if that was a lie—and he was so certain Dylan never lied—then how well did he know his brother? Was it possible Dylan *had* taken off on his own?

Were the events of the last twelve hours nothing more than a bizarre coincidence, and Dylan was off on a tropical island somewhere drinking his troubles away?

Dylan had told her about his divorce. He'd said—and she'd believed him—he wasn't ready to start dating again. Then there was this weird dynamic with Sylvia. Maybe he had been attracted to his boss after all, and given his broken heart, he didn't know what to do about it?

But she still didn't believe he'd assaulted Sylvia. It was the one piece that never rang true. People revealed their true selves on difficult field projects like this one, and she believed to her core that Dylan Slater hadn't laid a finger on his boss. The person she didn't trust was Sylvia Jessup.

She'd seen the woman come on to Dylan in small ways that made him uncomfortable. Subtle aggressions that were hard to call out, especially when the male-female dynamic was flipped. When a guy was sexually harassed, he was supposed to feel like a stud, or some kind of bullshit like that. Plus, Fiona had seen the move Sylvia had made the night before Dylan was supposedly sent home.

But she was utterly exhausted, and there was no convincing Dean tonight that there was nothing between her and his brother, so she pressed a kiss to his cheek and said, "Good night, Dean."

He smiled and pressed his lips to her forehead. "Good night, Fiona."

She completed another sixty-point turn, then settled in again, with his knees behind hers and her ass tucked against his hips and crotch. There was a small—very small—gap of air between them, so they weren't quite snuggled tight, but she was blessedly warm, and his arm draped over her shoulder, making her feel safe.

She closed her eyes and listened to the patter of rain on the fuselage. Slowly, sleep overtook her, and thankfully, she didn't dream.

SEVENTEEN

The rain had stopped. It was the first thought that crossed Dean's mind as he slowly came to consciousness. The second thought was that he held the beautiful woman his brother wanted in his arms and he was at half-mast. He gave thanks it wasn't a full-on morning missile.

Sorry, bro. But she's just as great as you described.

Dean slowly extracted his arms from the sleeping woman and unzipped his side of the bag so he could slip out. He wasn't about to do anything that could be construed as making a move on Dylan's girl while he was out of commission.

Thankfully, Fiona didn't stir as Dean slipped from the bag and zipped it up again. If he was lucky, he could get the fire going and have the place warmed up, with coffee at the ready, before she woke.

He hadn't held a woman as she'd slept since Violet died. He'd spent the night with other women, sure, but holding them after sex—and especially holding them without sex ever being part of the equation—wasn't something that had happened in more than ten years.

Sometimes, it was hard to believe it had been ten years since the love of his life had passed. And yet, at the same time, it felt like it had been forever since he'd held her. The day after her funeral, he'd boarded a plane and departed for Tanzania, the trip he and Violet had planned as their college graduation present, before she got sick.

She'd gotten a payout from her trust fund upon graduation, and she'd been eager to finance the trip for them both. A celebration of their wildlife biology degrees. Violet had dreams of being the next Dian

Fossey, and Dean was ready to be by her side, taking photos that would show the world the wonders of great apes and other fauna in equatorial Africa.

But before they could depart, she'd gotten sick. After her diagnosis, Violet had begged Dean to marry her—she didn't want her parents to have medical power of attorney, knowing they would cut Dean from her life if she became incapacitated. They'd married in a small ceremony that included Dylan as best man and his father as the other witness less than a week before her first surgery.

They'd agreed then that their African adventure would be a belated honeymoon, after she got better, but in the end, she'd made him promise he would take the trip without her, after she was gone. Boarding that plane without her after she'd been laid to rest was one of the most devastating moments of his life. He never would have done it if he hadn't given her that solemn vow.

He'd lost his father to H1N1 a few months after their hasty wedding, two years before he lost his wife to cancer. He'd lost his mom to kidney failure when he and Dylan were nineteen.

He'd ended up staying in Africa—traveling from country to country, taking photo after photo of incredible wildlife—for nearly nine months, far longer than the original expedition was meant to be, because he had nothing to return to.

Well, except Dylan, who'd encouraged him to explore the world and live life to the fullest after two and a half years of taking care of Violet. Of watching the tumors in her brain rob her of her ability to move, speak, and see.

That first solitary expedition had been for her. He saw all the animals in their natural habitats that she'd never been able to lay eyes on herself. He touched the vines and trees in the jungle, because she never got to feel that texture beneath her fingers. He imitated the sounds of birds, because she never got to experience the joy of making a birdcall and hearing a response.

Violet would have loved every minute of his African adventure, and for her, he tried to enjoy it too. And he did, but it took time. In a way, part of what made it possible for him to find pleasure in the trip was the hardship of it—nothing was easy or comfortable.

It wasn't some deluxe grand safari, even though that had been well within his budget.

Between diagnosis and death, Violet had turned twenty-five, and her trust fund came into her control. She'd left it all to Dean. But he had no interest in a rich tourist's pampered excursion. He'd wanted to get down and dirty in the thick of things. To see the animals up close and feel the heartbeat of the wilderness. He'd wanted to leave no mark on the land or animals while meeting them on their terms.

He wasn't naïve, so he hired guides, but they didn't *do* the work for him. They taught him the skills he needed and made sure he didn't die from his own ignorance. The end result was that the expedition was grueling. Hot. Miserable and dangerous. He carried his own pack and cooked his own food. There were times when food or water was scarce, and he and his guides survived on grubs and whatever else they could scavenge.

It wasn't *fun* in any normal sense of the word, but it had been utterly exhilarating. He was, well and truly, alive and living to the fullest extent possible, pushing his limits to the edge.

Dylan had worried upon Dean's return that he'd come back a daredevil, someone who felt the need to test the boundaries of mortality. And to a certain degree, that was probably true. But he'd dialed back the recklessness after that because he wouldn't risk leaving his brother alone in the world. They'd lost both their parents in a short time. It would be too much if Dylan lost Dean too.

Which was another reason he knew Dylan wouldn't take off without a word. Ten years might have passed since Dean lost Violet, but Dylan wouldn't do that to him.

They'd made a lot of pacts over the years, but the number one most important was communication. They were the only family they had.

After Violet died, Dean shut off the part of his heart that allowed for a deeper connection to anyone other than his brother. He wouldn't open himself up to that kind of loss again. He had friendships, but they were superficial. He refused to *care*.

His gaze landed on the sleeping woman, and he didn't like the concern he felt for her. When he'd found her facedown in the mud yesterday . . . his heart could have stopped for the pain that had ripped through him.

But that was because *Dylan* cared about her. And because it was Dean's fault she'd been in danger in the first place. It was guilt, not any deeper kind of caring.

And it had felt right to hold her last night only because it was safety and security for them both. Warmth and comfort, which they both needed.

If Fiona didn't feel for Dylan as his brother did for her, she'd change her mind when they found him, alive and well. He'd make sure of it. Dylan deserved happiness. Deserved a good woman by his side, and Fiona was . . . impressive.

Maybe even glorious.

He slipped outside to visit their makeshift latrine to see the snow that had fallen last night had all melted in the rain that followed. It was now sunny and clear, no sign of the storm that had whipped through yesterday.

He had no clue what the updated forecast would say, but as of two days ago, the storm was supposed to be confined to one day, and then it would be clear for two to three days. If they could get the side-by-side up the muddy road, this would be a good window to visit the village. If the weather stayed clear, even satellite phones might work.

Not that they had a satellite phone, but still.

Back inside the plane, he found Fiona up, shivering in his T-shirt as she bent over the small pile of coals and blew slowly on the flame until it glowed a hot red and caught the kindling she'd piled on top.

Her position—on hands and knees with her head bent low toward the flames—was unintentionally sexy, with her loose hair tousled around her shoulders. He felt a possessive heat burn in his gut. She wore *his* shirt and had slept in his arms. His cock thickened even as he tried to will the sexy associations out of his mind.

She's Dylan's.

Besides, he didn't do relationships, and she didn't do field flings.

She glanced up, and he prayed she didn't see the bulge in his sweatpants. He could hardly blame it on proximity now. He dropped down to a squatting position on the other side of the fire pit, hiding his reaction, which was thankfully deflating. "Morning. I was hoping to get water boiling for coffee before you woke."

"I blew it by getting out of bed. Lesson learned."

"You sleep okay?"

She shrugged. "Better at first than after the rain stopped. It was fitful after that. You?"

"Like the dead," he lied. He didn't want to tell her how much holding her had felt both right and wrong, interfering with his sleep.

She gave him a look that said she knew he wasn't telling the truth. He'd have to hope she assumed it was worry for Dylan that kept him awake. It was certainly part of it. He fed a few sticks of ammo box to the growing fire. "I'll break up the other boxes and tie them in bundles. We should take as much as we can carry with us to the side-by-side."

"It's safe to head out today?"

"Yeah. No snow on the ground. Blue sky."

She nodded. "I think we need to go over Dylan's maps, figure out where he worked on and around the volcano. He said he was going to the volcano that last morning to look for meteorite debris."

Dean nodded. "I wish we'd been able to find his phone in your tent. If I could get a look at the GPS data . . ."

She glanced down, biting her bottom lip, hiding the freckle that had so fascinated him that first day.

Still did, actually.

His belly dropped as he realized the nervous lip-biting was a tell. "Please tell me you have his phone."

Slowly, she nodded. "It's in the clipboard. I tucked it away before we left camp yesterday morning. I didn't want to leave it out. I just . . . I had that weird vibe from Victor, and then I thought you might have searched my tent the night before while I was in the office tent. I didn't want it out on the table."

He sat back on his heels, taking a deep breath. Her instincts had been spot-on. "I *did* go into your tent. I wanted to see if the phone was Dylan's and if it still worked."

"And what did you learn?"

"Yes on both counts. I left it because I was pretty sure you'd notice if it was missing."

"I would have. You know his passcode?"

He nodded.

She shook her head. "Man, I'm a little jealous. That's some deep trust."

He laughed. "Well, it's our birth date. So not so much trust as lazy."

She gave him a soft smile. "I stand corrected. But still, it's sweet."

Dean supposed it was. Dylan knew all his most important passwords and vice versa. But then, it would be a lonely life if he didn't have anyone with whom he could share his ATM PIN, wouldn't it?

Did Fiona have that? A personal identification number buddy? Did she even have siblings? Was she close to her parents?

He knew nothing about her.

When they had more time, he'd ask her all the important questions. But today, the search for Dylan had to take center stage. "Why didn't you tell me where the phone was when I was looking for it?"

"Because I was freaked out that you were searching so desperately for it, after you'd gone for Dylan's clipboard before the sleeping bag. I thought you might be behind the other sabotage."

She must've been terrified of him right then. "Tell you what. I'll make coffee, and we'll take a look at the map and the phone."

She nodded and rose. "I need to use the latrine and get dressed. Then I'll help make breakfast."

Fifteen minutes later, they were sitting side by side by the fire, each with a mug of coffee in their hands, Dylan's phone and clipboard between them. Dean had powered up the phone. Now he unlocked it with the PIN.

He went straight to the letter icon on the bottom of the screen to access the email accounts. Dylan had both his free, personal email account and work email configured on the phone. Given that they didn't have Wi-Fi to download recent emails, only the previously down-loaded messages from six weeks ago populated the screen.

Dean had seen these same emails on Dylan's computer in his Seattle apartment. He was more interested in emails *sent* from the phone by Dylan in his last days on Chiksook. Emails sent from this phone hadn't been on Dylan's home computer. Dean had had no way to access those messages until now.

He went to the Sent folder for Dylan's personal email and found a dozen emails from the last days he was on Chiksook. Two were to Dean—upbeat messages about the project and Fiona, including that last, unequivocal email that couldn't have been written by anyone but Dylan.

Dean showed her the phone, and the crease between her brows deepened as she read the last one he'd sent, in which he'd described going to see the archaeological site and how Fiona had looked on the bluff as she'd gazed across the landscape. He'd said he wished he had Dean's photography skills, because only Dean knew how to capture the light just so to do her justice.

She set down the phone and said, "Okay. I get it now. He *does* sound infatuated. But I swear, he *wasn't*. Dylan wasn't even a casual flirt, like you or Roy." She lifted the phone again. "Besides, it's irrelevant. We're looking for emails you haven't already read sixty times."

"A hundred, minimum. I've got all his emails memorized at this point."

Fiona's hand dropped to his knee. "I'm sorry. I know how terrifying this is, and you've been living with it for weeks."

He frowned. "Have you . . . lost a sibling?"

She waved a hand, as if to push away his question. "I mean, I only learned Dylan was missing last night. This is still new to me. And reading his email . . . I get it now. Dylan is *gone*. And you've been alone in your nightmare."

He caught his breath, realizing this was the first genuine sympathy offered by someone who also knew Dylan, and it . . . meant a lot. So much that his eyes burned, but he held it back.

He had friends who'd understood the gravity—like the reporter who helped him get the Bill Lowell ID—but the reporter didn't know Dylan. She didn't care beyond the abstract. "We're going to find him," Dean said.

She nodded. "We will."

He squeezed her hand and took another deep breath. He wasn't alone in his search anymore.

———

The last thing she wanted was to tell Dean about her own family. Not now. So it was with relief that he accepted her deflection, but also, it was true. It was finally sinking in.

Dylan Slater hadn't left Chiksook willingly. If he'd left the island at all.

She scrolled through the sent emails and paused when she saw the name of a lab in Nevada. She tapped the cracked screen to open it. "Dylan said he wanted to send the metallic rock to this lab. He said they'd run a mass spec to identify the mineralogy. There was something about light signatures for different minerals, look at the geometric shapes or something. Between those tests, they'd be able to determine what metals are included in the stone."

She read the email, and her heart rate picked up as a wave of relief washed through her. "Dean, he sent the rock and the harpoon head to the lab!"

He didn't lose or steal the artifacts.

Oh, sweet lord, she could cry at this news. *Thank you, Dylan.*

She cleared her throat and continued. "He emailed the lab to give them the heads-up that the samples had been mailed from the Unangax̂ village, so they would take a few extra days to ship, and to send receipt confirmation to the billing email address he'd set up for the samples he sent in July." She held up the phone so Dean could see the billing email address Dylan had included in the message. It wasn't one of the preconfigured email accounts on the phone. "Does this address look familiar to you?"

He shook his head. "Why wouldn't he send this email from that account, if it's the one he used when dealing with the lab?"

"It's not preconfigured on his phone, so he'd have to access it via the internet. Given the extra layer of going online and logging in, and the spotty internet here, odds are it timed out before he had a chance to type the email, let alone hit 'Send.' Internet is seriously dicey here. Even when using preconfigured accounts, we get timed out, and things aren't delivered. Sending from the preloaded email server would skip the step of logging in via the web and loading the account."

"That makes sense. He didn't want Pollux to know about the sample. He bypassed his work email in sending this from his personal account on his phone, and he paid for the analysis using an account he'd set up in advance with an online-only email account. Plus, he used the tribal mail system to send the sample out instead of using the camp mail service provided by the navy."

She nodded. "The locals have a regular weekly pickup and delivery. He must've stopped by the village after visiting the site and mailed it. But why the secrecy from Pollux? I mean, they should be the ones to pay for the test."

"Maybe someone in the village can answer that."

"I bet he was more suspicious of Sylvia than he ever let on." Dylan Slater was taking a different shape in her mind with each new detail. He'd sent weird-ass emails to his brother that made it sound like he was enamored with her, he bypassed the mail system available to fieldworkers, and he used a secret email address to conduct geologic tests.

And why had he left his phone and clipboard behind? The cracked screen *could* explain the phone. He wouldn't have had reception in the volcano anyway. But why the field notes? And if he never left Chiksook, then Sylvia had lied about his taking the helicopter with her.

Why hadn't *she* taken the phone and clipboard?

If one were trying to cover up a person's disappearance and claimed they'd left the island willingly—wouldn't it be prudent to pack *all* their belongings?

Trevor had been Dylan's roommate during the previous expedition, and he was the person who told Fiona about Dylan's expulsion from the team. What did Trevor know? Was he as clueless as Fiona had been, or was he also involved? Why had he been pulled from the jet at the last minute and replaced by Victor?

The fire popped and sizzled, bringing her focus back to the interior of the plane and not the office tent that evening nearly six weeks ago now, when Trevor had told her about Sylvia's allegation and Dylan's removal from the team.

"I feel like we have too many chess pieces and no actual board," she said.

"That's easy. Chiksook is the board."

"Is Dylan a pawn or a king?"

"I think he's a knight," Dean said. "He can jump over other pieces and move in asymmetrical patterns but isn't powerful like a queen or nearly as limited as the king."

"He can be taken without it being game over."

"Isn't that exactly what happened? Hasn't the game really just begun?"

She was a little surprised Dean could talk about it so analytically, but then, it was a testament to his sharp mind. She guessed he was compartmentalizing. It must be the only way he'd managed to cope these last weeks.

She really did know that pain and didn't wish it on anyone. She certainly couldn't share her experience now, when he was in the thick of it.

"So . . . what we need to do is cross the board without being killed and bring back Dylan."

"Yes," he said with a firm nod.

"What you're saying is we're pawns."

"Unfortunately, also yes."

"Sylvia is the queen?"

"I'm starting to think so. She's the only person who we're certain lied." He glanced sideways at her. "I will never, ever believe my brother would assault her. Not unless it was self-defense."

Fiona agreed. She believed in believing women, but in this instance, she knew the woman and knew the man. And nothing about the allegation rang true. What they needed was Sylvia's motive for lying.

Unfortunately, the most obvious motive was that Dylan was dead, and it was Sylvia's fault. She'd covered it up with her claims so she could pretend to send him home. As his immediate supervisor, she'd have no problem accessing his work email and sending the one Dean received to friends and colleagues.

But there was no way in hell she'd share that theory with Dean. He still had hope. And he needed to hold on to it as long as he could.

She grabbed a chunk of wood that had the overall shape of a two-foot-long two-by-four and set it on the fire, then bent down to blow on the coals to encourage it to catch quickly. She'd donned her long underwear, and it was warm enough inside the plane that she wasn't shivering, but it wasn't exactly hot either. Not shivering was a relatively low bar when it came to thermal comfort, but she'd take it.

She cleared her throat and asked, "So who is king? How do we end this game?" After all, finding Dylan's body would only answer the question of where he was. It likely wouldn't explain why.

"I have no clue."

Was Victor still on the island? How could they find out if he was here? Aside from tripping over him, of course.

Dean picked up Dylan's phone and flipped through the apps. "Browsing history can't load, and if it did, it would be overridden with null data, given the weeks that have passed." He tapped the screen several more times. "Same with messages. They won't load without internet."

They'd gleaned all the information they could from the phone.

She'd found her artifact, but they weren't really closer to finding Dylan.

She closed her eyes as the memory of a spring afternoon in Eastern Washington came to mind. Five years and four months ago. The moment when the last vestige of hope had died. She'd lost two siblings that day. But then, maybe Aidan had already been gone. After all, their mom's illness had taught her that a person could be alive and gone at the same time.

She wished she could save Dean a pain she knew all too well.

She didn't want Dylan to be dead. But really, what other option was there? This was Chiksook, and it had been nearly six weeks since Dylan was last seen.

She set the phone down and reached for the stack of field notes, flipping through them until she found a hand-drawn map. "This is Dylan's handwriting?" She was fairly certain, but she hadn't seen enough of it to speak with authority.

"Yes."

She stared at the contours and symbols. "I think this is a schematic of the lava tubes and caves on the coastal side of the mountain. He said it was an elaborate network."

"What does *'Kanuux̂'* mean?" he asked, pointing to a label on the map. He'd done a decent job with the Unangam Tunuu—the Unangas' name for their language—pronunciation.

"*Kanuux̂* means *heart*, I think. *Kanuux̂* is the native name for Mount Katin. Katin was some Russian guy's surname, but the locals have called the mountain *Kanuux̂* for centuries, even millennia. Long before the Russians came and renamed their mountain after a foreigner." It was true for many of the Aleutian Islands and their volcanoes. Russian names might mark the map, but the locals still used the names they'd given. Much as Denali was now Denali again and no longer named for an American president who'd never even visited the state.

"So the volcano is the heart of the island."

"It is."

"I bet Dylan loved that," Dean said.

"He did. He said it made sense, since the lava tubes were the veins and arteries. Dylan really loved his work."

"Loves," Dean corrected.

She covered his hand with hers. "Loves," she repeated, taking a deep breath to hold back tears that would reveal far too much.

EIGHTEEN

They hiked back to the side-by-side in silence, each loaded down with heavy packs and bundles of wood tied to the frames. Dean kept an eye on Fiona, making sure she wasn't favoring her leg. He wasn't sure she'd admit if she wasn't up to the hike, and she'd refused to allow him to carry more than his two packs, as that would mean they'd have to leave the bundles of firewood behind.

He was tempted to return to the plane once their gear was dropped off and she was safely tucked inside so he could retrieve more wood, but his gut said separating would be unwise.

Their plan for the morning was to go to the village. The locals might have information, and they would have a phone. Fiona would get in touch with her boss, and the cavalry would be called in, and then they could head to the volcano.

They had Dylan's map of the lava tubes plus another map with the locations of the sensors he'd set up on the surface. The volcano was Dylan's last-known location, so that was their starting point.

Hopefully.

It all depended on the side-by-side still being parked by the side of the road. And operational.

They descended a steep slope, the last hurdle before they reached the side-by-side. Dean's heart pounded as the vehicle came into view.

It looked fine. He circled it, checking the tires and studying the ground to see if anyone else had found it and potentially tampered with it. Not that footprints would be visible after the heavy, icy rain.

The tires were fine, the spare fuel can strapped to the back remained full, and the door was locked.

Relief filtered through him. Without the side-by-side, they would be in trouble. He doubted Fiona was up to the long hike to the village with the heavy pack, plus she needed to save her energy for the volcano.

He was eager to head to the volcano, but going straight there without going to the village first could be reckless, and possibly deadly.

His heart had thundered this morning when he'd looked at the map drawn by his brother. He was going to find Dylan *today*. He knew it in his gut.

But first, to the village . . .

He unlocked the back, and they piled the firewood and heavy packs inside. As before, field packs went into the back seat because the storage compartment was too small to hold everything, especially now that they had wood to burn.

The drive to the village was slow going over pathetic roads. "I'm going to assume they don't use this road very often," Dean said as they hit a particularly egregious gap in the road.

"They don't. There's another road to the north—we'll take that to the volcano—that's slightly better for them to come and go, but mostly they use boats. The village is situated on a sheltered deepwater bay that's easy for larger vessels to moor. Of course, it would be perfect for the submarine base. There was even some admiral, who didn't understand the sovereignty of Alaska Natives, who proposed seizing the village through eminent domain and making it the study area."

Dean let out a low whistle. "Just when you want to think our colonizer days didn't extend into the new millennium."

"Right? He apparently didn't get the updated history lesson that *manifest destiny* was a horrific excuse for genocide then, and would be deemed a crime against humanity now."

"Why did the Unangas agree to let the navy use this island in the first place?"

"The navy has promised them a whole lot of new infrastructure for the island. The village could be expanded, and there's going to be a new school that will make it possible for families to relocate here—and some will be able to get jobs on the base. Plus, they'll have stable electricity, internet, and cellular service. There were two years of public meetings before the navy settled on Chiksook for the base location, and there's another team looking at an alternate location in case the environmental analysis or engineering specs find a fatal flaw."

"I'm surprised you aren't also working on the alternate location."

"I was supposed to, but delays and difficulties with the Chiksook evaluation meant I didn't have time for the other project too—which is suffering from similar weather and infrastructure problems. Some of the fieldwork has happened concurrently, and I have difficulty being in two places at once."

"Aww. C'mon. Slacker."

She laughed. "David, the archaeologist who's working the other project, was super jealous when I told him I'd found an intact house. He grumbled that he doesn't even have cool World War II debris to record, let alone a full base like on Chiksook."

"He'd have loved our plane."

"Totally." She gave him a knowing look. "By the way, I saw you slip a whiskey bottle into your pack."

"Busted." He gripped the wheel tight as they rounded a slippery curve. "Are you seriously going to get in trouble for burning the boxes and opening the whiskey?"

"I suppose it's possible, but I doubt it. Nor do I care. We didn't desecrate remains, and believe me, I gave plenty of thanks for the refuge and supplies the plane provided. I am eternally grateful to the men who were on that plane, and when this is all over, I'll redouble my efforts to find out who was on that supply flight and reach out to their descendants to thank them, if they have any."

Dean had photographed the plane exterior before they left. The morning sun had glinted off the metal in a few places, but mostly it was buried under dirt and vines in a way that made it look like a living thing. "If you find them, I'll give them framed and mounted pictures of the plane."

"Oooh. They might like that. I think I would, if I were in their place." She glanced sideways at him. "In fact, can I have one?"

"Of course. I owe you the owl pictures you took too."

"Good Lord. Was that only three nights ago?"

"I'm pretty sure it was a decade."

"Back when you were Bill, and I was Dylan's lying girlfriend."

In his mind, she was still Dylan's . . . and it was making his growing attraction very uncomfortable.

"Are you still going to give me photography lessons?"

"Well, probably not *today*."

She snorted. "I didn't mean today. I just . . . I'm trying to set goals. Give me a reason to believe we're going to survive this."

"Put that way, yes. Absolutely. Hell, I'll take you on an expedition if you want."

"Can you do that? I mean, wouldn't *National Geographic* balk?"

He shrugged. "I finance my own expeditions when I want to."

"Must be nice."

"It is."

"Okay, where are we going? On our expedition, I mean. Give me something to fantasize about."

All at once, a thousand fantasies filled his mind. Every single one of them in some kind of exotic setting with Fiona naked beneath him. Or on top of him. Or he was behind her, thrusting deep into her wet heat. Under a waterfall. In an ice cave. In the middle of the desert. She would be his oasis. His paradise.

He shook his head, trying to dispel the thoughts and answer the question that had triggered them. "Depends on where you want to go. You mentioned Egypt."

"I'd love to go to Egypt, but if I'm going on a wildlife expedition, that wouldn't be it. What's your favorite place you've been to?"

"That's an impossible question."

"Go with your gut. First impulse."

"The Galapagos Islands." The destination came out almost of its own accord. But yeah. Galapagos was a wildlife biologist's dream.

"Ohhh. Yes please. Thank you. But . . . aren't the Galapagos ridiculously impossible to get access to?"

He looked at her askance. "Fiona Carver, do you even know who I *am*?"

She laughed. Full, warm, rich. "My bad. It's just that . . . the Galapagos are on my bucket list. You've really been there?"

"More than once."

"Oh my. Those might be the sexiest words I've ever heard."

It was his turn to laugh. "Good to know." He forced himself to think of Dylan, even as he wanted to flirt and tease. "I've been wanting to get Dylan to join me on an expedition forever, so this is perfect."

"He's never joined you?"

"No. He was in grad school when I first started, and after that . . . work and then his ex-wife got in the way."

"And after the divorce?"

"I tried. But he took the job at Pollux and couldn't get the time off. He said he was content to visit his volcanoes, and we'd go next year." He cleared his throat, as if that would dispel the emotion from his voice. "I'm afraid after this, I'm going to insist on now, instead of next year."

"Good plan," she said softly. "And, well, the Galapagos are volcanic, so no excuses there either."

"It will be the perfect expedition for all three of us." How much would it ache to watch Fiona and Dylan hold hands as they explored the birthplace of the *Origin of Species*?

She leaned toward him to peek at the dashboard. "We should probably refill the tank soon. Maybe we can buy more gas in the village."

He nodded, glad for the change in subject. "We should be getting close."

"We are. Another half mile or so."

They drove the remainder in silence. But then, Dean didn't know what else he could say.

At last, a series of small structures came into view, and at the center of it all was a Russian Orthodox church, identifiable thanks to a single small onion dome. Russian churches were central to every Unangax̂ village, and Fiona had mentioned this one was recorded as an historic structure.

He parked the side-by-side just outside the unofficial boundary of the village and turned off the engine. Fiona placed a hand on his knee and said, "Don't take this the wrong way but . . . let me do the talking, okay? I've consulted with the Chiksook chair several times. They know me, and they can be prickly with outsiders. For good reason."

He shrugged. It didn't matter to him one way or the other who did the talking, as long as she asked about Dylan. "Have at it."

They climbed from the vehicle and entered the village, walking down the center of the main . . . *road*, for lack of a better word.

A few people stepped outside and stood on their porches, watching without greeting. Fiona waved and said, "Hi. I'm Fiona Carver. I'm hoping to talk to Marion Flanders about what's going on with the navy base. Is Marion on the island today?"

A middle-aged man said nothing; he simply pointed, and Dean assumed Fiona knew where she was going, as she made a beeline for a small house in the center of a cluster of homes that were placed without regard to the roads or grid patterns that most Americans would be familiar with. But Dean had visited small villages all over the world and didn't find the layout disconcerting as he knew some white people would.

"Thank you," he and Fiona said in unison, giving the man friendly nods.

A woman stepped outside the house Fiona was aiming for before they reached the porch. She gave them both a polite nod. "My nephew said there was an explosion on the other end of the island yesterday. We were promised the navy would use care every step of the way and already they have polluted the air and poisoned the water."

"The explosion wasn't . . . I mean, I don't think it was the navy." Fiona waved in the general direction of the camp on the other end of the large island. "Well, certainly someone . . . but it could be a contractor . . . You see, we're not . . ." She huffed out a breath. "We were there. Saw it. It was horrific, but it didn't contaminate the water."

The village council chair simply cocked her head and waited.

"Well, except the runoff during the storm, I suppose, but we were gone by then. I didn't think . . ."

Dean marveled at the fact that calm, take-charge Fiona Carver was deeply flustered. She'd been caught off guard by the accusation and didn't know how to respond.

Dean stepped forward and offered his hand. "Hi. I'm Dean Slater. I believe you met my brother, Dylan, six weeks or so ago, if not before then. He's missing, we're trying to find him, and we think the explosion might have something to do with his disappearance."

The moment he said Dylan's name, the woman's face lit up. "You're Dylan's brother? Dean Slater? *The photographer?*"

The light in her eyes was a surprise. "Yes. I'm Dean. The photographer."

She waved to her door. "Come in! Come in! I must show you."

To the gathered villagers who now stood behind them, she spoke in a combination of Unangam Tunuu and English. The English part was basic: "This is Dean Slater! *The photographer!*"

He turned to see the faces of the others, and they transformed from concern and possible hostility to . . . *joy.*

"This is weird," he whispered to Fiona.

"I've changed my mind. You can do the talking," she whispered back. She nudged him forward, urging him to follow the chair into her home.

Inside the tiny house, Marion Flanders led him to a framed image on the wall, and her initial reaction now made sense. "He was our most revered elder, and your photo showed him great honor and respect."

Dean studied the framed cover of *National Geographic* with its iconic yellow border. Dean did *not* specialize in people, but, when nearing the end of a long expedition that had been permitted by the Aleutian Pribilof Islands Association, and one of their most esteemed elders—who'd offered his services as a guide for several days—asked for a portrait, Dean would never say no.

The man had donned his traditional clothing and stood in the ruins of his village—which had been destroyed during World War II. He'd been among the group that was taken to Japan for the duration of the war, while other Unangas had been relocated elsewhere in Alaska. When the war ended and he'd returned to the Aleutians, he hadn't been allowed to return to that village—no one had—except to visit.

He'd been his only family member to survive and return to the islands, and five years ago, Dean had photographed a proud man who represented his people today and a history that included colonization by Russia and America, as well as war and imprisonment by the Japanese. Every item in the portrait was selected by the elder and had meaning to him and his people.

It was, simply put, the best portrait Dean had ever taken, and it was because the subject commanded so much respect. Dean worked best with natural light, and he could swear even the sun cooperated that day.

He'd sent the elder a mounted and framed copy of the final image, along with a request from *National Geographic* to publish it on the cover. The elder had agreed as long as a donation that matched the amount they'd offered to pay him was made to the schools funded by the Aleutian Pribilof Islands Association.

The magazine had complied, and Dean had made his own donation as well.

He'd had other images make the cover over the years, and his work had been the subject of two one-hour-long documentaries, but the image framed on the wall here was probably his most famous photo.

"I was on assignment last year when I heard he'd died," he said to the council chair. "I was deeply sorry I wasn't able to attend his memorial and pay my respects to such a great man." By the time he'd received the invitation, it was weeks after the funeral.

Marion bowed her head and said something in her native language, then looked up and smiled. "It was an honor to meet your brother, and it is an honor to meet you. Tell me what has happened to him and how we can help."

NINETEEN

Fiona considered carefully whom she should call and decided her best bet was her boss. Graham might have some idea of what was going on and when a boat or helicopter would be sent for them. For all she knew, there could be a boat at the dock now, and he could call and tell the captain they were on their way.

As usual with the Aleutians, the connection was spotty. Every other word cut out at first, and it took a bit for Fiona to understand that Graham didn't know she was still on Chiksook. "Where did you think I was?" she asked.

"I was—old y—er on—ak."

She rubbed her temples and tried to fill in the gaps like a high-stakes Mad Libs. "You were . . . told we're on Adak?"

"Yes—ak."

"But who told you that? How?"

"Heli—er picked you—fly to Ad—"

Then he said something about the boat, then something about the helicopter again, and she slapped her hand over her mouth as cold dread sank in. "Wait. Graham. Is it possible the group on the helicopter was told a different story from those on the boat?" Did both groups think she and Dean had been rescued already? One being told the helicopter would pick them up and the other being told the boat would wait for them?

With different destinations—Unalaska and Adak—it was possible no one would've realized the truth for days.

"I can—eck with—eam. But, Fiona, I—on't think any—knows—on Chiksook."

"No one knows we're on Chiksook," she repeated so Dean would hear. "No one is coming for us. Not yet anyway." Into the phone, she said, "Is there anyone else the helicopter was supposed to pick up?"

For a brief, blessed moment, the connection was clear. "The new geologist guy. The one you emailed me about."

"Victor Neff."

"Yeah. Told the heli—er picked up you, the orni—and Neff." The phone cut out.

She pulled the small, low-tech cellular phone from her ear and checked the screen: *Signal Lost.*

She tried to call him back, but the bars disappeared from the upper left corner, the words *No Signal* taking their place.

"We've been having trouble for the last few days," Marion said. "It might work in a few hours."

Fiona met Dean's gaze. "No one is coming for us, and Victor is still here. The helicopter supposedly picked up all three of us."

"I don't want to wait a few hours. I want to go to the volcano and look for Dylan." He faced Marion. "Will you try calling again for us? Please? Follow up with Fiona's boss? Let him know we went to the volcano?"

"I will."

"Thank you," Fiona said as she wrote down Graham Sherwood's phone number.

"One more thing," Dean said. "When Dylan was here, did he ask about the lava tubes? Did he show you his map?"

The chairwoman's face shuttered, and her voice turned guarded, a first when addressing Dean. "He did."

"Have you ever been inside the caves?"

Marion pursed her lips. "I have not. It is our preference that the caves should not be unnecessarily disturbed."

Fiona realized the woman was uncomfortable because it was highly likely that oral tradition indicated some—maybe even many—of the caves contained burials. Across the Aleutians, several burial caves had been found over the decades, as the Unangas had been burying their ancestors in caves for millennia.

She would explain this to Dean on the drive, as clearly, the chairwoman did not wish to discuss it. "We will tread with respect when we enter the tunnels," Fiona said. "And won't disturb anything we might find there. Our only goal is to find Dylan."

The woman nodded. "I know this. Dylan understood the importance of *Kanuux̂* and made the same promise."

She had no doubt Dylan had understood what it would mean if he came across a burial cave in Mount Katin, but still the words made her feel a rush of warmth for the man, followed by the unavoidable ache that he'd been missing for so many weeks.

She'd failed Dylan too, when she hadn't questioned his abrupt departure.

"We'll return here after we've found Dylan," Dean said, pulling her back to the moment.

The woman nodded. "A boat will be here in three days. Be here by then, and we can get you back to Adak."

"That will be Plan B," Dean said. "Plan A is we find Dylan today, bring him back here, and a helicopter comes to pick us up."

The woman cupped Dean's hand in hers. "On Chiksook, it is always good to have a Plan B. C too. You need a plan for shelter and food."

"We have food, and we will be back here for shelter, if you offer it."

"Of course. Be careful. Find your brother. And be back here by nightfall. The volcano road is treacherous in the dark."

———

At last, they were on their way to the volcano. They even had a full tank of fuel, a gift from Marion. Dean gave thanks to the Unangax̂ elder who was surely seeing to their safety this day. Dean didn't even believe in that sort of thing, but today he did. If it meant he'd find Dylan—alive and well—he'd believe anything.

Marion hadn't been lying about the volcano road. It was scary as hell and rivaled some of the mountain passes he'd traversed in Africa and South America. A slip off the sheer cliff would send them into the northern Pacific Ocean. Their chance of survival would be nil.

The pass had been cut by the army during the war, because they had a radio tower on a high slope of Mount Katin, and this had been the best access route. The tower had been in service until the midseventies, and the road had been maintained by the military. After that, the Unangas had maintained the lower portion—that skirted the mountain inland—but let the cliffside road to the top fall into disrepair.

Dylan had taken this road many times during his expeditions, though, so they knew it was passable to a point, and there was a lower road that would bring them to the cave and lava tube network he'd mapped for them.

According to Marion, Dylan and Trevor had visited the village after their field trip to the archaeological site. Dylan had given her a package to mail, but she couldn't remember if Trevor had witnessed that exchange.

That was the last time any of the Unangas on the island had seen Dylan—the day before he'd disappeared. His hope Dylan was safely ensconced in the village had been feeble at best, but now it was gone.

Fiona made a low, screeching sound as the vehicle slipped on the narrow road. This curve was protected and set back enough that there was no reason to fear, but up ahead, it narrowed, and the cliff was sheer. The icy ocean—a hundred feet below, at minimum—crashed against jagged rocks.

"I'd be happy to get out and walk," she said with something of a whimper.

"We've got another mile until we get to the caves."

"I know."

"Your knee—"

"Is fine."

"Dylan drove this route many times during his expeditions."

"Yeah, and he never came back." She slapped a hand over her mouth. "Shit. I'm sorry. I'm just a bit terrified of dying right now."

"I get it," he said softly. "But you know if Dylan had died on this road, you'd have been told. Hell, it would have been easy to make it happen. It would have been the perfect cover. The fact that it's not the excuse you heard means the road is passable."

"Why didn't they use that excuse?" she murmured, and he guessed her focus on that might have eased her terror a bit.

"If Dylan had disappeared on this road, there'd have been a search—helicopters, boats, the works."

A glance showed her grip on the passenger bar was white-knuckled. She kept her gaze averted from the cliff as they approached the narrow section. He pressed his lips together as he gave navigating the road every ounce of his focus.

They rounded the long curve in silence, at last reaching a section where the road widened again and was set back from the edge.

"I think that was the longest thirty seconds of my life."

"I'll tell you about a road I was on in the Andes sometime."

"No thanks."

They reached the fork, in which one route went up to the radio tower and the other went down to the cave system. Dean took the low road, feeling a strange excitement in his belly. This was it. They were getting close. They would find answers here. He knew it.

"I think the worst part is knowing we have to drive back up."

She had a fair point.

"I've driven a lot of roads like this, Fi, and this rig was made to handle it. I'll keep you safe. I promise."

She didn't say anything. With his peripheral vision, he caught her slight nod.

If he could have left her in the village, he would have, but she'd insisted on coming. And frankly, it wasn't a good idea to set out alone. He needed her if he was going to find Dylan.

He drove slowly down the slippery, narrow road, keeping close to the mountain and away from the cliff, glad they didn't have to fear oncoming vehicles. This road wasn't made for two-way traffic.

At last they reached a wide, flat cove that was only about ten feet above sea level, and he parked the side-by-side. Water splashed on the rock wall that jutted from the sea, but only the most determined droplets reached high enough to splash the road.

This must be where Dylan had parked a dozen times.

Dean climbed from the vehicle, secured the door closed against the wind that whipped along the cliff face, then stretched his legs and flexed fingers that had gripped the wheel so tightly, they'd threatened to cramp.

Fiona peeled herself from her side of the vehicle and circled to the back to stand beside him. "You're a good driver in these conditions; sorry I was such a whiner."

"Sweetheart, you were justifiably terrified. That's not whining."

She looked up the side of the mountain, along the road they'd just driven down. "Jeez, it looks even worse from this angle."

He placed a hand under her chin and gently turned her to face him. "Don't. It'll only add to your anxiety over the trip back."

His gaze held hers. The early-afternoon sun lit her braided hair, drawing out the red hues he'd noticed when they'd first met. She was achingly beautiful in the sunlight, and he wanted to press his mouth to hers.

His adrenaline was still coming down after the stressful drive, and the reaction was natural. She leaned into him, like she wanted that kiss, and he reminded himself she'd had her own fight-or-flight reaction—her body choosing flight—and was likely suffering from the same impulses that demanded they celebrate survival, even if it was just a drive down a dangerous road.

He leaned in, but at the last moment, his lips found her forehead as he pulled her close, bringing her body flush with his. Her arms wrapped around him.

He'd held her last night, but that had been necessity to fit in the sleeping bag. This was an actual embrace . . . and it felt as natural as breathing.

Just as no one who knew Dylan had offered comfort, Dean hadn't been on the receiving end of a hug since he'd first learned Dylan was missing. His arms tightened around her of their own accord, and he buried his face in her neck as she did the same, tucking her forehead against the collar of his coat.

Wind whipped at the rocky flat and mountainside, and a spray of water dappled his coat as he held her, breathed in the chill salt air, and tried not to give in to the emotion that swamped him.

After a long moment, she lifted her head, and he straightened, still holding her tight. Their gazes locked, and even though there was nothing sexual in their embrace, there was a new heat between them. The pull of attraction had been there from the start, but now, she knew who he was and why he was here, so any attraction she exhibited was real in a way it hadn't been before.

She wanted to kiss him. And he wanted to kiss her. He could get lost in the comfort and escape of her mouth. Her body.

A strong gust sent another spray of water up the cliffside, this one just shy of drenching them. The nonmetaphorical cold blast of water was just what he needed to stop himself from doing the unforgivable.

He released her and stepped back. He wanted to thank her for the comforting hug, but that moment at the end there had changed things, making him feel awkward. He turned and reached for the rear door of the side-by-side, lifted it, and began sorting through the items they'd need for spelunking.

"Wow, for a guy who has a reputation as a playboy, you are seriously lacking finesse right now."

He dropped the bundles of rope and planted his hands on the rear bumper, leaning down. He let out a soft laugh, because it was that or groan. "I didn't know I'd be getting a critique, or I'd have done things differently. I also forgot you know my reputation."

He remembered that first night on Chiksook, when they'd found the clipboard and she'd shared what Dylan had told her about him. It was telling that Dylan had said Dean was a womanizer. After all, he'd mentioned more than once that the moment he told dates about his twin the wildlife photographer, all they did was ask questions about Dean.

Dylan hadn't wanted Fiona to fixate on Dean as other women had, so he'd told her the truth about his semifamous brother.

"I suppose it's worth noting," Fiona added, "that Dylan also told me you sleep around without emotional involvement as a coping mechanism."

He faced her, afraid to ask the obvious question but compelled to nonetheless. "Did he say why?"

"No. And I didn't ask. I admit, I'm curious now, but I have a feeling this isn't the time."

"It's not. And I'm not sure I agree with Dylan's assessment anyway. But know this: my reputation is earned, and it's exactly who I'm content to be."

Not only was that the truth, but it would also stop her from wanting to pursue this inconvenient attraction, making it clear he wasn't the right Slater brother for her.

TWENTY

Dean Slater was a puzzle she absolutely should not be trying to solve, but she couldn't help herself. Puzzles could be addictive, especially when they came with a rock-hard body and extreme competence. The man had saved her life last night, and today, she'd watched the Unangax̂ chairwoman deservedly fawn over him.

The portrait he'd taken of the Unangax̂ elder who'd survived internment in Japan during World War II showed that not only was he an amazingly skilled photographer, but also he knew how to interact with people from other cultures in a nonappropriative and honoring way.

She remembered reading about Anthony Bourdain after his suicide that one reason his food and travel shows worked for the people he featured was because he showed up with a desire to learn, not to teach and not to appropriate. He didn't say, *You've been cooking this dish for a thousand years? Let me show you how I can make it better!* as several TV chefs did. No. Bourdain bought food from roadside vendors and asked questions about the culture that developed the culinary style. He was open and curious and didn't speak to locals with condescension. He asked questions and, more importantly, listened to the answers.

She'd always loved his travel shows and never quite knew why, until reading that and recognizing the truth in it. She grieved the loss of Bourdain as if he'd been an actual friend. Now she looked at Dean and figured he likely shared many of the famous chef's finer traits, except instead of food, he sought to learn about the local population's relationship with wildlife. She supposed he also shared a similar ego to Bourdain, and figured it was equally justified.

She'd crossed a threshold at some point in the last day, and her mild attraction to the ornithologist had become a full-blown infatuation with a semifamous playboy wildlife photographer.

Huh. She never would have guessed that of herself, but in her defense, he *had* saved her life last night.

They divided their food between packs, keeping the frozen bricks of meat together so they'd remain frozen longer. They grabbed flares, rope, and paracord from the extra emergency pack they'd collected from Fiona's tent. Dean strapped the sleeping bag to the outside of his larger frame pack. They had every intention of returning to the side-by-side in time to drive up the cliff road before dark, but they wouldn't risk entering the caves without supplies to see them through an emergency.

Food, water, and heat were essential.

To that end, they debated about bringing a bundle of firewood, then decided to bring a few sticks that could be shoved down the sides of their packs. If their flashlights gave out, they could make a torch by dipping the wood in one of their cans of Sterno.

Thankfully, Dylan's map indicated where there were underground streams—meaning they wouldn't have to carry a lot of water.

At last, their packs were loaded, and items they needed but which wouldn't fit inside were tied to the outside, as streamlined as possible.

They both decided to leave their thick yellow rain gear behind, as they'd be sheltered from rain and snow inside, and the thick outerwear restricted movement. Odds were they'd be doing more than a little crawling. Thankfully, Fiona had kneepads for digging, which she cinched over her field pants. They would protect her bruised knee and also help prevent more injuries.

Dylan's map replaced her USGS quadrangle in her clear plastic map pouch so they could check it often without fear of it getting wet or torn. Dean tucked the pouch in the deep pocket inside his polyfill coat. He would lead on this expedition, as he'd done actual caving before, and Fiona had only visited tourist caves that she'd walked through with a guide who gave a canned speech.

There were several openings along the shore, some below them, at the waterline, and some above. Fiona would have liked to enter via the large opening that was only a hundred feet from where they parked the side-by-side, but according to Dylan's map, that opening was a dead end after a few hundred yards. The tube they needed to enter through could be accessed only after hiking up a narrow switchback.

Fiona studied the rock face. It looked sheer and like this would be a rope-less climb up the face, but she could just see the ledge.

"You can do this, Fi," Dean said.

She nodded. She had to. But still, thoughts of her father and sister made her want to turn around and hike up the switchback road to return to the village. She cleared her throat. "We might not find anything." Or they might find the very worst thing.

"We will. This is the last place we *know* Dylan was. Mount Katin, or rather"—he touched his chest, over his heart, where the map was in his pocket—"Mount Kanuux̂ is the key."

She had a strange feeling that in normal life, Dean was more of a pessimist, but in this, he absolutely didn't permit pessimism. With good reason, she supposed.

But damn, if they found Dylan's body today, it was going to break him, and she'd have to find a way to get him back to the side-by-side and drive the terror road herself.

But she'd do it. It was why she was tagging along now. She would *not* leave him to make the awful discovery by himself. It was an agony no one should suffer alone.

They made their way up the narrow ledge, single file. It was the kind of narrow that usually she'd walk with her back to the face, looking out and scooting along, but with her bulging backpacks adding about sixteen inches to her depth, that wasn't possible, so hip to the wall it was, one slow, careful step at a time.

Thank God it wasn't raining. She couldn't imagine Dylan would have done this in the rain.

A hundred feet in and Dean pointed to a hook embedded in the rock face. "Look. Dylan must've set up a handhold."

The fact that the loop was empty of rope now and Dylan had felt the need for a handhold did not bolster her confidence. Today was truly a day for facing her fears, between the terror road and now the terror trail.

She tried to think if there were any phobias she had left and decided it was a good thing the Aleutians didn't have snakes.

"Talk to me, Dean. Get my mind off the sheer drop to my left."

"Ask me questions."

This still wasn't the time to ask why he was committed to sleeping around, so she searched for a better topic. "How many countries have you visited?"

"I've lost count. But I've been to every continent. I've visited more than half the countries in Africa. Two-thirds of South America. I've never calculated what percentage of Asia, but I've been to at least ten countries there."

"I'm envious. I got into archaeology because I love to travel and work outside . . . but it's a field where you must specialize, so even if you're an academic who does regular field seasons, you're just returning to the same place over and over. As a CRM archaeologist, I get to travel here and there—like, look at me now; I'm climbing a volcano in the Aleutians—but it's nothing like the kind of travel you've done."

"I've been lucky. I inherited a large sum that has made the travel possible. Photography proceeded to make it worthwhile."

"When did you start taking pictures?"

"I got my first fancy camera for my fifteenth birthday. When I was eighteen, I built a darkroom in our basement."

"So you always knew it was what you wanted to do?"

"Yeah. I studied wildlife biology because I knew I didn't want to be a portrait photographer."

"But you're clearly very good at it."

"Thank you. But also, that subject was special." He paused, then added, "My best portraits are of people I find special. I am not knocking portrait photographers at all. I'm saying I don't think I'm good enough to do weddings or family portraits because there isn't time to develop the connection. I've got mad respect for portrait photographers and how they can capture the essence of a stranger. So many people *hate* having their picture taken, and they have to deal with that. Cheetah cubs don't care about the camera unless they see it as a threat."

"I've never seen your work. Until this morning at Marion's house, I mean. I guess I'll have to google you when we get back to reality."

"I've got two hour-long documentaries you can watch on the Nat Geo channel."

"Do you like them?"

"I don't know. I haven't seen them."

"*What?*"

"Well, I'm kind of one of those people who doesn't like having their picture taken."

"You have *got* to be kidding me."

"Nope. Totally true. Ask Dylan."

And there she caught her breath . . . because deep down, she didn't believe that would ever be possible.

———

They reached the top of the switchback trail—which Fiona handled like a terrified champ—and the path widened for a bit. He was about to tell her they'd made it through the worst when he saw the narrow, ten-foot-long natural rock bridge that spanned a thirty-foot drop they'd have to cross to get to the cave entrance.

He came to a dead stop, at a loss for words, and she bumped into him, then looked around him and said "Fuck me" under her breath.

He studied the landform. It was at least four feet wide, and the arch was several feet thick at the apex. It was as safe as a natural bridge of arching rock could get, given that natural bridges didn't come with railings.

"I don't think I can."

"I need you to, Fi."

"Please don't make me."

"I'm sorry. But it's the only way. And better to do it now when the sun is out. It could rain later." Given their luck, it probably *would* rain later. If it did, they'd need to explore the tubes and get back down this hillside before the path became too slick. And rain would mean they'd have to camp in one of the caves near the parked side-by-side, but at least there they'd have firewood and shelter.

Fiona closed her eyes and took several deep breaths. "Would it have killed Dylan to put 'tightrope walking required' on the damn map?"

"Well, it's not *exactly* a tightrope."

She crossed her arms and glared at him. "You're right. It's *worse*, because tightropes have a net!"

"You're adorable."

"Don't patronize me."

"Fine. Then you're wildly hot, and I think the fact that you're going to overcome this fear and walk that bridge is incredibly sexy."

Okay, so maybe he shouldn't have said that, but it was true. Because he had no doubt she'd cross that bridge and, when she did, he'd be so impressed, he'd want to press her up against a wall and kiss her silly.

She caught her breath, and her eyes got a little smoldery.

He swallowed and leaned into the pleasure of this. Surely Dylan would understand. Whatever it took to find him. He grabbed the strap at her hips and gently tugged her toward him. "You can do this, Fi. I know you can. Because you are *amazing*."

"I'm no world-famous wildlife photographer. I'm not a volcanologist."

"And the fact that you are neither of those things but are going to do it anyway just proves my point."

"I don't think you're playing fair."

"I'm only speaking the truth." He smiled, employing his very most endearing grin. "And when you get to the other side of that bridge, you know what I'm going to do?"

"What?" Her voice was soft, breathless.

"I'm going to give *you* the chocolate peppermint LUNA bar."

She tilted her head back and laughed, pressing her hand to her chest. It was deep and real and the most beautiful sound in the world. Finally, she managed to speak. "But we only have one, and you have to cross the bridge too."

"I'll make do with another flavor."

She rose on her toes and brushed her lips over his, startling him with the softest, sweetest, most fleeting kiss he'd ever received. "Okay. Fine. I'll do it."

"I knew you would," he said smugly to hide how thrown off he was by that nothing of a kiss, which somehow seemed more important than any of the more passionate variety he'd enjoyed in the last ten years.

Fiona Carver was dangerous in so many ways.

She stepped back from him and studied the bridge. After a moment, she said, "I'm going first. I would crawl, but I think the pack on my back might throw off my weight more in a crawling position."

"You want me to take your pack, or better yet, you leave the pack here and take a rope across, then we pull it over?"

"No. Too risky. If something happened and the pack fell, we'd be in deep trouble. I'm okay wearing it. It's heavy but balanced, and I'm used to the weight and how to adjust for shifts." She took a deep breath and raised her foot to step, then set it down. "The wind is freaking me out, though."

That was his main concern too. It whipped through the crevasse and bounced off the slope of the volcano. The only way to protect herself was to make a smaller target—like crawling.

"You can do it." There was really nothing else he could say.

She nodded and took the first step. Then the second. By her fifth step, she was nearing a normal pace. She reached the middle and stopped and whispered something under her breath he didn't catch; then she started moving again.

She'd neared the far side and safety when a loud boom sounded.

She startled, and her body twisted as her arms windmilled. She teetered on her feet; then one foot slipped out from under her as she tried to lunge forward.

Dean shot out, running across the open bridge as another boom sounded. Did it come from a different direction? No time to consider what it was or what it meant. He just had to catch Fiona if she lost her footing.

Just before he reached her, she got her feet beneath her and dropped forward, crawling to the safety of the wide, flat ground on the other side.

Dean was right beside her, diving forward to get off the bridge as it registered that the sound might have been a gunshot. His mind replayed Fiona's twisting motion before she lost her footing.

The jagged basalt surface snagged his coat and pants as he scrambled for cover. He reached for Fiona, pulling her to his side as he scooted back to press against the hillside, no longer visible to anyone above or below them.

"Was that a gunshot?" she asked, her voice high-pitched with fear.

"I think so." He put a hand on her shoulder, urging her to keep her back to the wall, under the slight overhang. "Stay there. I'm going to inch to the edge and have a look down." He pulled out his camera, a small one that had a decent zoom, and soldier-crawled to the edge of the flat. He held the camera over the edge and took a video without looking at the screen and exposing his head.

He then rolled over, shifted to a better position to see the slopes above them, and got another video by holding the camera out and away from him.

Another boom sounded. Something stung his cheek. A spall created when a bullet hit the rocky ground next to him?

"Get in the cave!" he said to Fiona, his words urgent but pitched so they wouldn't carry up- or downslope.

She scrambled to her feet and ran for the entrance that was more than seven feet high and ten feet wide. He bolted to his feet and followed her. Hoping, praying they weren't running right into a trap.

TWENTY-ONE

The lava tube branched in several different directions. Fiona tried to remember which one had been the route Dylan indicated.

All paths ahead were dark, and she grabbed the headlamp from her coat pocket, where she'd put it for easy access. She placed the elastic strap around her head and switched it on, using the red lens to give their eyes a better shot at adjusting to the dark sooner.

"To the left," Dean said.

She ran in that direction as instructed, but almost immediately there was another fork. "Which way?"

Dean cursed and stopped beside her to pull out the map. He also wore his red headlamp, and in the dim glow, she could just see the markings and Dylan's handwriting.

"Right this time," she said, once she'd determined where they were.

They moved as quickly as they could, going deeper and deeper, taking two more forks before they reached an underground stream that made enough noise that they could rest and talk in whispers. It would take anyone following them at least twenty minutes to catch up to them anyway, given that they'd been either above or below the only path.

And if they didn't have a map of the tunnels, they could spend hours searching, given the network that converged right at the entrance.

But before she could speak, she needed to catch her breath. She wasn't sure if she was winded from running through caves with a heavy pack or if it was the terror of being hunted.

They sat side by side on the cold stone floor with their packs on, ready to bolt if needed. She took a long drink from her water bottle, downing much of it. She could refill it in the stream, so there was no need to conserve.

She set the bottle down, and when she lifted her gaze, she saw Dean was holding out the chocolate peppermint LUNA bar.

She made a sound that was half laugh and half cry, took the bar from him, opened it, and snapped it in two.

He took his share without a word, and they both ate the best protein bar in their limited stores. Then she leaned against him, and he wrapped an arm around her, over the bulky pack on her back, and they just breathed quietly.

"So," she said after a long moment.

"Yep," he responded.

"That was . . . unexpected."

"I told you the volcano was key."

"You did *not* just say '*I told you so*' after we were shot at."

"Well, you aren't the only one who's always right."

She tilted her head back and laughed, remembering Cara's joke on the boat that second day.

"I also told you you're amazing and would conquer that bridge. I was right there too."

"I almost failed. Of all the things I was afraid of, being shot at wasn't one of them."

She shifted and kissed his jawline, her lips brushing over the bristly hair of his no-longer-perfectly-trimmed beard.

Part of her wanted him to turn his head and take her mouth with his, but she knew that was the adrenaline talking. She didn't do field flings, but she also didn't do nonfield flings. Dean Slater could only *ever* be a fling. He'd made that more than clear.

She tilted her head back, a mark on his cheek catching her attention. She touched the spot, just above where she'd kissed, and felt something wet on her fingers. She held her hand in front of the red glow of her headlamp. "Is that blood?"

"I think a bullet hit the ground near me, and a spall zinged my cheek."

"It was that close to you?" Fear threatened to make her lose the precious LUNA bar in her stomach. He could have been killed in an instant.

"I'm not the only one." The hand he'd wrapped around her pack tugged at something, and she heard the snap as he unclipped her field kit from the larger frame pack. He pulled the smaller backpack between them and set it on her lap, then poked one finger through a new hole in the fabric at the top. "This is why you lost your footing on the bridge. A bullet went through your field pack."

She stared at her backpack. On the side, three inches from the first hole, there was a matching exit wound in the sturdy waterproof fabric.

"I—I had no idea. I thought I just jolted at the noise."

"You, sweetheart, were spun around by a bullet, and yet you still crossed that scary bridge. That's . . . damn impressive."

She rolled the torn fabric between her fingers, completely out of words.

He leaned over and kissed her cheek, much as she'd done to him a moment ago.

As much as she wanted to lean into him and catch her breath after this startling development, she knew it wouldn't be wise to dawdle. "We need to see if you caught anyone on the video."

He pulled the small camera from his pocket and held it between them. Not surprisingly, the camera was high-quality. The screen was the size of a credit card, and the video was stabilized even though his hand hadn't been steady.

"There's someone down there. On the lower path beneath the arch."

"So the shots came from below," she said.

"Maybe. There might have been two people." He pressed a few buttons and zoomed in, then replayed the first video.

"That could be Victor, I suppose. It's hard to be certain with the layers of clothing and hat."

"Yeah. Let's see if I captured the person up top too." He switched to the second video.

"You're certain someone was up top?"

"They had to be. No way your pack could have been shot like that from below, same with the bullet that hit the ground next to me."

"Right. Not unless they're magic bullets."

He hit "Play" on the second video, and she flinched when the bullet sounded, even though she knew it was coming. Her gaze drifted up from the screen and fixed on the cut on his cheek. It would likely scar. "You're pretty darn impressive too."

He smiled but said nothing, just zoomed in on the hillside and replayed it again in slow motion. After watching several times, he finally broke the silence. "There has to be someone up there, but I didn't get anyone on the video."

"With someone above and someone below, we're trapped in here, aren't we?" The LUNA bar threatened to surface again. "And if they follow us into the tunnels . . . we're cornered."

"Not if there's another way out," Dean said. He pulled out the map in the plastic pouch.

"Dylan didn't mark a way out. All these tunnels dead end." She traced the hand-drawn lines.

"Then we'll have to go off the map. Take a tunnel he marked but didn't explore."

"We'll have to add to the map or we'll get lost. Maybe, if we lose Victor—or whoever it is—in the tunnels, we can double back and exit the way we came."

"We'll keep that open as an option, but I have a feeling one of them will stake out the entrance. Plus, there could be more than two of them."

"But *why*? Why did they shoot at us? Why did they . . . disappear Dylan?"

He gave her a grim smile in the dim red light. "Thank you for using that verb and not the one you were thinking."

She placed a hand on his thigh right above his knee and squeezed. After being shot at, Dean had to recognize that the odds they'd find Dylan alive were decreasing down to nil.

Dean's focus remained on the map, his breathing slow and steady. There was a calm about him that was unexpected. She suspected he'd entered some sort of hyperfocused survival zone. The ability probably served him well in his work. She knew just enough about wildlife photography to know those who were at the top of the game exercised extreme patience, and they often weren't risk averse.

Was Dean calling on those skills now? Was that why he wasn't falling apart after they'd been shot at?

"Dylan came back here because he wanted to see if he could find more metallic stones, to confirm there was a meteorite debris field," Dean said. "I don't know a whole lot about meteorites, but I remember reading about the one that is theorized to have killed the dinosaurs. They found the crater under the sea, and it's massive, as fitting of something that could wipe out megafauna across the entire globe. Do you know how old Mount Katin is?"

She shook her head. "I remember Dylan saying something about . . . a hundred thousand years? Maybe? It's earlier than the fifteen thousand years max I'd be looking at for cultural history, so I didn't really pay attention."

"Okay. So what if a massive meteorite hit somewhere near here sometime in the last seventy-five thousand years? The main crater could be underwater or incorporated into the volcano, and as the cone grew and lava tubes formed, pieces of meteorite could be embedded in the walls. Hundreds of years ago, the Unangas explored these tubes, collected some of the rocks, and used them in their homes. They even buried their dead here."

She nodded. It was not just plausible; it was probable. "And when the village was wiped out by the mudslide, it's possible knowledge of the tube network was lost, or the routes they knew had shifted with new lava tubes. After that, they might have been content to leave the burial caves alone and undisturbed through the centuries."

"Yeah, so for whatever reason, they didn't come back here and gather more of the metallic rocks. And this hasn't exactly been accessible to those who might want to explore the tubes since then. It's part of the Aleutian wildlife preserve, and between that and the military's development plans, access is severely restricted—believe me on this point, I tried for weeks to find another way to get here—so the volcano was monitored by USGS but went largely unexplored until Dylan was hired to do a more extensive evaluation for the EIS. And Dylan, being basically obsessed with volcanoes, was extra thrilled to discover there was a vast network of tubes that hadn't really been mapped or explored."

Fiona nodded and tapped the map Dean held. "This is far beyond the scope of work for the EIS. But he had downtime he could fill with exploration. His job wasn't like mine; he didn't have a gazillion historic and prehistoric items to record. And Mount Katin's been pretty quiet for the last few decades."

"So Dylan stayed busy during his downtime by exploring the cave system."

"And after I showed him the meteorite artifacts, he decided to come back here and see if he could find more of the debris field."

"That's my guess." He tapped the map again. "In July, Dylan ordered a bunch of two-way radios—the kind that can be used as relay stations to extend communications in caves. I found the receipt on his computer. I spotted two radios on our way here." He pointed to two locations Dylan had marked with the letter *R*. "He must've come here with Trevor or someone else to set up the relays so he could communicate from deep in the cave. Dylan never messes around when it comes to safety."

"So he wasn't alone in creating this map."

"Probably not."

"I wonder why he didn't have this map with him that last day?" She stared at the crisscrossing lines, smooth and true, despite being hand-drawn.

"My guess is he'd made a copy. There was a scanner and printer in the office tent."

"True. He might've done that regularly, copied his original and added notes to the copy while he explored, then updated the original when he returned to camp." It explained the lack of cross-outs. Map making was messy work, with lots of mistakes and erasures, and this map was drawn in ink. "So he came back that last day with a copy of the map to find the meteorite. But why would that lead to his disappearance?"

"Meteorites are valuable," Dean said. "Some contain rare earth metals that are used in cutting-edge technology like cell phones and automobiles. If this meteorite is big, it could be very, very valuable."

They studied the map and came up with a plan, then refilled their bottles with water from the stream, dropping tablets inside to purify the contents, although given that this was an underground stream likely fed by a caldera lake or rain runoff, it was probably safe already.

They pulled their packs back on, and Dean led the way, backtracking through two tunnels to get to the passage marked with an *M* on the map—which could stand for *meteorite* or *metallic*.

"Is the ocean floor being mapped as part of the study?" Dean asked.

"The coastline of the study area has been mapped already. More extensive mapping will be done outside the bay if the navy moves forward with base construction. You think they might find the impact crater in the ocean?"

"It's possible. The crater could have been disguised in the immediate vicinity by volcanic activity, but intensive mapping would likely reveal it."

"If the meteorite hit close to the island, who would it technically belong to? The United States? The state of Alaska? The Aleut Corporation?"

"That's an excellent question. I'm sure Alaska has comprehensive mining laws regarding ownership, but how would that apply to the ocean?"

"You think someone else—maybe someone from Pollux—found either the debris field or the crater and wants to harvest and sell it, and they were concerned when Dylan started searching for it?"

Dean nodded, his head bob making the red glow from his headlamp bounce across the walls. Fiona had turned off her headlamp to limit the spread of light through the tunnels. "Yeah. That's my theory. You told Dylan and the geologist—Trevor—about the metallic artifacts. And they both visited your site."

"Sylvia was in the tent the night I showed Dylan the stone. As were John and Roy. It was dinnertime. Even the cook and pilot were there."

"But Victor is the guy who's still on the island with us, and he might've been below the natural bridge."

"And he's not a geologist. Or if he is, he's never worked in California."

"Someone worked very hard to get Victor on this project."

"Yes," a male voice said from behind them. "They did."

TWENTY-TWO

Dean's first thought was to protect Fiona, who was behind him and couldn't see the path ahead. He snapped off his light, plunging them into absolute darkness, which would give Victor the advantage only if he had night-vision goggles with an infrared illuminator.

He grabbed Fiona's hand and dropped down, scooting on his knees into a large crevice he'd spotted. He placed her hand on his sleeve and felt her grip, freeing him to use both his hands to grope in the darkness to prevent either of them from bashing their heads on a rock or slipping into a crevasse.

Once he was certain he and Fiona were safely out of sight from the main passage, he peeked out, eyes wide open in darkness so complete, he could believe he was blindfolded, and looked for a pinpoint of red light.

He spotted it—and quickly snapped on the white beam of his handheld Maglite. Aiming it right for the NVGs, blinding Victor, at least for a moment.

Then he grabbed Fiona and again placed her hand on his arm. She gripped him without a word, and they crawled forward together, putting distance between them and the man who hunted them, unable to see the path ahead or behind.

"You won't find your brother," Victor said. "He's dead. His body tossed in the sea."

Dean didn't respond. Didn't react. He just groped in the darkness to find a path. He'd process the words later. Right now, he had to save

Fiona. He was the one who'd insisted she explore with him. It was his fault she was in danger. Again.

Movement behind indicated Victor was advancing, and he flashed the light at him again, this time using the strobe setting.

He hoped the guy had cheap NVGs and not the military-grade ones that recovered quickly. Victor had a gun. Dean's best weapon was a knife. If Victor got close enough for him to use it, it would be all over. Their only hope was to lose him in the tunnels.

There was a chirping sound—a two-way radio signal—and a tinny-sounding voice echoed in the chamber. "Where are you?"

All at once, Dean realized his mistake. He'd assumed the relay radios had been left by Dylan, but it wouldn't have made sense for Dylan to place the relays that last day if he'd been here alone.

The relays had been a sign that Victor and his accomplice had been exploring these caves.

And they had a copy of Dylan's map.

Victor's position was hard to gauge as his voice also echoed off the stone walls. "In the west tunnel. I found them."

The radio chirped again, and the same voice responded. "Perfect. Charges set. You have five minutes to get to the entrance. Plenty of time if you're in the west tunnel."

Victor cursed into his radio. "Asshole. I told you to wait."

"And I said trapping them was our best bet," the other man said. "Better run. Four minutes, fifty seconds."

Dean shone the strobe light in Victor's direction again. The man cursed, and Dean caught a muzzle flash accompanied by the deafening bang of shots fired.

The sound echoed through the tunnel, loud enough to dull his hearing, but he thought he heard rocks skittering on uneven ground.

He risked the light, which revealed the passage was empty. Victor had run for the exit.

"Blinding him as he pulled the trigger might have saved us," Fiona said, her voice shaking.

"I don't think he was really aiming, so much as trying to make a point not to follow him." But yeah. One of them could have been shot.

"He made his point, then."

Dean nodded. "I think . . . I think they're blowing up the entrance."

"If Victor doesn't make it out, he'll be trapped too."

"I think I'm going to hope he makes it, then." It was a strange thing to say about a man who'd just told him Dylan had been murdered. Who'd just shot at them. But they had a far better chance at survival if they weren't trapped with a man who'd shot at them multiple times already.

Dean wrapped an arm around Fiona and pulled her to his side. He snapped off the flashlight, once again plunging them into absolute darkness, this time without even a tiny red glow.

He needed to think, but his brain was spinning.

Fiona's arm slid around his waist, and they sat in the darkness, side by side, arms wrapped around each other, the only sound in the tunnel that of their soft breathing.

He focused on his breath, imagined he was in a blind waiting to take the perfect shot. He tried to sink into the Zen nothingness of waiting, but he couldn't do it.

Is Dylan dead?

He reached out with his twin energy and tried to feel his brother in these caves. He came up blank, empty. But that meant nothing. He and Dylan hadn't shared that kind of connection in years. Decades, even.

Dylan didn't *feel* dead to him. But he didn't feel alive either. And that, more than anything, was what scared him.

When the blast came, he was almost certain only two minutes had passed, not the five promised, but then, time was truncated and elastic with adrenaline.

Fiona's grip tightened on his waist, and she let out a soft whimper as the entire cavern shook.

He pulled her onto his lap, turning her sideways to accommodate the bulky pack, and held her even as he held his breath, wondering if the tunnel they were in was compromised now and would crumble down on them.

TWENTY-THREE

Fiona clung to Dean, practically burrowing into him. If they were going to die, at least they had this comfort of holding each other. Not alone. As Dylan must have been.

As Regan had been.

Her heart ached for what Dean must be feeling right now. For herself too as her memories of the search for Regan played on repeat in her mind.

She couldn't even process all the emotions she was feeling. They were trapped inside a volcano, and the cavern they were in could collapse at any moment. If they made their way to the entrance, they would probably find it blocked, and if it wasn't, they were sure to be greeted by Victor, his partner, and their guns.

She racked her brain to think if the voice she'd heard on the radio was familiar—someone on the team—but between the static, relays, and echo of the cave, it was impossible. It could be anyone, even Sylvia, although she was almost certain it had been a male voice.

After a long moment, she said, "Our only option is to keep going deeper. Look for another exit."

"I was thinking the same thing. We were going to go off the map anyway. That was the whole point of coming here."

"There really could be another way out," she said hopefully.

"I choose to believe there is." He said it with such conviction. If anyone could will another exit into existence, it would be Dean Slater.

She kissed his cheek, her lips brushing against his whiskers; then she placed her forehead on the spot she'd kissed and took a deep breath. "I think"—she exhaled, long and slow—"you're amazing."

"I think you're pretty incredible too. Plus, I just thought of a bright side."

"Oh yeah? What's that?"

"We don't have to cross the bridge again, or climb down the narrow hillside, or drive back up the crap road."

She laughed. It felt so good to laugh. "You're right. That *is* a bright side."

He reached up and cupped her cheek. "I'm going to get you out of here, Fi."

She wondered if he wanted to kiss her. If she turned on her light, would she see desire in his eyes? She wouldn't object to being kissed right then, but also . . . the man had just been told his brother's body had been tossed in the northern Pacific Ocean. His emotions had to be in deep turmoil. Bad timing for something that would change the dynamic between them, no matter how much they might want to pretend it wouldn't.

She gently extracted herself from his lap and got to her feet. "I'm going to assume that since this tunnel hasn't collapsed yet, it's stable." It's not like they had any other choice. "How far are we from the end of the map?"

He shone his light on the page and pointed. "I think we're here." He ran his finger along the line. "Two more forks, then we reach the end of the known universe." He met her gaze. "How are you with tight spaces?"

"Thankfully, claustrophobia isn't one of my issues."

"Yeah, but crawling through tight, unmapped tunnels would freak almost anyone out. I'll admit I'm not excited about the prospect."

"We don't have a choice. I'll deal."

"You really are amazing, you know," he said softly.

She smiled at him. "Ditto."

It was possible to find another way out. She knew just enough about lava tube formation to know there was hope. Tubes were formed when a thick flow of lava, what Hawaiians called *pahoehoe*, flowed down the volcano. The top layer, being cooled by the air—and the air in Alaska was quite cold, so she imagined it cooled quickly compared to other climates—would form a skin and solidify, creating an insulated tube that the lava continued to flow through, down the mountainside, eroding the ground it flowed over, carving tunnels in the rock.

Here the flow went to the sea, where the molten rock would sizzle and steam as it met frigid water, and entrances to these caves were impassible due to arctic-cold water pounding the shoreline. It was why only the upper entrance they'd used was accessible and also why, if they wanted to find an exit, they needed to follow tunnels that went up, not down.

The amount of lava and the speed of the flow contributed to the cave's depth and height. And when the volume of the lava increased, or if debris blocked the path of the tube, the molten rock under pressure, like toothpaste being forced through a blocked tube, could punch through the ceiling rock—opening "skylights" or cracks in the rock, creating new tubes and surface flows, that themselves could have been paved over by later flows.

What they needed was to find one of those skylights that hadn't been paved over.

They set out again, walking single file and crouching more and more as the ceiling dropped. In a few places, they had to crawl, but then the tube opened up again, and they were back to hunched-over walking. It would have been an incredible tour if Dylan were along to narrate and explain more about the creation of these tunnels. He'd be able to identify which flows came first.

She also had questions about the underground streams. Did they flow all the time, or was this the result of the rain yesterday? Were they fed by cracks in a caldera lake, the water seeping through rock, or was the flow just a collection of water runoff that seeped through a thousand cracks in the hardened magma?

If they could follow a stream, she presumed they'd find an opening in the surface, but unfortunately, the water they'd seen couldn't be followed. The source they'd found so far was nothing more than a flow that seeped through a fissure in the rocks too narrow to pass through.

The basalt tunnels were cold, these lava tubes having formed thousands of years ago. There wasn't any kind of sulfur smell to indicate magma chambers were in the vicinity. Dylan had told her the most active part of the volcano faced the land, and this seaward side was cut off from the main activity. The eruption fifteen hundred years ago that triggered the mudslide that covered the village had blown out the southwest flank of Mount Katin, much as the Mount Saint Helens eruption in 1980 had taken out a side in addition to the top of the volcano.

Both were stratovolcanoes, so that made sense.

She hadn't been born yet when Saint Helens blew, but she'd grown up in Western Washington and heard all the stories. She'd hiked the mountain several times and explored lava tubes that were open to the public.

Dylan had explained that the fifteen-hundred-year-old explosion was the reason there were more fumaroles on the southwest side of the mountain than on the northeast. It was one of the reasons the sub base would be placed along the eastern shore of the island, a fair distance from the bottom slopes of the mountain. That side of the mountain—and therefore the island—was more seismically stable.

Mount Katin, according to Dylan, was relatively quiet, especially in comparison to other Aleutian volcanoes. He'd set up sensors to better monitor seismic activity, to determine if the mountain was becoming more active and, if so, whether it presented a problem for the engineers designing the base.

They reached the end of the mapped tunnels and, as expected, found that the tunnel they were in continued; it was just much smaller. Probably too small for Dylan to continue without a partner.

"We won't fit with the packs on our backs," Dean said.

"I can wear my smaller pack on my chest, but the big one will have to be tied to a rope and pulled through."

"I'll go ahead, without the pack, letting out paracord. If I get somewhere wide enough for the both of us, I'll pull both packs through; then you follow. If I hit a dead end, I'll crawl backward, and we'll try a different tunnel."

"We might run out of paracord before you find a wide-enough opening." They had several hundred meters of paracord, plus at least fifty meters of rope, but they couldn't begin to guess how much they'd need.

"If I start to near the end of the line, you need to tug on it. I'll tie it to my waist."

"And what if the rope pulling the packs through gets caught on a sharp rock and snaps?"

"Then I'll crawl back, grab the packs, and back out, dragging them. You can crawl forward and push."

She nodded. At least they had a plan. It wasn't a good one, but it was a plan. It was unlikely Dylan had ever explored this place alone, but maybe on his last trip, he'd been desperate enough to try. As desperate as they were.

They both decided to remove their bulky coats for the crawl. It wasn't *warm* inside the volcano, but without wind, rain, or snow, they'd both be more likely to break into a sweat while crawling than shivers.

"We need a system for two-way communication," she said. "In case you get so far away, we can't hear each other through the tunnel."

"We'll tie the paracord to your waist too, and I can spool it out as I crawl. That way, I can signal you with three distinct tugs, to make sure it's not confused with the paracord getting caught on a rock. Things get bad for either of us, and we tug away. Shout as needed."

"Oh God. I really hope we don't need this."

"Me too, honey."

In another situation, a coworker calling her *"honey"* or *"sweetheart,"* as he'd done last night, would infuriate her, but they weren't coworkers and so far past any kind of normal. As it was, she liked the endearments, as much as she liked him calling her Fi. Regan had called her Fi.

"Do you have any nicknames, Dean?" She wanted to give him the same comfort.

"Not really. Dean doesn't shorten well, except to D, and when your twin's name also starts with D . . ."

"On the flight from Whidbey, I dubbed you Hot Bird Man."

He grinned. "Did you, now?"

"I did. But it turns out you aren't a Bird Man at all."

His grin deepened. "But I *am* hot."

She laughed. "That you are."

He winked at her. "It was only a matter of time before you succumbed to my charms."

She rolled her eyes but silently agreed.

She'd been warned by both Dylan and Dean that he engaged only in superficial flings. He might date a woman for a few weeks, but that was the extent of it. A few weeks of fun, then it was over except for friendship that may or may not continue.

Could she ever do that? Have a breezy relationship with a friend she was deeply attracted to?

It wasn't a one-night stand—which she'd tried and enjoyed in the past but decided wasn't for her because sex was simply better with an emotional connection. And it wasn't friends with benefits, in which the sex was an ongoing part of the dynamic. It was a short-term liaison that had a beginning and an end and no deeper emotions allowed.

No. She didn't think she was capable of that. She'd find herself on the hurting end when it was over, all alone in her deeper feelings.

She stared at the dark tunnel before them. This *might* not be the time to worry about starting something with Dean, considering they were trapped in a volcano.

But one thing she did know she'd do if—*when*—they survived this: she'd take more risks. With her heart and with her career. With her friendships.

She might even sign up for a dating app and meet new people. Go on uncomfortable first dates and take up rock climbing again.

No. Rock climbing wasn't an option. She scratched it off her mental list of risks she might take. Instead, she'd return to Jamaica and drink rum and dance in the sand to reggae music. Have a vacation fling with a handsome stranger.

But first, she had to help Dean find a way out of this damn volcano.

———

Crawling over jagged, rocky ground through a cramped tunnel wasn't the most unpleasant thing Dean had ever done on assignment, but it ranked pretty high on the list.

"You good?" Fiona called, her voice echoing down the tunnel. There had been a few serpentine curves, so she could no longer see him, but he wasn't so far that they couldn't talk. That was a relief. He didn't like having her out of his sight—what if Victor hadn't gotten out and would strike now that she was alone?—but it would be worse if he couldn't hear her.

"Fine," he called back. If only they'd thought to grab the relay radios. But then, for all he knew, Victor could listen in if they used those.

He rounded another bend, and the tunnel widened a bit. He crawled forward to see it widened more, and the ceiling was rising as well. Several feet later, it was wide enough for two people, then three. Finally, it was tall enough to stand, although he'd have to hunch over in some places.

"Fiona!" he shouted.

Her voice echoed back, distant now. "Dean?"

"I've reached a larger room. There are"—he scanned the rock walls—"maybe two openings we could explore from here. I'll see if they keep going. If they do, I'll pull the packs while you push."

"Roger. We're almost out of paracord."

He crouched low to reach one of the dark gaps in the rock, then directed the white beam of his flashlight into the void. It was a tunnel. Taller than the one he'd just crawled through but very narrow. Twenty feet in, something reflected off the light.

He debated if he should enter. He could wait for Fiona.

No way could he wait.

He untied the paracord from his waist and hoped she wouldn't freak out if she felt the slack. He'd be quick. He shuffled sideways, the rocks brushing his chest and back, and reached the piece of reflective material.

He sucked in a breath. His light had caught the silver inside of a food wrapper. He picked it up and turned it over. It was the wrapper of a peanut butter fudge LUNA bar.

Dylan's favorite flavor.

TWENTY-FOUR

Fiona followed the bags through the tunnel, pushing and unhooking them whenever they got caught on the jagged ground—which was often—but with Dean pulling the bags forward, it was a lot easier than she'd dared to hope.

It took at least twenty minutes to make her way through the tunnel, and she spent each moment trying not to think about the cramped feel of it. She hadn't been claustrophobic before, but this experience could change that. It helped to know there was a bigger room up ahead, and Dean was very excited by something.

She couldn't wait to find out what.

At last, she reached the point where the tunnel began to widen, and she felt the pressure on her chest ease. She hadn't even noticed that pressure until it began to lift. All at once, Dean was scooping the bags out of her way and she was on her feet.

It was such a relief to be with him again. He must've felt the same way, because he dropped the packs and pulled her into his arms, giving her an exuberant hug. Or, at least, as exuberant as the low ceiling would allow.

She pulled back to meet his gaze, and they both immediately blinded each other with the white light of their headlamps. In unison, they snapped off their lights; then he turned on a handheld light and directed the beam toward an opening on the opposite wall. "It's just wide enough to walk through sideways. I found this in there." He held up a LUNA bar wrapper. "It's Dylan's."

"What makes you so certain?"

"It's his favorite flavor."

"Blasphemy," she muttered.

"I know. But I love him anyway."

She knew he did, and she was afraid he was reading too much into one protein bar wrapper. "It could be Trevor's. Or another volcanologist from the study last year, before Dylan was hired."

"But Dylan never added this segment to his master map. What if he made it this far that last day?"

If that was the case, they might find Dylan's body up ahead. Victor had said he'd been tossed in the sea, but she wasn't about to put much stock in his veracity.

Why would anyone hurt Dylan? And why had they trapped her and Dean in the lava tubes? Hell, why had they shot at them? And blown up the camp. And sabotaged her phone . . .

It was an absurd list of things to happen. Was Victor a Russian agent? Was he trying to stop the submarine base from being built?

At best, this sabotage would just delay construction. The new base would happen. The navy was eager to establish a stronger presence in the North Pacific and Bering Sea, so when global warming opened up that new Northwest Passage, it wouldn't be entirely under Russia's or China's control.

If that was the case, Victor and his allies had jumped the gun. They should have saved the sabotage for actual base construction.

This only ensured that security would be tight when construction was underway.

She wanted to share Dean's excitement, but she was more confused—and worried—than before. Was it possible for them to find a way out of this labyrinth? And what would await them if they did?

"We should explore the tunnel where you found the wrapper. If we hit a dead end, we should come back here and eat and think about setting up camp. It's getting late enough that even if we find an exit, we might not want to leave until morning. We won't have a vehicle, and we don't really know where we'll end up. And for all we know, a storm could be raging outside."

"You want to leave our supplies here?"

She shook her head. "It would be faster, but too risky, I think."

"Agreed. We only leave our supplies if one of us scouts ahead. Like we just did."

It was hard to know what to expect, because Alaskan volcanoes weren't known for having extensive lava tube networks. The only other volcano that she knew of that had them—according to Dylan—was Akutan Peak on Akutan Island. There was another volcano with lava tube caves in the Pribilof Islands, but that was much farther north, and as far as she knew, neither island's cave network had been well explored.

Dylan had said the entrance to these tunnels had been exposed by a storm five years ago. Prior to that, no one had known Mount Katin had such an extensive lava tube network, although the Unangas had likely explored and used these caves for burials.

Fiona looked to the ceiling, where pointy spikes of lava hung down, looking a lot like stalactites, but this wasn't a karst cave system, where stalactites and stalagmites formed as water eroded away limestone. This was primarily basalt with rhyolite, dacite, and andesite that came from the lava flows of the stratovolcano.

She knew the basics of lava tube formation, but didn't know if it was different here than from Hawaii's shield volcanoes. Shield volcanoes were known for their vast cave networks, because that was how the mountain grew and formed, one layer of *pahoehoe* flow at a time, while Aleutian volcanoes were primarily stratovolcanoes, which were conically shaped because they had a central vent—a top crater—where eruptions occurred. They built their steep sides as lava erupted from the top and flowed down, depositing layers of lava, hardened ash, and anything else spewed by the central vent. Cone building, one eruption at a time.

Stratovolcanoes could have smaller vents on their flanks. Mount Katin had such vents—fumaroles—which were mostly on the land-facing slopes of the island, where the volcano remained active. Any vents they found on this side—assuming they were still on the ocean side of the volcano—would be, hopefully, dormant, and their escape route.

"What are the pointy things called?" she asked, her gaze on the ceiling. "Do you know?"

"Dylan always called them lavacicles. I don't know if that's the official name."

They did look a lot like icicles. Except, ironically, they'd been made with burning-hot molten rock, not freezing-cold water. Opposite in every way. "It should be the name if it's not."

"Need a break, or are you ready to go through the narrow tunnel?"

"I'm ready."

Because it was too narrow to have their packs on their backs, they would carry them at their sides, dragging with cord if need be. Again, she followed Dean into the gap, glad she could stay close this time, see him every step of the way.

The lengths he would go to for Dylan were both heart melting and heartbreaking. She desperately wished they would find him alive and well. She wanted Dean to have the happy ending she'd been denied.

She would love the chance to see the Slater twins together.

They must've been quite a pair to hang out with, both brilliant in their fields, charming and appealing. Athletic and empathetic. Achingly handsome. The full package, both of them, and her attraction to Dean was growing by the minute.

An inconvenient infatuation to have at this time, in this situation, but it was an unreasonable situation. Maybe she should just lean into it. Take joy where she could find it in the hours they had left.

She knew they had a chance at survival, but her hopes diminished with each passageway that offered no exit. They climbed ever upward, the slopes getting steeper, which she wanted to believe meant they were closer to the surface, but there were no telltale cracks of light or streams of water. Nothing to indicate they neared any kind of exit.

They inched forward in the narrow passage, until eventually they were both crawling and dragging their packs, but at last they reached a large, open oval chamber, with jagged lavacicle teeth pointing down from the ceiling.

To the left on the far side of the chamber, it looked like there was an offshoot tunnel that continued into a dark, serpentine void. They hadn't reached a dead end yet.

The white light of her headlamp flashed on streaks along the basalt walls. It could be water seeping down. Before she could examine the walls, she needed to catch her breath. It had been a steady upward climb, and her thighs burned from the effort of lugging herself and the heavy pack ever upward, plus having to crouch. It was like doing a zillion squats in a row.

CrossFit would be a breeze after this nightmare.

She dropped the pack and collapsed next to it. "Break time. I need water and protein. And if you slipped that bottle of whiskey into your pack, I could use some of that too."

She poured water down her throat with one hand and searched the outer pocket of her pack for a pepperoni stick with the other, then felt like she'd scored when she found the one that had a strip of cheese with it.

She ripped the pack open and took a bite that included both, letting out a happy sigh as she chewed with closed eyes. "Damn. This beats dinner at Canlis."

"Canlis?"

"A restaurant in Seattle. I went on a first date there once. The food was amazing."

"And the date?"

"Full of himself. A bigwig in his family's empire and in line to be the CEO. He figured his future greatness plus expensive dinner equaled owed sex on my part."

"I presume you set him straight."

"Hell yeah. Sex can be many things between consenting parties, but unless someone is a willing sex worker, the one thing it's not is a transaction, owed, for any reason. It's a gift. Shared and received. And I have no time for anyone who thinks otherwise."

Dean's smile was genuine as he offered her the bottle of whiskey.

She took it and held it up in a toast. "Good man. I knew there was a reason I liked you."

"So you like me now?"

She took a swig, then said, "You know I do. You're just fishing for compliments."

He laughed. "Probably. I like you too. And I want to take you to Canlis when this is all over—because a fancy dinner after all we've gone through is the minimum of what you're owed. And I do mean owed."

"I don't know. I think I owe you more."

"I'm going to insist you let me treat you, and I won't even expect sexual favors in return."

She handed him the bottle. "That's good. Because I don't do flings with friends or coworkers, and rumor has it that's *all* you do."

He took his own drink. "Rumors rarely lie."

They each took another drink; then he tucked the bottle away. "I'm going to explore. I want to know what that stuff is sparkling on the walls."

She set down her snack. "I'll help."

"No. Rest. Eat. I got this." He stood and stretched, then promptly hit his head and one hand on a lavacicle. It shattered, and he cursed.

Fiona slapped a hand over her mouth so she wouldn't laugh. It shouldn't be funny.

"Dylan is going to be so pissed I broke his volcano."

"He's the one who littered the LUNA bar wrapper."

"Good point. I'll be sure to tell him that."

Sitting directly on the cold rock floor should have chilled her, but she was sweaty from exertion, so she unzipped her polyfill coat and slipped it off to give the other layers a chance to dry. The air was cold in the tunnels, but with no wind or rain, she'd be fine without her coat for a bit.

She watched Dean as he approached the wall, ducking to avoid the ceiling teeth. "About now I'm really wishing I'd listened to Dylan when he went on and on about lava tubes and volcano geology."

She laughed. "I've been thinking that for the last several hours."

"I crammed Volcanology 101 for this trip, just like I crammed Ornithology for Dummies, and we know how that went. Too much info to take in at once, and I didn't know what I'd *need* to know. It doesn't help that I couldn't find any data on Aleutian lava tubes."

He reached the wall and shone the handheld light over the surface. "That's not water."

His words brought Fiona to her feet. "It's not?" The lines tracked down the walls in streaks. She'd been certain it had to be moisture of some kind.

She crossed to his side and reached out to touch the cold rock wall, tracing the silver streaks. "It's metal," she said in wonder.

"Meteoric metal."

She nodded. It was strangely exhilarating. Like being strapped into Space Mountain at Disneyland and seeing the stars streak across the ceiling for the first time. But without the roller-coaster part.

"It must've struck during an active cone-building period for the volcano," Dean said. "It—or pieces of it—hit a magma chamber, and what we're seeing here is the iron or other space metals becoming embedded in the lava and ash that form the cone. The meteorite melted as lava flowed down, causing the streaks we're seeing here."

"I wonder if an impact like that could have triggered an eruption? I know even less about meteorites than I do about volcanoes, but I researched what I could when I was home."

"Meteorites wouldn't be Dylan's specialty either, but he must've seen something that raised questions about how Pollux was handling the project."

She nodded. It was the only scenario that made sense. Otherwise, why bypass Pollux in sending in the meteorite sample?

She wished she had the test results.

"What does this all mean? Is there more meteorite embedded in the volcano? Or did it land in the North Pacific and this is just debris? I presume a meteorite with a debris field this extensive would have been large, which would mean a massive crater and a tsunami. There'd be evidence in the geologic record."

Her own words sank in, and she grabbed Dean's arm. "Core samples would have been taken a year or more ago by a Pollux geologist as the navy was evaluating the most likely sites for the base. They'd have recognized a tsunami in the profile then. I wonder if they had other reasons to believe there had been a meteorite strike tens of thousands of years ago?"

"Maybe someone found a cache of metallic stones. Were there accounts of military personnel bringing them home as souvenirs from World War II?"

She shrugged. "I haven't delved deep into the personal histories of WWII. My job is to record the ruins of the base and that's all. But that'll be worth looking into when we get home."

He took her hand and squeezed it. "I'm glad you said *'when,'* not *if.*"

"We're going to get out of here. I refuse to let that bastard win. Plus, I really want a free dinner at Canlis again."

He released her hand and walked along the wall, his light tracing the shiny streaks of metal. The flat rhyolite sheets under his feet made the tinny clanging sounds that were unique to rhyolite flows when pieces knocked together as he trod upon them.

He stepped away from the wall as the room opened up and the lavacicles were higher, allowing him to walk with ease. The sounds of his footsteps changed from tinny clanging to the tinkling notes of cracking glass.

He turned his light to the floor beneath his feet, and Fiona stepped closer to see what the light would reveal. The entire floor from where he stood, extending into the darkness beyond, had a glass-like sheen, which had cracked when he'd stepped on it in his heavy hiking boots.

"It's rhyolite, not obsidian," she said. "I'm guessing this was a lava pool once upon a time." She pointed to the distinct delineation between the dark basalt floor behind them, with its lack of shine, and lighter-colored rhyolite with a glassy sheen. "The magma forming this lava would be felsic, having a high silica content—certainly more than the basalt around it—which is why the rocks formed when the lava cooled were silica-rich rhyolite, which could have a glassy texture and be high in quartz. Hence the shine."

"You did cram some volcanology," Dean said, clearly impressed.

She laughed. "More that I've surveyed the outside of enough volcanic areas to know rhyolite when I see—and hear—it and why it can mimic obsidian. Plus rhyolite artifacts aren't uncommon." She pointed toward marks—more cracks—on the surface of the rhyolite pond, her stomach dropping as their meaning clicked in place. "Do those look like footsteps to you?"

"Holy shit. They're spaced about right."

He started to take a step forward, but she grabbed his arm. "Photograph them first. This is proof someone was here before us."

"Good idea."

He pulled out his camera and began snapping away as Fiona ran her own light all across the floor, very carefully walking along the edge, looking for other marks on the surface and finding them. "Dean. More footsteps here. I see tread marks."

"Two people were here."

"At least. Maybe three."

He joined her along what she figured was the east edge of the pond. Rhyolite could mess with compass readings, not to mention the metallic inclusions in the wall. "We should've been adding all the tunnels we've been through to Dylan's map."

"We'll write a description tonight. It's not like we were measuring anyway."

"True."

After he finished with the photos on the edge of the pond, they carefully crossed the glassy surface, taking photos of the footprints on the way. They were nearly halfway across the surface when she saw a gap ahead.

Dean must've seen it at the same time, because he suddenly said, "Fuck." She heard cold fear in that single curse.

They inched closer, stepping carefully. The two paths of footprints converged, and there were streaks and cracks and a jumble of marks across the surface.

"A fight?" she asked.

"Looks like it." He shone the light on the mess of footprints . . . and there were dark-brown splotches that stained the glassy surface. "That could be blood."

She nodded and knew his heart had to be as ready to leap out of his chest as hers was, because just beyond the marks on the floor that indicated a fight and injury was a gaping hole where the rhyolite floor had given way.

TWENTY-FIVE

Dean managed his breathing with the same degree of icy control he employed on a shoot when the lioness was finally in the frame, but not yet the perfect shot. He could not lose his shit now.

He took a dozen photos, then inched forward, stepping carefully on the floor that had more in common with thin ice than he cared to think about.

"We need our packs," he said. "In case we fall too."

"They'll make us heavier."

"Maybe you should go back to the packs. I'll lie on my stomach, scoot to the edge, and look down."

"That might not be safe either."

"I have to try."

After a moment, she said, "I know. Okay. I'll retreat to the packs, but I want it on record that I *hate* this plan."

"Duly noted."

She retreated and grabbed both their bags, then returned to the edge of what she called the pond. "Time to break out the rope and make you a harness or something. In case the ground gives way. I can tie it off on one of the basalt pillars."

He nodded and returned to her side, wanting to kick himself for not thinking of that. This was exactly the kind of thing they'd been saving the rope for. Paracord was great for their packs and signaling, but rope could hold his weight if he went through the hole. He just hoped it wasn't too deep, or they might not have enough. "I'm glad you're thinking straight."

She gripped his coat and pulled him to her. "Until we know how deep that fall is, you need to be careful. I'm not going to survive this without you."

He raised a brow. "So your interest in saving my ass is primarily selfish?"

"Damn straight. You promised me dinner."

He pressed his lips to her forehead. He wanted to hold her like this forever, but instead he released her and said, "I always keep my promises."

"You'd better. Because I'm an excellent grudge-holder."

That made him smile. "I expect nothing less from someone who excels at everything she does."

In an alternate universe, he'd met Fiona before Dylan. In that same universe, he wasn't relationship averse, and they spent lazy Saturdays when he wasn't on assignment—and she wasn't in the field—in bed.

But right here and now, he had to deal with this universe, and he didn't want her to see his hands shake as he looped the rope together to make a harness that might keep him from falling to his death.

Much as he'd spent the last six weeks denying the possibility, he feared what he was going to find in the chamber below this one.

He managed to keep the shaking to a minimum and stepped into the makeshift harness. He'd done enough climbing to know how to improvise, and his knot skills were better than average. He'd suspended himself from rock walls more than once to get just the right angle on a photo, and when a knot was the only thing to keep a man from falling into a pit of jackals, said man learned proper tying techniques.

There was a sturdy basalt pillar not far from the edge of the glass-like floor, and he looped the rope around it. "Until we know how deep the hole is, we don't want to tie off the rope. Which means you need to be my anchor and slide me down slowly if necessary. Can you do that?"

She nodded. "I don't know how I'd get you out of there, though. I don't have the strength to pull you up."

"I know how to use Prusik knots to work as ascenders. I can climb back up the rope if the floor holds, but it wouldn't be easy. Best to think of going down the hole as a one-way trip. I'll make a second harness for you, and you can tie on and lower yourself after I'm down."

"Have I mentioned I hate everything about this?"

"You have."

"You know there's another tunnel to the side? We can explore that. Look for a way out."

"If Dylan went through that hole, then that's where I need to go. You can lower my pack to me and explore the other tunnel, looking for an exit. If you find one, you can come back for me."

"I'm not leaving you."

He held her gaze. "Let's see what I find down there. We'll keep it open as an option."

He tied the rope to her waist and showed her how to let it out, using the pillar as a brake as needed; then he walked to the edge of the hole, lowering to his knees when he was ten feet away and then his belly. He used his forearms to pull himself forward, pausing after each six inches of progress to test the strength of the floor beneath him.

He made it all the way to the edge, then closed his eyes and took a deep breath, bracing himself for what he was about to see. He was at once terrified and hopeful. His eyes burned with the intensity of the conflicting emotions.

One more deep breath, and he opened his eyes. The white head-lamp light shone down into the void. The floor appeared to be about a dozen feet below.

His first thought was relief at not seeing a broken body on the smooth floor. It must've been the bottom of the lava lake that Fiona had speculated this was, but the lake had drained when the lava was molten, leaving only the cooled and hardened skin on the surface, which was now the floor he lay upon.

There was something down there, though, and he couldn't make out what it was with the diffuse beam of the flashlight, so he pulled out his camera and zoomed in, snapping pictures with a flash.

"What do you see?" Fiona's voice was low—as if she feared sound would shatter the floor—but it easily carried in the open chamber.

"Not sure. Just a floor and another chamber." He rolled over so he could look at the screen of his camera to see what lay below them. The rock floor was smooth, similar to this one but not as shiny. He zoomed in on the items that littered the floor.

Tears slipped from the corners of his eyes as he lay flat on his back, holding the camera above his face.

It was an empty MRE bag, a protein bar wrapper, and a cream-colored cloth of some kind. The cloth was covered in streaks of dark brown.

———

"I'm going down there," Dean insisted. He'd crawled away from the edge, then carefully walked back to what they knew to be solid ground and showed her the photos on his camera screen.

She couldn't argue with him, even though she wanted to. Desperately. Instead she said, "We need to measure the depth first. I have a long tape."

She rummaged in her bag and found the twenty-meter tape and handed it to him, along with a small roll of duct tape and her plumb bob. "Tape the plumb bob to it to give it weight."

He nodded and quickly taped the pointed weight to the end of the measuring tape, then made his way back to the gap in the floor of the cave. A minute later, he called out, "Ten feet, five inches."

She let out a breath. That was doable. He was over six feet tall, and she was five nine. If he could find a handhold, he could lower himself, then let go, dropping just over four feet, and he'd be able to grab her if she did the same thing.

"Okay." She paused. She hadn't told him she was an experienced climber. She even knew what a Prusik knot was. But it had been nearly two decades since her last ascent, so she couldn't make one to save her life—which was exactly what the knot was intended to do. She was as good as a novice and there was no point in claiming otherwise to give him false confidence in her abilities. "But it still seems risky—it could be a dead end."

"I think as long as we knot the line at intervals, the drop is short enough we wouldn't even need Prusik knots to climb out," he said. "No climbing skills required."

She nodded. She could climb a knotted rope—it was the *getting over the lip* part that would be the problem. "The floor would also have to hold with your weight hanging from it."

"That's the risk. You don't have to come with me, Fi. You can take the other tunnel. But I have to go."

"Maybe we should check the other tunnel first? See if it's a way out?"

He nodded. "Okay. But then I'm going down."

It took less than five minutes to discover the tunnel was a dead end.

This was the end of the line. In a strange way, it was a relief. She wanted to follow Dean into the hole but didn't want to worry she'd made a mistake.

She backed out of the cramped one-way tunnel and found Dean waiting for her at the opening, as promised. "Okay then. Let's prepare to descend."

He'd already rigged the ropes, so it didn't take long to get ready. The plan was he'd go down first, she'd lower the packs, then she'd follow.

He'd tripled the rope and knotted it so he could climb down. They'd have to leave the rope tied to the pillar behind, hanging through the hole, so they could climb back up if needed. But they would still have paracord and their rope harnesses to see them through the rest of their journey through the caves. All they could do was hope it would be enough.

Harness on, with just enough rope measured out so he'd land short of the floor of the lower chamber—presuming the fragile floor of this chamber held—Dean crawled to the edge and looked for the easiest spot to go over. "Found a decent handhold."

He pivoted his body, sliding so his legs dipped over the ledge. There was a cracking sound as his weight pressed down, and she held her breath. But once his legs and hips were over, the rock held.

He met her gaze as she stood by the pillar with their packs, just in case the entire floor should shatter. The rope was firmly tied to the pillar now, no need for Fiona to act as a brake for him.

They'd both switched their headlamps to red so they wouldn't blind each other, and she couldn't see his blue, blue eyes in the red glow that filled the chamber. "Be careful," she whispered.

He nodded and slipped over the edge, his fingers shifting from rock to rope to control his descent. After a moment, he said, "I'm on the ground. It's solid."

She was desperate to run to the edge, but she knew better. Instead she called out, "You okay?"

"Fine."

When he didn't say more, the tension that clawed at her belly sent bile up her esophagus. "What do you see?" Yesterday, she'd asked that question and he'd said, *"Wonderful things,"* quoting Howard Carter.

"Blood," was his answer today.

She closed her eyes. She'd give him a minute. Hell, she'd give him an hour if he needed it.

He didn't find a body.

241

Right now, that was all that mattered.

After a long interval, Dean said, "I'm ready for you to send the packs down."

Lowering the packs was easy and accomplished in a minimum of time, and then it was just Fiona, clipping her harness to the knotted rope.

She crawled to the edge of the hole and looked down. "Ready for me?"

"I'll catch you," he promised.

She closed her eyes and held her breath. This was far less scary with Dean below her, but still, thoughts of her dad and Regan were unavoidable. Plus, she worried about the floor giving way and rocks tumbling down on him. They didn't even have helmets, which, she knew, Dylan had always worn inside these caves.

Slowly, she slid her legs off the edge.

A shoelace caught on a sharp rock protruding from the thin, three-inch-thick floor lip, and she shook her foot in an attempt to free it. When that didn't work, she kicked back more forcefully. The lace came loose, but her hands also slipped on their hold as the floor cracked.

She grabbed for the rope but missed and didn't have time to blink before she was in free fall, a shriek coming from her throat.

Strong arms caught her. Dean pulled her to his chest as his knees bent with the impact of her weight, but he stayed on his feet, even as rocks rained down.

She grabbed at his neck, holding him tight. "I'm sorry!"

He held her to his chest. "What for?"

"Are you hurt? Did any of the rocks hit you?"

He released her legs so she could stand, wobbly though she was, and the arm behind her back pulled her tight against him. "I'm fine. Are you fine?"

"I think so."

"Then we're good."

"I screwed that up."

"Doesn't matter. We're both fine. Now shush and let me hold you."

She gripped him tight as tears poured down her cheeks. She cried silently, but he had to know she was crying from the way her body shook. He said nothing, just held her, stroking her back and hair.

She finally lifted her head and met his gaze. They still used the red headlamps, and his skin glowed like a blood moon. She stroked his beard. "I'm so sorry for everything that's happened, but at the same time, I'm thankful that of all the people in the world, you're the one who's with me."

His look was intense but somehow still warm, fierce even, as he held her. "I was thinking the same thing. I hate that you're having to deal with all of this and yet so grateful for your help."

She gave a sharp, bitter laugh. "You mean like I helped by collapsing the very fragile floor-slash-ceiling?"

"Sweetheart, cut yourself some slack. No harm, no foul."

She wanted him to kiss her, to escape this horrific situation with passion, but all at once she remembered where they were and why they were here, and she was a little horrified by her selfish desire.

She pulled out of his arms. "Show me what you found."

TWENTY-SIX

The blood-soaked cloth was one of the ubiquitous Pollux Engineering light cotton tote bags. It could belong to anyone, but Dean knew in his gut it was Dylan's. Had he left it here on purpose? The floor all around the bag had dark-brown stains that were likely more blood. How badly had he been injured?

The amount of blood looked bad, but some wounds bled a lot without being serious. Of course, any injury down here would be serious.

But if he'd eaten the MRE, that meant he had his pack, right? He had food. Maybe first aid. Maybe that bloody sack and empty food bag were nothing but a *fuck you* left behind for whoever he'd been fighting with up above.

Had they left him for dead when he fell?

"We need to explore this tube," he said to Fiona. "See if—I mean *how*—Dylan got out."

She nodded.

He could see the exhaustion on her face. They'd been going for hours and hours, one terrifying moment after the next. She needed a break.

"Scratch that," he said. "We'll have dinner here, then grab a few hours' sleep." He glanced at his watch. "It's dark outside anyway. Even if we find an exit, we need shelter for the night."

She gave a sharp shake of her head. "I'm exhausted, yes, but we need to keep going." She glanced up at the gaping hole in the ceiling and the rope that hung down through it. "I can't sleep under this opening. What if Victor comes after us? That rope would lead him right to us."

"Okay, we'll explore a little more; then we'll stop for the night."

They donned their packs once again and set out. There was only one direction they could go from here, and after a day of hard decisions, Dean was glad this was one he didn't have to make.

Unfortunately, the only tunnel was small, and they were on hands and knees. He led the way, as he'd been doing all day, and now he had an added fear of what he might find around every corner.

Is Dylan dead?

He didn't want to imagine it. Didn't want the words to cross his brain, but he had to acknowledge the possibility after seeing evidence of a fight in which his brother was surely the loser.

All at once, the tunnel seemed to close in, and he couldn't breathe.

He stopped and attempted to take gasping breaths, but no air entered his lungs.

"What's happening, Dean?" Fiona's voice was surprisingly calm even as she asked the alarming question.

"Can't . . . b-b-breathe."

Sounds behind him—barely audible over his gasping breath—told him she was crawling closer. He felt the press of a hand on his calf, and she squeezed, making sure he could feel the contact through all his layers of clothing. "I'm here with you. I've got you."

He was so damn thankful for her voice. Her touch. She was a pinpoint, a star in the vast heavens to fixate on and find his way. He couldn't see her in the dark tunnel that pressed around him so tightly, he could only face forward. But he could feel her. Hear her.

He was Orpheus and she was Eurydice, following his path out of hell.

He wouldn't make Orpheus's mistake. He'd keep moving forward. And when they got out of this tunnel, they'd set up their one sleeping bag, and he'd hold her in his arms. He wasn't alone in this. He wasn't alone in his quest for answers either. She was right there with him, hoping to find Dylan almost as much as he was.

She cared about Dylan.

And Dylan had wanted her. *Goddamn it*, he'd make that happen. He couldn't give up hope now.

Air filled his lungs. Panic receded. He had a goal now. Reunite Dylan and Fiona, so Fiona could fall in love with the best, most worthy man Dean knew.

Slowly, he began to crawl again. After a long stretch of silence, he spoke softly into the void behind him. "Thank you."

"You're welcome." Another moment passed; then she added, "And thanks for being human. I was starting to feel so inadequate."

He snorted. "Sweetheart, I am far too human." Like the fact that he wanted his brother's girl for himself. That was all flawed humanity right there.

"Nah. I'm pretty sure you're a superhero pretending to be mortal."

"Who's your favorite superhero?"

"Male: Black Panther or Captain America, with a soft spot for Spider-Man in an Aunt May sort of way. Female: Wonder Woman. Who's yours?"

"Totally Black Panther. I want to go to Wakanda on assignment. I mean, it's not even the hero so much as the world. The continent of Africa is amazing, but Africa without colonization? That would be . . . I don't even have words for it. I just want it to be true."

The walls of the tunnel widened a bit. His breathing was steady now, but he was ready to quit for the night too and hoped there was a chamber up ahead that would make a good campsite.

At last, after nearly thirty minutes of achingly slow crawling, they reached a wide spot on the inside-the-mountain corridor. The ceiling was low—only five feet in places that didn't have spikes hanging down ready to jab them in the head—but it was an irregular heart-shaped room that was about twenty feet wide at the apex and fifteen feet from the notch in the heart to a rounded point at the bottom. It would work as a camp for the night.

Fiona joined him in the wider space, and they both turned on their white lights to examine the chamber. His heart rate kicked up as it appeared to be a dead end.

No. No. No. No. *No.* This couldn't be it. It wasn't the end of the line.

He crawled toward the rounded part of the left side of the heart, where there was an irregular pile of rocks, gravel, and cobbles. It was . . . different. They hadn't encountered anything like it in the other tunnels.

"It looks like the ceiling collapsed over there," he said. "Closing off part of the room?"

"Or a tunnel."

His light scanned the jumble of rocks and stopped on a mark on one of them. He crawled forward to get a better look. He was a foot away when he was certain of what he was seeing.

A bloody fingerprint.

He shone the light over the gravel and cobbles, and the truth became clear. It had been an opening, not too long ago. But something—an explosive maybe—had collapsed the tunnel, sealing it shut.

Had Dylan been inside the tunnel when it collapsed?

———

Dean must've snapped a hundred photos of the bloody fingerprint and collapsed tunnel. Fiona didn't dare interrupt him as he processed what it all must mean. She was just beginning to process it too. They were going to have to crawl back and climb the rope and make their way back, retracing their steps to the entrance they'd run through so many hours ago, in hopes that it wasn't filled with rubble.

"We can . . . see if we c-can dig our way out," she said softly. "Either here or at the front."

Dean's eyes were red-rimmed and haunted when he turned to face her. "Most of these rocks are too big. No way can we move them."

"We have rope and tools. Leverage. We can try." She refused to give up this last hope without a fight.

"You see the thumbprint? You know what that means?"

She nodded. "Dylan was here."

"And he went that way." He nodded toward the wall of piled rocks.

He didn't say the words, and she wouldn't make him. They both knew what it all meant. The evidence of the fight on the glassy rhyolite floor. The blood in the chamber below. Dylan was injured and he'd tried to escape, but they caught up with him and destroyed the tunnel, killing him in a way that ensured no one would ever find his body.

But then, what were the odds of anyone tracking him this deep in the volcano? No one but Dean would have gone to these lengths to find a man they'd made sure everyone believed had flown home with Sylvia Jessup.

And they'd smeared his reputation in such a way to practically guarantee everyone would hesitate to reach out to him.

Including Fiona, but for a different reason. She'd wanted Dylan to reach out to *her* for help, instead of offering to vouch for him when she didn't know the details.

She'd played right into their hands.

She realized Dean had gone frozen, staring at the fingerprint, and placed a hand on his shoulder. "We need to set up camp. Eat. Decide on a location for the latrine."

They were breaking every rule of volcanology and Aleutian field-work with their *every rock can be a latrine* policy, but they didn't have other options and survival came first, last, and always.

If she got written up for this, the navy could enjoy knowing she'd piss on her resignation letter before sending.

248

For the first time, she realized she was *very* pissed—pun intended— at her boss and other higher-ups in the navy for giving Pollux so much free rein on this project.

She tugged at Dean's arm, then crawled away, hoping he would follow to the smooth patch of floor where they'd left their packs. Even if he didn't, she'd set up their bed and cook their dinner. The fish would be thawed by now, so they'd have salmon cooked on a skewer over a Sterno flame.

It took only a few minutes for her to set up the inflatable insulated pad and tuck it in the bands beneath their one sleeping bag. She then went into the most private alcove there was in the mostly open room and relieved her bladder. She washed up with hand sanitizer—saving their precious water, as it had been hours since they'd crisscrossed with a stream—and pulled out the fish steaks they'd enjoy for dinner.

She was absolutely starving, and not entirely certain they'd ever find an exit, so she decided to splurge and cook all four pieces of fish. Fish didn't keep after thawing anyway.

She had the Sterno can lit and the first two pieces cooking on a skewer before Dean finally joined her.

"Sorry," he said softly.

"No worries. It was my turn to cook anyway."

After the fish was cooked through, they left the small can burning, giving them a tiny bit of heat and a semblance of candlelight as they ate their dinner.

It was uninspired, plain food but still better than dinner at Canlis with an entitled jerk. She leaned against Dean as she ate, licking the juices that dripped onto her fingers.

Like her, he made noises of appreciation as he ate. It was amazing how good food could taste when you were on the run in a volcano after being shot at and almost dying a few times. Or something. She'd kind of lost track of the situation.

After they finished, they split a strawberry shortcake–flavored protein bar for dessert and drank a small ration of water. They had plenty of MREs and other food, but water would be limited unless they could find another stream.

After washing up with more hand sanitizer, she leaned against him again. They'd been largely silent as they ate, but now there was nothing to occupy them but their thoughts, and she had a feeling he was as eager to escape his as she was hers.

"I'd kind of like to get stinking drunk, but I know this isn't the place to risk alcohol dehydration."

"Same. But we can have a few sips without risking harm."

He pulled out the bottle and took a long drink before handing it to her. With only the blue flame from the Sterno can lighting the room, it felt so very intimate. Romantic even.

Without thinking, she asked the one question she shouldn't. "Why does Dylan think your playboy lifestyle is a coping mechanism?"

TWENTY-SEVEN

Of all the questions for her to ask him tonight, that one was a sucker punch. But also, he *wanted* to answer. Wanted her to know why he was off-limits. Then she could choose Dylan freely. Without hesitation.

Every time his brain strayed to what he'd found in this chamber, the collapsed tunnel, he shut that thought stream down.

First, he had to focus on finding a way out of here for him and Fiona; then he could process that.

For now, he had to convince Fiona he wasn't the guy for her. Dylan was. "My wife died when we were both twenty-five. Violet had a brain tumor. After taking care of her for two and a half years, watching the woman I loved lose every part of her life, one piece at a time, and hating the universe for the fact that when she finally took her last breath, it was a horrific relief, I decided that I was done with relationships. I had my great love. Now sex is . . . just sex."

Lonely, maybe. But still, a connection with pleasure, no matter how brief.

Fiona had gasped when he first started speaking, but by the time he'd reached the end, she'd gone completely silent. He wasn't even certain she was breathing.

Finally she said, "I'm so sorry. I can't imagine how horrible that must've been."

"Thank you." His words were the barest of whispers. It had been so damn long since someone had offered him sympathy for losing Violet. But he knew that was because he told no one about her. The only person in his current circle of friends who even knew he'd once been married was Dylan. He'd cut off all the friends he and Violet had shared when his life had been consumed by taking care of her. He'd seen them at the funeral, but he'd left the next day for Africa and never looked back.

He hadn't been able to return to that world, that circle of friends, because it made Violet's absence all the more painful. The jokes she would have laughed at, the tears she would have shed—both happy and sad—as their friends experienced marriage, childbirth, and their own tragedies.

He didn't regret that choice now. He couldn't. He'd done what he'd needed to survive. But now it was ten years since he'd last held Violet in his arms. Since he'd kissed her beautiful face and said goodbye. Only Dylan knew what September 23rd meant to him. The day she'd left the earth. Both freeing him and breaking his heart all over again.

At least now Fiona knew why he couldn't love. Why he was only fling material, while Dylan was the real deal.

"How about you, Fi? What's your story?"

"Not much worth talking about. Some long-term relationships that didn't pan out. In my early days, a few field flings that ended up hurting more than they should have."

She was holding something back. "That's all?" he pressed.

"For now, yes. But . . . let's just say my no-flings code came about for good reason."

He chuckled. "Is it a code or guideline?"

"You won't trap me with your *Pirates of the Caribbean* logic."

He took another drink of whiskey, then passed the bottle to her. "To having a code," he said. "Mine is flings only; yours is flings never."

She took a drink. "To codes that prevent us from being rash."

"Those might be the wisest words of all time."

"I think you're getting drunk."

"Punch-drunk, maybe, because a few sips of booze don't usually affect me."

"'Kay. Punch-drunk, then. Either way, it's time to put the whiskey away and crawl into the sleeping bag."

He took her advice and closed the cap on the whiskey bottle, setting it aside. Booze was too risky, given how he was feeling tonight. One sleeping bag meant another night of holding her tight. He ached for it, to hold her and to be held, but it also terrified him. What if, in the morning, he couldn't let her go?

He stood as much as possible, thanks to the low ceiling, and walked hunched over to the alcove that served as their latrine. He made a silent apology to Dylan and Mount Katin as he urinated on the stone floor.

When done, instead of returning straight to the pallet he'd share with Fiona again, he circled the chamber, shining his light on the walls, looking for telltale streaks of silver that indicated this was part of the meteorite debris field. The walls had a sheen here—more rhyolite with a glass crust, and he wondered how thin the ceiling was, if it was anything like the broken upper chamber floor.

Midway up one wall, he spotted a dark crevice and moved closer to examine it. He shone his light in . . . and felt a tiny flicker of hope. The crevice was deep, but it looked like the wall itself was thin. Only two or three inches thick.

Three inches of rock, but still, rock that could be broken.

He crossed to the collapsed tunnel and grabbed the biggest cobble he could carry and wield.

"What are you doing?" Fiona asked.

"Just checking something." He didn't want to get her hopes up. That would be cruel.

He returned to the crack in the wall and tried to figure out the best way to leverage the cobble. It was hard to throw hunched over as he was. But he'd been a baseball player once upon a time, and he had a good arm. The rock easily weighed ten times that of a baseball and was the size and shape of a pineapple.

Thank goodness he'd tossed a lot of footballs to his wide receiver brother. This would be a football toss, not a baseball pitch.

He stepped back far enough that if it failed, the rock wouldn't ricochet back on him, but not so far back that there wouldn't be enough force when it hit the wall. He dropped to his knees and took a deep breath, then brought his arm forward, releasing the heavy stone at the right moment, even giving it a bit of a spiral twist.

The rock smashed dead center into the crack in the wall and broke through, revealing a tunnel just wide enough to crawl through.

They agreed to sleep for several hours before attempting to crawl through the tunnel Dean had found. Or created through sheer will. Fiona was ready to believe the guy was magical.

They were both too exhausted to attempt anything strenuous, and the tunnel could pinch out after ten feet. It would be best to keep hope alive for one night, as they slept and rejuvenated. Fiona brushed her teeth using only a sip of water, then crawled into the sleeping bag. A few minutes later, Dean crawled in beside her smelling fresh and minty-breathed as well.

At least they had toothpaste. The rest of her was rank. But he was too, so it didn't exactly matter.

She rolled over to face him after he'd settled in. It was different, being chest to chest with him, but she wanted the intimacy of the position, to hold him. In the last hour and a half, they'd discovered that Dylan was most likely dead, and Dean had potentially found them an escape route.

It was a low and high beyond imagining.

She wrapped her arms around him, pulling him close as she tucked her head against his firm chest in the pitch-blackness of the cave. The extreme dark was less disconcerting when her body was pressed to his.

His arms encompassed her, holding her snug to his chest, as if he needed this moment as much as she did. Possibly more.

His fingers slipped into her hair, cradling the back of her head, holding her to his heart. She could hear the firm beat beneath her ear. Right now, they were both alive thanks to him. And they had hope, also thanks to him.

His body trembled against her, and he took a gasping breath, and she knew he was crying. There was nothing she could say to ease his pain. Nothing she could do except hold him and cry with him in the dark cavern, deep in the belly of a volcano named "heart" by the people whose lives it had shaped and even destroyed.

TWENTY-EIGHT

Dean woke with the dawn. At least, he assumed it was dawn outside. Inside Mount Katin, it was nothing but deep, endless darkness, but his wristwatch indicated it was morning.

Fiona slept in his arms, her body wrapped with his. They'd fallen asleep facing each other, and the tight fit of the sleeping bag didn't allow for much shifting of positions. They were both exhausted enough to have slept wrapped together in a way that would have been uncomfortable in another time and place.

She felt so damn good in his arms. Like she was meant to be there, and not just temporarily.

But he couldn't do more than temporary. He didn't know how anymore, even if he wanted to. And Dylan . . . It would just feel wrong to fool around with the woman Dylan had wanted for himself. Especially because for Dean, it couldn't be more than a fling.

Thankfully he'd survived the night without getting a proximity-induced erection. But then, his mind wasn't exactly on sex or attraction. Grief was front and foremost, followed by guilt, because wasn't it too soon to grieve? Wasn't it wrong to give up hope?

Had Dylan been dead this whole time?

He didn't want to believe it. Wasn't sure if he did, really. But at the same time, he knew he needed to brace himself for that eventuality.

Life without his parents. Life without Violet. He'd learned to live with those losses. But Dylan? How could he live with that on top of everything else?

Fiona stirred in his arms, and he figured he knew the moment she realized their entangled position, because her relaxed body went stiff. Instead of releasing her, he pulled her tight and kissed her forehead. "Good morning, sunshine."

She let out a soft chuckle. "I'd give anything to see sunshine today."

"Be careful what you promise, because I'm determined to make that particular wish come true." He pressed his face into her neck, enjoying the intimacy of the moment. What would it be like to wake up with her for real after a night of lovemaking?

He'd woken up with a woman in his bed many times in the last ten years, but this, with Fiona pressed against him, was the first time in so very long that he hadn't felt a disconcerting loneliness at the same time.

He forced that thought away and released her, but given the tight bag, letting her go didn't change much. "I'll start water boiling for coffee."

"You think that's a good idea? I mean, it's a diuretic, and we don't have much water left."

"We'll each get only a half a cup, then. But if I have to, I'll hike all the way back to that stream we found yesterday and get you more water. Without a pack, I should be able to go there and back in only a few hours."

"If it wasn't cut off by the explosion."

She couldn't see his face in the pitch-black room, but he smiled at her anyway. "Don't you go getting pessimistic on me now."

"Isn't it called realistic?"

"I don't need realistic either. Today, we need pure, unadulterated hope. Can you give that to me?"

"I'll try. But I don't know if that's really my strong suit."

"I have faith in you."

Her fingers stroked his beard. He liked the way she did that. Like she wanted to grab the whiskers and pull his face close for a deep kiss. Yeah. He liked that a lot.

"I have faith in you too."

"Good." He brushed his lips over hers, then wiggled out of the bag and her arms. It was cold without being trapped next to her body heat, and he wasted no time pulling on all his various layers before setting a tiny amount of water to boil over the can of Sterno. They didn't have cones and filters, just instant coffee flakes he'd learned to appreciate in times like these when being a coffee snob was counterproductive.

The water boiled, and he dissolved the coffee concentrate in it, then poured them each half a mug. They sat in the quiet cave, lit with a flashlight that doubled as a lantern, with the LED lights set to a soft yellow-orange that mimicked firelight.

She held up her mug. "Never have I ever slept inside a volcano before," she declared, then took a sip of her coffee.

He laughed and, following the rules of the game, took his own sip, then said, "Me either. I'd venture that's new for most people."

"I've also never slept in a cave before." She took another sip.

He held up his mug and drank. "That I've done. But it was wide open on one side, not fully enclosed."

"I could see doing that. But I don't think I'm up for deep-cave camping ever again. It's a little too . . . unsettling."

"I'd say that might have more to do with our situation, but I know what you mean. It's an intense lack of light and hard for the brain to accept."

"Every time our lights are out, I wonder if my eyes are open or not. At first it even triggered a panicky feeling when my eyes didn't adjust and begin to see. Like I'd lost my eyesight."

"But that doesn't happen now?"

She shook her head as she cradled her mug. "Not really. My brain has learned to stop waiting for my eyes to adjust, I guess."

They finished their coffee, then packed up their supplies, stuffing the sleeping bag in the compression sack and cinching it as small as possible. Once they were packed, Dean returned to the hole in the wall he'd created the night before.

The pineapple cobble had rolled several feet after it landed inside the opening, so he returned to the collapsed tunnel and grabbed three more good-size cobbles. His first toss hit the lip and ricocheted back without opening a wider gap. Either he needed to throw harder or the rock was too thick there.

After several more throws, he'd managed to create a two-foot-wide opening in the face. He grabbed one of their sticks of firewood from the Japanese ammo box and bashed at the jagged edges of the hole until it was wide enough to squeeze through and pull the pack. Unfortunately, the length of the tunnel he could see didn't appear to get any wider, and it disappeared into darkness the beam couldn't reach.

"Should I go ahead and scout with paracord tied to me, like we did yesterday?"

Fiona bit her lip, hiding the freckle that had so fascinated him that first day. He wanted to pull that plump bottom lip between his teeth and gently nibble, then dip his tongue inside her wet mouth and explore.

Damn. He wanted this woman, and it was strange how sharply that realization was hitting him now. He'd been sexually attracted to her from the start, but that had been simple physical attraction to a beautiful woman. Now he knew her.

He'd told her about Violet, and later, she'd held him as they both cried. He'd never been that vulnerable with a woman other than Violet before. He kind of hoped to never be so again. But if he had to go through it with someone, he was glad it was her and that she'd been right there with him, just as raw and vulnerable.

If he ever fell in love again, it would be with a woman like Fiona. She was nothing like Violet, and that was important to him. He never wanted to see traces of his dead wife in a lover. It would make him question everything about the attraction and any feelings he developed.

"Dean?" Fiona asked. "You okay?"

He realized she'd answered his question, but he'd been so focused on her lip and freckle and the wave of lust they triggered to pay attention to her answer.

He shook his head, even as he said, "I'm fine."

Her smile was a knowing smirk with an added eye roll. "King of mixed messages."

"But still king."

"Well then, it's time to get going, Your Highness."

"So, uh, how did you want to do this? Am I scouting?"

She tilted back her head and laughed. "What was your brain doing while I was talking?"

Undressing you.

He cleared his throat. "You don't want to know."

"I think I do. But you get a pass this time." She picked up the paracord and approached him. She reached behind his back and passed the line from hand to hand, encircling him, then tugged it forward so he was pressed against her chest as she met his gaze in the dim orangey-yellow light. She licked her lips, then bit that plump bottom one, her teeth touching the freckle that drove him wild.

She stepped back just far enough to tie a knot at his waist, just as he'd shown her yesterday. It was hot, the way she wielded the line. It made him think of bondage and other fun things. He wondered if bondage was her kink and if he'd ever get to find out.

He wanted to. So much.

"I said, Mr. Slater, that you should go in first but only as far as where the light doesn't reach, and if the tunnel continues, we'll tie on the packs and I'll follow."

She'd Mr. Slatered him, and damn, that was hot too.

He was going to have this woman. He needed to figure out how to square it with his conscience, given that Dylan had wanted her, but he *would* have her.

Did want her. Dylan wanted her.

Shit. He was mentally shifting verb tenses. His eyes burned.

And just like that, the sexy spell was broken. He took a deep breath and cupped her cheeks. She was an amazing woman, and he was grateful for both her strength and the distraction. If it weren't for the need to get her out of here, he might have given up last night. "Okay. Let's find a way out. Because dammit, I want a full cup of coffee this morning."

He turned to the tunnel. The smallest one they'd yet faced.

She slapped him on the butt and said, "Go get 'em, tiger."

"Aww. C'mon. I need a more original nickname than that."

"Fine. Go get 'em, Hot Bird Man."

He laughed. "That's more like it." He placed his hands on the shelf of the tunnel and boosted himself up, ducking his head inside. He pushed with his hands on the lip and propelled himself into the tunnel, snapping on the bright white light of his headlamp as soon as he was inside with a free hand to flip the switch.

The tunnel was long and narrow. It was going to be a squeeze. His shoulders scraped against the wall on either side. He could get stuck if it narrowed any more.

He closed his eyes and took a long, slow breath. Right now, this was their only exit. If he wanted to see daylight again, he had to go forward.

He moved slowly, inching along in an army crawl, forearms doing the work. The tunnel sloped downward, unlike most of the tunnels they'd traversed yesterday. It was the downward slope that made the path difficult to see from above, but now that he was making progress, he could see an opening ahead.

Please, please, please be a chamber with a way out.

It had to be, because backing up while going uphill would be difficult as the slope increased from an easy five degrees to a much steeper fifteen.

A sound carried up the tunnel, and he held his breath to listen. It wasn't wind—that would be too good to be true—but it was rushing water. Whatever they found up ahead, it would include water.

He shouted the news to Fiona, who responded, "Should I follow?"

"Not yet. I'm almost to the next chamber. I'll check it out and come back if it goes nowhere."

At least he might be able to turn around if necessary. But the sound of water gave him renewed hope.

The tunnel widened a bit as the slope got steeper, until he was crawling face-first down what he figured was a sixty- to seventy-degree slope, his hands forced to act as brakes, but then it leveled out, and he found himself in a large, dome-like chamber.

In the center of the room were at least a dozen human skeletons, lined up in a row.

TWENTY-NINE

Fiona gave a final shove, and the bulky chain of backpacks that Dean had been reeling toward him reached the steepest angle of the slope and slid down with ease, clearing her view of the chamber ahead for the first time.

Dean grabbed the packs and shoved them aside as Fiona tried to stop herself from sliding down face-first in an undignified end to this stage of the journey. Dean was there to catch her, lifting her to her feet before she landed in a heap.

"Thank you," she said, leaning against him.

He wrapped an arm around her waist and hugged her to his side. "My pleasure." He nodded toward the center of the chamber. "Wanna see?"

She nodded, and they both turned, switching on their white lights as soon as they faced away from each other. They'd gotten so practiced at the move of switching from red to white so they didn't blind each other, it had become second nature in the . . . how long had they been in the volcano? Twenty hours?

It felt like a lifetime, but it hadn't even been a full day.

"Yes. Definitely a burial cave," she said as she approached the remains in the center of the room. "As I mentioned before, there are known mummy caves on other islands. It makes sense that they placed remains here after they found an entrance—which we knew they did, because they had pieces of the meteorite in their homes."

"If they found a way in, it means there's a way out."

She nodded. "Assuming it wasn't covered up by the eruption fifteen hundred years ago."

"Even if it was, we might be able to break through, like I did when I threw the cobble at the crack in the wall."

She nodded as she kept her gaze fixed on the remains and their funerary objects. "The tools are made with hammered metal. Like the harpoon head. We're certain now the metal is from a meteorite, so this confirms they were shaping meteoric iron into tools just like the Inuit did in Greenland." She stared in awe at the tool assemblage. "Can you photograph the tools? Just the tools. Not the remains. That would be disrespectful. But I do think the Unangas would like to see the tools their ancestors made."

She scanned the walls of the room, and again, there were silver streaks. Had the Unangas found a larger piece of the meteorite in this very room? The size and number of metal tools—what looked like a knife, plus an ax and more harpoons with metal tips—indicated a good supply of meteoric iron, similar to what the Inuit had thirteen hundred years ago in Greenland.

She hurried back to grab her pack. "Wait! Let me get a scale and north arrow." She grabbed the plastic north arrow, which had one-centimeter black-and-white checkers, and set it next to the tools with the arrow pointing north—or at least as north as they could guess, given that the compass was thrown off by the iron tools, and volcanic rocks could have their own magnetism. It was more for scale than direction anyway.

While Dean photographed, she took notes in her yellow field book, describing everything with as much detail as possible without physically touching the remains or disturbing them in any way. The north arrow was never placed near a bone.

For several minutes, she was so engrossed in her work that she forgot their situation, until Dean said, "If this is going to take a while, I'm going to check out the stream and boil water for coffee."

She let out a surprised laugh. "I'm sorry. I went into automatic work mode there. I . . . I can't believe I did that."

"It was kind of adorable."

"I bet it was irritating as hell. We need to find a way out of here."

"Hey. I'm all for making lemonade when you can. This will be important to the Unangas. With this documented, the cave will be protected, won't it?"

She nodded. "This find makes further exploration of this area completely off-limits. It's a protected burial site on land that belongs to the Aleutian Pribilof Islands Association. In the unlikely event that this part of the island were to be granted to the US Navy, it would then be federal land and subject to NAGPRA protections. One way or another, no one will be allowed to disturb these remains."

"Well then, anyone who wanted to exploit the meteorite find is going to have a problem."

She grinned. "Yes. Yes, they will."

"Should I make coffee?"

She tucked her notebook away. "Between your photos and my notes, I've got enough. We can make coffee if you want, or we can try to find how the Unangas got in here fifteen hundred plus years ago, so we can get out."

———

The stream ran in a deep groove near the far wall, seeping in from a large crack above. It was three feet wide and just as deep, rushing rapidly, making Dean wonder if a storm raged outside. But then, it could be fed by a surface lake, and the flow wouldn't vary with rainfall or snowmelt.

They refilled their water bottles, both taking long drinks, then refilling again. They didn't bother with water purifying tablets. No time to wait the required thirty minutes or so for it to work. Plus, odds were this was clean, given the flow was filtered through cracks in the volcano.

Topped off with water, they decided to splurge and finish off the open Sterno can and heat water for ramen noodles and more coffee.

Fiona leaned against the cave wall, holding her bowl and making happy sounds as she slurped noodles and broth. "When we get back to civilization, I'm going to check into a spa and get three massages a day and eat room service while I lounge in bed. And I'll take lots of hot baths in a giant tub. In fact, I think I'll eat in the tub too."

Every word from her mouth was a turn-on as he imagined joining her, giving her those massages. Lounging and eating in bed and in the tub with her. His menu would include her, and he'd explore her body with his tongue.

He was thankful the lighting was too dim to reveal his erection.

He knew she was attracted to him, but was it anything like the lust he felt? He couldn't help but wonder if the lust was just a mental escape from the moment. He needed some good fantasies to keep him going.

Especially since he was finding it harder to imagine Dylan waited at the end of this quest.

It felt horrible to even think it, but he was slowly allowing the thought to stab him infrequently. Perhaps with repeated cuts, if the worst news came, the hole in his heart wouldn't kill him.

Once Violet had reached a certain stage in her illness that it was clear there would be no miracle, she'd insisted he start visualizing life without her. To prepare him. She'd had him sit by her bed, and hold her hand, and talk about the trips he would take and the things he would see. And those conversations had gutted him, but at the same time, the memories included Violet, holding his hand, asking questions. So when he was in Kenya, photographing elephants, he could hear her voice, asking him to describe the moment, and he'd felt her with him.

And the visualizations had helped him to accept that he would have a life that didn't include her. But he didn't know if he could do the same with the brother he'd known in utero.

As always, thoughts of Dylan blocked out the sounds Fiona made and words she said, effectively squelching his libido, which was a necessary thing.

He tucked away his empty noodle bowl and cradled his coffee in both hands. "Do you think Dylan is dead?"

The words came out without forethought. He didn't even know he'd been about to pose the question.

She set down her mug. "Please don't ask that."

"Because I won't like your answer."

"It's more complicated than that. I have my own reasons for not wanting to answer, but I can't share them now." She sighed and added, "I can tell you this, though: I don't want to give you unnecessary hope, and I also don't want to take away your hope. That's not my role here."

Part of him thought her role was that of guide. She was Beatrice guiding him through heaven or Virgil leading him through the nine circles of hell. Either way, without her, he never would have been able to navigate this island. He might have died the first night after the explosion, looking for shelter. But he said nothing, wanting to hear her thoughts.

She waved her hand toward the human remains in the center of the room. "This is probably going to sound . . . *out there*. I don't even know if I can sort it out in my own mind, but I'll try. This is a sacred place. It's not my religion or belief system, and I'm going to venture to guess it's not yours either, but even so, I respect and hold the beliefs sanctified here true and real for this place. Right now, you and I, sitting here in this sacred home of the dead, are in a kind of in-between, not on the earth but in it. At a meeting place between the living and the dead. And . . . I just don't want to speak words in here that speculate on life and death."

Her answer was so far removed from anything he'd expected. He studied her in the dim light and said, "You're a fascinating woman, Fiona Carver."

She gave a nervous laugh and said, "I think the word you mean is *ridiculous*."

He shook his head. "Learn to take a compliment. I think you're fascinating. In a good way."

She held his gaze, then finally whispered, "I find you a little *too* interesting, myself."

"Is there such a thing as *too* interesting?"

"When something becomes an obsession, yes."

He wanted to explore that line of thought, but her words about the sacred nature of the space they were in made him feel a tad superstitious. He took her hand and threaded his fingers between hers. He brought the back of her hand to his lips and pressed a kiss on her cold skin. "Thank you for not taking away my hope, and for not building it either. And for respecting the beliefs represented here."

He released her hand and added, "Now, I would like to get out of this in-between place and join the land of the living. After all, I promised you sunlight."

She smiled her beautiful, alluring smile. "If anyone can give me sunlight, it's you."

Damn if he didn't wish he could be Apollo and drive a sun chariot across the sky just for her.

———

Three tunnels extended from the room, one of which was wide and tall and easily explored. They chose that one first, but the tunnel came to an abrupt end after thirty meters. The second one was tiny and narrow and would require a scout first, so they opted to explore the third, which was the channel the stream flowed through. It was risky, though, because they would certainly get wet following it, which could kill them with hypothermia far faster than they'd die of starvation. And if at any point the channel was only big enough for the water to flow through, they couldn't risk attempting to swim out, as there might not be any air pockets.

"You up for this?" Dean asked.

"I think it's our best option."

"That's not what I asked."

"Someone once told me I'm amazing and I can do it. So I shall."

"Whoever told you that was absolutely brilliant and obviously a hundred percent correct about everything, all the time."

"And hot. Don't forget hot."

He laughed, and she felt a low, happy ache in her belly at the sound.

"Let's do this," she said and cinched her pack like she was gearing up for battle.

Crawling through an icy-cold volcanic underground stream proved to be . . . not fun. But thankfully, the passageway got wider, not smaller, at least for a while. Then it closed in again. By the time they reached the point where it was too narrow to crawl any farther, she was shivering from being soaked through from knees to feet and hands to elbows.

Dean was ahead of her, on all fours. Their packs were being dragged through the stream at that point, but at least neither she nor Dean was fully belly down in the water. The rapid flow made dragging and pushing the packs a little easier, in her opinion.

He stopped abruptly, and she accidentally pushed the packs forward, and they slid toward him. She grabbed them so they wouldn't slam into his back, aided by water.

"It curves a bit up ahead. And it gets very narrow. So narrow, we might have to submerge."

That was . . . *utterly and completely terrifying.* "We can't do that."

"But . . . I think I see daylight on the other end."

269

THIRTY

Dean dunked his waterproof camera in the tunnel and snapped several shots. He pulled it out and looked at the screen, examining the photos he'd just taken, and tried to estimate the length of the tunnel. Twenty feet to daylight?

There was only one way to test it. "I'll put the rope harness back on, in case the current's so strong that I can't fight it and it pulls me down. We've got enough rope left for this, and I'll need your help to pull me back if I can't swim through."

"You'll have to decide fast. Once you're under, you'll have, what, a minute to get out?"

"It's not a long tunnel. I can do it."

"But you won't have room to move your arms."

"Dolphin kick, baby. Have I mentioned that I was captain of the swim team, and butterfly was my stroke?"

"Oh my. I never knew that sentence could be so hot."

He smiled. Impressing Fiona was his new favorite thing.

"After I'm through, we'll tie the bags on the paracord line, and I'll pull them out. Then you'll clip your harness to the rope, and I can pull you through. The current will be on our side."

"We're really getting out of here?" she asked. Her voice was sweet, hopeful, and sounded about ten years younger than it had five minutes ago.

"I promised you sunshine."

Her grin lit the dark chamber. "Then take me to the light."

He stripped down to his boxer briefs—there was no point in getting everything soaked—but it wasn't an easy maneuver, given that they were both crouched in several inches of icy water with no room to stand.

She helped him strip and rolled the dry items in his waterproof raincoat. Then he did the same for her, helping her undress down to sports bra and underwear. Both rolls of clothing went into the center of the large frame packs, where they had the best chance of staying dry.

It was strange to undress each other now, after the other intimacies they'd shared and two nights with only one sleeping bag.

"Damn," she muttered. "I told myself I was delirious when you stripped down in the plane and you couldn't really be that ripped."

He laughed and flexed, showing off for her avid gaze, then letting his travel over her rapidly goose-bumping skin. "All I had until now was my imagination. You have exceeded it."

If it were the right time or place, he'd ogle Fiona's hourglass shape, but those goose bumps meant they needed to hurry.

But still, he paused when he noticed her gaze on the violet tattoo. He took her hand and pressed her cold palm to the ink that covered his heart. Words weren't necessary as she leaned forward and pressed her lips to his cheek, with her hand pressed to his rapidly beating heart.

He kissed her forehead, then released her. It was time to get out of here.

He donned the rope harness, this time placing his arms through the loops and using a carabiner to cinch it at the breastbone. The rope was snug around his shoulders, providing the necessary leverage should she need to reel him back.

"I'll swim straight through if I can. If you feel the line slack, like I'm struggling to swim backward, pull hard."

She nodded.

He helped her with her harness; then he tied on their last length of rope to connect them. It was the line he'd use to pull her through after he'd been freed. Last, he tied on two long lines of paracord, which would be used to pull the packs through the water-filled chute.

They were both quaking with cold by the time they were ready, so he didn't waste a moment. He positioned himself in the center of the channel, told himself this was just another day at the waterslide park, took a deep breath, and dunked, hands in front of him, arms outstretched with palms pressed together, how he'd always met the water at the gun from the starting block.

The water was a level of cold one didn't find at swim meets, but he'd jumped in enough glacier-fed lakes to know what to expect. He shot through the tube, heading toward daylight like a torpedo.

The current was swift, but his body offset the pressure in the tunnel just enough for the pressure to back up. He thrust with hips and knees, letting his whole body absorb the ripple, a rhythm with the water that was as natural as breathing. His lungs began to ache as he kicked his way through the tight space. He was in danger of being a cork that plugged the waterworks, and he straightened, his hips and knees moving in a shallower, gentler motion.

His lungs burned, but daylight loomed. He was so damn close.

He hit the opening, but it was small. His arms were before him, and his shoulders scraped against the sides. He got stuck, his arms projecting into the outside world while water rushed over his head and around, threatening to drown him.

He hadn't come this far to drown at the final moment, and he kicked with his hips and knees as the rocks scraped against his shoulders. His head cleared the water and he gasped a breath before the next surge of runoff came.

He kicked and wriggled and was pretty sure his numb skin tore, but finally, his shoulders cleared and his upper body was pushed out of the small gap in the hillside like a cork popping free. All at once, he was birthed from the volcano.

The noon sky was gray as wind whipped across the hillside. He shivered at the instant cold of the strong wind on wet skin as he took in his surroundings. The stream babbled down the hillside in joyous freedom on the cold—frigid, really—late-summer day. He'd landed on a hillside on the North Pacific side of Mount Katin. A few feet away from where he'd popped out, the slope came to an abrupt stop, and the stream fell into a sharp, hundred-foot waterfall that poured directly into the icy North Pacific.

———

If ever Fiona had taken a leap of faith, it was this. There was no way to communicate with Dean except for the pull of the ropes. When his harness rope went slack but then he'd tugged on it, she'd followed their agreed-upon instructions and tied on the packs for him to pull through. If he'd made it, he was naked but for boxer briefs on the side of a volcano, and she internally laughed and cried at the idea of him freezing his ass off.

In daylight. Free of their volcano prison.

She'd yanked the cord when the packs were tied and watched them disappear in the tunnel. Minutes later, the rope on her harness nudged her toward the dangerous stream.

She wasn't the swimmer Dean was. She didn't know how long she could hold her breath, didn't have faith her strength would hold up in icy water.

She closed her eyes and remembered his face as she'd stood by that archway bridge a lifetime ago, and he'd told her she was amazing and could face her fear and quite literally cross the bridge she'd come to.

Now she had to face a fear she didn't even know she had. Drowning in an arctic tunnel trying to escape an Aleutian volcano. Really, was that on *anyone's* bingo card?

This game better have a *stellar* prize at the end. Like, it better be epic.

She jerked the rope to signal she was ready, then counted to three and plunged into the icy stream.

———

It might have been the longest minute or two of Dean's life. Even with the current on their side, it was harder to pull her through than he'd expected. He imagined her body scraping against the rocks, but there was no help for that. Fast was the one and only goal.

He pulled on the rope, hand over hand, reeling her in like the biggest, greatest fishing prize of all. The rope snagged at least twice, and he released some slack to give her room; then he pulled with renewed vigor.

She broke free all at once, sliding from the narrow opening, coughing and gasping. She rolled over and looked up at the overcast gray sky. She burst into tears, her body rolling into a ball in a natural reaction to the cold wind after being submerged in icy water.

The first words she managed to say after coughing the stream water from her lungs were, "I was counting on more sunshine."

THIRTY-ONE

Fiona didn't think she'd ever be warm again, but at least she was alive. And there was daylight. Sweet, precious natural light. Plus, she'd gotten a solid rinsing in the stream and almost felt clean. Dean was still only in his skivvies, and she realized he hadn't gotten dressed even though he was exposed to the cold wind, simply because he didn't want to delay in pulling her out.

They both stripped out of their wet underwear, then hurriedly pulled on their wool base layers, which were warm in spite of being damp below the knees and from elbow to wrists. Next came fleece and wool layers, then wind- and rainproof outer layers. She crammed her feet back into her wool socks and sturdy but wet boots.

She didn't know if she should throw these boots away or have them memorialized in bronze when this was over. They were good boots that had served her well, but her feet ached from the constant walking over uneven ground. She had blisters that were beyond the help of moleskin.

Funny how she'd been able to ignore the pain in her feet until now, when they were freed of the volcano. It just hadn't been something she'd allowed herself to focus on. But now that the most urgent concern was behind them, there were new urgent concerns moving up the queue.

"We need shelter and a fire. ASAP," Dean said, pretty much echoing her thoughts.

She pulled out her USGS quadrangle map from the plastic case where it was tucked behind Dylan's hand-drawn map and looked around for landmarks to get her bearing. Thankfully, there wasn't a layer of fog today, and she could make out the point of a nearby island, as well as the shape of the shoreline below.

She held out the map to Dean. "It looks like we're about here." She glanced up; they were a fair distance below the snow line, closer to sea level, and shifted her finger down several contour lines. "Or rather, here."

He let out a low whistle. "I knew we'd gone a lot of miles inside the volcano, but I didn't expect us to be this far east."

"Me neither. I don't think it's possible to hike back to the side-by-side."

"I'm pretty sure it will be gone or disabled anyway," Dean said.

"Yeah. Me too."

"So what's our closest shelter? The airplane is on the other side of the mountain. That's gotta be a two-day hike, given the terrain, and the village is at least a half day's hike from the plane."

No way could they make that hike without a tent for shelter.

"The nearest place where I know we can find shelter is the World War II base." She traced the route on the map. "About a third of the base was covered by a lahar mudflow in 1963—it's one of the reasons the historic base wasn't considered a suitable site for the submarine base— but there are a few bunkers and magazines that are extant. Plus, we can salvage wood—maybe even coal from storage drums if they're still intact. Build a toasty fire. It'll be more comfortable than the airplane."

"Looks like it's only a few miles from here," he said.

"Yeah, but they won't be easy miles."

"Nothing is out here."

They quickly repacked their packs, redistributing the weight for hiking now that some of their food had been consumed and there were multiple streams they'd cross, so they wouldn't have to carry much water; then they set out.

Dean used his high-powered zoom lens to scout their route when- ever they were forced to make a decision. They had to zigzag up and down the slope at times when they reached uncrossable crevasses or streams. After several hours of hard hiking, they took a break for a late lunch by a stream, boiling water with precious Sterno for a hot tea drink. "Tonight, I want lamb roast for dinner, with a lemon-rosemary glaze and scalloped potatoes on the side. For dessert, I want pavlova with fresh strawberries and cream."

He laughed. "How about grilled chicken with sliced cheese and whiskey for dessert?"

"I suppose that will be satisfying."

"I'd suggest we bag one of the caribou that were introduced to the island for hunters, but then we'd have to drag the carcass to the base and figure out how to smoke it."

"Plus, without fog and rain, that much smoke would give away our location," she said.

"Would you believe I used to be vegetarian?" he asked.

"Oh, totally. I mean, given your work."

"Yeah. But that's also why I gave it up. Too many expeditions where I needed a high-protein diet to get through the day and didn't have the luxury of not eating meat to survive, especially when that's all the locals had to subsist on."

"And when you're home in LA? Are you vegetarian then?"

"No, but I do eat a lot less meat than I do on expeditions. My wife was vegan, and I learned to cook from her, so I have a pretty good array of vegan and vegetarian recipes to choose from that are satisfying when I'm home. I've never really developed my meat-cooking skills."

"Can I just say that I find it particularly cruel that a woman who was vegan and probably doing everything right health-wise was struck down by brain cancer?"

He nodded. "Hell yeah. I was so pissed about that. I still am. It was just all so . . . unfair. Violet always said the one thing she really missed being vegan was ice cream. In the last months of her life, she enjoyed a lot of ice cream."

Her heart squeezed. The strength of this man—who'd been in his early twenties at the time—taking care of his dying wife who was barely an adult herself. She reached over and placed a hand on his thigh just above his knee. "I'm so glad you had each other."

He smiled. "Me too. I wouldn't trade a single minute, not even to avoid the pain of losing her."

That might be the loveliest thing she'd ever heard.

She had a feeling he didn't talk about Violet much, and she appreciated that he'd shared that facet of his life with her.

They finished eating and again packed up the remains of the meal, adding to their growing bag of garbage, but each stop lightened their load a small fraction.

The wind whipped at them as they descended the volcano, and a fog rolled in, which made picking their path carefully impossible. This was the worst kind of hiking conditions. If they had any other choice, they'd do the smart thing and stop. But they couldn't afford the luxury of being cautious. Not when there was no shelter to be found. Some rock outcrops provided wind block, but the slope was too steep. They might sled down the mountain in their sleeping bag hitched to the inflated thermal pad.

They had no choice but to keep going, even as night fell and they were socked in.

They used their red headlamps and hoped anyone searching for them wouldn't see the light in the thick fog, but at last it paid off, and they reached the bottom slopes of the volcano, leaving uneven, rocky ground behind and returning to muskeg and marsh. They were close to sea level with less than a half mile left to hike to the WWII site.

The fog thinned, but darkness had descended, and without stars due to cloud cover, it was almost as dark as inside the volcano. Worse, the grasses here were high—nearly six feet, as they'd been near the archaeological site that first morning—and she knew for a fact there were collapsed structures hidden in the tall grasses.

"I'm starting to not love this island so much," Fiona said. "I think it might be out to get us."

He laughed. "If Chiksook were out to get us, I think it would have swallowed us whole already and then maybe spit us out for good measure."

"I'm pretty sure we *were* spit out of a volcano earlier today."

"Huh. You're right. I take it back. The island hates us. Or maybe it's just Mount Katin."

"But Mount Katin is *Kanuux̂*, the heart of the island. I think it's all or nothing with Chiksook—volcano and island are one."

They picked their way slowly across the marshy, high-grass terrain, and even with all their caution, they still made a mistake.

They were on the outskirts of the base, away from the uneven ground of the lahar flow that was difficult to traverse, with grasses that had grown around the rocky volcanic debris. Here, the ground was more even but covered in sloppy muskeg.

Fiona knew the moment she'd placed her weight on her forward foot that something was off, but her body was already pitched forward, so there was no backtracking. A scream tore from her throat at the sudden drop as she plunged through the thin ground cover into a pit, with Dean falling along with her.

She landed on her back, knocking the wind from her, and tried not to panic as she struggled to breathe. At last, she wheezed in a breath with a groan as she shone her light upward.

Holy hell, they were eight feet down, in a narrow hole with corrugated metal sides. Getting out would be difficult.

Dean shone his light on the hole up above and cursed. "This was a trap."

She studied the remnants of the ground cover above and saw what he did—paracord rope holding what remained of the muskeg mat together.

"Holy shit," she said, her heart sinking. "After all this, we've been caught by Victor and his crony?"

"He must've known that if we got out, we'd head for the nearest shelter. He's probably lying in wait for us in the ruins, in case we didn't fall in this or another pit."

Victor'd had time—nearly two days—to rig all sorts of traps. This wouldn't even have been hard, as the US military had left so many structures behind to rot, many of them dug deep into the earth.

"I'm sorry, Dean. It's my fault we walked straight into this." She'd failed him now too.

He pulled her close. "Oh, sweetheart. This isn't on you."

"I should have realized he'd guess where we would go."

He threaded his fingers through her hair, cupping the back of her head. "No. This isn't your fault. Blame Victor and whoever he's working for. But don't blame yourself. The whole reason we're even alive right now is because of you."

"And you," she said, cupping his cheek with one hand, stroking his beard.

"It's been a team effort, all the way." The hand at the back of her head pulled her closer; they were a hairbreadth apart. "You're amazing, Fiona. I hate that you've been in danger but so thankful to have you by my side." He brushed a thumb over her cheek. "And if this is it for us, I'm going to have my ice cream before I go."

He moved forward that final millimeter, and his mouth was on hers.

It wasn't a chaste or comforting kiss. It was a full-on, *I want you now* sort of kiss. His tongue slid between her lips and *oh damn*, it felt so right. So perfect.

She responded with the same passion. The same need. She'd craved this since that first night, when life was simple and she'd gone for a walk with ornithologist Bill. But nothing was simple now, and Dean was ten times more enticing than Hot Bird Man had ever been.

His tongue slid against hers, and she let out a soft moan of thankful joy. *This. So much this.*

Their mouths were locked together as he cradled the back of her head and she ran her hands over his pecs, wishing there weren't so many layers between her fingers and his skin.

If she was his ice cream, she was melting in his heat. She didn't know if any single kiss had ever been this powerful, but then, just this morning, she'd been certain ramen noodles were the greatest meal ever created, so her scale might be skewed.

No. No, it is not. This kiss is absolutely, positively exceptional.

He released her mouth, and she could just see his fine features in the gray light of a rising moon. His mouth curved just slightly. Perfectly. It was a bad-boy smile. A playboy smile. And *ohmygod* it was utterly delicious. "I've wanted to do that since day one."

"Me too," she whispered. "You were mysterious Bill, and I wanted to let you kiss me in the moonlight."

"I—he—never mind," he said, and then his mouth was on hers again, taking and giving.

She would have happily let the kiss go on forever, but they were interrupted by a sharp laugh from above. "I *knew* you two would hit it off."

THIRTY-TWO

Dean jolted backward, breaking the kiss of a lifetime.

He hadn't heard what he thought he'd heard.

No. It was a dream. Or maybe a nightmare.

After all, Fiona was *Dylan's*. And he was kissing her in a way that could and would only lead to sex.

He looked up, toward the gap in the matting they'd fallen through, and snapped on the white light of his headlamp.

His belly plummeted, and his heart raced. His eyes teared. *Please, please, please don't let this be a dream.*

"Hey, Dean. What brings you to Chiksook?"

He met Fiona's gaze, unwilling to believe his own eyes. "Do you see—?"

She nodded and looked up. "Hey, Dylan. Think you can toss us a rope?"

Dean's brother grinned, his teeth showing through a scruffy beard. "Sure thing, Fi. But it won't be easy for me to pull you up. I'm not at my best after the last six weeks. How about we start with you, and together, you and I get Dean out?"

Of all the scenarios he'd imagined, his brother rescuing *him* from a pit was not on the list.

The corrugated metal walls were rusted and had enough gaps that climbing would be possible with help from a rope, and as long as one wore gloves.

As Dylan suggested, Fiona went first, with Dean giving her a boost and pushing from below as she found toe- and handholds while Dylan pulled from above. It took only a few minutes for her to clear the top edge, and then the rope was tossed back for Dean.

The metal buckled under his weight, and he needed more help from Dylan and Fiona than he wanted, but with the rope wrapped around a metal pillar—all that remained of some long-ago structure—for leverage, they were able to hoist him to the top. From there, he scrambled from the pit and collapsed on the squishy, muskeg-covered ground as soon as he was free.

Dylan and Fiona both fell backward, gasping for breath right along with him. They'd been sitting in a line with Dylan as the anchor, legs outstretched as they pulled him to the surface.

Wind whipped around them, slightly louder than their combined gasping breaths. Finally, Dylan said, "Sorry, man. That trap wasn't meant for you. It was in case anyone from Pollux came looking for me."

A gazillion questions circled through Dean's mind. But first he needed to breathe. Then he needed water. And food. Probably fire too. He was damn cold. When he could speak again, he said, "Please tell me we're close to shelter and can build a fire."

"Gotcha covered, bro. Soon as we can all move again, I'll take you to my humble abode."

Fiona scooted toward Dylan and gave him a hug. Dean watched his brother's arms enfold the woman he'd just spent some seriously intense days with, and he tried to release his jealousy. This was what was meant to be. His brother. Alive. With Fiona.

It was everything he wanted.

His eyes teared with joy, even as his heart split with pain.

———

Every part of Fiona's body ached, and there was a good chance she'd sprained something either in the fall or while climbing out or while pulling Dean up. Who knew? Adrenaline had cloaked everything in the moment, but now that they were safe, ensconced next to a warm fire deep inside an elephant magazine, all the little aches and pains came alive and demanded attention.

She scanned the inside of the magazine. "I love what you've done to the place, Dylan."

He laughed. "It's a fixer-upper, for sure, but it's served me well."

Months ago, on her first trip to the island, she and Dylan had visited this base together, so they could both gauge the work they'd be doing here. He'd pointed out the chimney sticking out of the lahar. She'd thought the chimney was debris, just another random piece of metal, displaced by the flow, but he'd then pointed to the dark gap at ground level. *"That's the entrance to one of your magazines or batteries."*

"No way," she'd responded. *"If that were an elephant magazine, the opening would be a ten-foot-wide steel pipe."*

"It was, once upon a time. The rocks and debris in the lahar came down and covered it." He'd crawled forward on hands and knees and shone a light through the hole. *"Yup. Lahar crushed the exterior end of the pipe, and debris covered it. Looks like a magazine. It's still sound. I mean, a fixer-upper, but still standing."*

"Once I realized where I was when I got out of the volcano, this was my goal. Knowing this was here was what kept me moving."

He'd moved more debris around the opening, further disguising the small tunnel. But even more magnificent was the hearth he'd rigged—a small, rusted, military oil/wood/coal stove he'd salvaged from one of the rusted-out Quonset huts—which utilized the extant chimney he'd spotted so many months ago.

He'd positioned the stove so the stovepipe—which he'd also salvaged from a hut—pointed to the vent at the top, drawing most of the smoke out of his hidey-hole. It provided warm, Franklin-stove-style heat plus worked as a griddle for cooking.

"This is amazing, Dylan. You've been using coal to heat?"

"Yeah. I tried diesel at first but couldn't get it to work—the rubber tubes all rotted, gaskets were unreliable, and I'm pretty sure I didn't have all the parts—so I gutted it and converted to coal and wood. Between driftwood and coal barrels, I've kept warm and dry."

"Diesel?" Dean asked. "Where did you find diesel?"

"There are a bunch of leaking barrels of the stuff, all piled together."

"It's how they heated the Quonset huts," Fiona added. "It's one of the things that's on my list of potential hazards to be recorded that the Aleut Corporation has been asking the navy to clean up for decades. It was actually supposed to be taken care of before this project ever started, but my boss argued for addressing it after the EIS to avoid more delays."

"Well, if that's why this stove and all the others—I had to cobble this together from parts—are still here, I'm glad for that," Dylan said. "As far as I can tell, they just threw some peat and moss over the various oil barrels and hoped no one would notice. It would have been great for heat if I could've gotten the diesel to work. As it is, I added more muskeg on top and hoped it would work as another trap, like the one you fell in."

The reference to the pit reminded her of Dean's kiss, which was probably the hottest of her life. Now Dean planted himself opposite her, with Dylan in between as they faced the WWII potbelly heater, and his behavior was strangely stiff toward her. Awkward, even.

Not what she'd expect from a guy who had a reputation as a playboy. Shouldn't he be a smooth operator?

She glanced at Dylan's right leg, which he'd stretched out, angling toward Dean. When they'd finally had the energy to get up and walk, Dylan had reached for a pair of driftwood crutches and struggled to stand, and she'd noticed the splint he'd fashioned to his upper right thigh.

Dean had shot up faster than Fiona and helped his brother to his feet. *"What happened to your leg?"*

"Broke it when I fell through a floor. Let's get a fire going in my town house, and I'll tell you everything."

Now Dean handed Dylan a full bottle of whiskey, and his brother let out a happy sort of groan. "Best. Brother. Ever."

Fiona frowned at the bottle. "You carted *two* bottles from the plane?" They were bulky, fragile, and heavy. It was such an extravagance for one, let alone two.

Dean smiled. "It's Dylan's favorite. Figured he'd want it when we found him."

"You were right," Dylan said, and he took a long swig. "Damn. Coulda used this six weeks ago."

"What happened, Dyl?" Dean asked.

Dylan huffed out a breath. "It's gonna sound outrageous. And unbelievable."

"We were in the volcano," Fiona said softly. "We found the shattered floor where you fell and broke your leg. We'll believe you."

Dylan's eyes widened in the orange light of the fire that glowed through the open door of the stove. "Holy crap! You were there? Did you get out through the same tunnel I did?"

"No," Dean said. "It was full of rubble. Probably collapsed with explosives. We saw your bloody fingerprint and thought you might have been in it when it blew."

"They must've found it after I escaped and closed it off. How the hell did you get out, then? Did you climb back up and go to the original entrance?"

"No," Fiona answered this time. "They blew that up too. Dean found a crevice in the thin rhyolite wall in the same room you escaped from, and he threw rocks at it to open it up. It was an older flow that had been closed off by a later one. We found a burial cave at the other end and escaped via an underground stream."

"Whoa. How did you—"

"We know how *we* got out," Dean said, cutting him off. "We really need to know what happened to you; then we'll tell you our story."

Dylan took another long pull from the whiskey bottle, then said, "Fair enough." He set the bottle down and tightened the cap. "On my first Chiksook expedition, there was another geologist on the team—remember Jay, Fiona?"

She nodded. "Vaguely. He left after a few days. Got really sick, right?"

"Yeah. He pulled me aside the second day, insisted we go for a walk outside camp. Made sure neither of us had cell phones with us—said he thought people were listening in—he sounded really paranoid, but I humored him. He went on to say he'd been working on the project for months and had seen preliminary reports that mentioned the potential for a meteoric debris field on the north face of the volcano, and a few stones were being sent in for testing to determine the mineralogy. Then, all of a sudden, the data disappeared from all of Pollux's correspondence. Like the data had never existed. Even his work computer's files had been replaced. But he had printed a few reports at home and had the original versions.

"He knew the lava tube opening was a relatively recent find—less than five years ago—and no one had really explored the tunnels. So he started mapping the caves, a little here and there when he could justify the time. And on the first day of the previous expedition—before you or I joined the team—he went back to the tunnels and discovered a bunch of new footprints. Someone had explored the caves—extensively—during the break between expeditions.

"He checked the trip logs and even talked to the Unangax̂ chair, and no one had been permitted access during the weeks in question. No one from the village had done any exploring. He figured the mineralogy for the meteorite came back and it was heavy with rare earth metals, something really valuable, and the debris field was such that there could be a mother lode somewhere in the tunnels or in the ocean. He'd confirmed there were tsunami soils that probably dated back fifty thousand years, the result of a significant strike."

Dylan shifted on the ground, adjusting his broken leg and massaging the muscles just above his kneecap as if they ached. "Anyway, he said he wanted me to look out for meteorite debris inside and outside the volcano, and if I found it, not to put it in the official report until we had enough data to sidestep Pollux and go straight to the navy with the suppressed data."

He shook his head. "I'll admit, I was sure the guy was having some sort of mental breakdown. Or he wanted the meteorite for himself. But then the next day, he got so sick. Then he was sent home and spent weeks in the hospital with some unexplained illness. I tried to see him in June, when I was home between expeditions, but he refused to talk to me."

"You're sure he's alive?" Dean asked. "Did you exchange texts or talk to a family member who'd seen him?"

Dylan frowned. "Exchanged texts. He told me to go away, then blocked my number."

"So he might be dead," Fiona said. "Does he have family who can confirm he's alive?"

"I don't honestly know. The hospital released him. That much I confirmed, so he was alive and well enough to go home." He reached for the bottle and opened it again, taking another swig before continuing. "It was all so peculiar, but after Jay got sick, I was sucked in. I couldn't help myself and took up the task of mapping the caves. I was only able to add a little bit to his work, though, because it wasn't easy to get the time to do it without looking suspicious and . . . caving alone is really dangerous, so I needed to convince Trevor to do it with me without sounding like, well . . . like Jay had sounded when he first approached me.

"Trevor seemed to treat it as a lark. He's done some spelunking and, as a geologist, was really into it. We set up relay radios so we could map separate areas at the same time. He didn't have a problem keeping it a secret—said he liked the idea of screwing Pollux a bit. But also, we *were* mapping the network, which would be useful, especially if we did find more of the meteorite."

"When did you realize Trevor was in on it?" Dean said.

Fiona glanced at him sharply. In all their conversations, Dean had never said he suspected Trevor. Or at least, not more than anyone else. "When did *you*?" she asked Dean.

"Just now. But also, the relay radios nagged at me. It was clear Dylan had set them up with someone. But Victor and his accomplice were using them. They knew where to place them, which meant they had Dylan's map or were working with the person who'd helped Dylan. That could only be Trevor."

She nodded and turned back to Dylan. "And you? Did you suspect Trevor?"

"I want to know who this Victor person is, but I'm sure we'll get to that . . . I was starting to suspect him the night you showed me the meteoric stone from the archaeological site. But even more worrisome was the way Sylvia responded. She got this unholy light in her eyes. Then, well, you saw how she was coming on to me when you stepped into the office tent later that night. I think she wanted access to my computer and papers, and she figured the best way to do that was to get into my tent and be there while I was sleeping. I was just paranoid enough by that point that I *never* left my laptop alone."

"But Trevor was your roommate. He could have gotten your laptop while you slept."

"Not exactly. He was sleeping with Cara and had moved into her tent. I think the only thing of his that remained in our tent was his sleeping bag, because Cara had a double—which she'd brought because her relationship with Trevor had begun on the previous trip."

Fiona shook her head. Leave it to Cara to come prepared for a liaison. But if she hadn't, Trevor might have remembered to grab his sleeping bag when they were forced to evacuate quickly, and she and Dean wouldn't have had the life-saving extra-wide bag.

"I'm amazed Cara kept her fling with Trevor secret."

"Well, he's married, and she knows you don't approve of cheating. She asked me not to tell you." He shrugged. "I don't like lying—or approve of cheating, for that matter—but since you never asked, there was no reason for me to say anything one way or the other."

She winced, remembering that Dylan's wife had cheated on him. "Oh. Yeah. I forgot Trevor is married. Yeah. I would—and do—have a problem with that. I guess when Cara left early, Trevor just stayed in her tent." She glanced at Dean. "It even explains the lingerie you found. If Cara left it behind, Trevor couldn't bring it home—not without the risk of his wife finding it."

Fiona's heart twisted. Did Cara also know about the meteorite, or was she just sleeping with Trevor because she enjoyed hooking up in the field, and there was nothing more to it?

"Anyway," Dylan continued, "Trevor was never in our tent when I was asleep, and even then, on that last trip, I kept my laptop under my pillow when I was sleeping."

"Wow. You were concerned."

"The way Jay got sick right after he clued me in . . . it didn't sit well." He nodded toward his backpack in the corner of the magazine. "I had it with me when I went through the floor. Fat lot of good having a computer has done me without Wi-Fi or power, but at least Sylvia never got it."

"But Trevor still had the map," Dean said.

"Yeah, I should never have told him. Shouldn't have asked for his help exploring the tunnels. But I did all that before I really believed we'd find something. Then we found a few meteorite streaks, and I started to think Jay's paranoia—and now mine—was justified. What we found

290

was nothing like the walls of the room where I fell through the floor, but enough to know we were onto something. And then you showed me the artifacts, and Trevor was super eager to interview the Unangax̂ elders on the island and ask about their oral history. When we left the site that day, I explained that was your job and they wouldn't take kindly to his questions, but I took him to the village anyway, because I wanted to take care of the samples you gave me without Pollux knowing about it."

"Was Trevor aware you mailed the samples?" Fiona asked.

"No. I gave the package to Marion privately." He cocked his head. "How did you know I mailed them?"

"We found your phone. And Dean unlocked it."

"You found my phone? Where?"

"In your footlocker, inside your clipboard with the map."

Dylan frowned. "I left my phone in my clipboard in the side-by-side that last day. There was no point in taking it into the tunnels where there was zero reception, and I didn't need the clipboard either. I tucked the clipboard under the seat, so it'd be out of the way if I dumped wet field gear in the back at the end of the expedition. So how did it end up in the footlocker?"

"Someone packed your things and returned them to your house," Dean said. "I found your field clothes with your dirty laundry, as if you'd come home and dropped off your dirty clothes before heading out again."

"I think I know!" Fiona said as memories slipped into place. "More than once I've seen the maintenance guy go through the vehicles at the end of the day—making sure they're gassed up, etcetera. What if he found your clipboard after you were supposedly sent home? It would make sense for him to drop it in your footlocker, figuring Pollux would deal with it at some point. Hell, he might not have even known you'd been sent home. It was all handled very weirdly by Pollux."

"What did they tell you?" Dylan asked.

She grimaced. "That you'd sexually assaulted Sylvia."

He reared back, his eyes widening. "What the . . . *holy fuck!*"

His unkempt beard, gaunt features, and shocked eyes gave him a wild look, and her heart ached at having to tell him this part of the story. He'd been through hell and had no idea what had been going on back home.

"Yeah. I'm sure it was no accident they claimed you'd done something we wouldn't want to repeat or ask too many questions about. We were told it was a legal issue that would be thoroughly investigated. You both left the project on the same helicopter, but Sylvia took a military flight home, and you flew commercial."

"And I was told you were on the military flight, but no one mentioned the assault allegations," Dean added. "It was implied you went home when the entire crew was evacuated the next day."

"I think that's why we were evacuated," Fiona said. "Someone sabotaged the generator so they could make it look like you left with the rest of us when your family asked where you were."

"Wow." Dylan ran a hand over his face. "When did you realize I was missing, Dean? When I was a no-show for our visit in LA?"

"Before that. A few days after you'd supposedly been evacuated, I received an email from your work email address that said you were taking a leave of absence and going off the grid for a few months for the sake of your mental health."

"Oh, man. I'm starting to understand why you're here now. You didn't believe it."

"Of course I didn't. I mean, I didn't know about the assault claims, but you'd never go off grid without talking to me first."

Dylan nodded, then turned to Fiona. He gave her a cynical smile. "And you? Did you believe it?"

"Well, I didn't know about the going-off-the-grid email. Just the assault allegation, and no. I didn't. It didn't make sense, given what I'd witnessed between you and Sylvia. Frankly, I was waiting for you to reach out to me to ask me to make a statement on your behalf. I discussed it with my boss, and Graham felt my reaching out to you would be unwise. He and I were both concerned about me having to return to the field with Sylvia again, especially if she knew I was willing to make a statement on your behalf. It was a relief when Pollux informed us that Sylvia wouldn't be on this expedition."

He nodded, his pursed lips lost in the scruff of his beard. "Thanks, Fi, for believing in me. For talking about it with your boss. It must've put you in an awkward position."

She placed a hand on his shoulder. "I wish I'd done more. Said more. I never suspected . . . any of *this*."

"I should have told you about the meteorite and Jay's suspicions. I thought I was being careful. But really I was just playing into their hands. I made so many mistakes."

"None of that, now," Dean said. "You aren't to blame. Now, tell us who is, exactly. Trevor and Sylvia, of course, but is there anyone else we don't know about?"

"I'm not sure. I mean, besides this Victor guy you mentioned."

"We'll tell you what we know after you tell us what happened those last two days," Dean said.

Dylan nodded, then paused, and she guessed he was trying to remember where they'd gotten off track. "After we left the site, Trevor and I went to the village. He started asking all kinds of questions about meteoric artifacts and if the Unangas had a history of exploring the caves. He's usually a smart guy, but he didn't pick up on the fact that they were really bothered not just by his questions but by how he asked them. No respect for traditional cultural practices. I was mortified and apologized to Marion when I gave her the package.

"I think he believed the mother lode of the meteorite might be in the volcano and the Unangas had found it, and that's why the site had several meteoric rocks and a hammered meteorite tool."

"It's possible," Fiona said. "We found a burial cave with several hammered tools, and there were a lot of streaks in the walls."

Dylan nodded. "I'm not surprised. The next day—that last morning—I decided to go into the caves one more time, just like I told you at breakfast. I set out early so Trevor couldn't come with me. I knew it was dangerous, but I didn't trust him anymore, and if the meteorite was there, I wanted to document it and get the info to the navy so Pollux couldn't steal it. Because I'm pretty sure that's either what they were already doing or why they were so desperate to find it. If it's full of rare earth metals, it would be worth millions. And remember, Pollux already had the mineralogy done. They knew what was there."

He rubbed a hand over his face. "I need to back up a bit again. It's all kind of jumbled, and I forgot something important . . . In the office tent the night before—about thirty minutes before the ugly scene you witnessed with Sylvia—Trevor had left his laptop open while he took a call from his wife. While he was out, I checked his search history, and there were a whole lot of links to articles about hafnon and hafnium, and meteoric finds. I only had a few seconds, though, and you know how bad the internet is in camp."

Fiona nodded.

"I know hafnium is an element that resembles zirconium, and it's not found in pure form on Earth, but there's always the potential for elements to exist in pure form in space, so a meteorite could have hafnium inclusions. I did a quick search on my own computer that night and was reminded that hafnium is spontaneously combustible in powder form. The dry powder reacts with moisture to produce hydrogen, which is of course flammable. The resulting fire can produce an irritating, corrosive—even toxic—gas. But hafnium is safe in bulk—non-powder—form."

"Which is why Unangax̂ tool makers could hammer a harpoon head from it without it exploding on them," Fiona said. "But if they tried to grind the metal into shape . . . that would've been dangerous."

"Yes. Exactly. And they probably did just that." His voice was grim. After a somber pause, he resumed his story. "It's possible hafnium is one of the elements behind the Tunguska event—the massive explosion that occurred over a remote part of Russia in 1908, and which is believed to be a meteor strike—so we potentially have a precedent for a meteoroid with hafnium inclusions entering the earth's atmosphere. I continued searching and learned hafnium is used in the control rods for nuclear reactors, and then a whole lot of hits for hafnium bombs and gamma ray weapons came up in the search.

"I couldn't get most of the articles to load, but the ones that did detailed experiments by the Defense Advanced Research Projects Agency to create massively powerful weapons from a hafnium nuclear isomer. In theory, the isomer can store, per gram, up to ten thousand times as much energy in the nucleus as TNT, and DARPA wanted to use that potential to make gamma ray weapons. So, if the meteorite is high in hafnium . . . without the highly technical and expensive process of separating it from zirconium, it could be very, *very* valuable to the weapons industry. Like to the tune of billions."

THIRTY-THREE

Dean's head was reeling, trying to take it all in. The euphoria of finding Dylan. The shock at his appearance—underweight, hobbling on a broken leg—and being led into the elephant bunker that had made up his hideout for the last several weeks.

And finally learning the truth behind his disappearance.

They'd been on the right track suspecting the meteorite was key, but the idea the material could be worth billions made the risks taken by Sylvia and Trevor more understandable. Not to mention bringing in Victor, whoever he was.

"So they found you in the tunnels that last day, or you found them?" Dean asked.

"Trevor and Sylvia followed me. Hoping I'd lead them to the meteorite, I think. He jumped me when I tried to leave, and we scuffled. Sylvia pulled out a gun and fired—trying to stop the fight, I think—but then the floor started to crack. Trevor shoved me down, I slammed into the crack, and the floor gave way."

Dylan rubbed his thigh, just below the splint. "I fell hard. I think I landed on a rock that snapped my femur. It's kind of a blur because I also hit my head. I lay there, bleeding. In agony as Trevor and Sylvia argued about what they were going to do. How they'd explain my disappearance without triggering a search party.

"I gathered the original plan was for me to slip off the natural bridge archway and die when I hit the rocks below. Then Trevor could say he'd watched me fall, yada yada yada. But without my body, they couldn't do that. No way could they have anyone searching the caves or hillside for me. They might find me. They might find the meteorite. Plus, they had plans to start harvesting the chunks from the walls, as soon as they could figure out how.

"I did the only thing I could and played dead. I was bleeding pretty badly, and my leg was busted. I figured I really *was* dead."

Dean's eyes teared as Fiona covered her mouth with her hand. How close had he come to finding his brother's body in that chamber?

Dylan continued. "They were worried about the stability of the floor, so they didn't get too close to the edge while they were talking. I knew they couldn't see that I was still breathing, but I didn't move other than that. Once everyone was gone from the island, they figured they could hire someone to retrieve my body and toss me out to sea. The same guys who would harvest the meteorite debris from the walls." He glanced up. "I'm guessing this Victor guy you mentioned?"

"Probably," Fiona said. "Supposedly, he's a geologist. Trevor's replacement."

Dylan nodded. "But before they could worry about how they were going to retrieve my body, they had to settle on a cover story. They left me there, broken and bleeding, while they argued over what they would say. Between the moment they walked away and hearing Fiona's scream as you fell in the pit, I haven't heard another human voice other than my own."

Dean had already hugged Dylan when they first got to their feet after he rescued them from the pit, but now he reached over and grabbed him to his chest and let his tears flow. "Dammit. I was so afraid I'd lost you too."

Dylan hugged him back, also crying. "I wasn't gonna do that to you. I couldn't. Not after you lost Violet." Then Dylan reached out and pulled Fiona into their hug. "C'mon, Fi. It's awkward if you just watch."

She let out a teary laugh. "I don't want to intrude."

"Nah. You're part of the family now. After what you've been through."

Dean placed a hand on Fiona's back, closing the triangular hug, but it felt weird touching her now, even though he'd held her so many times in the last few days. He needed to let the fantasy of her go.

She must've sensed his awkwardness, because she pulled away. "Why don't you two talk while I find the latrine. Then I'll make dinner."

"I've been using one end of the Quonset hut as a latrine and the other end as a makeshift shower. Set up a fire pit for heating water by the barrels that collect rainwater through the leaky roof."

"Got it. I'll be back. You guys talk."

She disappeared through the round opening—yet another tunnel, albeit this one very short—leaving them alone.

"Isn't she great?" Dylan asked. "I knew you guys would hit it off."

"She's amazing," was all Dean could say, his belly churning. Dylan had seen them kissing. He must be cut up inside but was putting on a good face because he was happy to be found.

"How did you two end up together? How did you get here at all? Chiksook is impossible to get to unless you're Unangax̂."

Dean let out a bitter-sounding laugh. "Yeah. I know."

"So how'd you do it?"

"Pollux put out a call for an ornithologist. They needed one in the field ASAP; someone reported seeing gray buntings. So I became Bill Lowell—remember him?"

"Oh, wow. Yeah. You first met him in South America, right?"

"Central. Costa Rica." Bill had met Dylan when the ornithologist visited LA several months later, and the two had hit it off. "Anyway, I called in some favors and got a fake ID and ended up on the flight from Whidbey with your girlfriend."

"Oh, man. My girlfriend. Shit! I forgot. She's, uh, not my girlfriend."

"Yeah, when she denied it, I figured it was wishful thinking. I get it. She's amazing. And, man, I'm so sorry about what you saw; that was the only—"

Dylan let out a sharp laugh. "What? What's to apologize for? She's great, and I *knew* you two would be great together."

Now Dean had to figure the whiskey had gone to his head. Or rather Dylan's, because, come to think of it, he hadn't had any tonight. He reached for the bottle and unscrewed the cap. "Man, you are *not* making sense."

The whiskey burned his throat, washing away the taste of Fiona's kiss. It didn't matter. He had Dylan back. That was the only thing in the world that mattered now.

"I knew you'd like her. From the moment I met her, I just felt this zing."

"Yeah. I get it," he said, not wanting to hear the finer details of Dylan's infatuation.

"I don't think you do. But you know what, I'm gonna wait until Fiona gets back, because I have a feeling she needs to hear this too."

"Please don't. I won't interfere. I *want* you to have her."

Naturally, that was the moment Fiona came crawling back into the bunker. "I'd apologize for barging in sooner than expected, but . . . given what I just heard, I'm glad my flashlight busted in the fall so I came back. Now, which one of you is going to explain how I'm an object that can be given away?"

———

Fiona was, in a word, furious. Did Dean Slater really think he got to decide who she'd be with? Aside from the fact that Dylan wasn't interested in her, it was galling Dean didn't respect her autonomy.

She crossed her arms. Her bladder could wait—it had only been an excuse to leave the brothers alone for a bit, and once she realized she didn't have a decent light, she'd dithered outside in the wind, trying to decide what to do. Clearly, crawling back inside had been the right choice.

"I'm waiting."

"You fucked up, man." This was from Dylan, and she couldn't help but laugh. He got a pass. It was Dean who'd offered to hand her off like a trophy.

The silence stretched out. Dean, the not-very-smooth operator, was at a loss for words. Finally, he broke the silence. "If Dylan is in love with you, I refuse to stand in his way. My feelings don't matter."

Dylan let out an audible wince. "Ohhh. Wrong way to go, bro."

"So you're saying *my* feelings don't matter either?" At least Dylan understood.

"Of course they do!" Dean said. "But if there is any chance you have feelings for Dylan . . . I just . . . I can't get in the way."

"Dylan, are you in love with me?"

"Nope."

She fixed her gaze on the impossibly handsome, incredibly infuriating photographer who was definitely not an ornithologist or even a halfway adept ladies' man, if the current situation was anything to judge by.

"Of course he says that when asked point-blank!"

Now Dylan was laughing, and Fiona sort of wanted to laugh too. But mostly she was irritated.

"Dylan, why did you tell your brother we were dating? Was it because of deep-seated infatuation or because you were trying to get him off your back about dating his model friend?"

"The second one."

"What?" Dean said, more than a little outrage in his voice. "You said you were head over heels for her. She was *the one.*"

Dylan rolled his eyes, and this time Fiona did laugh. Was there anything more absurd than hiding out in a WWII magazine on an Aleutian island with two hot fraternal-twin brothers after escaping a volcano and finding out about the possible existence of a billion-dollar meteorite and a scheme to harvest the rare earth metals for gamma ray weapons, then having the brothers argue over which one of them had the right to *date* her?

"I was really, really tired of you trying to fix me up with your model friends. I didn't want to hook up on my vacation. That's not my speed. Never has been. I just wanted to hang out with you, so I lied to get you to drop it."

"But you named Fiona because you like her."

"Yeah. *Like* being the operative word." He flashed a grin in her direction. "I think you're great, Fi. And the moment I met you, I . . . I don't know, I just wanted Dean to meet you. He'd been doing the no-emotion, no-commitment thing for so long, I just thought you'd be . . . I don't know. Different. Right somehow. So when I had to come up with a name, yours popped into my head. I ran with it, thinking that when I told him the truth during our visit, I'd tell him I wanted you two to meet the next time he came up to Seattle. No pressure or anything. We could go out for drinks or catch some live music. I just wanted you two to meet."

She smiled at Dylan, her heart filling as she felt the genuine warmth of what had been a budding friendship blossom into something so much deeper after this bizarre, intertwining adventure. He'd been innocent of the assault on Sylvia and didn't have any weird, unfounded obsession with her. He was just Dylan, a good man, who'd wanted to catch Pollux in their scheme. And after everything that had happened, as he'd said earlier, in an odd sort of way, she was family now. A Carver branch on the Slater tree.

She met Dean's gaze. He looked . . . well, *deer in the headlights* might be apt. "So do you believe me now when I say there's nothing between Dylan and me?"

Dylan's gaze bounced between Dean and Fiona, and he said, "I think I'm going to visit the latrine. And I won't be back for a while. At least, not without announcing myself. Loudly." And then Dean's brother stood with the aid of his driftwood crutches and hobbled to the opening before expertly crawling out, dragging his broken leg and pushing the crutches in front of him.

"I still want to know how he escaped and got all the way down here with a broken femur," Fiona murmured, saying exactly what Dean had been thinking.

"I think my brother is pretty badass."

"Agreed."

She looked at him askance, and he saw the hurt in her eyes. He really had fucked up. Reduced her to an object. Like that dickhead who'd figured a fancy dinner at an expensive restaurant should result in a sexual transaction.

Fiona deserved so much better than him. So much more than a guy who no longer knew how to feel. How to open up.

She'd seen him at his most vulnerable, but even then, he hadn't been putting his heart on the line. He didn't think he'd ever be able to do that again. He'd given his heart to Violet, and she'd taken it to the grave.

"And I think you're amazing, Fi."

She smiled and waited.

He cleared his throat. "And I want you. So much, it killed me thinking I needed to let Dylan have you."

"And that's where you messed up. You don't get to decide who I screw."

He flinched. It wasn't the word she chose; he was a huge fan of mindless sex—it was one of his favorite things. It was the *way* she said it. The emotionlessness, which he never wanted to hear from such a passionate woman.

One thing he knew about her was that if he did get her into his bed, the last thing it would be was a screw. It would be hot. Wild. A night to end all nights. A fling, but not a *screw*. Because Fiona didn't do anything without passion.

He rose from his seat by the flickering fire and approached her, his intentions—in his mind, at least—finally clear.

He pushed her back to the cold steel wall, his body blocking her in. "I don't want to screw you, Fiona. I've never wanted anything so pedestrian. I want to *possess* you. To make your body quiver at my touch. To make you beg for more. For my touch. For my mouth. For my cock. I want you so wild with need, you forget everything and let me fuck you like you've never been fucked before."

Her beautiful green eyes widened with each word that fell from his lips as he hovered above her, pressing her to the wall.

"Have you ever been utterly *possessed*, Fiona? Ever been reduced to nothing but nerve endings demanding *more, more, now?*"

She shook her head. Her voice came out breathy. "No. I've never lost control like that, ever."

"Well, now I have a new goal."

Her nostrils flared. "You think you can just snap your fingers and I'll beg? After everything that's happened?"

"Oh, no. That's what makes this special. I am everything you think you don't want. But still, you want me."

He saw his moment, and his mouth descended on hers. He hadn't mistimed it. She was all in, right there with him. Heated up with nowhere to direct the passion until his tongue was stroking hers in a deep, carnal kiss that made all sorts of promises he couldn't wait to deliver.

He might not get to keep Fiona, but he would have her. And it would be glorious.

THIRTY-FOUR

Dean's kiss was, quite simply, raw perfection. It was fire and passion and joy and celebration and chocolate and vanilla and strawberries topped with fudge. His tongue stroked hers, and her knees turned to jelly. But thankfully, his arm snaked around her waist, and he kept her upright so she didn't miss a second of this sweet escape.

She didn't do field flings, but maybe this didn't qualify as a fling. It was a *reward*. One she'd earned through quite literal sweat and tears, with a little bloodshed along the way.

"Glad to see you two made up."

Dean tore his mouth from hers and sprang back from the wall. She might've collapsed without his support, but she locked her knees. No point in giving him *that* satisfaction.

"I'm still deliberating," she said to Dylan.

"Looked to me like you were all in."

She shrugged. "He's a good kisser; what can I say?"

Dylan laughed while Dean gave her a look that promised delicious retribution.

"I thought you were going to give us a heads-up when you returned," Dean said.

"Uh. I did. Like, repeatedly."

She was pretty sure Dylan was lying, but she loved him for messing with his brother that way. She pressed her fingers to her lips and blew him a kiss. She totally got Dylan. And he was the *best*.

"All right, boys, I think we've earned a fancy dinner. We've got a few more thawed pieces of meat before we're down to MREs. Dylan, as our host, you choose: chicken or beef? We finished off the salmon last night."

"I'm tired of fish anyway. We should probably eat the chicken before it goes bad, but frankly, I'd prefer steak if you have it."

"We have three strips of top sirloin," Dean said.

Dylan let out a soft groan. "That. *Please.*"

Fiona could totally relate to his calculus. Life was short. Eat steak first. She glanced at Dean. *Or have ice cream before you die.*

And that was the thought that gutted her. The realization of the truth he'd uttered before he kissed her the first time. Her anger evaporated; her ego slipped away.

He cared about her. More than he wanted to. More, even, than he knew *how* to care, because he'd cut off that part of himself when he buried Violet.

But she couldn't get herself wrapped up in the idea that he'd give her more than a one-night stand. He wasn't capable of more, and she really couldn't blame him.

Could she be satisfied with that?

But then, would she be happy if she *didn't* give in to this wild attraction? After all they'd been through?

She pulled the food from her pack, determined to focus on something else. She laid out the vacuum-sealed pouches of thawed meat. "How did you escape, Dylan?"

"It's kind of a blur. But mostly anger and determination. I just didn't want those assholes to win."

He sighed and leaned back against the wall, tossing another piece of driftwood into the stove. "I had to listen to Sylvia and Trevor talk about how they were going to cover up my death. When they agreed they'd hire someone to collect my body and toss me out to sea, I knew I had to be gone before anyone came back. No matter what it took."

With a long stick, he poked at the fire through the open door on the side of the stove. Fiona could tell from the look in his eye that he wasn't here, with them. He was back in the well of the chamber, after he'd fallen through the fragile floor. A place she and Dean had been just last night, and she could see it in her mind with the same terror Dylan must've felt.

"I couldn't bandage my head wound right away. I mean, they might hear me moving around and realize I was still alive. So I grabbed the only absorbent thing that was easy to get to—the damn cotton Pollux tote bag—and maneuvered it so it was under my head and turned, face-down, so I'd look like I was dead while I pressed the cut into the bag."

"We found it. The bag with your blood soaked through," Dean said.

The brothers exchanged a look, and she wanted to hug them both. The pain and fear they'd both suffered was intense but, unfortunately, not unfamiliar to her. What she wouldn't have done for a moment like this with Regan.

This was so many of her fantasies come true. Just not for *her*.

Neither man knew what she'd gone through, and she was glad for that, because it had shadowed her pessimism. Made her ache and not believe in happy endings. It was why she'd refused to tell Dean not just her thoughts but her story.

Dean and Dylan were now getting the reunion she and Regan never got. She didn't feel bitter about that. Instead, she just felt happy that these two men—both of whom she cared about in very different ways—could have a joy denied her. Denied Regan.

There was justice somewhere, at least.

Of course, they still had to survive this and bust Sylvia and Trevor and Victor and whoever else was involved.

"After I was alone, I think I was delirious. Pain and blood loss. I ate something—I'm not even sure what, but I knew I needed to eat, then get the hell out of there. They would come back for my body. My leg hurt like a bitch, but I didn't have anything to splint it with. I just . . . started crawling, dragging my leg. Thinking about how Jane Goodall said—at least, I think it was Jane, but it might have been Margaret Mead—that once archaeologists started finding skeletons with healed femur fractures, it was a defining moment of civilization. Or maybe a benchmark. Because leg fractures can't be survived alone, without a community. An australopithecine breaks a leg, and they're *dead*."

"It was Mead," Fiona murmured. "And a brilliant observation about communities and civilization."

Dylan smiled and waved his arm in a circle in front of his chest, like he was bowing with just the arm gesture and dip of head as he lay with his broken leg spread out in front of him. "Welcome to my one-man civilization."

Fiona's eyes burned once again. "Thank you for being the exception to the rule."

He gave her a cocky grin. "We Slater men are all exceptional."

She snorted a laugh. "Your brother has dug his own hole. Let him dig himself out."

"Roger that." He smirked. "So I dragged my *exceptional* self—very painfully, I might add—across the chamber and to the nearest tunnel. I had a minimal first aid kit and wrapped my wound"—he touched his forehead, which sported a nasty, still fresh-looking scar—"in gauze and took two ibuprofen. I want it on record here that ibuprofen doesn't dampen the pain of a femur fracture very much."

"Noted," Fiona said. "You are badass."

"Damn right. Okay, so then I made it to the chamber with the escape tunnel, and . . . I'm not entirely sure. I think I passed out for only a few hours, but it might have been more? No daylight to tell and"—he waved his arm around—"I had no way to know how much time I'd lost. I didn't have my phone, and my smartwatch battery died the first day."

She noted he still wore the dead watch on his wrist. Which was kind of sad but also endearingly sweet.

"I woke up at some point and realized I needed to go through the tunnel and hope for an escape. With my leg broken, it wasn't like I could back up and find a different route. All balls in one basket."

She guessed his choice of the word *balls* over *eggs* hadn't been a mistake, and really, they were the gender equivalent of the same thing.

"It was the most painful . . . who knows how long . . . of my life, but in the end, I found myself delirious and in a ton of pain but outside the volcano. I remembered visiting the World War II village with you, Fiona, and knew it was the closest shelter. Plus, it was by a sheltered cove. I could fish when the MREs ran out.

"All I had to do was survive. So I crawled, knowing I was going in the right general direction thanks to the water when it was clear and the *sound* of the water when it was not. I had a heavy coat, hat, gloves, and a couple of emergency shelter tents. I holed up against tephra mounds in my pathetic Mylar shelter for two nights. Frankly, I thought the emergency tent was ridiculous that first night, giving me false hope. But it saved my life. Mad respect for it by the second night. I was ready to name it Wilson and declare it my best friend after that, but then I reached the base and moved into this sweet little condo."

He nodded to a shredded pile of Mylar and rotting piece of canvas far enough from the fire to prevent the tent from melting and cloth from burning. "I only use the Mylar when I don't dare risk a fire in case the smoke will be spotted. But the weather here is more fog than clear, and I've had plenty of wood and coal."

Her heart ached at all that Dylan had needed to do to survive. The pain he must still be in with an improperly set leg.

She cleared her throat. "And food? How have you gotten enough to eat?"

"I tried spearfishing in the bay. When that failed, I found some old nets in the ruins. Way easier and more effective. Rodents when I couldn't fish."

He was lean—far leaner than he'd been the last time she'd seen him, but that was hardly a surprise. The fish he'd been able to catch probably hadn't been large. Just enough to keep him going.

Dean brushed aside her efforts to help and cooked the steaks, dropping them on the hot stove. The meat smelled utterly delicious, sizzling on the flat grill top. But when the time came to eat, Fiona found she couldn't enjoy more than a few bites, and she passed the remainder to Dylan. "Please. Eat this."

He resisted, but then Dean did the same. Finally, Dylan said, "Listen, I'll eat Fiona's, but you two split the other one. My stomach couldn't take more anyway."

She and Dean split the remainder of his steak, and it was more than enough to fill her belly, knowing that they'd be limited if they didn't figure out how to get off the island sooner rather than later. Dylan needed medical help. Sheer will could only carry a man so far.

That night, they opened the sleeping bag, and the three of them slept on the cold ground, sharing the not-nearly-wide-enough thermal pad beneath them with the open sleeping bag as a blanket above. Fiona slept in the middle, with each Slater brother pressed on either side against her.

THIRTY-FIVE

Dean slept deeply for the first time in weeks. As he drifted off, he had Fiona pressed to his side and could hear the even breathing of his brother just inches away. He'd never quite lost hope, but at the same time, he didn't know if he'd ever quite believed this outcome was possible.

He was almost afraid to wake up and find it was a dream. But when the gray light of dawn penetrated the small opening of the short entrance tunnel, he opened his eyes to see Fiona and Dylan, facing each other and curled together in sleep. Fiona had shifted closer to Dean, with her backside against Dean's hip, giving Dylan as much of the thermal pad as possible, which meant Dean was completely pushed off the pad on his back on the cold, hard ground. He was glad for this, as there'd been much arguing the night before as they tried to convince Dylan to take both pad and sleeping bag. The current arrangement was a compromise.

Seeing his brother and Fiona entwined triggered a mild ache, but it wasn't jealousy or anything negative toward either person. It was just the ongoing question if Fiona and Dylan might be better suited. After all, Dean wasn't interested in anything more than a fling. What if Dylan could offer her a future?

If that were the case, he'd have to step back. Fiona deserved a man who'd love her until the end of time, and he had no doubt she could and would fall in love with Dylan, given the chance.

It was bizarre to have these thoughts, even as he woke with her in his arms for the third morning in a row, their survival still far from assured.

But dammit, he'd get her and his brother to safety. Whatever it took. Whatever sacrifice necessary.

He scooted back, attempting to extract himself from her side, and she shifted at the loss of his body heat, her eyes fluttering open with reluctance.

He pressed his mouth to her ear and whispered, "Sorry I disturbed you. Don't wake up. It's early still, and you both need more sleep." Then, because he couldn't help himself, he did the thing he'd wanted to do the previous mornings they'd woken together and pressed his lips to her neck, kissing her soft skin and breathing her in at the same time.

She let out a soft, contented sigh and wiggled her ass, brushing against his hip. If they were spooning, her ass would be fully met with his ready erection, but as it was, he fought the urge to roll to his side and pull her back against him so he could grind into her.

Decidedly not the time or place for it.

Later. When they were alone. With a full box of condoms.

Setting his reservations aside, it was exhilarating to know he *could* have her. She wanted him as much as he wanted her. She wasn't Dylan's and never had been.

He kissed her exposed neck one more time, then slid away, slipping out from under the open sleeping bag and tucking it around her to keep her warm.

As quietly as possible, he pulled on his outer layers and boots, then crawled through the opening to face the day.

He rose to his feet and was greeted by sunlight undimmed by clouds or fog. Bright and clear and, he knew, a rarity in the Aleutians.

But clear skies would bring new problems. Smoke from the coal stove would be readily visible. Dylan had been careful to keep the smoke to a minimum when the weather was clear.

At some point, someone had returned to the cave to recover his body, and they must've freaked out when they'd realized he was not only alive, but he'd escaped. When had that happened?

Weeks ago, he guessed. Given the difficulty of getting to the island, perhaps Sylvia and Trevor had managed to plant someone on the team hired to fix the generator. Those repairs had begun a month ago, and it was someone from that crew who'd reported the gray bunting call that led to the ornithologist job posting.

Was Victor supposed to pose as an ornithologist so he could search for Dylan, but Dean was hired instead? It would explain Trevor's last-minute replacement.

Was Trevor the man who had been above the natural bridge? If so, how did he get here? Was there a boat offshore, or had he arrived on the helicopter before the camp was evacuated?

Whoever Victor was, Dean suspected he was on Chiksook to tie up Sylvia and Trevor's loose ends before they could start harvesting the meteorite in earnest. Somehow, he'd figured out Dean was Dylan's brother, so separating him and Fiona from the team had been necessary.

Trapping and killing them in the volcano had been plan A.

Did Victor guess they might have escaped, or had he simply returned to the task of searching for Dylan?

According to Dylan, a vehicle had driven to the World War II base yesterday morning. Dylan had been inside the magazine and heard the engine. He always left the front covered with the rusty camouflage and had extinguished his fire with the dawn. He didn't worry about heat signature because no heat would be noted from the steel magazine buried under several feet of dirt.

The vehicle had stopped, and he'd heard footsteps just outside the magazine. Fifteen minutes later, the vehicle had driven off.

In the previous weeks, Dylan had woven together mats of leaves and vines to cover a few of the deeper debris pits that lined the road. Some were small, collapsed structures, and others were storage pits where the military had tossed debris in a feeble attempt to clean the place up when they'd abandoned the base. He'd hoped anyone searching for him would stumble into one of the pits, but as far as he could tell from the footprints and tire tracks, the person had stuck to the road.

Fiona and Dean had been caught because they'd been actively avoiding the open road. But thankfully it hadn't been one of the debris pits, or they could have found themselves landing on jagged metal parts of rusty vehicles, sharp rebar, or even coated in diesel fuel if they'd landed in the pit with the leaking barrels. Luckily, they'd dropped through a now-roofless magazine, the floor of which had filled in with a thick layer of soil and vines, cushioning their landing at least a little.

It had to be Victor or his unknown crony who'd searched the base. But if not Trevor, was it possible his partner was John or Roy? Neither Dylan nor Fiona knew of any connection between either engineer and the meteorite find. And Fiona's boss had only mentioned Victor as being the third party who was supposed to be picked up by the helicopter, which meant John and Roy were probably accounted for. Cara too, for that matter.

Everyone was a suspect at this point.

Dean was convinced the second man had arrived on the helicopter just before the camp blew up. There had likely been a lot of confusion in the off-loading of supplies followed by whatever had triggered the initial evacuation of the camp.

There'd been misdirection in telling the people on the boat that the helicopter would pick up some people and telling people in the helo that the boat would wait for the missing team members. It would be easy for the new arrival to get lost in the same shuffle, which made Trevor the most likely suspect.

Dean kept coming back to the same questions: Who was Victor Neff? Who else was involved in the scheme to harvest meteorite debris from Mount Katin? And had the conspirators found the mother lode?

With no answers to be found in the cold morning sun, Dean visited the Quonset hut Dylan had established as the latrine and shower, then stepped out again into the chill daylight. He could happily spend every moment in the daylight after almost twenty-four hours of being trapped underground. Stories of miners being trapped would have new resonance now, as his and Fiona's experience was minor compared to what others had faced.

Hell, what Dylan had faced, crawling down a mountain with a busted leg. Dylan had always been his hero, but now, the guy had just added *super* in front of the word.

Yet he knew more than anyone how mortal Dylan was, which only made it all the more amazing.

Dean walked to the beach, the protected cove where Dylan had collected driftwood and fished, always on the lookout in case a boat chose this port for shore. The sea was a crisp, cold blue today with larger waves breaking outside the cove. If they were at a more southern latitude, the deep-blue water would look inviting for a swim. A fish jumped, and Dean wished he'd grabbed Dylan's homemade spear or, better yet, the net he'd used to good effect these last weeks.

Hunger had driven Dylan to enter the water without the benefit of waders and stand there, up to his thighs in icy water, waiting for a fish to swim near. His legs must've been numb with cold—possibly a benefit for the broken one—as he waited for his meal.

Success meant a fresh fish cooked on his potbelly stove, the coal fire inside drying his clothes and thawing his frozen leg muscles. Failure to spear or net a fish meant risking hypothermia for nothing.

How did he do it?

Sheer will. Desperate survival instinct.

He needed to get Dylan real medical attention. ASAP.

They couldn't wait for a rescue. They didn't even know if Fiona's boss had called for an emergency search. They hadn't seen any helicopters yesterday, but then, clouds were low, and what were the odds a helicopter search would include the coastal side of the volcano?

They needed a plan.

Dean looked at the piles of driftwood on the beach. Dylan said there was half a fifty-gallon barrel left of coal. Between that, their remaining Sterno, and the remaining whiskey, could they create enough smoke to get attention? But should they dare to risk their fuel that way? Fire was survival here.

Plus, there was one big drawback to sending smoke signals: it would draw Victor and his crony to their hideout before the real rescuers could arrive.

Team Victor had guns and explosives, whereas Team Slater—and Carver—had knives, a trowel, and whatever tools they could round up here.

They had a flare gun, but that should be used only if they spotted a helicopter they knew was friendly.

What they needed more than anything was a vehicle. Then they could drive to the village and call for help or simply take a boat to another island. To Adak, where they could fly to Anchorage and a hospital.

It was too far for Dylan to walk on his busted leg, but if they couldn't get a vehicle, they'd have to try it. Without a tent, though, the journey could kill all three of them.

No. Walking wasn't an option with Dylan. And leaving Dylan behind was absolutely not an option.

Everything was risky. They needed to look for an escape while preparing for an attack. He looked toward the water, where fish were jumping in the morning sun, in no danger of being caught or speared.

What he needed was bait.

———

They spent the morning inside the magazine, going over their options. Each was more bleak than the last, and Fiona hated every single idea because they all were risky. And she feared Dylan didn't have enough in reserves after six weeks with an untreated broken femur and malnutrition.

They loaded him up with protein, vitamins, electrolyte water, and painkillers, and by the early afternoon, there was more color in his cheeks than there'd been the day before, but it was clear to her—and Dean agreed, in private—that they couldn't attempt any of the more proactive plans with Dylan's questionable health.

He'd powered through for weeks, surviving as best he could, but it appeared that now that he could rest with others to watch his back, his body was begging for the much-needed break.

It was hard to guess what was going on in official channels. The navy was probably scrambling after the camp had been blown up, and she didn't doubt the fact that she was missing with Dean—who'd been impersonating an ornithologist—was now part of the cover story. The camp explosion had probably been placed firmly on Dean's shoulders, and they could easily claim he'd abducted her and gone nuclear because he blamed the military for his brother taking off without a word.

The more she thought about it, the more she realized Dean was the perfect scapegoat, a gift Trevor and Sylvia hadn't counted on. Dean was just famous enough to make it an extra-salacious story.

But if this plan to get Victor's vehicle worked, there was no way everything could be laid at Dean's door. One, Dylan would share his story with the world, and he had a broken leg and scar as proof. And two, there was proof of the meteorite. In the site and sent to the lab.

The Unangas would vouch for them. Fiona's boss could confirm she'd called him. Their bases were covered, as long as they could get a vehicle and cross the island to the village and get off this rock.

After their lunch of MREs, protein bars, and electrolyte powder dissolved in water, Fiona convinced Dylan to rest in the shelter of the magazine while she and Dean explored the historic ruins and looked for anything they could use to defend themselves if Victor showed up before a rescue team arrived.

She tucked Dylan in as she would a younger brother, zipping up the side of his sleeping bag and pressing her lips to his forehead—which wasn't feverish, thank God.

He caught her wrist before she could crawl away. "Don't believe Dean," he whispered. "When he pushes you away. And he will. It's all he knows how to do after Violet."

She nodded. "He told me about Violet."

Dylan smiled. "I'm glad. She was . . . the best. But it's time for him to move on."

Maybe that was true, but she didn't think she was cut out for being Dean's transitional woman. She had her own issues to deal with and wasn't eager to be someone's test relationship. Especially when said person had never indicated he wanted more than a fling.

She brushed her lips on Dylan's forehead again. "How about you worry about you and not your brother?"

"Can't do that. We always look out for each other. It's what brothers do."

Her heart squeezed. She'd had siblings like that. Until she didn't.

The image of Regan's body splayed on the rocks was one of those memories that had the same impact every time it flashed in her mind.

She'd read somewhere that every time a person remembered something, they were really remembering the last time they'd remembered it. So the memory became infused with the emotions triggered at each later instance of it. Memories could be tainted and twisted with each visitation.

But her memory of finding Regan's body would always be raw and pure. Each time she remembered it, the vivid pain cut across her chest, like a blade across her heart.

Her fault. Even Aidan agreed on that point.

Every instance of remembering hammered home it was her fault.

She'd never trusted the smarmy bastard Regan had worked for. And she was 100 percent certain Regan's death was no accident, no matter what the investigators had said.

———

Dean paused while digging a hole for a photography blind and leaned on the handle of the rusted shovel as he watched Fiona cross the site. Her hair glowed with red in the natural light, and he wished he had his camera in his hands. She was a lioness, queen of her domain, sleek and mesmerizing.

Damn. He'd never guessed he could be so infatuated, especially not after such a short time.

But then, watching Fiona go through one wringer after another in the handful of days they'd known each other had taught him more about her than the women he'd *enjoyed,* for lack of a better word, in the years since he'd lost Violet.

Was it time to open the lock on his heart?

The idea terrified him. He did not want to feel again. At least, not that kind of feeling. He'd loved every minute of being married to Violet, but he never wanted to *choose* that kind of pain again. And loving like that, hurting like that, it felt like a choice now.

Ahh. But damn. Fiona. Beautiful. Brilliant. Bold.

Mesmerizing.

As long as she knew the rules and as long as he didn't engage his heart, they could enjoy this spark that had been there from their first conversation on the jet.

"How's Dylan?" he asked.

"A fighter."

His heart burned along with his eyes. *Yes. Yes he is.*

She gave Dean a heartbreaking smile. "But . . ."

He nodded. "You're worried. I am too."

"I feel like he was hanging on as long as he could, and now . . ."

"We need to get him to a doctor."

"Maybe we can salvage a boat from all the junk here. There's got to be something that will float. Isn't that what duct tape is for?"

"I've considered that. But damn. You know how many miles we'd have to row to get to the village or another island? If the seas get rough . . ." His voice trailed off. A rowboat could be a death trap.

Fiona squinted as she looked across the water. "You said something earlier about needing bait to get Victor out of the vehicle. This gives me an idea . . ."

THIRTY-SIX

They were as ready as they'd ever be. Everything was in place. They just needed Victor and a side-by-side with a full tank of gas.

They'd spent yesterday afternoon and evening and all of the morning setting it up. It was now the afternoon of Dean's sixth day on this island and less than forty-eight hours since they'd found Dylan. His brother was holding his own, but damn, it was like the minute his body knew he could relax, his energy gave out. Every time he went to sleep, Dean was terrified he wouldn't wake up.

He was exhausted and strained to the limit of his endurance.

They'd planned to wait for Victor and his crony to show up again, but given Dylan's condition, he and Fiona had agreed to desperate measures. They would set a bonfire to draw Victor to them.

Everything burnable they could scrounge was in a massive pile, ready to be set off. They had one shot at this. If Victor didn't see the smoke, didn't show up, they'd have burned half their resources for nothing.

They made it look like a signal fire, with the goal being as much thick, dark smoke as possible.

Dean held the bottle of whiskey he and Fiona had shared in the volcano. It was half-full. Or half-empty. Both were true.

They'd soaked much of the wood and charcoal they'd gathered in the pit of diesel, in hopes the fuel wasn't too diluted with runoff water and would accelerate the burn.

"Once the fire is going, we get into position," Fiona said.

He nodded. "It might take hours for Victor to get here. It'll be cold, the waiting."

She turned to Dean and said, "Then give me something warm to think about."

He smiled. *Damn.* She was everything.

The move came naturally. Smooth like fine wine. He cupped a hand behind her head and tilted her back, then covered her mouth with his, his tongue sliding between her lips, taking everything he wanted while giving her what she'd asked for.

Her mouth was silky sweet and smooth, his body rocking with the pleasure of the easy kiss, the feel of her tongue sliding against his. The heat and passion of her. He forgot about everything. Life. Death. Breathing. He simply pulled her body flush to his and took her mouth, utterly possessing her as he'd said he wanted to do when they were alone in the magazine the night before last.

She kissed him back, giving him all he demanded and taking what she needed in return.

He finally raised his head, not wanting to end the moment but knowing it had to be done. He brushed her hair from her face. "When we get out of here, I want one night with you, so I can worship you as you deserve."

She gave him a small, inscrutable smile; then she whispered in his ear, "That sounds lovely, but . . ." Her voice dropped an octave deeper. "I don't do flings." She then bit his earlobe and slipped from his arms. "Now, let's light this sucker up and end this nightmare."

———

Fiona took the cloth coated with Sterno gel and set it in the heart of the bonfire pile, next to wood that had been soaked in diesel and whiskey in hopes the fire would take off in spite of the wood being wet due to the recent storms. She lit the cloth, and the flame caught, burning slowly.

It wasn't dramatic, like an action movie; it was a slow burn that seeped into the damp driftwood and debris that made up the woodpile, each piece catching slowly, in turn, until finally, after several minutes, the fire was raging.

From slow burn to inferno in . . . fifteen minutes or more.

She smiled at the comparison. Relating to it more than she should.

It was the fires that burned slow and hot that did the most damage. Sneaking up and consuming you like a frog on boil.

When the fire was steady, she left to take her position by the water, ready to play her part should Victor show up. Dean would check on Dylan, make sure he was safely tucked away in the magazine; then he'd get into the blind he'd made to hide.

Hours passed as Fiona waited, feeding the bonfire as needed, keeping the smoke level thick and high, letting the fierce Aleutian winds carry it up. Anyone searching for them would see the smoke. No doubt about it.

It was possible their real rescue would arrive before Victor, but she wouldn't bet on it.

An hour before darkness fell, a fog rolled in, thick and white. There was no point to keeping the bonfire going. She and Dean quickly spread out the burning wood, making a big, blackened patch in the middle of the road right as it ended next to both covered and uncovered storage pits. More toxic waste on the base.

They both returned to their positions. Now there was nothing to do but wait as the fog closed in.

Darkness was descending when the hum of an engine sounded in the distance. Dean made the birdcall that meant he heard and was sliding into his hiding place.

Timing was everything. Fiona's role was to push the decoy into the water, but if she went too soon, it would be too far out, lost in the darkness and fog, and if she went too late, Victor might spot her.

And shoot her.

She took a deep breath. Better early than late.

She pushed the boat they'd spent the last day repairing with duct tape and sweat. They'd managed to make three human-looking dummies to ride the boat. The fact that it was twilight and foggy worked in their favor.

With a hard shove, the boat was launched into the small, shallow bay, veering toward the entrance to the cove. She said a silent prayer, asking for it to remain on that course; then she tucked herself into her hiding place to wait for Victor.

———

Dean planted himself beneath the muskeg matting, telling himself this was no different from positioning himself in a blind and waiting for his moment to take the perfect shot. The only difference was, he wasn't waiting for the perfect photo—he was waiting for the perfect moment to attack, and the animal in question was a predator out to kill the only family he had left.

He sank down into the wet earth with his camera, leaning into the cold pain of the long wait. Later, when all this was over, he'd get warm by a fire with Fiona in his arms.

But first, victory over Victor.

He knew their plan was too simple. Their odds of success minuscule. But hope had guided him through this entire dangerous journey, and he wasn't about to give up that drug now.

The vehicle stopped in the middle of the road before the smoldering, blackened circle that marked the bonfire. Close to the magazine but two hundred yards from the shoreline.

The bright spotlight mounted to the top of the vehicle lit, creating a white beam in the fog that touched the water, just catching the decoy boat as it went out to sea in a haze of fog.

They didn't need the decoy to distract Victor for long. Just long *enough*. Long enough for him and his companion—Dean could see there was another person in the front seat—to step out of the vehicle.

The companion took the bait. Victor did not.

"What the fuck? There are three of them?"

"Obviously Slater and Carver escaped the cave, because you were a dumbass and set the charges too soon. If you'd given me the time I needed, they'd both be dead."

Dean had a theory about that . . . and wondered if Neff did too.

He was pretty sure the explosion happened much faster than the declared five minutes but had to admit time had all been relative those minutes in the cave, when Neff had shot at them in the dark.

The second man's goal could have been to get rid of Dean, Fiona, *and* Victor. Perhaps he wasn't pleased with the guy's job performance. Or he wanted his share of the bounty.

The man took several steps toward the water, his gaze on the rowboat with the three human shapes propped up inside.

"Get back here, you idiot! Can't you see it's fake? No one is rowing."

Well, it had been worth a shot.

Dean wished he had a gun so he could shoot the companion in the leg. Let these men know the fear and pain they'd inflicted on Dylan.

Instead, the only weapon in his arsenal was patience. He willed Victor to get complacent and climb from the vehicle.

His companion ignored the demand to return to the vehicle and instead took more steps toward the rocky beach. "I just saw someone move."

Dean would snicker if it didn't risk making noise. *A wave jostled the boat, asshole.*

"That was just a wave, fool." Victor had even less patience with Tweedledum than Dean did. He wondered what their connection was. Mentor and mentee assassins? Or two unconnected guns for hire?

The man turned, his profile to Dean as he looked inside the side-by-side at Neff. Dean pressed the zoom button on his camera. He was recording the entire scene, and this was his first chance to capture the guy's face.

"If it's fake, then maybe Dylan Slater set it up by himself, and his brother and Fiona are dead after all." The second man shouted the words to be heard over the engine and wind. The camera's microphone shouldn't have a problem capturing the conversation.

Victor twisted the key, shutting off the engine while muttering, "Fucking moron. Damn engineers think they know everyone's job."

The guy was an engineer? He must be from Pollux, then. But he wasn't Roy or John.

Victor climbed from the vehicle with his gun drawn. He'd clearly been around the block a few times and knew bait when he saw it. Unlike the Pollux engineer, who was in way over his head.

"And how would Dylan Slater know to place *three* people in the boat, not just one?" Victor shouted.

The other man cursed. "Fiona Carver cannot leave this island or we're all fucked."

Victor pointed his gun at the man's chest. "You should have thought of that before you planted the explosives and tried to kill me."

"*What?* I didn't! I wasn't trying to kill *you.*"

"Bullshit."

"I radioed you! I told you I'd set the charges. Why would I do that if I wanted to trap you in the cave?"

"You needed to know if I'd found them and how deep I was in the cave. When you realized how close we were to the entrance, you reset the timer, giving me less than three minutes." Victor took a menacing step toward the man. "The thing you need to understand is, I don't work for you. Once you brought my team on board to fix your problem, you bought yourself a new boss. Bratva doesn't take well to stupid Americans who think they can cut a deal, then back out at the first opportunity."

"*Bratva?* Jesus. Sylvia hired the Russian mafia?"

Victor let out a sharp laugh. "You are slow, my friend, but eventually you catch on."

"You were hired to kill Dylan Slater and stop anyone else on the team from finding him first." The increasingly agitated engineer waved toward the boat that rocked in the water, heading out to open sea. "And you were supposed to do it without crippling the project. You haven't found Slater, my camp is in ruins, my archaeologist is missing, and I can't hold off a search team much longer. You've ruined *everything.*"

Who was this guy? Dean hadn't met anyone from Pollux face-to-face—at least, not until he'd boarded the flight on Whidbey. Everything had been done online or by phone. But he'd interviewed with the top brass on the project, yet he had no clue who this man was.

Fiona might know, but she was hidden on the other side of the rotted-out Quonset hut.

Of the two men, Dean had no doubt Victor was the most dangerous, even though the other man was clearly desperate. It must be just dawning on him that Victor didn't need him now that he had a line on Dylan's location.

Once Victor had Dylan, Fiona, and Dean contained, he wouldn't need the engineer anymore. No reason to keep him alive, not when his Bratva cronies would swoop in and take what they wanted anyway.

Had Victor already located the impact crater and mother lode? Rare earth metals would be enough to make this venture profitable, but if what Dylan suspected about hafnium's nuclear isotope was correct, a cheap source of pure hafnium to experiment with gamma ray weapons would make the Russian Bratva—and their government—very happy.

"I think," Victor said, "I don't need you anymore. So I shall let Ms. Carver and the Slater brothers kill you."

"What? You aren't making sense."

Victor took a step forward, toward the engineer, walking slowly.

The man took a step backward, but all at once he seemed to remember that he had a gun and pulled it out, pointing it at Victor.

Victor didn't so much as flinch. "You think I'd let you keep bullets after what you did?"

The man pulled the trigger repeatedly, but all it did was dry fire. Clicking on the empty chamber.

Victor continued to approach the man at a slow, undaunted pace. And that was when Dean realized Victor was corralling him, backing him toward one of the pits Dylan had covered with a blanket of muskeg. The pit was full of diesel barrels and sharp metal rods pointing upward. It wasn't deep, but falling backward into it could do some damage.

When had Victor spotted it? And what else had he noticed?

His words, *I shall let Ms. Carver and the Slater brothers kill you,* were ominous.

Victor knew they were watching. Listening. He was a step ahead of them. And he was armed with a gun.

The engineer pitched backward, falling into the pit. He howled in pain. The fall hadn't killed him, but he was in agony, likely landing on a rebar spike or something equally terrible.

Dean thought of Dylan and figured that was a small justice.

Victor stood on the edge of the pit and stared down at the wailing man inside. "I think we should leave your boss here to suffer, don't you, Ms. Carver?"

THIRTY-SEVEN

Fiona had been reeling from the moment she'd caught sight of Victor's partner. Graham Sherwood. Her *boss*. He was a civilian engineer and head of the department that included cultural resources. The man she'd called from the Unangax̂ village to ask for a rescue.

He'd been here, on the island already at that point. He had to be for them to cross paths at the volcano just hours later. He must've been on a satellite phone. He'd set up the charges to close off the volcano entrance and probably taken down the tunnel Dylan had escaped through too. Of course he had. He was a structural engineer, and decades ago he'd served as a demolition expert for the navy. He knew explosives.

Hell, he probably had opened—or planned to open—another portal into the volcano with his explosives. No need to use the front door when a secret entrance was better.

She wondered if Victor realized he still needed Graham to access the volcano.

But then, the Russian mafia would probably bring in their own experts. Obviously, Sylvia, Trevor, and Graham had lost control of this scheme the minute Sylvia brought in Victor.

But why did Graham do it?

She knew he'd been upset at being passed over for the position of chief engineer for an Echelon-III-level job—the next echelon that would have relocated him to Hawaii, where he'd have been in charge of engineering projects for the entire Pacific region. But was he bitter enough over that to betray his country?

"Come out, Fiona. Don't you want to ask Sherwood some questions?"

Yes. Yes, she did. But revealing her location to Victor didn't seem like it was in their best interests right now.

"You don't understand, Ms. Carver. If you don't show yourself now, I will be forced to start using Sherwood's explosives to blow up every building on this base. Surely one of them contains you or the Slater brothers."

If he hadn't identified the tephra- and lahar-covered magazine as a structure, his threat was meaningless. What had her worried was how easily he'd spotted the covered pit.

Fiona crept forward so she could see Victor as he stood over her boss, who continued to moan in pain.

"Fi—Fiona. Please. *Help me.*"

What the hell did the guy expect her to do? And why would she? He'd probably told Victor the minute she'd reported something was off about him. Which was why Victor had disabled her phone and radios, cutting her off from the team. He'd probably removed the emergency tent and sleeping bags from the side-by-side, hoping she and Dean would die of exposure that first night.

The fog thickened even as the night deepened, casting everything in inky, clouded darkness.

All at once, a light shone up from the pit, landing in Victor's face, lighting him in a bright-white glow. Graham wasn't going to go quietly.

Victor snarled and closed his eyes, even as he leaned over and pointed his gun into the pit.

The rest happened so fast, she nearly missed it.

Dean launched himself at a blinded Victor, shoving him into the pit. The gun fired as he pitched forward, and she caught the flash.

Dean, carried by momentum, fell in on top of him.

Fiona gasped and bolted from her hiding place. She had to get Dean out before Victor managed to shoot him.

The three men grappled in the pit, the oily muck sloshing as Graham wailed and Dean and Victor fought for the gun.

"Get Dean clear, Fi," Dylan said, his voice low and steady.

She looked up to see him standing twenty feet away, leaning on his crutches, pointing the flare gun at the pit.

She hadn't even heard him slip from the magazine. He must've done that when she was launching the boat. The vehicle engine would have cloaked the noise.

She and Dean hadn't wanted him to be part of this showdown. Clearly he'd made his own plan.

She didn't have time to question his actions now. She needed to help Dean.

In the pit, Dean landed a blow on Victor's chin, then crawled forward, over his body, reaching for the far side of the narrow pit. Fiona ran to him and grabbed the hand reaching for a hold. She dug her heels into the soft earth and yanked. His skin was slippery due to the oil slick, but she got a grip thanks to his tight wristwatch.

He planted a foot on Graham's head and pushed forward, launching himself up and out, aided by her pull on his arm.

He landed on her, slick with mud and oil, and they both scrambled backward, away from the pit, Fiona moving as fast as she could in a crab walk, Dean crawling beside her. They needed distance. Dean was coated in the same diesel Victor and Graham were.

They'd gone ten feet. Fiona watched as Victor emerged from the pit, coming after them. Dylan pulled the trigger on the flare gun at that moment, sending the projectile into the Bratva assassin's back.

The man pitched forward, landing on the muddy muskeg as his back erupted in flames.

The fire spread, engulfing the pit.

Both Victor and Graham let out wails of pain. Victor got to his feet and stumbled toward them, his head wrapped in an orange halo of flames as his diesel-soaked hair burned. She and Dean got to their feet and easily avoided his dodging approach.

He turned to go after Dean but, at the last second, spun and ran down the rough slope, heading for the icy sea.

THIRTY-EIGHT

The first thing Dean did—after pressing a fast, oily kiss to Fiona's mouth—was grab a second camera and hit record. He turned, capturing the fire pit where Fiona's boss writhed, as well as the burning man trying to run for the water. Victor tripped and fell on the uneven ground as he burned, slowing his progress as he fled toward the sea.

This video would be evidence. Proof of what happened here. His other camera remained in the blind, facing the pit, where he'd focused once he realized that's where Victor was corralling Fiona's boss. It was still recording, and between that and this video, they'd have what they needed for authorities.

No way would he, Dylan, or Fiona take the fall for other people's crimes.

Victor stumbled twice more on his way to the water. He should have rolled while he was down, but the uneven lahar wasn't covered with damp leaves and mud like the muskeg, so perhaps he made the right choice in continuing to stumble toward the water.

He reached the shallow edge and stumbled again. It wasn't deep enough to submerge himself, and the burning fuel on his clothes transferred to the water. He was surrounded by floating flames. He struggled to rise, to get to deeper water so he could submerge himself, and at last he did, plunging forward, leaving a burning slick of fuel on the surface.

He remained underwater for a long time, then finally surfaced, out farther than Dean had expected. But now his clothes were saturated, and he was in over his head. He was injured and uncoordinated and struggling for air.

"What do we do?" Dylan asked. "Our only boat is out to sea, and we don't have any life preservers."

Dean turned to the pit, where Fiona's boss had gone silent. There was nothing they could have done for him. They didn't have fire extinguishers to douse the oil fire, and he'd been hopelessly trapped in the burning pit of diesel and other oils.

Dean remembered Fiona mentioning Graham had put the kibosh on cleaning up the leaking barrels sooner, even though the locals had been asking for the cleanup for years.

"We can throw Neff a line," Dean said. "But none of us risk our lives to save him."

"Agreed," Fiona answered, and he saw she had already tied paracord to her silicone collapsible field bucket. She handed Dean the other end of the line, then flattened the bucket and tossed it like a Frisbee out over the water, toward where Victor struggled.

It landed several feet short, and Dean reeled it in. This time, he threw the disk. It was short again but closer, and Victor swam toward it and grabbed on. It slipped from his grasp, and he went under.

Dean waited for him to surface. After a long moment, he reeled in the disk again and tossed it one more time, aiming for where he'd last seen Victor.

Minutes later, a body floated to the surface, facedown.

He took Fiona's hand in his and squeezed.

He held his breath, his heart pounding as he watched the water for signs Victor was alive. After a minute, he released Fiona's hand. Much as he didn't want to, they were out of options unless they wanted the body to float out to sea. Without overthinking it, Dean stripped down to his underwear.

"You can't swim out there," Fiona said. "The water is freezing. He's not worth it."

"It'll rinse a little of the oil from my skin, and that body is more proof Sylvia hired Bratva to hunt Dylan." He handed her his clothes. "Rinse what you can from the outer layers. Keep the long underwear dry."

Then he stepped into the frigid water up to his thighs and pushed off, torpedoing for the body that floated on the surface, heading for the narrow entrance to the small, shallow bay.

His body burned with the cold, making it hard to breathe. But still, he was careful as he approached Victor, in case this was some kind of trap, treading water next to the body for a period of time, making sure the head never turned to take a breath.

Once he was certain Victor was dead, he grabbed the man's jacket and tugged him toward shore. It wasn't long before Dean's feet touched bottom, and he stood, dragging the body up the beach and over the rocks, finally laying him on his back next to the rusted-out Quonset hut.

Dylan shone a light on his face, and it was clear why Victor had struggled in the water and had been unable to breathe. His face must've been coated in oil, as what remained of his facial skin was raw, red streaks, the musculature beneath charred.

Even if they'd pulled him from the water the moment he'd doused the flames, he probably wouldn't have survived.

It was stunning he'd lasted as long as he did.

Fiona pressed Dean's long underwear into his arms. "You can wear this in the car and ride in the front with the sleeping bag." She turned to Dylan. "You'll be in the back so you can stretch out your leg as much as possible. I'll drive."

"What do we do with him?" Dylan asked. "His body won't fit in the rear storage. Not with our gear."

"We'll put him in the magazine and plug the hole," Fiona said, "so animals won't get to him before investigators arrive. Maybe there's still a chance to identify him."

If the guy was really Russian Bratva, identification wasn't likely. But given what he'd said on video, Sylvia would probably be desperate to cut a deal and answer questions. Not that there was anyone else she could implicate other than Trevor.

"I've got video of everything that happened tonight. He's in shadows, but maybe I managed to get his face. Plus, he would've needed to show some kind of ID to get to Adak and Chiksook."

"Yeah, but he didn't take a military flight; they won't have copies of his ID. We don't really know *how* he got to Adak, come to think of it. He might have been there already when we arrived."

Dean turned to face the diesel pit. It still burned, pumping out black smoke. "No way can we put this out." He placed an arm around Fiona and pulled her to his side. "I'm sorry, Fi. Sorry he betrayed you."

She leaned her head on his shoulder. "I'm still kind of in shock about that. I always got along with Graham. I wonder if this was simple greed or something more?"

He pressed his lips to her hair. "We'll get answers."

After a moment, she pulled away. "How are you not shivering?"

He nodded toward the burning pit of oil. "Adrenaline, and that thing is pumping out a lot of heat."

"Oh. Right."

Still, warming oneself by a diesel fire that had, essentially, killed two men was kind of macabre. So he doffed his wet boxer briefs and pulled on his wool long underwear, then grabbed his boots. He hadn't even noticed the pain of walking barefoot on the rocks up the beach after pulling Victor from the water. Adrenaline was a dangerous drug, because now he saw gashes on his feet that he'd have to treat with antibiotic ointment.

Later, when Fiona was driving them toward safety, he could deal with his feet. Right now, they needed to get the hell out of here.

After all, they were fairly certain Sherwood and Neff had been the only hunters on this island, but they had no way of knowing for sure.

THIRTY-NINE

The drive across the island would take at least three hours in the dark fog. Thankfully, it hadn't rained in a few days, and the roads weren't as slick as the first time Fiona and Dean had set out in that direction. But still, the dark and fog meant she had to go slow, which was the opposite of what her nerves wanted.

Holy hell. Her boss had betrayed not just her but their country. He'd taken the same oath to protect the Constitution that she had when he'd signed on for federal service. Worse, he'd been in the military, a combat engineer. From there, he'd taken a civilian job with the US Army Corps of Engineers before switching to the navy about a dozen years ago, where he'd moved up the ranks until he was the head of their division for the Pacific Northwest.

What would bring a man who'd honorably served in the military, who'd then worked as a civilian for the Department of Defense, to decide to cash in on a project in this way?

Did he think finding the meteorite was a winning lottery ticket, his to redeem? Was he bitter about being passed over for promotion? There had to be something more for this sharp turn in allegiance.

Whose idea had it been? The only things they knew were that Sylvia Jessup and Trevor Watson were both fully on board, and Sylvia had brought in Victor when things went south. Now she couldn't help but wonder if there was some undisclosed relationship between Graham and Sylvia? That would be blackmail-worthy, considering he was managing the project for the navy and she was overseeing several sections of the EIS.

She paused on that thought as the vehicle took a particularly hard bump. "Sorry!" she said to Dylan, who grunted in pain from the back seat.

"I'm thinking it's time to dig out that bottle of whiskey," Dylan said.

"An open bottle in the car?" she said in mock horror. "What if I get pulled over?"

Dylan laughed. "Oh, man. Wouldn't that be sweet? I've never wanted to see flashing red and blue lights in the rearview so badly."

She thought about it and decided she agreed. It would be lovely if there were a battalion of cops on this island.

Dean grabbed something from the small pack between his feet and handed it back to his brother. "Gotcha covered."

"You put the booze with the road trip snacks?"

"Yep. But road trips aren't the same without Cracker Jack."

"Cracker Jack?" she asked. "What are you, eighty?"

"Our mom never let us have Cracker Jack except on road trips," Dylan explained. "And Dean . . . he'd always eat the entire box slooooowly, before he even touched the prize."

"Whereas Dylan dug through the box, spilling half the contents, just to get to the temporary tattoo."

"And then we'd spend the next half of the drive bargaining for more Cracker Jack or arguing over who got the better prize," Dylan added.

"Lord. I bet you were adorable as kids, but your parents were exhausted."

"Pretty much," Dean said. "Dad said he always wanted two . . . but not necessarily at the same time."

"Mom decided she preferred flying with flight attendants delivering alcohol at regular intervals." In the rearview, she saw Dylan hold up the bottle Dean had handed him and take a long sip.

Their story brought back memories of her own family on road trips. Three kids crammed in the back seat, fussing and fighting and laughing. Her father at the wheel while her mom tried to entertain them with license plate games and verbal puzzles. She missed them all so much, her heart ached with it. Both her mother and her brother were still alive, but both were lost to her in very different ways.

"If you want, Fi, I can take over driving," Dean said. "I'm warm now. Feet bandaged."

"I'm fine."

Truth was, she didn't want to give up the driver's seat. The minute she stopped having to focus, she might just fall apart. She couldn't let that happen. Not now. Not in front of these two men who'd been through so much.

She had to hold it together.

She tightened her grip on the wheel and fixed her gaze on the foggy road visible in the glow of the headlights. She would deliver them to safety. Then, when she was alone, she'd fall apart.

———

It was after eleven p.m. local time when they arrived at the village. Dean was pretty sure Fiona was operating on fumes, but somehow, she managed to give the village chairwoman a coherent description of what had happened, and the leaders of the village were all called to a meeting as phone calls were made and they each were handed phones to give their accounts to different authorities. Some tribal, some state, some federal.

The FBI said they'd send a team from the Anchorage field office first thing in the morning. Promises were made for a medevac airlift for Dylan at the same time. Sometime in the wee hours, there was nothing left to be said. Their hostess was asleep in her room, while Dylan was asleep in Marion's guest bed, where he'd crashed after enjoying a hot meal prepared by one of the elders.

Fiona was unsteady on her feet, suffering full adrenaline crash, and Dean wasn't doing much better.

"You should sleep in the guest bed with Dylan," she said. "I'll take the couch."

It was the first time in days they didn't *have* to sleep curled up in the same sleeping bag, and . . . he didn't like it.

He hadn't shared a bed without sex with a woman in more than ten years, and now, he didn't want to sleep alone. It was a little unsettling, but he figured given the week they'd had, he could tell that part of his brain to shut the hell up. He wanted to lean in to this feeling. "I want to hold you. Now. Tonight."

"I don't know if I can do that."

"Why not? I've held you for the last four nights."

"Because you had to. Not because you chose to."

"Tonight, I choose to."

"Why?"

"Because I care about you."

"Because you want to seduce me."

"I don't want to seduce you tonight. Not here. Not like this."

"I know. But that's your end goal. It's not me. It's sex."

"I want you *and* sex. Sex with you. I want you. All of you. But tonight, I just want to hold you. We've been through hell together, and I want to feel you, alive and breathing in my arms."

Those words were truer than he wanted to admit. In the end, when Violet had faced her last weeks, all he'd wanted was to lie by her side in the hospital bed they'd set up in their living room and hold her. To live every minute they had left with her in his arms.

This wasn't that. He wasn't trying to repeat what he'd shared with Violet, but he did understand the deeper intimacy of holding someone you cared about and just experiencing the preciousness of life and being together. Sharing the same breath and orbit.

He wanted to hold Fiona so he could be there for her if she fell apart. As she'd been there for him that night in the volcano, when he'd cried at the possibility of losing Dylan.

Fiona had held back her story from him. He knew it. Tonight, he wanted nothing more than to give her the space to feel.

She leaned against him. "I'm afraid I might cry."

"All the more reason to let me hold you."

"I don't want you to see me cry."

"Then we'll turn out the lights. Just like in the volcano."

She gave in then, her whole body relaxing against his. "Promise me you won't turn on the lights."

"Promise."

They set up a bed on the floor, once again employing the narrow sleeping pad and extra-wide sleeping bag, but now they had pillows and extra blankets for padding, so they opened the bag as they'd done when Dylan joined them in sleep.

After brushing teeth and using the bathroom, Dean turned out the side table lamp and crawled into their makeshift bed beside her and pulled her into his arms. She smelled of soap and flowers—they'd both taken showers between phone calls, and Dean had helped Dylan wash as well.

Dylan had grumbled at the indignity of needing his brother's help to bathe, but after six weeks of sponge baths without soap, he wasn't about to refuse, and Dean was skilled in this area after taking care of Violet.

It was glorious to be clean again, the diesel fuel scrubbed from his skin, but the sleeping bag had absorbed the odors of their journey, including the black smoke of the contaminated gas fire, making sure his olfactory senses kept the memory of what happened tonight front and center.

He pressed his nose to Fiona's clean hair and breathed deeply. "There's something you've been holding back."

He felt her nod against his chest.

"If you want to tell me, I'm here. Listening."

"I was certain Dylan was dead."

He nodded in the dark, his arms tightening around her. He'd suspected that, and he understood. She didn't need to feel bad about it, but he sensed she did. "I understand. I probably would have too, in your shoes. But for me . . . I just couldn't."

"It's not that. I mean, yeah, that's part of it. But there's more. You see, five years ago, my sister went missing."

His heart squeezed. This was an ominous beginning. She'd never once mentioned having a sister, even as he'd spent days talking about his brother. He'd . . . assumed she was an only child?

But all he said was, "Your sister?"

"Regan. My baby sister. I have an older brother too, Aidan. But this is about Regan, who was three years younger than me and brighter than the sun."

The name Regan rang a bell. Why was that? But what he said was, "You're using past tense for Regan."

"It's the only tense that applies."

"I'm so sorry. You don't have to tell me, but I want to be here for you."

"That's the thing. I couldn't tell you before. Because I didn't want to take away your hope." Her hand settled on his chest, over his heart, pressing on the violet tattoo. His clothes were all rank, so he'd stripped to his underwear for sleeping inside a warm house, and she wore underwear and a T-shirt. They were closer to naked than they'd ever been together, and her hand was on his bare skin. But nothing about this touch was sexual, and he didn't want it to be, didn't react as if it were.

"Tell me."

"She went into archaeology because of me."

Again, the name Regan tickled at his brain, but he shoved it aside so he could focus on her words.

"When I was a junior in college, I did my archaeological field school—it was like summer camp for people who could drink and screw around without consequences, and it was a blast, if you liked that sort of thing. Regan visited the camp for a weekend—eighteen and a senior in high school, it was such an adventure for her—and this guy from my field school was all over her. I'm pretty sure she lost her virginity to him, and while I wasn't thrilled, because he'd been hitting on every woman in camp before Regan showed up, it was also a case of her body, her choice, and I wasn't going to freak out and get judgy on her. She wasn't that into him, so it's not like he broke her heart or anything.

"She decided to go into archaeology after that—she wanted her own field school and the adventure of dig bumming. It can be a nomadic existence if that's what you want, and that was totally Regan. I was the one who wanted the stability of working for one company and living in the same place. She wanted to live out of her car and bounce from project to project. She was a free spirit all the way, dig bumming in California, Oregon, Washington, Idaho, and Nevada. She had half a dozen companies she worked for, and some projects lasted only a few days, some several months. More often than not, she hooked up with one of the guys on the crew."

"Did that bother you?" he asked as his hand stroked her back.

"Not at all. Except for the guy at field school, she was generally a good judge of character, and she always got involved on her own terms. She was so much better at flings than I was—I'd had a few field . . . *relationships* at that point, and they never ended well. Found out when it was over that one guy had a girlfriend—who was pregnant! Another guy just never intended for it to be more, even though he said otherwise when we were sharing a tent for a month. I was pretty sour on the whole field-fling thing out of the gate, but not Regan. No. She loved the ephemeral nature of fieldwork and fieldmen."

So she came by her aversion to flings both naturally and in response to some assholes. He felt a surge of anger for the cheater and the liar and the scars they'd etched into this amazing woman's heart.

"Anyway, five years ago," Fiona continued, "she was on a project in Eastern Washington, near Coulee Dam. It was a survey of the Lake Roosevelt area for flood control. She was twenty-seven years old, and this time the guy she was sleeping with was her boss, the owner of the small consulting firm. It wasn't a sexual harassment or pressure issue—she had no trouble getting field jobs and didn't care if she advanced with his small company. I'm fairly certain she was the one who pursued him. She'd first hooked up with him on a project down in Richland, but when that ended, he didn't want her to move on, so he convinced her to do the Lake Roosevelt job with him.

"She had misgivings—she had a longer project lined up in Eastern Oregon she wanted to take—but he begged her, said he needed her, and she *liked* him, so she decided to take the job. She showed up at the campground her boss had reserved, expecting to find a full field crew, but it was just Jeff. She drove to town—there was no cell reception at the campground—and called me that night. Freaked out. Said she was worried there wasn't even a project, that it was all fake.

"I begged her to quit. To drive to Seattle. Told her she could live with me for a few months until she lined up another job. I knew a company that was hiring lab techs. She could have worked for them and been safe." Fiona's voice broke on the word *safe*.

And now he knew why Regan's name was familiar. He cleared his throat. "I spent weeks looking for you. Online. All I had to go on was the name *Fiona* and *archaeologist*."

"You found Regan instead."

He nodded and pulled her close. He couldn't hold her tight enough now that he knew what she was about to tell him. "The news article didn't identify you as an archaeologist, so I set it aside."

"There was no need to identify my profession. I was just the sister who found her body."

That was the part that was the sucker punch. This past week, as he was searching for Dylan, she was reliving the nightmare of finding her sister.

Of course she hadn't believed he'd find Dylan alive. How could she believe anything else?

He knew from the article that when it was reported that Regan was missing, a huge hunt ensued. Her sister had driven out from Seattle to join the search and was the one who'd found the body.

According to Jeffrey Koster, who'd given a statement to the reporter, Regan Carver had fallen from a cliff into the lake during the archaeological survey, and her body had been swept away.

"You don't think Regan's fall was an accident," Dean said.

"I don't. For good reason. I mean, aside from Regan's call when she told me she was uncomfortable with Jeff." She cleared her throat. "You see, when I was sixteen and Regan thirteen, our dad died in a climbing accident."

Dean's breath left him in a rush. He should have guessed when she'd said her climbing days were over, and then there was her fear of the steep cliffside hike and natural bridge.

"Yeah," she said, proving she could read his thoughts. "That's where my fear of heights comes from. We all loved climbing with our dad, but after that, neither Regan nor I could stomach it. Given that, I know there is no way she would have been standing close enough to that cliff edge to fall."

He tightened his arms around her and stroked her back.

"She wasn't ever diagnosed with acrophobia or basophobia—which is fear of falling—so there was no real proof except my word. And Jeff *did* have a survey project there. Regan was wrong about that."

"Is he still working in the Pacific Northwest?"

"Yes. He's the reason I don't go to local conferences. I'm not part of the Pacific Northwest archaeological community—beyond the job, that is."

He pressed her head to his chest, so close to his heart. "I'm so sorry, sweetheart. I'm so sorry you lost your sister. So sorry you were the one who found her. And so sorry you had to relive it all this week, as I was relentless in my need to search for Dylan."

"But you found him. So maybe I can start having hope again."

"*You* found him. Or maybe he found us. I'm not entirely sure about that part."

She let out a soft laugh. "We found him. Or we all found each other. I'm elated the outcome was different. Happy for you and for Dylan." But still he heard a sad note in her voice, and his heart ached. He never wanted this woman to feel pain. He wanted to protect her from grief and loss. But it was too late for her, just as it was for him.

He threaded his fingers through her hair. "It's okay to let go, honey. I've got you."

"I know you do."

It was her confidence in him that made his heart surge. Her utter trust. He kissed her hair and held her close, and after a long while, she let out a shuddering breath; then he felt her body quake against him, and he knew the dam had broken, and she was letting out the trauma of reliving her sister's death over and over as they searched the caves for Dylan.

He rubbed her back and held her, and as she'd cried with him when he let loose his fears for Dylan that night in the cave, now he cried with her, deeply saddened that there had once been another amazing Carver archaeologist whom he would never get a chance to meet.

FORTY

Marion Flanders watched as Dylan Slater was loaded into the navy Osprey; then his brother the photographer and the archaeologist climbed inside. She and the rest of the people in her village had gathered in the schoolyard to watch them leave, and as one, they waved when the military aircraft lifted from the ground like a helicopter.

Once they were high enough, the helicopter would become a plane, and Dylan Slater would be ensconced in a hospital in Anchorage far faster than if a simple helicopter had been employed for their rescue.

She turned to her people and nodded to the elders. It was time for their meeting. They had decisions to make with far-reaching implications.

The families dispersed, but all the adults of the village—twelve people; eight women, four men—headed straight for the meetinghouse next to the church. They each took their place around the table, with her at the head.

Henry led the opening prayer. He was brief this morning, a sign they were all in a hurry to discuss the issues at hand.

Without preamble, Marion passed around her iPad with photos downloaded from Dean Slater's camera. Photos of the sacred site her people had protected for well over a thousand years.

"It can't be a mistake that the photographer was Dean Slater," Henry said.

There were murmurs of agreement around the table. Slater had been approved by their most esteemed elder five years before. And his recent photos were respectful. No images of the ancestors, just the arti-facts that proved the stories handed down by the generations.

"They found it, then. The stone." The speaker was Lorraine, the vil-lage teacher, who made sure the children learned English and Unangam Tunuu.

"Yes," Marion said. "But they don't know they found it. Don't real-ize the meteorite was hidden by the remains of the ancestors. They have no idea how close they were to the source stone."

"And now that the remains of the ancestors are known to be there, law prevents anyone from legally entering the chamber," Noah said.

She nodded. "Fiona Carver has assured me the burial chamber will be protected—at least from legal desecration. We will have to remain vigilant for Russian looters."

"What about that geologist Trevor Watson? He asked far too many questions about the meteorite when he was here with Dylan weeks ago."

"He was arrested this morning," Marion said. "Carver was notified of the arrest before the sun was up."

"Good," Lorraine said, and heads around the table nodded in agreement.

They'd all been concerned when the geologist asked so many ques-tions that day. Her people had been protecting the secret of *Kanuux̂* for centuries. *Kanuux̂*—heart, in their language—wasn't the name of Mount Katin, as they'd told Dylan once upon a time; it was the name of the stone buried in her depths. Their oral history of the volcano went further back than they'd ever told any anthropologist or colonizer.

"If what is said about the meteorite's elemental content is true," said Virgil, the youngest among them, "then shouldn't we consider claiming it for ourselves? We could buy so much for our people. We wouldn't need the submarine base to get the navy to build us roads and a reliable power plant."

She'd known to expect this question and also knew Virgil would be the one to raise it. And it wasn't an idea she could dismiss out of hand. There were Alaska Native Corporations who did sell access to their prehistory, and while it was easy to cast judgment, it was harder to survive. Their decisions, she knew, while they might not match her own, would never be taken lightly.

Henry was not so gentle with his feelings on the matter. "Absolutely not." The words, delivered with steely calm, were as good as a shout coming from him.

Lorraine placed her hand on her husband's arm. "We will hear out the pros and cons and then vote."

The pros were long, and all were about money and infrastructure for the island. The cons were fewer but deeply felt.

"We will get the navy to pay for those things anyway," Noah said, adding to the cons. "They will build everything we need if they place the submarine base here, plus they will protect *Kanuux̂*. Russian looters will not be able to access the island as long as there is an active US naval base here."

Lorraine stood from her seat, and Marion saw the teacher rising to impart knowledge to her students. "One thing we must remember is the warnings that were passed down by the ancestors, the reason we protect the secret of *Kanuux̂*. They felt the explosive power of the meteorite. Many were injured and a few died. Remember what the ancestors said: *'The end of the earth will come from a sickness of the heart.'* They referred to the explosive reaction, but now we know hafnium is even more dangerous. If it can be used to make gamma ray weapons, that is indeed a sickness of *Kanuux̂* that could destroy the world. I hereby motion we continue keeping the secret and charge the generations that come after us with doing the same."

The motion carried unanimously.

———

Fiona leaned against Dean in the small hospital waiting room. They were alone in the room outside the surgery suite. Both their gazes were fixed on the twenty-four-hour news channel offering up headlines. Dylan had been in surgery for hours, and the story of his rescue from Chiksook Island was on repeat on the TV.

Sylvia Jessup had been arrested at the same time as Trevor Watson. Dean felt a spike of hostility every time they showed the clip of Sylvia's perp walk from the FBI vehicle to the federal detention center in Seattle, where she would be held prior to her arraignment.

The FBI had worked fast, but they'd had to, knowing she was likely to flee the moment she learned Dylan had been found alive. Same with Trevor, although he, apparently, was already on the run and had been found thanks to his Good To Go! pass, which registered an early-morning trip over the Tacoma Narrows Bridge on the way from his Gig Harbor home to SeaTac Airport.

Dean picked up the remote to the TV. "I can't watch anymore." He flipped channels, finally landing on the first Indiana Jones movie. "Ahh. A classic."

"You do realize this movie opens with our hero stealing an artifact, destroying the site in the process, and then running from the natives who were just protecting their heritage? He's basically the worst archaeologist ever."

Dean laughed. "Yeah. But it's fun to watch if you tell yourself he's a looter and a thief and try to forget he's supposed to be an archaeologist."

"That's fair. But worth noting universities have to include lectures in their Archaeology 101 classes to break down all the ways these movies spread terrible misinformation about the profession."

"Ouch. I can change the channel if you want."

"Nah. I like watching Marion. She's smart and strong and takes care of herself."

"Marion is totally hot," Dean said. "You know what we should watch . . . the movie with Kathleen Turner and Michael Douglas.

Romancing the Stone. She's trying to find her sister, and they follow a map to a treasure—a stone—called 'the heart' in Spanish."

She laughed softly, leaning against him again. "Don't they spend the night in a drug dealer's crashed airplane at some point?"

"Yeah. A Douglas DC-3." He wrapped an arm around her shoulders. It felt so right having her at his side.

"You know the *plane*?"

"I like planes. I think it comes with testosterone."

"Is this your way of trying to tell me you were after the meteorite all along? Because I don't believe it. I mean, we *did* find your brother."

He chuckled. "But . . . this is the reverse. You're the one who was after the stone. You said so that first day—you wanted to get back the stone that had been collected from the site."

"Maybe, but . . . the hero—or antihero?—was collecting birds to sell at the beginning, I think. And you're Hot Bird Man. Not me."

"Oh my God. You're just pretending to not remember the movie. I mean, who remembers that Jack was collecting *birds*?"

"Jack?" she said suspiciously. "You remember his name?"

He pursed his lips, feeling somehow sheepish for not admitting it from the start. "I might have watched it on Netflix or HBO in the recent past. There's a Land Rover in it. I never pass up watching movies with Land Rovers. I like them even more than airplanes."

"Uh-huh." She paused. "So did they get stuck in a volcano at some point?"

"No. Now you're thinking of *Journey to the Center of the Earth*. The one with Brendan Fraser and the kid from *The Hunger Games*."

"Oh yeah. Hey. They were looking for a volcanologist brother in that one."

"They find him too . . ." His voice trailed off as he remembered that scene in the movie, which in turn reminded him of her sister. He cleared his throat. "But there are also dinosaurs, so I think that's pretty much where the similarities end."

The door to the waiting room opened, and they both rose to their feet to greet the surgeon. The man had a confident smile on his face—very different from the tempered demeanor he'd had prior to surgery. "Dylan came through with flying colors, and I'm happy to say the bone looks good. Better than I expected. We had to make some adjustments and screw him back together, but with a lot of physical therapy, he should get full mobility back."

Dean felt a weight lift from his chest. "Oh, thank God." He'd worried about Dylan's weakened condition going into surgery. What if his heart couldn't handle it?

"Thank you so much, Doctor. When can we see him?" Fiona asked.

"He's still in recovery. He should be moved to his room in an hour or two. You can visit him then."

After the doctor left them alone, Dean turned to her. "Why don't you go to the hotel and get settled in? Maybe rest a bit? I'm fine alone here."

The FBI had set them up in two rooms in a large hotel that they'd yet to visit. She looked exhausted, and he still had adrenaline to keep him going. Plus, nothing would pry him from the hospital before he'd had a chance to talk to Dylan, see that he was okay.

She nodded. "I suppose I could use a good soak in the tub. You'll call me as soon as he's awake?"

"I promise."

He kissed her softly and watched her leave, his heart still in a jumble. This intimacy between them was dangerous. He wanted her. All of her. But she didn't do flings—and now that he knew why, any idea of crossing that line was impossible. He could not, and would not, offer her more.

But what if she initiated it? Could he take what she offered, knowing in the long run it would hurt her?

Could he sleep with her and walk away?

Two hours later, he was no closer to an answer as he walked into Dylan's hospital room. His brother was propped up on the bed, eyes closed, but he smiled at the sound of footsteps and cracked open one eye. "Hey, bro," he whispered. "Was kinda hoping your better half would be here."

Dean smiled and moved to stand next to his brother's bed. "She's much nicer to look at, that's for sure."

"Take good care of her, man. Or I'm gonna break *your* leg."

He didn't know what to say to that. Fiona wasn't his. Wouldn't be his. "You know I don't do relationships."

"Sh-she's worth being an excep-ception." His voice slurred a little, having a bit of a dreamy quality that came with heavy sedation.

Dean had no doubt about that. But he didn't think he had it in him to love like that again. But this wasn't the time to tell his brother that.

He placed his hand over Dylan's and squeezed. "How about you focus on healing?"

"I mean it. If I didn't want you to be ha-happy, I'd go after Fiona myself. Don't blow it."

Dean's entire body tensed. "What do you mean? I thought you weren't interested in her?"

"Of course I was interested. Shhhhe made it clear shhe wasnn't interested in coworkers, s-so . . . thought of you."

Dylan had wanted Fiona all along?

Dylan, who would love her without reservations?

Dean took a deep breath and dropped into the visitor's chair. He fixed his gaze on his beloved brother's face and tried not to think about anything except how grateful he was that his brother was safe and recovering at last.

FORTY-ONE

It was strange, crawling into bed by herself in her hotel room, but the FBI had booked two rooms without asking, and it would have felt even stranger to tell them they only needed one room and one bed.

She'd figured Dean would ignore the second room and join her in her bed, but after a late dinner in the hotel restaurant, he'd accompanied her to her door, politely kissed her good night, then sauntered down the hall toward the stairs, heading to his own room two floors below.

She'd stood in the foyer of her room in indecision for minutes as she debated what his walking away like that meant. Last night he'd been insistent on holding her. Tonight, he hadn't even offered.

But he was likely as confused as she was, his emotions in turmoil after all they'd gone through. Elation topped the list, certainly, but there was still trauma to process.

She took a long bath—her second one today—as she tried to force her brain to relax. In the tub, she decided it was a good thing he'd walked away. After all, she was flying home to Seattle tomorrow, and he would remain in Anchorage until Dylan was discharged and able to fly home.

She needed to sort out her life—including facing her job after she'd watched her boss cook in a vat of oil.

Her coworkers were being investigated. Others in the office could have been in on Graham's scheme. There weren't a lot of places she was comfortable working in the Pacific Northwest, considering everyone in her field knew she believed Jeff Koster had murdered her sister, and the man was a respected archaeologist in the CRM world.

If she couldn't work for the navy anymore, there weren't a lot of places for her to go.

And what would Dean do now? He'd said he wanted Dylan to move back to Southern California, live with him while he recovered and went through physical therapy. Dean would probably resume his carefree playboy lifestyle between jaunts around the globe for lengthy expeditions.

She didn't feel *jealous* of the women he would sleep with, per se. After all, they didn't get his heart. All they got was sex.

Fiona, quite simply, wanted both.

So now she slipped between the clean sheets of her hotel room bed and had neither.

She lay there in the darkened room, eyes wide open as she stared at the ceiling. Dean had promised to drive her to the airport in the morning. He'd rented a car so he could go to and from the hospital with ease while he was stuck in Anchorage.

After she passed through security, would she ever see him again?

She had no doubt she'd see Dylan. He'd insist on it, and so would she. But Dean was different. He didn't *want* to feel. The best way to avoid feeling things was to avoid people who made you feel.

She'd bet money that Dean would be conveniently out of town if she flew south to visit Dylan. And she was certain he'd avoid Washington altogether.

If tomorrow would be the last time she ever saw Dean, was she really risking anything if she went to him tonight? After all, she knew the rules. He wasn't married and didn't have a pregnant girlfriend. Wasn't lying about his feelings to get her into bed.

He'd said he wanted to possess her, and damn, but she wanted to be possessed like that, just once. To have a wild, perfect night with an incredible man she admired. She wanted his heart, yes. But she also

354

wanted a simple, pure, raw, and carnal connection. With him. Only with him.

She tossed off the covers and practically sprang from the bed, her mind made up. She pulled on the jeans and top she'd purchased earlier when she'd taken a few hours to herself while he waited in the hospital. The one thing she didn't think to buy was condoms. But she could remedy that. The hotel had a small store in the lobby.

She checked her appearance in the mirror with a small laugh. She'd spent days with the man without a real shower, and *now* she worried about how she looked?

She hurried to the elevator and jabbed the button impatiently. She didn't want to lose her nerve, and with every second that passed, she was in danger of doing just that.

In the lobby, she grabbed a three-pack of condoms, then on impulse grabbed a bottle of champagne and a box of prepackaged chocolate cupcakes with peppermint frosting. They weren't LUNA bars, but they'd do. "Do you have champagne glasses I can bring to my room?" she asked the cashier.

"You can get some from the bar. Just give them your room number."

"Perfect. Thanks."

The woman bagged her purchases, and Fiona crossed the lobby for the dark bar, nearly empty at this late hour. She made a beeline for the bartender, and he gave her two flutes.

Feeling an excited rush, she turned, holding the glasses in one hand and a bag of goodies in the other. Her gaze landed on a couple standing next to a booth. The woman wore a skintight cocktail dress that was out of place in Anchorage. Her body was pressed to the man's, her hand on his chest in an intimate pose as the man wrapped his arms around her.

No. No. She was imagining things. It was dark, and her brain was filling in details.

He must've heard her gasp, though, because he looked up, and the light hit his face, highlighting his blond hair, trim beard, and blue Newman eyes.

The champagne flutes slipped from her fingers and shattered with a loud crash on the bar's concrete floor.

———

The look of shock and horror on Fiona's face was enough to rip Dean's heart out. He pushed Becca away. "Sorry! I'll call you tomorrow." He shouted the words over his shoulder as he bolted after Fiona, running from the bar and into the wide, brightly lit lobby. "Fiona! Stop!"

She jabbed at the elevator button at the far end, and the door opened. She slipped inside.

He had no choice but to continue the gruesome scene for everyone in the lobby to hear, and he shouted, "She's my wife's sister!" as the doors closed in front of her.

The Black man behind the reception desk shook his head. "My dude. That does *not* make it better."

Dean let out a pained laugh and ran a hand over his face. "My *dead* wife," he clarified for the man. At least Fiona would understand.

A moment later, the elevator doors opened again, and there was Fiona, white as a sheet and still the most beautiful woman alive. "I'm listening," she said.

He stepped into the elevator. "Thank you."

He reached to pull her into a hug, but she stepped back, clutching a shopping bag to her chest. "Start talking."

He looked at the panel of buttons. "Your room or mine?"

"My room. So I can kick you out if I need to."

He jabbed the button for her floor. "Fair enough."

"You didn't tell me your wife had a sister."

356

"I didn't tell you anything about my wife's family. And I didn't realize Becca lives in Anchorage now or I *would* have mentioned her. I didn't know I would see her tonight. I set up my new phone this morning but had it turned off in the hospital, per their rules, and didn't bother to call in to my old number to check messages until after we had dinner. She'd seen the news. They named the hospital Dylan was in, so she guessed I was in town and asked if we could meet. I figured my life is already an emotional wreck, so why not?"

The doors opened on her floor, and they headed to Fiona's room. "You don't get along with your wife's family?" she asked.

"No. Only Violet's grandmother liked me. Everyone else thought I was after her for her money. You see, Violet had a massive trust fund."

"And you inherited it."

"I did."

She swiped her key card in front of the sensor, and the light clicked green. Fiona pushed open the door, and Dean followed her inside, thankful she was hearing him out.

She made a beeline for the fridge and then grimaced at the contents of her bag before pulling out a bottle of champagne and stuffing it in the fridge.

He remembered the shattering glasses, and his heart squeezed as he realized she'd been clutching two champagne flutes in the bar.

Two. This was her last night in Alaska, and she had a bottle of champagne and two flutes. "What else is in the bag?" he asked, his throat feeling dry.

"None of your business."

He had a feeling it was but didn't say as much.

"Tell me about your wife and her supermodel waif of a sister."

Come to think of it, Becca *was* pretty and waiflike. And she'd been dressed in a form-fitting cocktail gown worthy of an heiress who'd just left some fundraiser for a politician running for the Senate. Becca was filling the stilettos her parents wanted her to fill as the socialite philanthropist who provided excellent PR for the family business.

Good lord. What Fiona had seen was ripe for misinterpretation, and his reputation only made it worse.

He explained the fundraiser, which in turn explained Becca's polished look, which wasn't exactly normal for Anchorage, Alaska, and Fiona probably knew it. He then returned to his unpleasant situation with Violet's family.

"Violet's parents pretty much hated me. But they were also damn controlling of Violet, so she wasn't too fond of them either. We weren't married yet when she was diagnosed, and when she got sick, she was terrified of the decisions they would make if they had medical power of attorney for her. Including the fact that they would prevent me from being by her side. She begged me to marry her. She trusted me with the big decisions and wanted me with her until the end."

"Oh. Damn. You weren't married yet when she was diagnosed? No wonder they thought you were after her money."

"Bingo." He dropped onto the foot of her bed, the emotional upheavals of the day too much for him to stay on his feet any longer. "Becca was in her teens when Violet and I married. Barely twenty when Violet died. She always believed her parents' take on the situation. But over the years, her grandmother has had some sway, and she's also experienced her parents' controlling behavior. She chose Alaska for her home to get away from them. Tonight, she said she'd wanted to reach out to me for some time. Today, when she realized I was in Anchorage, she saw her chance. Got my cell number from the family's trust attorney."

She stepped close to him, and he reached out and pulled her onto his lap and buried his face in her neck. "Fi. I would never do anything like that. Would never hurt you in that way."

"I-I'm sorry I jumped to conclusions like I did."

"I get it. I realize what it must've looked like. But please know, I'm not such a hound dog that I couldn't even give you one night to come around. Sweetheart, at the core of my job is patience. It's all about waiting for the right moment, the right shot. And you, Fiona Carver, are what I want."

Even as he said the words, he hesitated. He wanted her. Yes. For today. Right now. But he couldn't give her more.

Fiona's mouth pressed to his, and he took what she offered. It was a sweet kiss as her tongue slid along his, deep, slow, and passionate. His erection pressed against her ass as she made a soft sound in the back of her throat.

They could follow this languid kiss all the way between the sheets. If he was correct about what he suspected was in the shopping bag, he could slide between her thighs and possess her completely, worshipping her as he'd promised.

But what of tomorrow? He would say goodbye and close off his heart to her. Would that be worse than never having her at all?

She pushed him back on the bed, then crawled up his body, straddling him. She rocked her center against his erection, and his mind went thankfully blank as her mouth found his again.

He wrapped his hands around her waist as she rolled her hips and their tongues met, stroking, tasting, exploring. Pleasure pulsed through him, radiating from each spot where their bodies met.

Fiona Carver was offering herself to him, without reservation. His hands shook with the glory of it, with the need to have her. Possess her. Pleasure her.

He tightened his hands on her hips and rolled, pinning her beneath him. His hips settled between her spread thighs, and it was his turn to control the rhythm as he thrust his hips, giving her a hint of how it would feel when he was inside her.

She groaned against his lips, her eyes closed as she tilted her head back, lost to the feel of him. "I need you, Dean."

"I know, beautiful. I need you too." He kissed her neck, trailing his lips down the vee of her shirt. He sat up, shifting his legs until he straddled her, then gazed down, taking in the sight of her splayed beneath him. His hands shook a bit as he slowly unbuttoned her top, revealing a satiny beige bra she must've purchased today. No longer confined by the tight sports bra she'd worn the last week, her breasts were fuller than he'd realized.

Tonight, he would explore and kiss and lick every perfect inch of her. Possess her like he promised. And tomorrow, he'd kiss her goodbye at the airport and close the door on the feelings that flooded him when he was with her.

"Take your shirt off, now," she said as she stared up at him, her green eyes hot with arousal.

"Yes, ma'am." He peeled off the long-sleeve T-shirt she'd purchased for him while he sat by Dylan's hospital bed.

She made a soft, happy sound, like she was eating the best ramen noodles in the world, and ran her hands over his bare chest and down his abs. He leaned down and kissed her again, his tongue stroking deep as her hands explored his torso and back.

He'd spent so many hours thinking of what he wanted to do to her, he hadn't considered what her touch would do to him. How *her* hands would feel somehow more intimate on his heated skin during foreplay because after all the holding and comfort, this was the first time they could show passion with touch.

He ran his lips over the tops of her exposed breasts. He wanted the bra gone, but at the same time, he wanted to draw out this moment. Tomorrow, all he'd have was a memory, and he wanted this to be one to savor. To call upon when he was on assignment and conditions were miserable.

Her hands cradled his head, and she pulled his mouth to hers and kissed him deeply, making more of those sexy sounds that lit him on fire. Her fingers stroked his beard, her nails lightly grazing his skin between whiskers. She lifted her mouth from hers, opened her eyes, and he held her smoky gaze. "Make love to me, Dean. Please. Now."

All at once, his body stiffened. She could have just as easily said, *Get inside me.* Or even better, *Fuck me.*

But she didn't. She'd used the one phrase that was like being dunked in a frigid volcanic stream.

What the hell was he doing? He *couldn't* make love to her. It was the one thing he didn't know how to do. Didn't *want* to do.

But he'd been on the verge of doing just that. He needed to pull back. Disengage his emotions.

Sex. This was just sex.

All he could give her was tonight. A brief moment of ultimate pleasure. Fleeting physical release. Spectacular, no doubt, but still fleeting. She deserved so much more. She deserved a man who could *be* so much more. A man who would love her without hesitation.

He pulled back from the kiss and ran his lips over her forehead. "I can't offer you anything more than sex, Fiona."

She frowned, and her eyes widened. "Shit. I just—It was just a phrase. I was talking about sex."

"I don't think you were."

"I want sex. With you. That's all."

Oh God. He'd brought her to his level. He didn't want that for her. He wanted her to *not* fear giving her heart away.

"But, Fi. I care about *you.* And now . . . Shit. I don't think I can have *just sex* with you. But I know I can't offer you more."

Making love to her, then walking away would be the worst thing he could do. For both of them.

She pushed at his chest. He sat up and gazed down upon her, seeing the confusion in her eyes. "Are you . . . turning me down?"

He closed his eyes, hating himself as he said, "I think I am."

"Why, Dean? It was just a . . . slip of the tongue. I'm meeting you on your terms."

"I don't think it was a slip." He opened his eyes again. "You don't do flings. This isn't the time to start."

"Shouldn't that be my decision?"

"Of course. But I also get to make decisions about my body. And I'm afraid I won't be able to walk away from you if we make love. And I don't want that. I don't want a relationship. Ever again. I've always been clear on that."

The light in her green eyes dimmed, and she took a deep breath. She was hurting, and he'd caused it. He hated being the cause of this amazing woman's pain, but it would only be worse later if they continued on this path.

"I'm sorry," he said.

She pushed at his thigh, which still straddled her hips. He shifted his weight, freeing her to move from under his body, putting some space between them. "I guess I understand. We both need to protect our hearts." She rolled to her side and curled into a ball.

He ached, seeing her in that position. But he couldn't waver in his resolve. Not without doing more damage. "We do."

"Is this goodbye, then?"

"I don't really know." He touched her back, running a hand down her spine.

She straightened and rolled over to face him. "Will you hold me tonight, one last time?"

He lay down beside her and pulled her to his chest in the same way he'd held her the last several nights. "Oh, sweetheart. I want that more than anything."

For the sixth night in a row, they crawled into bed together, but this was the first time they shared an actual mattress. And this time, the bed was big enough that they didn't need to hold each other close. But he held her anyway.

He drifted off to sleep holding her tight, wondering how in the world he'd find the strength to let her go with the dawn.

AUTHOR'S NOTE

As stated in the beginning, Chiksook Island and all the cultural, historical, and geological features described in this book are fictional. This of course includes Mount Katin and the meteorite, *Kanuux̂*, as well as the lava tubes and caves explored by Dean and Fiona. The World War II ruins are based on what can be found on other Aleutian Islands, including but not limited to Adak and Attu.

Likewise, I have created a fictional village whose residents play an important role in the story. When writing characters whose cultural history and affiliation is different from my own, my goal is always to provide respectful and meaningful representation. If as a reader you were surprised to learn of the World War II incursion into the US in the Aleutians or the internment of the Unangas during the war, you might appreciate exploring the Aleutian Pribilof Islands Association (APIA) website at www.apiai.org, where you can learn more about the Unangax̂ people's past and present.

The navy project that sent Fiona to the Aleutians in the first place, while fictional, is something that may be in the works in the near future. The US Navy is indeed looking at the Aleutians and the Alaska coastline for future submarine bases as global warming opens up a new Northwest Passage through the Arctic Ocean.

ACKNOWLEDGMENTS

Enormous thanks to Kelly, an Alaskan archaeologist and fangirl who was extremely helpful in describing field conditions and protocol for projects similar to the Chiksook EIS presented in this story. Kelly provided fantastic, interesting, detailed, and accurate information. Mistakes and misrepresentations, whether due to error or fictional license, are on me.

Thank you also to Patrick Barnard, PhD, for answering my very random and sometimes rambling geology questions. I am solely responsible for any incorrect geologic data or descriptions in this story.

Thank you to environmental planner, biologist, and avid birder Doug Lister for helping brainstorm ways to get my fake ornithologist to Chiksook and selecting gray buntings as the ideal species for "Bill" to search for.

Thanks to Darcy Burke, who was my first sounding board for most—if not all—of the key plot elements that shaped this story.

In addition to Darcy, Toni Anderson, Gwen Hernandez, Jenn Stark, Annika Martin, Julie Kenner, Serena Bell, and Kate Davies were rocks of support as 2020 hurled new, unfathomable challenges our way. Thank you, ladies, for helping keep me sane. I hope I was able to offer you even a fraction of the support you gave me.

Huge thanks to my agent, Elizabeth Winick Rubinstein at McIntosh & Otis, for your endless support over the last decade. This book wouldn't have been written if not for you.

Thank you to Lauren Plude, my editor at Montlake Romance, for making Fiona and Dean's story possible. It's a thrill and a joy to be working with you!

Thank you to my children for being the amazing people you are. One of the rare blessings of social distancing was getting to spend more time with you both.

As always, thank you to my husband, US Navy archaeologist David Grant, who makes sure I get my NHPA and NEPA details right. Every moment I spend with you, I'm living my best life.

CONNECT WITH RACHEL ONLINE

Follow Rachel on Facebook
facebook.com/RachelGrantAuthor

Follow Rachel on Twitter
twitter.com/rachelsgrant

Find Rachel's books on Goodreads
goodreads.com/rachelgrantauthor

Email Rachel
contact@rachel-grant.net

Visit Rachel's website
Rachel-Grant.net

ABOUT THE AUTHOR

Rachel Grant is the *USA Today* bestselling author of the Flashpoint series and the Evidence novels. She worked for over a decade as a professional archaeologist and mines her experiences for story lines and settings, which are as diverse as excavating a cemetery underneath an historic art museum in San Francisco, surveying an economically depressed coal-mining town in Kentucky, and mapping a seventeenth-century Spanish and Dutch fort on the island of Sint Maarten in the Netherlands Antilles. In all her travels and adventures as an archaeologist, Rachel has found many sites and artifacts, but she's only found one true treasure: her husband, David. Rachel Grant lives on an island in the Pacific Northwest with her husband and children. For more information visit www.rachel-grant.net.